W9-BEG-228

EX LIBRIS

Romance Treasury

THE ROMANCE TREASURY ASSOCIATION

ASSOCIATION

NEW YORK·TORONTO·LONDON

ROMANCE TREASURY
Copyright © 1977 by The Romance Treasury Association. All
rights reserved. Except for use in any review, the reproduction or
utilization of this work in whole or in part in any form by any
electronic, mechanical or other means, now known or hereafter
invented, including xerography, photocopying and recording, or in
any information storage or retrieval system, is forbidden without the
permission of the publisher.

All characters in this book have no existence outside the imagination
of the author and have no relation whatsoever to anyone bearing the
same name or names.

These stories were originally published as follows:

THE PRETTY WITCH
Copyright © 1971 by Lucy Gillen
First published by Mills & Boon Limited in 1971

WITHOUT ANY AMAZEMENT
Copyright 1948 by Margaret Malcolm
First published by Mills & Boon Limited in 1948

STORM OVER MANDARGI
Copyright © 1973 by Margaret Way
First published by Mills & Boon Limited in 1973

ROMANCE TREASURY is published by
The Romance Treasury Association, Stratford, Ontario, Canada.

Editorial Board: A. W. Boon, Judith Burgess, Ruth Palmour and
Dust Jacket Art by Will Davies
Story Illustrations by Muriel Hughes
Book Design by Charles Kadin
Printed by Kingsport Press Limited, Kingsport, Tennessee

ISBN 0-919860-29-X

Printed in U.S.A.   A030

CONTENTS

THE PRETTY WITCH

The
Pretty
Witch

Lucy Gillen

Isobel's first impression of mystery writer Lucifer Bennetti was one of dislike. But since his brother, Nigel, had persuaded him to hire Isobel as his secretary, she was prepared to fill the position.

Not that Nigel's motives were entirely unselfish. Confined after an accident to his grandmother's home, he wanted Isobel close by in the hope of persuading her to marry him.

Lucifer was a disconcerting man, as baffling as his notorious namesake. It came as no surprise to Isobel that, living in the Cotswolds where ancient cults and superstitions abound, he was involved in witchcraft. And he did seem to have a magical power to attract her.

Inevitably, Isobel was faced with a crucial decision!

CHAPTER ONE

Isobel glanced yet again at her watch and sighed despairingly. It was already five minutes past nine and still the hot, overcrowded bus had not reached her stop. If only she had thought to check how long the bus took to get to Green's Corner she could have caught an earlier one, and twenty minutes had seemed plenty of time to cover the journey from Greenlaw.

It had seemed a much shorter distance when she had come for her interview a couple of weeks ago, but then, of course, she had been very extravagant and indulged in a taxi. The taxi had made little of the distance and none of the stops that the bus was required to make. Not that it wasn't a very pleasant journey, especially now, with the Gloucestershire countryside at its summery best, but she was not traveling to Green's Corner just for the pleasure of enjoying the scenery, but to take up a new position as secretary. Being late was not going to make a very good first impression.

Actually she had been more keen than usual to make a good impression, because she felt as if she had won the post more through influence than because her prospective employer had been impressed with her skills. Indeed he had seemed barely interested in such things as typing and shorthand speeds and had been very offhand and casual with her for the brief time he'd seen her.

Although the interview had been short Isobel remembered it all too vividly and, not for the first time, wondered if she had made a mistake in changing her job so impulsively. Of course the pay was a lot higher than what she'd been making at Frome's, and it should be quite exciting working for someone as well known as Luke Bennett, although he had made her rather uneasy at their first meeting.

She had expected a famous writer of crime novels to be somewhat impressive, but he had been so much more than she expected. For one thing, he was a tall man, and her own meager five feet two had seemed even less than usual when he stood up to greet her. He had said little during the short time they were together, but she thought she would never forget those rather startling black eyes and the dark, disturbingly attractive features. He was so completely unlike Nigel that she had been quite unprepared and had plainly shown her surprise, a fact that had appeared to amuse him.

Of course they were only half-brothers. Luke Bennett, or Lucifer Bennetti to give him his true name, had the same mother as Nigel, but his father, so Nigel had rather reluctantly informed her, was an Italian count and their mother's first husband. Evidently the older brother had inherited his looks entirely from his father, but Isobel had expected them to have at least one feature in common.

Nigel's brown hair and blue eyes and his regular features were in great contrast to his brother's black hair and eyes, and Nigel was at least a couple of inches shorter, too. Thinking of Nigel, she pulled a wry face, remembering that it had been he who had persuaded her to apply for this job and no doubt, too, persuaded his brother that she was suitable for it. But now here she was, on her first morning, at least five minutes late and getting later every minute.

Lateness was one thing Nigel would never tolerate, and she felt she was letting him down badly. She had been a little surprised at first when Nigel had suggested her leaving Frome's, where she had been ever since leaving secretarial college four years ago. Thinking of it later, however, his reason became clearer. Nigel had been away from the firm for several weeks now, and she had no idea how much longer it was likely to be before he returned.

Several male members of the staff had made no secret of the fact that they found her very attractive, and only Nigel's presence had kept them from doing anything about it. With Nigel away things might be different, and Isobel thought the idea was that Nigel would be able to have her near him and also out of the way of temptation.

She sighed with more than relief when at last Green's Corner came into sight around another bend, and she was on her feet ready to alight well before the bus had come to a halt, thanking heaven that the bus stop was only a couple of yards from the gates of Kanderby House. The conductor smiled at her as she passed him, attracted, as most men were, by her fairness and the lovely, soft smiling features.

Her thick corn-gold hair curled slightly, and she wore it tied back with a brightly colored scarf at the nape of her neck. At the moment a small anxious frown drew her brows together above huge, brown-fringed grey eyes. It was too warm for a coat, but her linen dress was neat and smart enough to please even the most fastidious employer, and also dark enough green to be considered suitable for a secretary about to begin a new job.

She remembered to turn right after she went through the double gates, because the lodge where Lucifer

Bennetti lived and worked had been built in the ample grounds of Kanderby House, his grandmother's home. The garden was bright and colorful and smelled of the dark loam that lay in permanent shadow beneath the shrubs all along the driveway and half hiding the lodge she sought.

She sent a swift, not very hopeful look along the driveway to the bigger house immediately opposite the gates, wishing she could catch just a glimpse of Nigel before she faced what she expected to be an irate employer.

It was a faint hope, of course, for while he was still so incapacitated it would be unlikely that he would be up and about so early. A bad car crash several weeks ago had put Nigel into the hospital for some time. Now he was staying with his grandmother, recovering slowly and chafing at the enforced inactivity.

Isobel crunched her way around the gravel driveway to the front door of the cottage and hesitated briefly before knocking. She felt very small and scared, rather like a child starting school for the first time, as she waited for her knock to be answered. When no one came after several seconds, she knocked again and eyed the shiny brass knob speculatively. Perhaps the manservant who had admitted her before was out or busy elsewhere and unable to hear her knock.

Her heart thumping uneasily, she turned the knob and pushed the door open a couple of inches. "Hello!" Her voice sounded very quiet and horribly uncertain, and she thought for a moment that the house must be empty; then a door to her right opened suddenly and curious eyes looked at her through the narrow opening.

"Judging by what I can see," Lucifer Bennetti said,

"you're my new secretary." He crossed the intervening few feet and opened the door wide while Isobel prepared an apology. "Come on in."

He left her to close the door behind him and went back into the room he had come from. Presuming she was expected to follow, Isobel walked in after him, remembering the bright sunny room from her last visit. "I'm very sorry I'm so late," she ventured, and he turned an unconcerned gaze on her, one black brow arched curiously.

"Are you? I hadn't noticed."

Isobel blinked. Friendly as she was with Nigel he would, even so, have commented on her arrival some fifteen minutes late. "It's a quarter past nine," she informed him.

The black eyes studied her for a moment, then he smiled. A crooked, sardonic smile that glittered wickedly and made Isobel feel strangely uneasy again. "I hope you're not a clock-watcher," he told her. "I don't work to the clock. This isn't a nine-to-five job; I thought you realized that."

"Oh, I do," Isobel hastened to assure him. "I was just apologizing for not starting on time, that's all."

Again he studied her in silence for a while. "I suppose you had to be right on the dot with Nigel, didn't you?"

She nodded. "Of course. In business you can't afford to be any other way."

"Of course." She thought she detected sarcasm in the reply, but gave him the benefit of the doubt.

She looked around at the untidy shambles of paper and reference books, boxes of carbon, pieces of scribble-covered paper and a typewriter half-hidden by a tweed jacket thrown carelessly across it. "What would you like me to do first?" she asked, and he too looked around the untidy room before raising a brow at her.

"Is it beneath your secretarial dignity to tidy up?" he inquired in such a way that she felt sure he expected her to refuse indignantly.

"No, of course not, Mr. Bennetti."

He looked at her curiously. "Oh, so Nigel's enlightened you now, has he?" He grinned at her and she was reminded uncomfortably of his satanic namesake. "I'm surprised he let the cat out of the bag; he usually prefers to keep quiet the fact that there's Italian blood in the family. He heaved a sigh of relief when I decided to use Luke Bennett for a pen name."

Isobel put down her bag and gloves and prepared to tackle the marathon of bringing some sort of order to the big room. "I've never heard him express any opinion about it either way," she told him, "so I think you must be wrong in that respect."

That expressive brow shot upward again, and he eyed her curiously as he perched on the edge of another desk, presumably his own, near the window. "Are you on familiar enough terms with him for him *to* say anything, Miss Hendrix?" he asked in a suspiciously quiet voice, and Isobel glanced up only to hastily lower her gaze again when she met his eyes.

"I'm . . . I'm not sure I know what you mean, Mr. Bennetti."

A deep chuckle startled her, and she flicked him another wary glance. "I mean, in fact," he told her, "are you Nigel's girlfriend?"

She stopped tidying for a moment, the discarded jacket

in front of her, her expression uncertain as she looked at him. "I . . . yes, I suppose you could say that in a way," she admitted.

"I thought so. He takes you out more than he does anyone else, doesn't he?"

Isobel nodded. "We have been out together quite a lot, before his accident, of course."

He was grinning again, the black eyes glittering wickedly. "I thought it might be that," he said. "He seemed so anxious to have you here and he hinted that I should keep my beady eyes off you."

"Oh, he shouldn't have done that," Isobel protested, feeling more uneasy than ever at his frankness.

A quiet laugh greeted her protest, and he stood up and walked around to the other side of his desk. "I don't imagine you mean that the way it sounds," he told her. "Anyway, my brother knows me a lot better than you do, and he doesn't approve of me in the least."

"Then why did he want me—" she began, and he smiled.

"Better the devil you know," he quoted softly, then laughed. "And while you're here he can keep an eye on you, can't he?"

It was an uneasy truth that she was obliged to face. She nodded but was unprepared to voice agreement. "I don't think that's quite true," she told him, looking up sharply when he laughed again.

"You're very young," he said bluntly, "and rather naïve too, from the sound of it."

"I'm—"

Her protest was cut short as if she had not even spoken. "You look as if a good strong wind would blow you away," he said, sweeping his black eyes over her small but attractive figure. "A real *fantoccia*. Nigel has excellent taste, I'll allow him that, but you look as if you'd be more at home with fairy tales than with my blood and thunder epics. Will you be able to cope?"

"Quite well, thank you, Mr. Bennetti."

His smile was a mere crooking of the wide straight mouth. "I think you will too," he said.

Whether or not he always finished at the same time for lunch, Isobel had no way of knowing, but she was relieved that today he told her she could go at just before one o'clock. She had to admit that the morning had gone far more quickly than she realized, and once he became absorbed in his work, he said little, so she finished tidying the room and then got on with a pile of typing that awaited her attention.

She was nervous, too, when she thought about lunchtime, because Nigel had asked her to come over to the house and have lunch with him and his grandmother. She had never met Mrs. Claudia Grayson, but she knew her to be an extremely wealthy woman. Isobel wondered if she would take kindly to having her grandson's employee as a luncheon guest.

"Are you going over to the house for lunch?" Lucifer Bennetti asked as she picked up her purse and gloves.

Isobel nodded. "Yes. Nigel asked me to come."

She looked at him, startled, when he put a hand under her arm and walked to the door with her. "I'll act as escort," he told her, grinning at her surprise. "Beppo has the day off. My man," he explained when she frowned curiously. "When he's off I eat with the quality."

For the first time Isobel realized that they must have been alone in the cottage by themselves all morning, and almost as if he guessed what she was thinking, he looked down at her and chuckled softly as he closed the door behind them. He really was the most disconcerting man, Isobel thought, and one she could very easily dislike.

He took her around the thick shrubbery at the back of the house and across a lawn to open French windows that led straight into a long, sunny, beautifully furnished room. Their appearance gave rise to simultaneous cries of welcome from Nigel, resting uneasily in an armchair, and from a small and remarkably bright-eyed elderly woman.

"Lucifer dear, I'm *so* glad you remembered you were lunching with us today," his grandmother told him as he bent to kiss her cheek.

"Of course I remembered, Grandmama, how could I forget?"

The old lady kissed him enthusiastically, obviously doting on her older grandson; then her bright blue eyes peeped curiously around his broad shoulders to Isobel. "And this must be the young lady I've heard so much about. Do introduce us, one of you."

Nigel, unable to leave his chair very easily, found himself forestalled, and Isobel saw the frown that condemned his brother's action. "Grandmama, this is Isobel Hendrix. Miss Hendrix, my grandmother, Mrs. Grayson."

The blue eyes studied her for a moment in friendly curiosity while she still held her hand; then the old woman smiled. "I'm delighted to meet you, my dear. I've heard a great deal about you from Nigel."

Isobel glanced at Nigel, relieved at her reception. "It

was very kind of you to ask me to lunch, Mrs. Grayson. Thank you."

Eyes twinkling, the old lady looked at Nigel. "I just had to meet you after hearing so much lavish praise of your prettiness," she told Isobel. "And he's quite right, you're a very lovely girl, Miss Hendrix."

"A real little *fantoccia*, eh, Grandmama?" Lucifer said softly, and the old lady shook her head in mild reproach.

"Lucifer, it may be a compliment to call a young lady a doll, but I feel it's not very polite at this stage of your relationship." She looked at Isobel, seeking understanding, while Nigel frowned blackly in the background. "How have you been getting along with my scoundrel of a grandson, Miss Hendrix?"

"Oh . . . very well, thank you, Mrs. Grayson." She flicked a glance at Nigel and smiled reassuringly. "I've been very busy, but I prefer it that way."

"She even tidied up without a murmur of complaint," Lucifer informed his grandmother. "At least she didn't complain out loud."

"Tidied up?" Nigel frowned. "Tidied up what? You don't mean that you actually had the cheek to ask Isobel to clear up that . . . that pigsty of an office of yours?"

"Was it a pigsty?" Lucifer asked. He was such a picture of innocence that his grandmother laughed.

"It was, well, untidy," Isobel said. "But it was soon tidy."

"You'd no right to use Isobel as a cleaning woman," Nigel told his brother shortly. "She's a trained secretary and that's what you're paying her to be."

Isobel supposed that his injuries and the subsequent enforced inactivity had made Nigel less amiable than usual, but she had not realized quite how bad-tempered his good-looking face could be, and the contrast was especially noticeable beside Lucifer's apparent good humor. Under the speculative gaze of his family, she walked over to him and covered his hand, which lay on the arm of the chair.

"I didn't mind, Nigel," she told him. "You know I had to tidy up quite often after Mr. Pogson."

"Pogson's an oaf," Nigel informed her gruffly. "You won't be going back to him."

"I know," Isobel agreed, "but I was just pointing out that there's more to being a secretary than shorthand and typing."

"Oh, there won't be any shorthand for me," Lucifer pointed out, "except for the odd letter or two now and then."

"Really I don't mind in the least," Isobel insisted, seeing that Nigel was bent on carrying it further and anxious to end the discussion. "You look very tired," she told Nigel, still holding his hand under hers. "Are you in pain?"

"No." He shook his head. "It's just that I've been getting around a bit this morning and it takes a lot out of me."

"Why don't you take it easier while you have the opportunity?" his brother asked with a grin. "It's not every man who has such a heaven-sent chance to be bone idle, in summer, too. You don't know when you're in clover, my lad."

Nigel's blue eyes glared at him balefully. "It's all right for you," he retorted. "You're not confined to a blessed chair all day, or most of it anyway. I'm sick of being inactive."

"Give me the chance!" Lucifer smiled, but Nigel glowered, determinedly ill-humored.

"You always were a lazy devil when you had the opportunity."

Lucifer's smile admitted it willingly, and Isobel thought that the slightly exaggerated shrug and spread hands, which emphasized his foreignness, were deliberately overdone just to annoy Nigel. "It's my Italian papa, I suppose, but I can imagine nothing more heavenly than a perfect excuse for doing nothing at all. Indolence comes naturally to me."

"Oh, nonsense, Lucifer," his grandmother protested with a laugh. "You're as industrious as anyone I know. You put most people to shame."

"Except Nigel," Lucifer argued. "He's a regular whirlwind when he's well. He lives, eats and sleeps work." A black brow quirked in Isobel's direction. "Well, almost," he added softly.

Nigel frowned. "If anyone listened to you," he told him, "they'd take me for an absolute bore, and I don't think I'm that."

"Of course you're not, dear," his grandmother consoled him. "Now I think we'd better go in and have some lunch before Mrs. Clay thinks we're not interested."

The meal was less of an ordeal than Isobel had feared, and her hostess managed to keep the peace between the two brothers with a skill that told of long practice. It was just as well, Isobel thought ruefully, that the two men did not usually live in the same house or there inevitably would have been more serious quarrels. Nigel still found movement of his legs difficult and painful, and he resented the slower pace he was forced to adopt. His condition probably made things more than usually uneasy between them.

"I was hoping to take you to the County Show next week," Nigel told Isobel as they finished lunch. "I'm sorry I can't, because I think you'd have enjoyed it, and I haven't been to see it for years."

"The County Show?" She looked interested. "If it's what I think you mean I certainly would have enjoyed it." She shrugged and smiled consolingly at him. "Never mind, perhaps we can go some other time."

"Not until next year," Nigel said. "It's only an annual event, and it's one of the best of its kind in the country."

"Oh well, never mind, it can't be helped. You can't hop about on your poor legs, can you?"

Lucifer, although apparently engrossed in conversation with the old lady, caught enough of what Nigel and Isobel were saying to get the general gist of it, and he expressed interest. "Do you like country shows, Miss Hendrix?" he asked, and Isobel looked surprised for a moment before nodding her head.

"Yes . . . yes, I really do." She told herself she had been rather rash to admit so much, and certainly Nigel anticipated his brother's next question, judging from his frown.

"Then will you come with me?"

She glanced uncomfortably at Nigel and hesitated when she saw the expression in his eyes. "I don't think so, thank you, Mr. Bennetti."

The look Lucifer gave his brother told her that he guessed the reason for her refusal, and the black eyes glistened with laughter, although he spoke seriously enough. "But why not, if you like going to things like that?" he asked. "I know Nigel can't go, but he isn't selfish enough to deny you the pleasure of going, surely. Are you, Nigel?"

Without appearing utterly selfish there was little Nigel could do or say other than to agree, and he nodded reluctantly. "Of course, go if you want to, Isobel," he told her. "I'm sure you'll like it."

"I do like that sort of thing," she admitted, sorely tempted but still uncertain. It was obvious that Nigel disliked the idea of her going without him, even though he was verbally encouraging her.

"Then you should come," Lucifer said as if the matter was now settled. "We'll start early and make a day of it."

Isobel said nothing, still wondering why she did not make more of an effort to resist being pressed into going with him. Lucifer Bennetti, it appeared, was a man who didn't hesitate in making up his mind and making sure that everyone else complied with his ideas.

There was a hint of stubborn dislike, however, in Nigel's expression as he looked toward his brother. "Will there be just the two of you?" he asked quietly; so quietly that Isobel sensed something other than mere curiosity behind the question.

Lucifer raised a brow, a half-smile crooking his mouth. "Just the two of us," he agreed, obviously following Nigel's train of thought but not prepared to meet him halfway.

Nigel's eyes glowed with malice and his voice was edged with disapproval as he watched the other's face. "What about Vanessa?" he asked.

If he had expected Lucifer to be discomfited by the question he must have been disappointed. "What about Vanessa?"

Isobel shifted uneasily at the tension between them,

although she thought Nigel was far more conscious of it than Lucifer, and it was obvious which one of them was going to come off best. She thought perhaps Lucifer always did, for Nigel already seemed less sure of himself.

"You usually take Vanessa to the County Show," he said. "I just wondered, that's all."

Lucifer smiled, a slow dark smile that foretold triumph. "Well, wonder no more," he told his brother. "Vanessa is otherwise engaged at an antique fair. She's flying out to Germany on the opening day of the show and she won't be back until the day after it closes. Does that answer you?" The question was quietly put and he smiled when he asked it, but Isobel thought it betrayed resentment at being questioned.

"I was only curious," Nigel said, on the defensive, while Mrs. Grayson sought hastily to restore normalcy.

"It would be a shame if Miss Hendrix didn't see the show," she said, smiling at Nigel consolingly. "And I'm sure she'll enjoy it quite well with Lucifer, dear."

"Of course," Nigel conceded, and Isobel felt more uneasy than ever about accepting the invitation, although in fact she had never really been given the chance to accept or decline. One way or another, however, she seemed to be already committed, and she thought Lucifer was watching her, perhaps expecting her to find some excuse not to go with him.

She smiled at him for the first time, wondering if he had made the offer because he wanted to accompany her or merely to annoy Nigel; either way she would hold him to the promise now. "I'm sure I shall enjoy it," she said. "If you're sure you can spare the time away from your work, Mr. Bennetti."

"Oh, we'll manage to get done, don't you worry about

that," he assured her with a grin. "We'll work late for a night or two to make up for it."

"Lucifer, you really mustn't," Mrs. Grayson objected mildly. "You mustn't overwork Miss Hendrix the way you did poor Mrs. Lomas; I'm not surprised she left you."

"Tottie Lomas," Lucifer told her, unrepentant, "was not only the most unattractive female in existance, she was also a clock-watcher. I've already warned Miss Hendrix not to expect a nine-to-five job with me."

"I'm afraid I've already blotted my copybook," Isobel confessed, her explanation mainly for Nigel's benefit. "I didn't arrive until a quarter past nine this morning."

"You . . . late?" Nigel looked flatteringly surprised. "I've never known that to happen, Isobel. Did you miss the bus?"

She shook her head. "No, but I'm afraid I didn't allow for it taking so long to get here. I hadn't thought of it stopping at every stop all the way from Greenlaw."

"It's a pretty murderous journey at that time of day," Nigel told her. "I've never used the bus, but I suppose it stands to reason that it's crowded with people going in to work and shop in Edgemorton."

"I realize it now," Isobel said ruefully, "but I just didn't think this morning. Tomorrow I'll get the earlier one."

"It's a wretched journey for you," Nigel sympathized. "But there's nothing else for it, is there, darling?"

It was not only unusual for Nigel to use such an endearment with other people there, but there was also some odd feeling of expectancy about him, although she could not for the life of her think why there should be. As if he, too, sensed and interpreted something other than sympathy for her, Lucifer smiled to himself.

"Where are you staying?" Mrs. Grayson asked, a concerned look on her face, while Lucifer's smile grew even more knowing as he looked across at his brother.

"I have a room in Mudlan Street in Greenlaw," Isobel informed her, increasingly puzzled.

"Oh, but they're such horrid little houses, if I remember correctly," the old lady said, and Isobel smiled wryly.

"It's a case of necessity, I'm afraid, Mrs. Grayson," she said. "So few people in Greenlaw rent out rooms, and it is nearer than Edgemorton. It's not much of a room, but the landlady's very nice."

"I see no reason," Mrs. Grayson declared, as if she had quite made up her mind, "why you can't come here."

The odd feeling of expectancy was at last explained when Isobel saw Nigel's look of satisfaction. "It would be very much more convenient," he said, and glared at Lucifer when he laughed.

"Very," Lucifer said softly.

"Oh, but I couldn't possibly," Isobel protested.

"My dear Miss Hendrix, of course you can." The old lady was adamant and Isobel thought ruefully that Lucifer had probably inherited his implacable will, at least in part, from his grandmother. "Did you notice the little cottage the other side of the gates across from Lucifer's?" Mrs. Grayson asked, and immediately answered her own question. "No, it's more than likely you didn't, because it's hidden by the rhododendrons. It used to be occupied by the gardener, but a full-time gardener is almost impossible to find these days and the cottage has been empty for some time now. It was too small for Lucifer and his man, so we had the other little house built, but it would be ideal for one, if you'd like to use it, my dear."

"I . . . I'd love to," Isobel said, too stunned for the moment to say much more, but intrigued with the idea of having her own little house, and not having to travel to work by bus each day. "If you're sure it would be all right." She could not have said why it was Lucifer she looked at briefly when she said that, for he seemed completely unconcerned with the idea.

"There's nothing simpler," Mrs. Grayson assured her. "It's in excellent repair and it only needs to be aired and the furniture moved back in. Say about a week or even less, and it'll be ready for you." She smiled at Isobel knowingly, her blue eyes mischievous. "I know Nigel will love having you so near at hand, my dear."

"I certainly will," Nigel agreed earnestly. "Do take it, Isobel, I'd like you to."

Isobel knew that he was watching her expectantly, but she was even more aware of Lucifer's black eyes fixed on her from across the table. "Then I will," she said at last. "Thank you very much, Mrs. Grayson, it's very kind of you."

"There, that's settled." The old lady beamed her satisfaction. "It will help Nigel's recovery no end, I'm sure of it, having you here, and save you all those beastly bus rides." She seemed pleased with her persuasive powers. "Apart from anything else," she added, "I shall have some female company sometimes, instead of all these men."

"Only two of us, *cara mia*," Lucifer protested lightly, and the old lady pulled a face at him.

"It seems more," she told him. "At least I shall be able to talk about things that interest only women, like fashions and such. I may be well over seventy, but I'm not old-fashioned and I like to talk about feminine things."

"Oh, you're certainly not old-fashioned, Grandmama," Lucifer assured her with a twinkle. "I wouldn't be surprised to see you blossom out in the very latest styles any day now."

"And so I might, you impudent rogue," his grandmother retorted laughingly. "Although I haven't the figure that Miss Hendrix has for showing it off."

The remark brought Isobel once again, embarassingly, under the scrutiny of those black eyes and she hastily lowered her own. "I have to agree with you there," Lucifer said softly, and sent her a wicked look that made his brother frown.

"At least I shall be able to see you more often," Nigel told her. "It means you can spend all your free time with me, Isobel."

"It also means I can be on time in the mornings," Isobel said with a wry smile. "I hate being late, and especially on my first day."

"Well, if you have such a guilty conscience about it," Lucifer told her, "you can make it up by working late tonight."

"Oh, that's not . . . " Nigel began, but Isobel shook her head at him, sensing a challenge behind the suggestion, as if he expected her to protest as Nigel was doing.

"Of course I'll work late, Mr. Bennetti," she told him quietly. "I owe you that much." He looked, she thought, quite disappointed because she did not argue.

CHAPTER TWO

After a week of working for Lucifer Bennetti, Isobel was still uncertain just what her feelings were toward him. He was not an easy man to know or to like, she thought, but at the same time there was something almost magnetically attractive about him and she had no difficulty in believing Nigel's rather sour comments about the number and variety of his brother's women friends. His grandmother adored him, that much was obvious, although she saw much less of him than she would like to have done, despite his living so near at hand.

Isobel had to admit to being very curious about the Vanessa that Nigel had referred to as Lucifer's usual companion at the County Show. She had got as far as discovering her name was Vanessa Law and that she and Lucifer had been friendly for quite a long time. Indeed, more than friendly, if Nigel's raised brows were anything to go by.

"She's quite a character in her own way," Nigel informed her on the day that Vanessa Law departed for Germany and the antique fair. "You'll probably meet her sooner or later, working for Luke, although she doesn't go to his place very often; he believes in keeping work and play strictly apart."

Nigel would never, Isobel had discovered, use his brother's more exotic first name, and she could not help wondering if he did it with the express purpose of bringing Lucifer down to his more everyday-type level. The older man's bland self-confidence, combined with his darkly foreign appearance, obviously discomfited Nigel, a fact that surprised Isobel who had, until now, known him always as a self-sufficient, rather unimaginative business executive. .

"Is she pretty?" she asked, and Nigel shrugged.

"I suppose so, if you like that sort," he allowed. "Although more accurately I'd have called her eye-catching, stunning, something less feminine than pretty."

Isobel laughed. "She sounds rather formidable."

He did not treat the remark as lightly as she expected, but frowned over it thoughtfully. "In a way, she is. I suspect she's as foreign in origin as Luke is, although her name's British enough."

It was difficult to believe, she thought, that he was talking about his own brother. The other's Italian father seemed to have condemned him as a foreigner in Nigel's eyes and nothing could redeem him.

"Is she dark like he is, then?"

"Dark as a cat," Nigel declared, as if even darkness itself was suspect. "Black hair and the most weird yellow eyes."

"Yellow?" Isobel looked startled.

He nodded, still serious. "They are yellow, especially in some lights, although she prefers to call them amber, I believe."

"I . . . I don't think I've ever seen a human being with yellow eyes. It sounds uncanny."

He laughed shortly but the laugh was devoid of humor. "She gives me the creeps, and God knows I'm not fanciful."

Isobel laughed, trying to shake off the strange feeling of uneasiness he had aroused in her at the mention of the woman whose place she was to take at the County Show. Somehow he had managed to make Vanessa Law sound not only striking but strange, and not the kind of woman who would take kindly to being replaced, for however short a time.

"She sounds most unusual," she said. He looked at her thoughtfully for a moment, as if debating with himself whether or not to say something that was on his mind. "I don't suppose you've ever heard of the Elgin Circle, have you?" he asked at last, and Isobel looking puzzled, shook her head.

"No, I don't think so. What is it? A club of some sort?"

"I suppose you could call it that," Nigel agreed cautiously. "They meet fairly regularly and discuss . . . well, their own particular interests." He looked at her again, warily, as if he was still making up his mind whether or not to confide in her. "Actually they're a group of people who are interested in the ancient arts of witchcraft."

"Oh!" She looked at him uncertainly. "I know . . . at least I've heard about people who take an interest in that sort of thing, but I never thought I'd be this close to it."

"Oh, you don't have to be worried about it," Nigel assured her. "They keep pretty well to themselves, though they make no secret of their existence. They make a study of the old methods and the ways and means of explaining some of the seeming miraculous spells that the old witches worked."

"It sounds spooky."

"Not really," he said. "In fact they're rather bent on explaining that things weren't as spooky as they were made to appear. The group caused quite a stir at the time they started a couple of years back, but that was mainly because of the people who formed it. They were all either well known or wealthy and therefore anything they did that was the least bit out of the ordinary was news, even if it didn't last long. It was mentioned in most of the more sensational dailies at the time."

"And Vanessa Law belongs to them?"

"She certainly does," Nigel informed her. "She founded the group."

An uneasy warning tingle shivered along Isobel's spine and she knew the answer to her question even before she asked it. "And your brother?"

He nodded, reluctantly, she guessed. "Luke was roped in by Vanessa right from the start," he told her, "although he treats it more of a joke than a serious study, and sometimes I think Vanessa gets furious with him."

That was something Isobel could well believe. "Of course this part of the world was once quite well known for . . . well, goings-on, wasn't it?" she asked. "I mean the idea of witches and witchcraft died hard in some parts of the country."

"In more parts of the country than you might suspect," he informed her, sounding defensive. "But I suppose the Cotswolds lend themselves to ancient beliefs and superstitions; there's a kind of atmosphere here that one doesn't find anywhere else."

"It's quite the most beautiful countryside I've ever seen," Isobel said, and meant it. "It's so soft and pretty and so . . . so old somehow."

"Does Mr. Bennetti find the atmosphere helps with his writing?" she asked, and laughed apologetically when he looked at her with raised brows. "I have to admit," she confessed, "that I've never read any of his books."

To her surprise he laughed, a rather short humorless

one, it was true, but he so seldom even smiled that she was encouraged. "That's marvelous," he told her, taking her hand in his. "I quite thought you'd be a fan of Luke's, and here you are admitting that you've never even read one of his wretched books!" He leaned across and kissed her lightly beside her mouth. "Isobel, you're wonderful, and very refreshing."

"I never have much time for reading," she said, feeling a bit guilty about the admission and his pleasure at it. After all, it would do no harm to read one of Lucifer's books and then she would not feel foolish if he asked her about it at any time. "I must get one and read it," she said, "out of curiosity if for no other reason."

Nigel smiled wryly. "Well, don't bother buying one," he told her. "Gran has them all in her room; I'm sure she'd be only too delighted to lend you as many as you want."

They were alone in the big sunny room with the French windows open to the garden and the heavy scented warmth of summer. Isobel could just see Mrs. Grayson at the far end of the lawn, busy among her precious roses, her white head bare in the bright sunlight and shining like silver as she moved. Just being here in the old house one felt more than ever the quiet serenity of the countryside; it seemed to envelop the old, mellow stone building, even encroaching into the beautifully kept garden where foxgloves and periwinkles grew along the hedge beyond the bordering trees.

"It's wonderful here," she sighed. "Almost too good to be true, and I'm so looking forward to moving in tomorrow."

Nigel still held her hand, smiling at her, with his serious blue eyes alight with something it was all too easy to interpret. "I'm looking forward to it, too," he told her softly. "I shall have you right here where I can see you as often as I like."

"Only when I'm not working," Isobel reminded him with a laugh. "Don't forget I'm still a working girl."

"I'm not likely to be given the chance to forget that you're working for Luke," he said shortly, then squeezed her hand. "But at least you'll be here where I can see you." He sighed. "If only you could drive," he told her, "we could go out sometimes and really see the country-side. Just the two of us, Isobel. I'd love to show you some of the places I knew when I was a small boy."

"You lived here when you were young?" She could think of no reason why that should come as such a surprise, but it did. Perhaps because he had always seemed such a city type that the thought of him belonging among these soft hills and sunny meadows seemed out of character somehow.

"Of course, it's my home, didn't you realize that?"

She shook her head. "No, no, I hadn't realized it."

"I spent all my time here when I wasn't at school," he said. "Both of us did. Kanderby and Gran have always been our . . . our haven, if you like. We'd have been pretty badly off without them, too, especially without Gran."

"She's a very sweet person," Isobel said sincerely.

"You don't know how sweet until you owe her as much as we do. She brought up both of us for most of our lives."

"Oh, I see, I didn't realize that. You . . . you didn't see much of your parents?" It was the first time they had ventured on to such personal ground and she was unsure how willing he would be to talk about it.

"Almost nothing." He sat back in his chair, his eyes

lazily half-closed, still retaining his hold on her hand. "Madge, my mother, was married before, you know. She was only recently divorced from Giulio Bennetti when she married my father. They'd traveled all over the world, she and Bennetti, and Luke went with them, but when she remarried and I arrived, the idea of carting two children from one racing circuit to another, wherever my father happened to be competing, was too much for them, so we were left with Gran here at Kanderby, although Luke was at school by then, of course. I was about a year old and Luke about seven."

"Oh, I see."

He laughed shortly but without humor. "I'm sure you do. Whenever my mother and father were in England I saw them, but most of the time I played second fiddle to a very busy social and motor-racing calendar." He shrugged. "Not that either of us bothered all that much, although I suppose Luke must have missed her more than I did; he'd spent a lot more time with her."

"He must have done," Isobel agreed softly, thinking how much less resilient Nigel had proved than his half-brother. Or perhaps he just showed his resentment more openly.

"Once we were both at boarding school," Nigel went on, apparently eager to talk now that he had begun, "we seldom saw each other except during holidays."

"Weren't you at the same school?"

"Oh, lord, no! Luke spent most of his early days at some fancy place in Rome, and came over here permanently only when he came to university."

"Oh yes, of course, I suppose he was near his father."

Nigel grimaced. "Bennetti was no more of a natural parent than mine was. Madge has a talent for finding unlikely fathers and giving them children. No, Luke's father paid the bills and that was as far as parental interest went. Gran was the center of both our worlds, although we're so different."

"And you certainly are different," Isobel agreed ruefully, remembering her own initial shock at the sight of Lucifer.

"Of course," Nigel said, "six years is quite a big gap between children anyway, too much for them to be really close, even if they're full brothers and share a common outlook."

"Which you and . . . Lucifer don't?"

"Certainly not!" He sounded so bitter that it came as a shock to her. She had always known, or at least guessed, that he and Lucifer did not see eye to eye on most things, but she had not realized quite how much he resented his brother, and resent him he undoubtedly did, although she could not imagine why. His own position as a child had surely been no more unstable than Lucifer's, rather less so in fact since Lucifer must remember being with his mother and father for the first few years of his life.

"What I don't understand," she said slowly, looking down at their clasped hands, "is why you persuaded me to come and work for him if you dislike him so much."

He looked up sharply, as if her choice of words startled him, holding her gaze steadily for a moment before shaking his head. "I don't know that I dislike him, actually," he denied, though he sounded uncertain, as if the idea had not occurred to him before. "Does it sound that way to you?"

"In a way," Isobel admitted. "Although I'm probably quite wrong," she added hastily.

"I don't know. I never have been sure how I felt about

Luke, he was always such a. . . ." He laughed shortly. "He's so different, I suppose," he admitted. "I never quite understood him."

"Why did you want me to have this job with him?"

He smiled, faced with something he was certain of for a change. "You know why . . . because I wanted you here, where I could see you. You were so far away in town." He raised her face to his with a hand under her chin. "You'll like it here, won't you, Isobel?"

Isobel smiled. "Oh yes, I'll like it here, who wouldn't? It's so beautiful and I love the countryside, I always have." She did not venture to ask what would happen when he was fully recovered and returned to London and to work again. Would he expect her to leave here and her very lucrative job with Lucifer to go back with him to Frome's? That was something that would no doubt have to be met some time or other, but better, at the moment, to leave things as they were.

"You get on with Luke?" Nigel asked, breaking into her thoughts. "I mean he doesn't drive you too hard?"

She laughed, shaking her head. "On the contrary, he just leaves me to get on with my work and says very little. It's very easy, much easier than I expected."

"That's fine, then." He sighed, apparently satisfied for the moment. "At least I don't have to bother about him. . . ." He shrugged, looking a bit sheepish and as if he was ashamed of his own thoughts. "Well, I know you'll be all right," he said, as if convinced at last. "He never takes much of an interest in girls of your age, he always sticks to the sophisticated thirties, they're his type."

"Are they?" She wondered if Nigel really believed that or if he was deliberately refusing to accept the possibility of Lucifer finding her attractive.

"Anyway," Nigel added, "he'll never be really serious about anyone, he's too much of the Latin lover to let anyone get near enough to mean anything to him."

"I can see what you mean." Isobel thought of the dark, satanic-looking face and the black eyes of Lucifer Bennetti and wondered if it was possible for anyone to get close enough to him to touch his heart. Perhaps Nigel was right; after all he was his brother and perhaps knew him as well as anyone did.

"Are you going with him to the County Show on Thursday?"

Isobel blinked hastily, realizing how deep in thought she had been. "Yes . . . yes, I think so, Nigel." She looked at him, wide gray eyes curious and a little anxious. "You don't mind if I go, do you?"

He did not answer for a moment, but ran a caressing finger over the back of her hand. "Yes, I mind," he admitted at last. "I mind like hell, Isobel, but as Luke says, I'd be utterly selfish to deprive you of the pleasure of going just because I'm out of action." He glared down at his legs, still encased in plaster. "I feel so damned helpless like this."

"I know," Isobel consoled him, "and I wish there was something I could do to help. Maybe," she added, suddenly inspired, "I could stay here with you, while my boss goes to the show on his own."

Nigel scowled, shaking his head. "You don't know Luke. He's made up his mind he's taking you to the show and he will, or neither of you will go. I'm as bad scalded as burned; either way he has your company and I don't."

Isobel had been wondering just how to broach the subject of her moving into the garden cottage the following day.

With two suitcases to carry it would be so much easier if she caught the later bus that would not be so crowded, but she was hesitant about asking Lucifer for the time off, especially in view of the fact that she would be doing no work at all the following day after that, when she would be at the show with him.

To her surprise, however, it was he who raised the matter as they were finishing work for the day. "I'll come and fetch you tomorrow morning," he informed her as she finished off a page prior to packing up, and she looked at him for a second or two in silence.

"Oh! Oh no, there's no need, Mr. Bennetti," she managed at last. "I can manage quite well on my own, I only have two suitcases."

"But you don't want to have to lug them on and off a crowded bus at that hour in the morning," he told her.

"I . . . I was going to ask if I could come on the later one," Isobel confessed. "So that it wouldn't be quite so crowded."

"Why catch a bus at all when I've said I'll fetch you?" The black eyes attributed all sorts of discomfiting reasons for her hesitancy, and she was forced, finally, to nod agreement.

"It's very good of you, thank you."

He came over and sat on the edge of her desk, looking down at her with that same disconcerting gaze. "You just don't trust me, do you?"

"I didn't say that," Isobel objected. "I've never even suggested it."

He grinned wickedly. "No, but I'll bet Nigel has and you've taken his word for it."

"Taken his word for what?" She determinedly began to

type another line, not waiting for him to answer, but he put a finger on the carriage release leaver and sent the platen shooting along out of her control, grinning at her frown of frustration.

"For the fact that I'm no better than I should be," he told her, unconcernedly. The black eyes drew and held her gaze no matter how hard she fought against it. "And you believe it, don't you?"

She refused to be flustered by his deliberate shock tactics and shrugged with apparent unconcern as she regained control of the machine and prepared to finish her line, despite the way her heart was hammering, almost in panic, against her ribs. "I think it's quite possible you lead a very busy social life," she agreed primly, and he exploded into laughter.

"What a delightful way of putting it," he told her.

Isobel got on with her typing. "I'm glad you approve," she said as she reached the end of the line. "Now if you don't mind, Mr. Bennetti, I'd like to finish this page before I leave."

"Are you in a hurry to leave?"

She sighed resignedly, looking up at him still perched on the edge of her desk. "No more than I usually am," she said, "Although I do have things to pack if I'm moving in the morning."

"And you are moving in the morning," he said. "Nigel worked it very neatly, didn't he?"

Isobel frowned. "Worked it neatly?"

He nodded, grinning in such a way that she could cheerfully have struck him before she even heard what he had to say. "I recognized his tactics that first day," he said, and Isobel remembered that knowing smile he had worn while Mrs. Grayson was making her the offer of the cottage. "I suppose he told you to get that particular bus that morning, didn't he?" Isobel nodded, seeing his reasoning at last and disliking the idea of the old lady having been tricked into making her the offer. "And he said himself," Lucifer went on, "that it was always crowded and therefore took longer than usual to get here. He knew you'd be late that morning."

"Oh, he wouldn't do a thing like that!" Isobel objected, knowing he was right but not prepared to admit it. "He knows I hate being late."

"He also knows that the cottage has been standing empty," Lucifer insisted. "And he knows that Grandmama has a very soft heart and would offer you the cottage to save you that journey every morning and evening."

Isobel kept her eyes lowered, typing forgotten for the moment. "He . . . he wouldn't do anything like that," she insisted.

"He would, you know." His smile teased her, as he recognized her unwillingness to admit it. "I know my little brother better than you do, don't forget. I've seen him work crafty little schemes like this before."

"But why?" she asked, still unwilling to face it. "Why didn't he ask Mrs. Grayson in the first place if he wanted me to have the cottage?"

He shrugged, shifting his frame off her desk and walking across to the window. "Grandmama knows it too," he said. "He probably gets more satisfaction out of maneuvering people without them realizing it."

"Oh, you have no call to say things like that about Nigel," she protested. "I know he's your brother—your half-brother—Mr. Bennetti, and you claim to know him well, but you shouldn't say things like that about him. It isn't as if you were ever really close, and—"

"Who told you that?" he interrupted, and she clenched her teeth at the indiscretion.

"Well . . . well, I can imagine you weren't," she said. "You're so different."

"For which Nigel thanks God, I imagine," he said, with such startling accuracy that she wondered for one crazy minute if he could possibly have overheard Nigel's words to her.

"It's obvious you wouldn't get on," she insisted. "It's like. . . ."

"Chalk and cheese?" he suggested softly, and laughed again at her discomfiture.

She lowered her eyes before the gaze that teased and disturbed her. "Will you let me get this page done?" she asked.

"Certainly." He grinned at her over his shoulder. "You don't like the idea of your Nigel doing anything underhand, do you?"

"I don't believe he . . . he intended it to be underhand," Isobel declared. "I've only your word for it and, if you'll forgive me saying so, I don't know that I care to rely on that too much."

"Why, you cheeky little. . . ." He stared at her for a moment, then burst into laughter again, shaking his head at her. "I should either sack you or slap you for impudence," he told her, "but I suppose you have some revenge owing to you, so I'll let you get away with it this time."

"Also," Isobel went on, determinedly righteous, "I wish you wouldn't refer to him as my Nigel. It's an incorrect assumption."

"An incorrect assumption." He rolled the words around his tongue. "What a grand phrase for telling me that you and Nigel aren't. . . ." He used one hand to such expressive purpose that Isobel flushed.

"Well, we're not!" she retorted indignantly.

"You may not be," he allowed calmly, "but Nigel definitely is."

"Well, either way it's no concern of yours."

"It will be if he talks you into marrying him," he declared with embarrassing bluntness.

"Mr. Bennetti—"

"And if he does," he went on as if she had not spoken, "that will make you my sister-in-law . . . half-sister-in-law," he corrected himself hastily, "so in the circumstances I think it would sound much friendlier if you called me Lucifer."

"I don't agree," Isobel argued. "For one thing you're my employer and I've never called my employer by his Christian name."

"Not even Nigel?"

She shook her head firmly. "Not during working hours," she said. "I always called him Mr. Frome then."

"How very proper," he taunted.

"It's quite usual in business, Mr. Bennetti. It's not really good for discipline to call one's employer by his Christian name."

His black eyes glittered wickedly at her for a moment. "I'm surely exempt from that rule, aren't I?" he suggested. "My name's more pagan than Christian, isn't it?"

By about nine-thirty the following morning Isobel was

beginning to think that Lucifer Bennetti had forgotten his promise to fetch her and her suitcases, and she had just decided that she would catch the later bus as she had first intended, when he arrived.

She heard the front doorbell ring loud and insistently and then her landlady's voice in the hall downstairs and Lucifer's deep quiet one. She was already halfway out of her room when the woman called up to her, "Gentleman for you, Miss Hendrix."

"Thank you." She put her suitcases out onto the landing and closed the door, turning in time to see a bemused and flattered landlady disappearing into her own sitting room and Lucifer just starting up the stairs with a wide grin on his dark face.

"Did you think I'd forgotten you?" he asked as he picked up her cases and started downstairs again, without waiting for a reply.

"I was just leaving to catch the bus," she replied. "I did think you'd forgotten, or else changed your mind."

"I seldom change my mind," he told her, putting her cases into the trunk of his car. "Not once it's made up." He saw her into the car and closed the door. "Your landlady thinks the worst," he declared as he slid behind the steering wheel, directing a villainous smile at her serious face. "The worst or otherwise, depending on your point of view."

"Judging by the expression on her face just now," Isobel said, "she suspects the worst and looks upon it as otherwise."

He laughed softly, shifting the long powerful car easily up into top gear as they picked up speed. "I rather think she fancied me herself," he informed her, not shy in

boasting of his conquest, and Isobel looked at him speculatively.

"I expect you gave her the full treatment," she
remarked. "She would be impressed."

"But you're not?"

She wished she could have sounded more convincing
when she answered him. "I'm not easily impressed, Mr.
Bennetti."

"Lucifer." She sat silently, refusing to be drawn, but
feeling some strange magnetism forcing her, quite against
her will, to look at him, and when she did the black eyes
gleamed briefly at her in triumph before turning back to
the road ahead. "Lucifer," he repeated.

"Lucifer," she echoed obediently, clenching her hands
at the soft sound of his laughter.

CHAPTER THREE

Isobel had decided to be cooperative. She was ready in good time and was waiting to be collected for her outing to the County Show. She felt far more nervous than was reasonable in the circumstances and told herself she was being utterly ridiculous, but outside of working hours she saw very little of Lucifer and the idea of spending almost an entire day in his company, without the normal distraction of work, gave her a strangely exciting feeling.

She had told him that he could find her at Kanderby House, as she wanted to have a word with Nigel before they left. She had dressed with care, hoping that her long-sleeved, flowery print dress would be considered appropriate to the occasion, and then at the last minute wondered if something more tweedy would have been better.

A last-minute, rather panicky check with a mirror had reassured her and she felt quite summery and light-hearted with her thick fair hair loose about her shoulders, instead of tied back as it usually was. Any doubts she might have had about her appearance were banished as soon as Nigel caught sight of her, drawing her down to him so that he could kiss her appreciatively.

"You look lovely," he told her. "Absolutely lovely, and I envy Luke being seen with you."

She dipped him a mock curtsy and sat beside him, her hand still held in his. "I do wish you could come, too Nigel," she said. "I feel horribly guilty about going of like this and leaving you here, and it's such a lovely day."

"Don't feel guilty," he admonished, kissing her gently. "Why should you?"

"Perhaps because I know you don't really like me going with your brother."

He looked downcast. "I made that pretty obvious, didn't I?" he admitted. "But please don't let it bother you, Isobel, I'm not really jealous of Luke."

"I should think not," Isobel said hastily, feeling nevertheless an irrepressible skip of excitement at the prospect of the day before her.

"I know I don't have to be," he said, and put a hand to her face, smiling. "I know you'll come back to me," he added softly.

"Of course I will."

"Are you quite happy working for Luke?"

The question was unexpected at this moment, although it was not the first time he had asked it, and she hesitated before answering. "Yes, I quite like working for him," she said. "It's very interesting work and not too difficult, not in the usual sense of the word. There's seldom any rush for anything and I can do it in my own time as long as I get it done, he doesn't seem to mind how. It's not hard work; I've no complaints on that score."

"On what score, then?" he asked, and she laughed, supposing she had made it sound as if there were other grounds for complaint.

"No score at all," she assured him hastily. "I've no gripes about anything, Nigel, so I suppose I must like working for him."

"That was one of the things that worried me at first," he admitted, and smiled when she looked at him, puzzled. "That you might get to like working for him too much," he explained, and she shook her head.

"I won't," she declared firmly, fully understanding his meaning.

Nigel sighed. "I suppose I was taking a bit of a risk asking you to come here," he said. "I know it's only because I'm here again," he admitted as if his own doubts embarrassed him, "but Luke's so—" he shrugged fretfully. "—I don't know. . . . It's simply that when I'm here I begin to believe all sorts of things I'd normally ridicule."

Isobel looked at him questioningly. "Well, if it concerns your brother and anything to do with me," she told him, "you needn't believe anything. No matter how persuasive he is," she added.

"It's not persuasion so much I'm thinking about," he said with a brief laugh. "Oh, it's ridiculous, I know, but sometimes I almost believe some of that silly nonsense they dabble in. Vanessa and her crew," he added by way of explanation, and Isobel looked startled.

"That . . . that black magic club you mentioned?" she asked, and he nodded. "But, Nigel, you don't believe in that sort of thing, do you?"

"Not when I'm miles away in London," he said, "but here, it's different, Isobel. You must feel it, even in the short time you've been here." His blue eyes begged for understanding. "Don't you feel that sometimes Luke is . . . is just that bit too . . . different?"

Isobel shook her head determinedly. "No. No, I don't, Nigel. He's just an ordinary man whose looks give him a slightly sinister appearance at times, that's all." It was not "all," by any means, and Isobel knew it. Ordinary was certainly not the right word to apply to Lucifer Bennetti, but she refused to recognize that his undeniable attraction owed itself to anything other than nature.

They both glanced up, startled, when soft footsteps sounded on the paved area outside the French windows. A second later, Lucifer walked in. He stood just inside the open windows, his dark eyes paying far more lavish homage to her looks than any words of Nigel's had done, sweeping over her from head to toe in one expressive look that brought the color flooding to her face.

"Good morning."

Whether or not Nigel was included in the greeting, he made little effort to answer to it, and it was left to Isobel to reply. "Good morning, Mr. Bennetti."

A black brow shot upward. "I thought we'd settled that 'Mr. Bennetti' business yesterday morning," he said, and Isobel glanced hastily at Nigel before answering.

"I still think—" she began, but was cut short by a quiet laugh.

"So do I," he told her adamantly. "Lucifer . . . whether Nigel likes it or not. I'm your boss now and I don't object, so I don't see why he should."

Nigel's look of disgust was intended to belittle him, but he merely smiled, watching Isobel steadily as if he dared her to argue. Isobel stayed stubbornly silent for a moment, then she got up from her place beside Nigel, her voice determinedly matter-of-fact. "I'm ready when you are, Mr. Bennetti."

"And I'm ready when you decide to be a little more friendly. If you're going to keep up this boss and secretary game, then we may as well stay here and work."

Isobel looked up at him, trying to judge just how serious his threat was, and one look at the dark face with its jaw stubbornly set was enough to tell her that he meant exactly what he said. "All right," she said shortly. "Have it your way, Lucifer."

He grinned. "I usually do," he told her with such unabashed pleasure at the fact that, had it not been for Nigel's black frown, she thought she would have laughed at the sheer impudence of it.

Isobel smiled down at Nigel, grumpy-looking in his chair, and bent to kiss him beside his mouth. "Goodbye, Nigel, I wish you, too, could come."

"Goodbye." He released her hand reluctantly. "Take care." It was a vague warning, but it sent a swift unexpected shiver along her spine as she stepped out into the sunshine with his brother, following his long-legged stride out to where he had parked his car.

It was, she thought as he helped her into the car, a vehicle typical of him. It was long, sleek and shiny and looked hot and red in the bright sun. Not quite respectable was the term that came to mind, although she dismissed it hastily as not only fanciful but ridiculous.

He slid his long legs under the steering wheel and turned to look at her inquiringly. "Do you mind the top being down?"

Isobel shook her head, anticipating the welcome breeze their movement would raise. "Not at all," she said. "It'll be nice and cool, and it's very hot at the moment."

He slammed the door shut with an apparently satisfied smile. "Good. I had a nasty suspicion you might turn out to be a hothouse flower."

"Well, I'm not," she said firmly. "I quite enjoy being outdoors with the wind through my hair, especially when it's like it is today. It's really lovely."

He looked at her golden hair shining richly in the sun and smiled. "I agree," he said, deliberately misunderstanding. "It's very lovely loose like that." Isobel did not reply, but merely lifted her face to the breeze as they turned out of the short driveway and onto the road.

She had to admit as they drove along that she thoroughly enjoyed the ride in the open car. The wind lifted her long hair from her neck and she was pleased she had thought to wear sunglasses. Dusty green leaves in the hedgerows flicked and twirled as they passed and dappled the car and their faces with tiny fleeting shadows.

She even found herself relaxing completely in the deep comfortable seat, her head laid back so as to catch the breeze as it skimmed above the windshield. She even took advantage of his preoccupation with driving to study her companion: the dark, Mephistophelean features, so appropriate to his unusual name, and the thick black hair blowing wildly awry in the wind and adding to the overall effect of turbulence. There seemed always to be an air of unrest about him, perhaps even excitement and she had never yet been quite at ease with him, no matter how she tried.

He drove well, but with the same rakish air that he brought to everything else he did, although she was pretty sure that some of it at least was put on with the idea of showing off to her. On second thoughts the idea of his even bothering to show off to her made her smile ruefully, thinking herself unobserved.

"You're smiling like a little kitten," he told her, turning suddenly, and she looked startled at having her reverie broken into. "Why are you so pleased with yourself?"

"I don't know that I'm pleased with myself about

anything in particular," she denied, certainly not prepared to let him know the reason for her smile.

"You looked it," he told her.

"Well, I'm not."

He raised a dark brow at her momentarily, seeking her reaction. "You looked rather like a bewitching little sorceress who's well pleased with her latest spell. A sort of prettily wicked look."

"Nothing of the sort," Isobel denied, her heart beating uneasily when she remembered Nigel's words about him being more than just different. His interest in witchcraft, she told herself, had nothing to do with his remark to her, it was nothing but coincidence and she was letting Nigel's rather unreasonable suspicions rub off on her. "I can't think why you should make so much of a perfectly natural reaction to a lovely day," she told him.

"I ordered this lovely day especially for you," he informed her, flicking a crooked smile at her over one shoulder.

A rueful, if uneasy, smile greeted his boast. "You must have a lot of influence with the weather man," she said, staring at the rugged, dark profile as his laugh shivered down her spine like a trickle of icy water.

"You'd be surprised who I have influence with," he told her softly, and turned his black eyes on her briefly.

"No, I wouldn't, not really," she denied. "I imagine you're very good at making things go your way."

He laughed. "You really believe that, don't you?"

"Yes."

"Do you mind telling me why?"

She looked at him uneasily, wondering if he was already laughing at her. There was a hint of a smile at the corner of his wide mouth, but his eyes were fixed straight ahead and half-hidden by long lashes, so she could not tell for certain. She shook her head.

"I don't know; I just think . . . imagine that you're strong-willed enough to get your own way, that's all."

That was not all, she thought wildly, as Nigel's words hammered away again at her brain. Her pulses throbbed at her temple and the wrists of her hands clenched tightly in her lap. Even the bright sunlight and her own common sense could not entirely dismiss that sense of slightly sinister unreality he gave her, and she started almost visibly when he appeared to follow her thoughts.

"Are you interested in witchcraft, Isobel?"

"No! Of course not, why do you ask?"

He shrugged. "I just wondered. A lot of people around here are."

"I don't take it as very much of a compliment that you think I'm a witch," she told him.

"I didn't say you were," he denied. "But you'd make rather a pretty witch if you were." She looked at him suspiciously and, as if he sensed her gaze, he turned his head again briefly and smiled. "A very pretty witch," he said softly.

"I haven't the least desire to be a witch, thank you," she informed him. "Pretty or otherwise . . . even if I believed in such things, which I don't."

He was silent for a second or two and she watched the dark face from under her lashes, curious now to see how he would react. "Oh, but you should," he told her solemnly, at last. "Especially in this part of the country."

"Well, I don't." She felt far less certain about it than she sounded.

"But you get a little cold shudder every time it's mentioned," he guessed, laughing softly at the swift, suspicious look she gave him.

"You're ... you're wrong, I don't."

"No? Okay, have it your way."

"Nigel told me you belong to a ... a club or something that believes ... studies witchcraft," she ventured, wondering if she was treading on delicate ground after her brave assertion of disbelief, but he appeared unconcerned.

"The Elgin Circle," he said. "It's amusing."

"But some of them take it very seriously, don't they?"

"Oooh, my goodness, yes!" He grinned at her briefly. "The rest of them are very serious indeed about it all."

"But you don't believe in it?"

"I didn't say that. I try to keep an open mind on most controversial subjects like that. I just believe in enjoying myself, that's all, instead of being gloomy about it." He laughed again, and Isobel could imagine how much his lighthearted attitude would annoy serious students of the occult. "In fact," he added with some satisfaction, "I think they'd throw me out if they dared, but I have the edge on them, of course, and they're cautious about actually sending me packing."

"Oh?"

He turned a wry smile on her briefly. "Well, wouldn't you think twice about giving Lucifer his marching orders from an order of witches?" he asked.

That involuntary shiver slid along Isobel's spine again. "It's nonsense," she insisted.

"You just wait," he chuckled, "Vanessa will convince you. If anyone can, she will!"

Isobel frowned. "I don't want to be convinced," she

assured him. "I've told you, I don't believe in such things."

She was curious because his apparent reluctance to dismiss it all as nonsense both puzzled and, to a certain extent, troubled her. "Forewarned is forearmed," he told her. "At least you should know something about it as you're likely to be involved at some time or other."

She stared at him, certain he meant what he said, but scarcely believing he could. "I have no intention of being involved," she declared, trying to steady her voice so that he would not suspect her hands trembled and her heart raced. "It's utter nonsense in this day and age. It's all ancient history and no good can come from raking over old ashes."

Surprisingly, he laughed. "When talking about witches," he informed her, "that's rather an unfortunate turn of phrase, isn't it?"

"You know what I mean," she said, and was surprised to hear herself sounding almost apologetic.

"Yes, I know what you mean," he admitted. "And here we are."

He turned the car into a field, presently being used as a parking lot, and Isobel's eyes widened when she saw the variety of cars and other vehicles already parked there. She had expected nothing as big as this, not nearly so many people even, and she saw Lucifer recognize her surprise with a smile.

Another gate gave access to the showground proper, already swarming with people, most of them much too warmly clad for the weather and looking uncomfortably hot. It was many years since she had visited a country show like this and she breathed in the hot, humid scents.

There was always a special sort of smell peculiar to such gatherings and it seemed universally the same, a smell she could never quite analyze. Crushed dry grass, hot engine oil and livestock predominated, with the whole overlaid with too much warm humanity in too small an area. But there was a sense of liveliness and excitement that Isobel responded to as they made their way through the crowd.

"Is there anywhere you'd like to go first?" Lucifer asked, rather surprising her by consulting her.

Isobel shook her head, content to follow his lead. "I don't mind in the least," she told him. "You know your way around better than I do, I expect."

"Possibly," he allowed, putting a hand under her arm as they made their way past a display of farm machinery. "I don't suppose you're interested in tractors and combine harvesters for a start, are you?" She shook her head, and he smiled down at her. "You didn't expect so many people, did you?"

"It's so much bigger than I expected," she admitted, and looked up at him curiously. "You seem to have somewhere in mind," she told him as he led her unhesitatingly along. "Where are we heading?"

"For the horses," he grinned. "You like horses, don't you?"

She blinked surprise at the accuracy of his guess. "Yes, as a matter of fact I'm very fond of horses of all sorts, but—"

His laugh cut her short. "First lesson in understanding witchcraft among other things," he told her, "is a basic knowledge of psychology. I watched your reaction when I mentioned horses and I saw the telltale look in your eyes that gave me the clue. If I hadn't seen it I'd have tried sheep, pigs and cows in that order, but the odds were pretty short on me being right first time."

So that, Isobel thought wryly, was how he could apparently follow her thoughts with such accuracy. How he had been able to impress her with his talk about witches so closely following on her own thoughts about his association with the occult. He had seen and noted her reaction to being called a bewitching little sorceress and taken it on from there. He was right; psychology was the basis of the seeming mystery and, for the moment, the thought comforted her.

"Very clever," she told him, eyeing him curiously. "But why this insistence on witchcraft? It's much too lovely a day to think about spooky, unpleasant things like that."

He shrugged. "Just in case," he said, and a moment later laughed. "Come on, let's go and find your horses."

It surprised Isobel how many people he seemed to know, until she remembered that he had spent a good deal of his childhood here, and that he still lived among the same people now and was therefore completely at home. Also, despite his dark, foreign appearance, he fitted into his surroundings surprisingly well; far better than she could imagine Nigel doing. Nigel always seemed so very much a city person, whereas Lucifer's dark face was much less noticeable among all the weather-beaten, well-tanned faces of the country people.

He wore no jacket and his shirt was open at the neck, his strong brown throat contrasting with fine white cotton. Hot weather suited him and he looked almost too attractive, drawing the eyes of every woman they passed, and taking it all in his stride, Isobel thought wryly.

Her own cheeks were bright with warmth and her eyes shot from one attraction to another, anxious to miss nothing. There were sideshows in one small section and a long white marquee sold refreshments, the latter catching her eye as she realized how thirsty she was.

"You could do with a drink," Lucifer informed her with a smile, and she nodded.

"Psychology again, I suppose," she guessed, and he laughed.

"You are thirsty, aren't you?"

"I am," she admitted, "and I suppose I showed it by licking my lips when I saw the refreshment marquee."

"Exactly," he laughed. "You learn quickly, *piccola*."

They sat in the half shade, stealing the edge of the shadow cast by a huge oak, the grass cool and soft as they sank down on to it. Isobel drank half her drink and sighed her relief as it cooled her dry throat, leaning back on her hands, her legs curled up under her. She glanced up when Lucifer waved a casual hand to someone over near the entrance of the marquee.

The man he greeted returned the wave and a second later Isobel glanced curiously at Lucifer when he started across the grass toward them, a big sketchbook tucked under one arm. "An artist?" she asked, and Lucifer nodded.

"And an old acquaintance." She may have imagined it, but she thought she detected sarcasm in the remark.

The man stopped in front of them, his eyes going curiously to Isobel before he spoke. "Hello, Lucifer, long time no see."

"Quite a long time," Lucifer admitted, as the

newcomer flopped down in the shade, the sketchbook on his hunched knees. "I'm surprised to see you here, Cal; I thought country fairs were a bit out of your line."

The shoulders under the rather stained shirt shrugged. "I'm earning an honest crust," he said wryly. "Sketching the county and the hoi polloi alike. A little money here and there."

"Oh, I see, you're working."

"Uh huh." The shaggy head nodded. "I don't know who your lovely lady is, but I would enjoy sketching her head."

Lucifer smiled, casting an oddly protective glance at Isobel, which she noted with some surprise. "I'll bet you would, but I doubt if you could do her justice in the time you have available." He waved a casual hand between the man and Isobel and performed perfunctory introductions. "Cal, Isobel Hendrix. Isobel, Cal Ford."

The man's eyes studied Isobel carefully for a short time before he summoned a dry smile. "Very nice, too," he remarked, and Isobel blushed at the obvious interpretation he put on her presence there with Lucifer.

"I'm Mr. Bennetti's secretary," she informed him, and saw Lucifer's smile of amusement.

"Oh, I see." The gaze was even more curious now and discretion was put aside as he gave voice to what had obviously been on his mind all along. "I thought you were a little bit out of Lucifer's usual line," he told her bluntly, "and much younger, too." He looked at Lucifer questioningly. "I expected you to be with Vanessa, as usual," he told him. "Is she missing or have you two . . . ?" His hands spread expressively and Isobel wondered if he too had origins similar to Lucifer's.

"She's in Germany."

"Oh!" Isobel thought he was disappointed and so, apparently, did Lucifer, for there was a hint of malice in his voice when he spoke again.

"Disappointed?" he asked softly, and the artist's thin face flushed.

"I told you," he said, "I'm working; meeting old friends is a bonus."

Isobel felt uneasy. Obviously the man was an admirer of Vanessa Law and Lucifer was being rather cruel in taunting him about it. She could feel sorry for Cal Ford if he was in competition with Lucifer for Vanessa's attention, for he would be formidable opposition for any man.

"Aah!" The black eyes recognized a half-truth.

The man's restless hands flicked open the sketchbook and he sat staring at the blank page as he spoke. "I seldom see Vanessa these days. She's busy, I'm busy and ... well, you know the way it goes."

"I know the way it goes," Lucifer agreed, and added so quietly that Isobel barely heard it, "You're a fool, Cal."

"Maybe," the man shrugged. "Beggars can't be choosers, but you wouldn't know, would you?"

"I don't believe in being a beggar," Lucifer told him quietly but firmly. "If I want anything I go out and get it, but thank God I've never yet let any woman get under my skin to that extent."

"You're a conceited devil," Cal Ford said bitterly, "but I wish I had half your nerve."

Lucifer smiled, shaking his head, glancing at Isobel a second later, as if he had only now remembered she was there. "Isobel's a pretty child," he told him. "If you're working, you can do a sketch of her." The artist looked at her again with curious eyes as Lucifer smiled at her. "Show the man your best side, *bella mia*."

The endearment, accompanied by the unexpected request, stunned Isobel for a moment and she stared at him. "But you can't be serious," she said at last.

"Of course I am." Despite his claim to be serious, the black eyes glittered with laughter, and he put out a hand to cup her chin, turning her head first this way, then that, his head on one side as he studied her. "Hmm," he decided at last. "Full face, I think, then it will show your beautiful eyes."

"Lucifer. . . ."

"Don't argue," he told her quietly, "just look at Cal and relax."

Cal Ford nodded approval, already making the first bold lines on the virgin page of the pad, nodding his head as he worked, while Isobel sat as still as she was able to, thinking she had never felt so uneasy in her life. Once she inadvertently moved her head and Lucifer's strong fingers turned her head back to its original position, his smile recognizing her embarrassment.

"Sit still," he told her. "If you fidget you'll put the man off his stroke."

"Nearly finished now," Cal Ford said, his smile sympathizing with her, as his deft strokes flew over the paper, shading and highlighting.

Isobel sat as still and patiently as she could, but it seemed an interminable time before Cal Ford raised his head, holding the pad out in front of him as he frowned over the finished work. "Lucifer's right," he admitted at last, "I haven't done you justice."

Lucifer took the drawing from him, his black eyes going from the original and back to the sketch, his expression impossible to interpret. "It's good," he declared at last. "It's very good, you've captured that soft and lovely look to perfection. You always manage to get to the heart of your subject, don't you, Cal?"

"Do I?" Cal Ford looked rather surprised at the praise. "I'm glad you're satisfied."

"I am, thanks." He detached the drawing from the pad and handed the pad back, rolling the sketch into a tube.

Cal Ford looked puzzled. "It's for you?"

Lucifer nodded. "Of course, who else?"

The narrow shoulders shrugged again. "I thought it might be for Miss Hendrix herself. I remember doing a drawing once before at your request and you declined to have the finished work then." The rather sad eyes had an envious look. "You said you didn't need a drawing when you had the original," he added, and Isobel had no difficulty in guessing the identity of the subject.

Lucifer smiled, tapping the rolled drawing against his chin. "This is different," he said softly. "I don't have the original of this one. Nigel has."

CHAPTER FOUR

Lucifer had said he would expect her to work extra hours to make up for the time they had spent at the show, and Isobel was not really surprised to find that he had meant it. In fact he kept her working late for the next week or more, and she began to wonder if he intended making it a regular thing.

Nigel took her continued long hours as a personal affront and he made no secret of his resentment when Lucifer lunched with his grandmother again one Sunday. Isobel too, had been invited and she kept her eyes lowered discreetly when Nigel tackled his brother about her working late so often.

"You delight in disrupting people's lives, don't you?" he accused, and Lucifer smiled.

"I didn't know I was doing anything so dramatic," he said. " 'Disrupting people's lives' is rather overdoing it, surely."

"I don't think so," Nigel argued. "You know Isobel spends her free time with me and you're just damned selfish enough to keep her late every night because you know it upsets our plans."

"I never even gave you a thought," Lucifer admitted blandly.

"Exactly!" Nigel glared at him so hard that even Isobel found it difficult not to see how self-righteous it made him look.

"As for plans. . . ." A black brow arched curiously. "Come on, Nigel, you can't possibly go anywhere plastered up like that."

"Lucifer!" Mrs. Grayson shook her head at him, but Isobel recognized the customary indulgence even in the reproach. "Poor Nigel has enough to contend with without you being so callous about it."

"I'm not being callous," Lucifer protested mildly. "But where can he go trussed up like that? I've offered to take him out in the car to give him a change of air and environment, but he turned up his nose at the offer. He won't budge."

"It's difficult," the old lady told him, seeing his point of view as usual. "Being driven when you're used to driving can't be much fun."

"It isn't," Nigel declared bluntly. "Especially when he drives like a maniac in that ghastly little horror of his."

"Like a maniac?" The black eyes turned appealingly to Isobel and her heart sank at the prospect of either lying or having to side with him against Nigel. "Isobel, be honest now, do I drive like a maniac?"

She was very tempted to lie, but she knew she would never be able to while he watched her like that, so instead she did her best to compromise. "You certainly drive very fast," she said after a moment's hesitation, "but you seem to have good control, so I suppose it's safe enough."

His gaze mocked her reticence and she knew Nigel was even less pleased with her answer. "There you are," Lucifer told him. "Grudging admission, but admission just the same." He looked at his brother, his eyes wickedly black. "One thing about my driving, old boy," he added softly, "at least I'm all in one piece, aren't I?"

"Oh, that was cruel!" Isobel objected, and even Nigel blinked at the vehemence of her protest, while Lucifer looked actually surprised, the first time she had ever seen such an expression on his face.

"It was unkind, Lucifer," Mrs. Grayson told him.

"All right, all right!" He held up his hands as if in defense. "I'm sorry I was cruel to poor Nigel and I'm sorry I kept poor Isobel from being with him. Okay?"

"Of course." It was the old lady who answered for them, only too ready to accept his apparently sincere apology. "No one holds it against you, but you really shouldn't make Isobel work so hard and so late."

"I don't think I do," he argued, and Isobel saw the strong jaw set stubbornly. "I know she works hard, but not too hard, and there may come a time when there's very little for her to do at all. She has to take the rough with the smooth; she knows that." The black eyes flicked briefly to his brother before settling on Isobel, curious and a little puzzled. "Has she been complaining to you?" he asked Nigel.

"No, of course she hasn't," Nigel said, "Isobel's a good worker, but. . . ."

"Then why try to make her otherwise?" Lucifer interrupted.

"I have to agree with Nigel on that point, Lucifer," Mrs. Grayson said, obviously reluctant to speak her mind. "Just lately you've kept her very late and almost every night."

Isobel noted the barely discernible tightening of his wide straight mouth as he looked at her. "Everyone seems to think I treat you very badly, Isobel," he said quietly, the dark eyes compelling her to look at him. "Have you any complaints?"

She felt herself the target for three pairs of eyes, but it was Lucifer's that still held her gaze. "No." She shook her head. "No, I don't mind having to work late. I . . . I knew I would have to sometimes."

"But not all the time," Nigel insisted, angry because she was not supporting him. "I scarcely ever see you before eight-thirty in the evening now."

"But it's not permanent, Nigel." She sought to stem the temper she could see threatening. "And I do spend every evening with you, which I never did in town."

"I know you do, but that was the idea of having you here, so that I could see you more often." The admission sent Lucifer's black brows swiftly upward and brought a wicked glitter to his eyes.

"So in other words," he said quietly, "my need for a secretary was intended to play second fiddle to your need to have Isobel within easy reach. You wanted her here to soothe your fevered brow and my wants came a very poor second. Now I know why you talked me into taking her on as my secretary."

"You knew all along," Nigel retorted. "And don't make it sound as if you were doing me a favor. You did need a secretary, and Isobel's a damned good one."

"I agree," Lucifer said, still far less disturbed by the argument than his brother. "But she *is* working for me, and she's said she doesn't mind working late, so I don't see that you've much room for complaint." A long hand reached out and covered one of Isobel's, the fingers curled firmly over hers. "Don't you like working for me, Isobel?" he asked softly.

"Yes, yes, of course I do." She hastily lowered her eyes against the reproach she saw in Nigel's. "I'm quite happy," she added, "and I'm very well paid."

"You see?" His shoulders shrugged off any further discussion along those lines and the strong fingers tightened briefly over hers, as if in thanks. He was, she thought wildly, quite the most uncrushable man she'd ever met.

Whether he had been influenced after all by his family's remarks, Isobel did not know, but the next day Lucifer called a halt to work much earlier than usual. She was not sorry at all for, despite her protests that she did not mind working late, she felt she had been doing rather too much lately, although she would never have said so to Nigel.

He saw her glance at her watch as she covered her typewriter; she looked at him sharply when he laughed. "Respectable hours today for a change," he remarked, and Isobel smiled.

"So Nigel's complaints did have some effect," she said.

He shook his head, coming over to perch on the edge of her desk as he often did. "None at all," he denied. "I don't allow myself to be influenced by anyone; it just happens to suit me to let you leave early today."

"Oh, I see."

He was watching her, his eyes glittering mischievously as he reached out a hand and brushed back a stray wisp of hair from her neck. "I expect you do see, *bella mia*," he said softly. "You realize who pays the piper and therefore calls the tune, don't you?"

Isobel moved away from him, hating the way her heart was thudding wildly against her ribs just because he touched her and used that name he often called her, mostly when they were alone. "I know you're entitled to call the tune, Lucifer, but I wish you wouldn't use Italian words I don't understand."

"Bella mia?" He smiled, and it was obvious he had no intention of enlightening her until it suited his purpose. "Why does everyone call you by your full name? Haven't you a pet name?"

"No." She overlooked a rather unflattering name she had been called as a baby, for it had never been carried over into adult life. "I'm always called Isobel, and I prefer it that way."

"Never Belle or Bella?"

"No, I don't like my name shortened, I prefer it as it is."

"Well, you'll have to bear with me if my more flamboyant tastes lead me into error sometimes," he told her solemnly. "I think Bella suits you much better."

"It's not my name."

He smiled and her pulse quickened alarmingly. "But it's so much more descriptive," he said softly, and laughed when she frowned.

"It's extremely rude to use words you know I don't understand," she objected.

"Ah, but knowing you, *piccola,* you'd probably take even more exception if you did understand," he told her. "You're such a proper little creature, aren't you?" He lifted her chin with one hand and spoke so close to her mouth that his breath was warm on her lips. *"Bella,"* he said softly, and in a gentle, liquid accent that did crazy things to her pulse. *"Bella, bella, bella."*

"Please don't!" She brushed away his hand and turned her face away, clasping her hands tightly to stop them trembling.

"Don't you want to know what it means?" he teased, and she shook her head.

"I don't suppose you've the slightest intention of telling me," she said, trying hard to ignore the watching eyes. "And I'm not sure I want to know anyway."

"But I'd love to tell you, if I can be sure you won't take offense in your funny puritan little way and slap my face for paying you a compliment."

"I am not puritan," Isobel objected indignantly. "How can you say that?" She looked down at the papers on her desk unseeingly. "Besides," she confessed cautiously, "I . . . I think I have some idea what it means."

"Of course you have," he told her, and she felt sure he was laughing at her although she dared not look at him to confirm it. "It means pretty and beautiful; everything that describes you so perfectly, *bella mia*." He spoke softly and, almost unwillingly, she turned her head and looked at him. "You're well named, little Bella."

"I'm not named Bella, I'm Isobel," she insisted, her voice barely under control.

"To me you're. . . ." He shrugged his shoulders and spread his hands, deliberately Italian, she suspected. "*Bella mia*."

"I do know what *mia* means, Lucifer, and it definitely doesn't apply." She busied herself in an attempt to restore normalcy, tidying her desk as best she could for his being seated on it, then she picked up her handbag, ready to go. "Now," she told him meeting his eyes with difficulty, "if there's nothing else, I'll go."

The black eyes mocked her. "Go by all means," he said, leaning forward as she brushed past him on her way out. "*Ciao, bella mia*."

It was no time to stay and argue the rights and wrongs of anything, she decided, and instead she walked to the door and out into the tiny hall. She was just in time to see the front door open and a woman come in. She made her entrance with all the self-confidence of a regular visitor and Isobel felt her hands tighten involuntarily when she realized who the caller must be, and why she had been allowed to leave so early today. Despite Nigel's rather lurid description of Vanessa Law, Isobel was not prepared for quite such a striking appearance, and she felt a strange chill of uneasiness when the odd, almost yellow eyes looked at her coolly.

She was several inches taller than Isobel and quite slim with jet black hair piled on top of her head in a style that should have been much too severe for her sharp features but which, in fact, added in some odd way to her exotic looks. Even on this bright and sunny August day she wore a very dark dress. Isobel could not be sure of its actual color in the shady hallway, but it gave the woman an appearance of being even taller.

"Good evening." Some gesture of acknowledgment was called for, Isobel thought, and she tried a half smile.

Whether the other woman would have replied or not did not arise, for almost at once Lucifer came out into the hall and took charge of the situation with his usual aplomb. "I thought it might be you," he told the visitor. "You're early."

As a welcome it could have been said to lack warmth and her mouth, surprisingly full-lipped in the thin face, pouted reproach before she tiptoed over and kissed him. "Flattering as ever," she said. "You are a brute, Lucifer."

He ignored the reproach and turned to smile at Isobel, already part way out of the front door. "Van, this is Isobel Hendrix; Isobel, Vanessa Law."

Isobel proffered a hand, ready to be sociable although a shiver ran through her, which she firmly quelled, when the odd, catlike eyes swept over her insolently. "Miss Law," she murmured, not noticing until it was too late the wide gold ring on the other's left hand.

Her proffered hand was ignored and instead a brief nod of the black head reluctantly acknowledged her existence. "Mrs. Law," she corrected her coolly, and looked up at Lucifer suspiciously. "Someone said you had a new secretary," she said, making it sound like an accusation.

"News gets around." He acknowledged the fact with a smile. "It's amazing, isn't it?" The look he gave her told her plainly enough that he guessed Cal Ford to be her informer. "Especially after the County Show."

"Cal told me," she informed him defiantly.

"Of course." Isobel felt horribly superfluous standing there, but it would be difficult to just leave without saying anything further.

"You didn't say anything," Vanessa Law accused, and Lucifer smiled.

"I saw no reason to tell you that I had a new secretary," he told her. "My business arrangements don't usually concern you. I didn't see why Isobel's arrival should." That, Isobel thought, with sudden and startling insight, was completely untrue. He had not only known that Vanessa Law would hate the idea of her being there but had put in a hasty appearance when he heard the two of them together in the hall.

"If you needed a new secretary," Vanessa told him, the catlike eyes sweeping over Isobel chillingly, "I could have found you a much more suitable one if you'd told me."

"More suitable?" Such innocence had to be assumed, and Vanessa Law recognized it too and frowned.

"You should have had someone older like Mrs. Lomas," she informed him shortly. "This one's far too young."

She would not, Isobel thought, even give her the benefit of a name and she looked at Lucifer, wondering what his reaction would be. "There's no law against young secretaries that I know of," he told her quietly, "and Isobel's very efficient."

"Hmm." Vanessa could see the argument already slipping away from her and decided to make the best of whatever power she had over him. She pushed an arm through his and looked up at him, her mouth pouted in reproach. "I wasn't aware that efficiency interested you to that extent," she told him, "but if it does, I'm very efficient too, aren't I, darling?"

"Very," he agreed amiably and with a smile that recognized surrender. "Vanessa," he explained for Isobel's benefit, "runs a very prosperous antique business in town."

"I know," Isobel said. "Nigel told me."

The yellow-colored eyes narrowed. "Nigel?" she queried, looking to Lucifer for explanation.

"Isobel," Lucifer explained, "used to work at Frome's, Nigel's firm."

"Oh, I see."

Lucifer laughed, evidently enjoying the situation. "I'll bet you don't," he declared. "Isobel caught the directorial eye while she was there and, since he's been laid up after his crash, he's been pining for her so much that he talked me into taking her on as my secretary."

Isobel flushed, looking at him with reproachful eyes. "You weren't obliged to take me on, Mr. Bennetti," she told him. "I wasn't desperate for work. I already had a perfectly good job at Frome's."

"Oh, I don't regret taking you on," he said, his grin taunting her for her touchiness. "As I said, you're very efficient and you're much, much prettier than Tottie Lomas."

The latter definitely did not please Vanessa Law, and she pursed her full lips doubtfully. "What happened to Lomas?" she asked. "Why did you get rid of her, Lucifer?"

Lucifer shrugged. "I didn't. She left."

"She left?" She looked as if she found that hard to believe. "But why?"

"If it matters," he informed her with a grin, "she said she'd had enough of me. She couldn't stand the pace." He looked at Isobel and smiled. "It gets pretty hectic at times, doesn't it, Isobel?"

"At times," she agreed, feeling uneasy each time those strange eyes came in her direction.

"Despite her fairy-tale princess looks," Lucifer went on, making things worse, "I think Isobel's made of sterner stuff, aren't you, *bella mia*?"

Why, oh, why, Isobel thought wildly when she saw the other woman frown, did he have to use that endearment when Vanessa was there? It was just about the most indiscreet thing he could have done, and Isobel felt a sudden, urgent desire to flee, to run as far away from there as fast as her legs would take her. There was something about Vanessa Law that gave her a cold feeling in the pit of her stomach. She wondered why Lucifer did not realize it and behave more discreetly. Except, of course, that it was the sort of situation he would probably enjoy.

"If . . . if you'll excuse me," she said, glancing at her watch, "I'll go now. Nigel's expecting me as soon as I've had dinner." She closed the door hastily behind her and hurried away, trying not to hear the cool hard voice of Vanessa Law raised in protest as she left.

"Lucifer, she's too young, get rid of her."

Gradually Nigel was getting about a little more each day, although he had still to take care and not overdo the time he was on his feet, and it would be a long time yet before he was completely fit again. It was the cool of the evening and the last of the red summer sun gave a curiously unreal look to the soft green hills and the toy village of stone cottages tucked away in their shelter.

The garden sloped a little at the very end and from there it overlooked a scene so beautiful it was breathtaking, a scene Isobel felt she would never tire of. She walked slowly beside Nigel as he hobbled along on crutches, breathing heavily from the exertion.

"Am I going too fast?" she asked, and he shook his head.

"No, no, I'm fine, thanks, even though I am puffing like an old man."

"If you'd use that wheelchair," Isobel told him for the umpteenth time, "I could push you and save you all this exertion."

"Well, I won't." He looked stubborn. "I refuse to be pushed about like a baby in a carriage. I'll go under my own steam or not at all."

Isobel smiled. "All right, obstinate, but don't say I didn't offer."

He leaned forward, awkwardly because of the crutches, and kissed her cheek. "I know I'm stubborn, darling, but I hate being dependent on anyone at all, and most of all you."

"Why most of all me?" she asked.

"Because you're special. I want to do things for you, not the other way round."

"You do do things for me," she laughed. "And it works both ways, you know. I like to do things for you too."

He stopped, perching rather precariously on a low wall. "Let's take a breather," he suggested. "I'm sure it's farther to the end of the garden now than it used to be." He took her hands and pulled her down beside him and Isobel felt her blood stirring uneasily at what she saw so unmistakably in his eyes. "You are special, you know," he told her softly. "You're very, very special, Isobel."

She shook her head, uncertain if she wanted him to be so serious. With Nigel there would be no lighthearted flirting, as with Lucifer; Nigel was much too serious about everything to indulge in anything so frivolous.

"I'm just a girl," she told him lightly. "A moderately good secretary and fairly good-looking, so I've been told; nothing so special."

"You are to me." He leaned across and kissed her mouth, his blue eyes looking incredibly dark, almost as black as Lucifer's in the red light of the dying sun. "You're beautiful, Isobel, you're beautiful, my darling."

His choice of words again reminded her of Lucifer and she hastily dismissed the memory of that idiotic discussion about her name. "You're very flattering," she told him, smiling gently, for Nigel would be easy to hurt, she thought. She brushed a fall of hair from his forehead, sensing that he was far less sure of himself than she had ever known him to be and wondering at the change. The self-sufficient business executive apparently had still quite a lot of the schoolboy in him and at the moment he looked a lot less than the twenty-nine years he claimed.

"I'm not being flattering at all," he declared. "You *are* beautiful and I'm more than half in love with you already. A few more days in this witching country with you and I'll be completely under your spell."

The words reminded her of Vanessa Law and she shook off the scene they recreated, smiling to take the edge off her words. "I don't want you to fall in love with me," she told him, and saw him frown suspiciously. "I . . . I want to be fancy-free for quite a few more years yet and see something of the world."

"You're not thinking of leaving me?" he asked, and she shook her head.

"Not for the present," she denied. "But I don't want to be tied down anywhere yet, it's too early."

He sighed, lifting her hands to his lips in an unexpectedly romantic gesture. "I suppose I'm being selfish," he allowed. "You're very young and I've never quite realized it until now. How old are you, Isobel?"

She remembered Vanessa Law's last words as she walked away from Lucifer's cottage earlier, telling him that she was too young to be his secretary, and wondered why Nigel, too, had raised the question of her age.

She scowled at him. "That's not a question a gentleman would ask," she said. "And you of all people should know how old I am. You interviewed me, or have you forgotten?"

"No, of course I haven't forgotten." He frowned in

thought for a moment. "Let me see, you came to us straight from school, didn't you?"

"Secretarial college," she corrected him, and laughed at his concentration. "That was four years ago," she prompted, "and I was eighteen then, so you work it out from there."

"Is it possible it's four years ago?" he asked. "I remember it very well, actually, but it doesn't seem so long ago as that. I remember I thought you were an enchanting little creature, even then, and I grudged old Pogson having you for his secretary."

"He frightened me to death," Isobel confessed laughingly. "And so did you, that first day."

"But not now."

"Oh no, not now."

"I'd hate to think you looked on me as an ogre of a boss, even if I am a bit stuffy at times, and I am, aren't I?"

"No, not stuffy," she denied. "Just serious."

His eyes studied her closely in the fading light, and she thought he had been reminded of something. "Luke's never stuffy, I suppose, is he?" he asked at last, and Isobel hesitated before she answered.

"No, he's never stuffy, but then he's seldom serious either."

"Hmmm. He let you leave at a reasonable hour tonight," he said. "Did you demand to go or did he have a change of heart?"

"Neither. He had a date."

"Oh? That early?" He was obviously curious and Isobel was not reluctant to enlighten him as they started walking again, down toward the grassy slope at the end of the garden.

"I met Vanessa Law as I came out," she told him. "*Mrs.* Law, although you'd omitted to tell me that."

"Sorry. Did you call her Miss?"

"I did, and was put firmly in my place for my pains. I . . . I don't think she liked me very much."

He glanced at her face and shrugged awkwardly. "She wouldn't," he stated bluntly.

"She's very striking, isn't she?"

"Very," Nigel agreed wryly. "How did she strike you?"

"You told me she gave you the creeps," Isobel reminded him, "and I'm inclined to agree with you. I felt cold shivers all over me when she looked at me. She really is a remarkable-looking woman and those . . . those strange-looking eyes have to be seen to be believed."

"They *are* yellow, aren't they?"

Isobel nodded. "Although they're more amber than actual yellow, I suppose, to be honest." She smiled ruefully. "The temptation to liken her to a witch, knowing what I know about her, is almost irresistible."

"Isn't it, though?"

"The last thing I heard her saying as I came away from the house," Isobel told him, "was that Lucifer should get rid of me because I was too young." Try as she would to conceal it there was an edge of anxiety on her voice when she asked the question. "Will he, do you think?"

Nigel shook his head. "Not Luke," he said with certainty. "Especially if Vanessa was issuing orders, as she has a habit of doing. I thought she would have known him well enough by now, he digs his heels in hard if there's any suggestion of being told to do anything. He's a terrible autocrat, he always was, even as a boy. I suppose he gets it from his father."

Isobel could not disguise her interest, no matter how she tried. "Was he an autocrat?" she asked.

"So I understand," Nigel said, his expression grim. "I suppose he still is. Count Giulio Giovanni Giuseppe Bennetti of the Palazzo Bennetti, Rome. Does that answer your question?"

Isobel laughed. "No wonder Lucifer has such illusions of grandeur," she said. "I suppose they're not really illusions, are they? Does he ever see his father?" she added, her curiosity thoroughly aroused, and Nigel laughed shortly.

"Not lately," he told her. "The last I heard there was a new and very beautiful young Contessa and . . . like father, like son. Papa Bennetti's not likely to put his young Contessa in the way of temptation by asking Luke to visit."

"No," Isobel admitted thoughtfully. "I can see he wouldn't if he's a wise man."

"I don't know about wise," Nigel demurred, "but he must be quite an old man by now."

"Oh, really? I hadn't realized that. The Count was . . . your mother's first husband, wasn't he?"

"Yes." He frowned as he always did when he was reminded that his father had not been first. "Gran knows all the sordid details, of course, and I've heard them at various times through the years. Mother eloped with Bennetti when she was only seventeen and he was nearly thirty. Luke was born less than a year later and the whole thing lasted only about five years, then she divorced him and married my father."

"Mrs. Grayson was telling me about your father," Isobel said, seeking a more popular subject. "Apparently

Andy Frome was a big name in motor-racing at one time, although it was before my time, of course."

"He was a very big name," Nigel agreed, with a note of pride for the father he could scarcely have known. "He was also shrewd enough to think of his family's future and he started Frome Engineering as a sort of insurance for when he retired. The only trouble was he didn't live long enough to retire."

"It was a chance he took in his profession," Isobel said softly. "I expect he knew that and left the firm for you when you were old enough."

"Yes." He sighed. "I would rather have liked to have known him a bit better, though." He sat down gratefully on a rough wooden seat under a tree, his eyes on the distant hills that were rapidly disappearing in the dying light. "I sometimes wish I'd had the nerve to follow in his footsteps," he said slowly, "but as you see, I can't even handle an ordinary, everyday car without bashing it and myself to pieces."

"Not quite to pieces," Isobel smiled. "You're getting on famously now, Nigel, aren't you?"

"I feel a lot better," he agreed, and reached for her hands as she sat down beside him. "That's largely due to having you here," he told her. "It was a stroke of genius on my part, getting you that job with Luke."

"Yes, yes, it was." She, too, gazed out at the fast disappearing hills, watching the color of the sky change from red to purple, and not for anything would she have let him know the brief thought that entered her mind and was hastily dismissed. The thought that evidently he shared none of Count Bennetti's qualms about trusting her in close proximity to Lucifer.

CHAPTER FIVE

Isobel was thinking one evening of her dinner. It was quite early and it would be some time yet before she was allowed to leave, but it had seemed such a long day today and she would be very glad of the half hour or so of relaxation that would follow her meal, before she was expected to go over to the house and see Nigel.

It had been so sultry all day, not pleasantly warm but heavy and oppressive and, even with the windows wide open, the room seemed close and airless. She finished the page she was typing and looked across hopefully at Lucifer and was disconcerted to find him watching her.

"Have you had enough for today?" he asked, running a hand through his hair, and Isobel nodded.

"It's so terribly hot," she complained, "and there doesn't seem to be a breath of air anywhere."

He stretched lazily. "It'll probably thunder before the night's out," he guessed. "It feels like it."

"Don't you know?" she asked, remembering his claim to have ordered the fine weather especially for the County Show.

"Not this time," he admitted. "But I'm pretty sure we're in for a storm."

Isobel shuddered. She knew she was an abject coward and frankly admitted it, but thunderstorms had always terrified her ever since she was a child, and no amount of logical explanations made a scrap of difference. Not that she made an exhibition of herself if there were other people around, but if she was alone she always hid her head and let her shaking limbs have their way.

"I hope you're wrong," she told him.

He frowned and studied her curiously. "You're not scared of thunderstorms, are you?"

Isobel hesitated before admitting it. "Yes, as a matter of fact I am. Oh, don't worry," she added hastily, "I don't go berserk or make a fool of myself, at least not when anyone's around."

"But you don't like it when you're alone?"

"I'm petrified, an absolute coward."

Surprisingly he seemed more interested than scornful as she had expected him to be, and he leaned back in his chair to catch what breeze there was from the open window behind him. "Why?" he asked. "I mean what actually frightens you?"

She shrugged, looking a little shamefaced for having admitted it. "I don't know, I wish I did, then perhaps I could do something about it."

"What do you do when you're alone?"

"I hide my head," she said, hoping he wouldn't laugh.

"Under the pillows?"

"Anywhere that shuts out the noise and the flashes of lightning. I told you, I'm a dreadful coward."

"Oh well," he cast a speculative eye at the brassy sky outside, "let's hope it keeps fine for you."

She echoed the hope fervently and picked up paper and carbon to start another page. "It may not come to anything," she said.

"I thought we agreed we'd finished for today," he said, getting up and coming to sit, inevitably, on her desk.

"Take that paper out again and pack up, it's much too hot to work."

Isobel glanced at her watch. "It's rather early," she said, willing to be persuaded, and he laughed.

"You're a glutton for work, aren't you?" he asked. "I'm surprised Nigel wanted to part with you."

"Well, he didn't exactly part with me, did he?" she asked.

He grinned wryly at her. "No, the crafty so-and-so pulled a fast one there. He wanted it both ways." The black eyes twinkled wickedly. "Not that I blame him in the least."

"That wasn't his only reason for getting me here," she protested. "You wanted a secretary, after all. You'd driven the last poor woman half out of her mind. Besides," she added practically, "this job is a much better-paid one."

"Little mercenary," he teased. "Is that the only reason you came here?"

She looked at him for a moment. "The main one," she said at last. "Although I like being near Nigel, of course."

"Of course," he echoed. "But you realize that he'll expect you to go back to Frome's when he does, don't you?"

It was something that had often crossed Isobel's mind since she had been there. What would happen when Nigel was well enough to return to London and whether he would expect Isobel to go, too. Almost certainly he would, she thought, and wondered if she was prepared to go when she had so much to give up. Not only was her salary considerably more, but she also had the little cottage to herself and at far less rent than she had been paying for her rooms in London.

"I . . . I don't think he will," she denied, so obviously not believing it that he laughed.

"You know damn well he will," he told her, and arched a brow in query, a query she forestalled.

"Well . . . well, maybe he will," she allowed hastily. "But it's logical really, I suppose."

He was still, she saw, going to ask her. "Will you go, Isobel?"

It was a difficult question to answer at any time and particularly so with that black-eyed gaze seeming to look right into her. "I . . . I don't know."

"Ah, I suppose it depends," he said mockingly, as if he guessed her reasons for hesitating.

She lifted her chin, her eyes glistening darkly. "It would depend," she told him.

"On what else he offers?"

The jibe angered her and she clenched her hands on the papers she was tidying. "I don't know what you mean by that," she said, "but I don't like the way you said it."

"Sorry about that, but you do know what I meant, don't you?"

"No, I don't."

"Oh, come on," he said. "You know he's crazy about you."

"That's not—"

"He might marry you," he guessed, giving her no time to finish her protest. "In fact I'm pretty sure he's serious about you."

"Which is more than you ever are about anything," Isobel retorted.

He laughed. "You don't know me well enough to make a crack like that, *bella mia*, now do you?"

She made no immediate answer, but was forced to recognize the truth of the accusation. Considering she spent so much of her time in his company she knew really very little about him except what Nigel had told her, and she doubted if she ever would. He was as enigmatic and elusive as his notorious namesake.

"No, I suppose not," she admitted at last as she put the cover on her typewriter and picked up her purse. "It's hot," she complained, "and I feel cranky."

"That's painfully obvious." He rose from her desk and held up a hand when she would have retorted. "I suggest we go and find ourselves a breeze," he said. "Freshen ourselves back into sanity with a long fast drive."

"But—"

"But me no buts," he told her. "We'll drive out as far as Reever's Beacon and back."

"It would be lovely and cool," Isobel said wistfully.

"Then why are you arguing?"

"I . . . I'm not . . . I'll let Ni—"

"You'll do no such thing," he retorted, taking her firmly by the arm. "You're not tied to Nigel's apron strings and you don't have to report every move you make to him, so let's go."

"You are a bully," she told him a little breathlessly as they left the cottage and walked out to his car. "An absolute bully!"

"I also eat pretty blondes for breakfast," he informed her, leering horribly as he half pushed her into the car.

Isobel looked at him loftily. "I can believe it," she retorted.

It was beautifully cool driving along and, despite Nigel's scornful reference to his maniacal driving, Isobel had no qualms at all for her own safety. He was a skillful driver: the strong brown hands firmly in control and taking no chances although they were traveling fast to create a breeze. The lanes were quiet and there seemed to be no other traffic about. She had little time to notice the countryside flying past, but sightseeing was not the object of their journey, just the creation of a cool breeze, and she leaned back her head and half-closed her eyes to make the most of it.

"Have you ever been to Reever's Beacon?" he asked unexpectedly, and grinned at her barely concealed start.

"No, no, I've been nowhere except into Greenlaw and to the County Show with you." She turned her head and looked at him lazily from under her lashes. "What is Reever's Beacon?"

He smiled. "Exactly what it says it is . . . a beacon. One of those fireplaces you find dotted over the landscape; the original telephone service, I suppose."

The idea amused her and she laughed lazily. "You're quite funny, aren't you?"

"Am I?" He briefly turned his head and grinned at her.

"I mean funny ha-ha, not funny peculiar," Isobel explained then added, almost without thinking, "Nigel scarcely ever laughs."

He smiled, his eyes on the road ahead. "He always was a bit of a sobersides," he told her. "That's probably why he thinks I'm crazy."

"Does he think you're crazy?"

"Of course, hasn't he told you?" Another brief grin over his shoulder gave lie to the assertion. "It's because

I'm not one hundred percent British," he explained solemnly. "You know the idea . . . all foreigners are a bit crazy."

"Do foreigners include Scots?" Isobel asked, and he nodded. "Of course. Why? Are you one?"

"I'm afraid so."

He shook his head solemnly over the information, lips pursed. "Then I'm afraid your girlish dreams won't materialize, *cara mia*. No wedding bells for you."

"I wish you'd stop harping on wedding bells," Isobel objected. "What about you hearing them first . . . you're a great deal older than I am."

"And you're sassy," he retorted. "You treat your elders with respect, my girl, or you'll be in trouble."

"Yes, sir."

"You needn't go that far, for heaven's sake!"

"Well, you *are* nearly old enough to be my—"

"If you say it," he warned, "I'll tip you out, so help me!"

"Well, you *are*," Isobel insisted, thoroughly enjoying the situation.

"Darn you, stop it, will you!"

"You started it."

He sighed resignedly. "So I did," he admitted, "but even I wasn't precocious enough at thirteen and three months and two days to have fathered you."

She looked at him a second in silence. "You're very precise," she said, sounding a little breathless and wishing there was something she could do about her heartbeat. "I didn't know it was that much."

"I like to keep the record straight." He turned and grinned at her and she found herself smiling in return, a warm glow of intimacy adding to the sun's warmth. "Anyway," he added, "it was your wedding bells we were talking about, not mine. I'm not the marrying sort."

"What makes you think that I am?" Isobel asked, and he shook his head, his mouth smiling, although he did not turn his head again.

"Oh yes, *bella mia*," he told her softly. "You must marry some time, you're too beautiful to be allowed to remain alone all your life."

"Well, I don't know who told you that I'm going to marry Nigel," she said, determined not to be defeated. "The subject has never even been raised between us."

"Yet," he added briefly, and Isobel frowned.

"I've no intention of marrying anyone for a long time yet," she told him. "Nigel knows that."

"He's not a patient man."

"For heaven's sake, Lucifer, he hasn't even asked me. There's nothing as serious between us as you seem to think," she added.

"But there soon will be."

He sounded so sure that she looked at him for a moment in silence, then she shook her head, smiling knowingly. "If you're trying to impress me with your powers as a forecaster," she told him at last, "you forget you've already told me how it's done."

"Have I?"

"Mmm. It's all done by psychology, according to you. You watch for a word that triggers a reaction, then take it from there."

"You catch on quickly, don't you? But how do you think I managed it in this case?" he asked. "I've not seen Nigel for more than five minutes in total unless someone else has been there, and we've certainly not discussed his feelings for you."

"Then it's probably guesswork," Isobel retorted.

He shook his head and grinned. "Nope, you're wrong, this time it's genuine seeing-eye stuff. Nigel's going to ask you to marry him much sooner than you expect."

She stared at him, suddenly uneasy. "I . . . I don't see how you can possibly know that," she told him, and added, "and why are you so interested, anyway?"

"I'm more interested in what your answer will be," he confessed.

She was quiet again for a bit, thoughtful too, for she did not even know herself what her answer would be. "I'd need to think about it," she told him at last. "I'd need to think about it a lot."

"I hope you will," he said quietly. "I'd hate to see you make a mistake, *cara mia*."

Reever's Beacon itself proved quite unexciting, but the view from the top of the hill was enchanting and it was so beautifully cool. It was not grand-looking countryside, but pretty and mellow, with little stone villages cuddled up in the rich old trees that both sheltered and guarded and looked as if they had been there for ever. Some ancient Cotswold farm girl could have looked out at exactly this same scene, unchanged except for the occasional glinting car windshield over on the main road.

They sat, part way down the slope of the hill, and watched the dark gray threat of clouds roll over the hills and down between them like a gathering frown, and Isobel shivered at the prospect of their arrival. The air was heavy with the gathering storm and she knew that before nightfall it would break and send her, coward-like, to hide her head. Unless by some chance it came before she left Nigel, and then it would not be so bad. It was never so bad when she was with someone.

"Here comes your storm," Lucifer told her, and turned to smile at her.

"I don't think it's funny," Isobel said. "Certainly not if it breaks while we're up here in the open."

He grinned widely, his disheveled hair giving him an even more satanic look than usual. "You can hide your head on my shoulder," he promised. "I won't mind."

"I'll do that." She glanced at the clouds again. "Shouldn't we go back, Lucifer, just in case it catches us here? We've no coats."

"We won't need coats," he told her, and sounded absolutely confident of the fact. "It won't get here yet. It won't reach us for another three or four hours."

"How do you know?"

He shrugged, grinning at her, mocking her fears. "I know," he said.

Isobel hugged her knees, shoulders hunched impatiently. "Oh, you know," she echoed. "You know so many things in advance, don't you? Sometimes I think you really are...."

She bit her lip on the preposterous suggestion she had almost given voice to, and he turned his head and looked at her, one black brow lifted high into the thick fall of hair on his forehead, his eyes glittering darkly in the brassy sunlight as if he knew exactly what she had been about to say. "I am?" he prompted. "What am I, *piccola*?"

"Oh, nothing!" She shook her head, refusing to look at him. It was so nonsensical it should never have entered her head in the first place, and yet here, on this ageless, quiet hillside, with those black eyes watching her, she could believe almost anything was possible. "Lucifer, let's go back, please."

"Why?"

Almost any other man would have complied with her plea, been anxious to please, but he merely watched her as if he had no intention of moving until he was good and ready. She flicked him an appealing look, her eyes wide and darkly gray, glancing away again hastily when her heart set up a rapid, almost panicky beating that she felt must surely be audible.

His broad shoulders hunched slightly to support the arms curled about his knees, the strong brown throat and chest dark against the whiteness of his shirt, open to the waist to catch the sparse breeze. There was something so right, so disturbingly right about him in this ancient place, that she felt herself not only alien but afraid.

"Please, Lucifer!"

"What's the matter with you?" he asked, and she shook her head hastily to deny it.

"Nothing's the matter with me, I just . . . I just think we should go, that's all."

"That's not all," he retorted. "Isobel, what is it?"

She sought to steady her voice, her throat feeling dry and parched. "I . . . I don't know." She attempted a laugh, but it failed miserably. "It's the storm, I suppose, I've got the heebie-jeebies."

A finger touched her arm gently and traced a long line down to her wrist. "So you have," he allowed, "though I can't think why."

She shivered involuntarily at his touch. "I told you . . . it's the storm."

"Just the storm?"

"Yes, of course. What else?"

He took her chin in one hand and turned her, reluctant, to face him. "Me?" he suggested softly. "Or perhaps old Reever's spirit?"

"Oh, Lucifer, don't!" She bit her lip. "I'm sorry, I'm being stupid, but. . . ."

"I'm sorry."

The apology was so unexpected that she looked at him for a moment in disbelief. "Why should you be?" she asked. "I'm just being silly. There's such an atmosphere up here, isn't there?"

"Yes, I suppose there is," he allowed, "and you're obviously susceptible to it."

"Can we go home . . . please?"

He looked at her for a moment in silence, still holding her chin in his hand, then he leaned forward and kissed her lightly on her mouth. "If you want to," he said.

"I do."

He got to his feet and reached down for her hands. "Your wish is my command," he told her, and she shook her head.

"It's nothing of the sort," she argued as he pulled her to her feet. "You just don't want to get wet when that storm breaks."

"You cheeky infant," he retorted, and held her hand tightly to pull her up the hill after him.

Instead of being earlier, Isobel was even later than usual

that evening going over to see Nigel, and his frown conveyed his displeasure almost as soon as she entered the room. "It's time Luke gave you an early day," he told her shortly, and she was tempted to keep silent about her drive to Reever's Beacon with Lucifer. She would have, but there was little point in trying to keep it secret if Lucifer told him about it, and he almost certainly would. That would inevitably lead to suspicion on Nigel's part if their stories conflicted.

"Actually I did leave early today," she told him. "It was much too hot to work."

"It's murder," he allowed. "But you've been a long time coming over here, if you left early."

"I . . . we went for a drive to cool off."

His eyes narrowed suspiciously and Isobel's heart sank. "You and Luke?"

"Yes. We went as far as Reever's Beacon."

"Why so far as there?" Nigel demanded.

"I told you; to cool off. It's been terribly hot in the office all day and it was lovely and cool in the open car."

"I've no doubt," he said acidly. "It wasn't very lovely stuck here with all this plaster on my leg."

"Nigel, I'm sorry." She wished she felt more sympathetic and less impatient as she sat beside him on a low chair. "I did need some air after being cooped up in that room all day, and the offer was too tempting to refuse."

"I can imagine."

"You surely don't object to my going for a drive for an hour, do you?" she asked, looking at him dubiously. "That would be unreasonable, Nigel."

He shrugged, reluctantly agreeing. "Yes, I suppose it

would," he allowed. "It's this ghastly heat, I feel terrible."

"I expect you do." She was more easily sympathetic now. "I wish there was something I could do to help. I always feel so helpless."

"Will you walk down to the end of the garden with me?"

"Yes, of course. It should be much cooler down there."

She helped him up from his chair and handed him the walking sticks which now took the place of the crutches he formerly needed, following him out of the French window and onto the lawn. "It's better already," he said, "although it's hot work struggling along on these things."

"But much better than the crutches," Isobel said, determinedly cheerful despite his grumbles. "You've done wonderfully well in the past few weeks, Nigel. At least walking sticks are a sign that you are progressing, aren't they?"

"It takes so damned long," Nigel complained. "It seems like years since I walked properly on my own two feet."

" 'Patience,' " Isobel quoted wryly, " 'is a virtue.' "

"It's one I don't possess," Nigel retorted.

She smiled, pulling a rueful face at him. "I had noticed," she chided him gently, and he shook his head.

"I'm sorry, darling, I shouldn't take it out on you. Please forgive me."

"It's this blessed storm brewing up," Isobel said. "It makes everyone edgy, I'll be glad when it breaks . . . in a way," she added hastily.

"It might pass us by, it does sometimes."

Isobel shook her head. "According to Lucifer," she

told him, "it should reach us about nine o'clock tonight."

"Huh!" He snorted disgust at the opinion. "How would he know?"

"He seems pretty sure of himself," Isobel said. "We'll have to wait and see how right he is."

"He's always so blessed sure of himself," Nigel declared, reminded of her absence earlier. "I don't suppose he gave you much option about going with him in the car, did he?" Her expression was confirmation enough and he scowled as he hobbled slowly along. "One of these days," he promised darkly, "he'll come such a cropper and I, for one, won't weep over him."

"Considering your opinion of him," Isobel ventured, "I'm rather surprised that you want me to work for him."

"I don't especially," Nigel confessed. "But I want you here where I can see you more often, and I know you have more sense than to fall for his line of smooth talk."

"I think I'm flattered," she told him wryly, and instinctively put a finger to her lips where Lucifer had kissed her.

He flicked her a brief glance, as if he suspected sarcasm. "You're much too intelligent to let Luke's continental flattery fool you," he told her. "I know you, Isobel. Anyway," he added, as if it solved everything, "he's too old for you."

Thirteen years, three months and two days, Isobel thought, and immediately dismissed the thought. She walked along slowly beside him, seeking a safer subject than Lucifer. "Shall we sit down?" she asked.

They had reached the end of the garden where the bank sloped away and what breeze there was blew sulkily in over the valley and barely stirred the trees. The air was as heavy as lead and the evening sky a dull metallic gold and gray that leaned weightily on the hills.

Nigel sat down with a sigh of relief, putting the sticks down beside him on the seat. "God, it's awful," he said. "Just look at that sky, it's almost touching, it's so heavy."

"It looks awe-inspiring from here," Isobel said. "Almost beautiful in a way."

"I don't call that beautiful," he contradicted. "It's threatening and ugly." He took her hands in his and smiled down at her, hazily fair in the fading light, her gray eyes big and lustrous. "You're what I call beautiful," he said softly. "You're very beautiful, darling Isobel."

"Nigel—" She would have protested, but he kissed her and very effectively silenced her.

"I warned you I was half in love with you the other day," he reminded her. "Well, now I'm completely in love with you. Do you mind?"

She did not know quite what to say to him, plainly hearing Lucifer's voice in her mind warning her. "I'd hate to see you make a mistake, *cara mia*." She was convinced that she was not yet in love with Nigel, although she thought she might easily be before very long, and she felt enough for him now, not to want to hurt him.

"I . . . I don't know, Nigel," she said. "I told you that I don't want to be serious about anyone yet. I don't want to commit myself to a promise I may regret."

He put a gentle hand to touch her face, his smile unexpectedly understanding. "You're so young," he told her softly. "I mustn't hurry you, but I'm here when you make up your mind, Isobel. Remember that, won't you?"

"I'll remember it," she promised, feeling ridiculously tearful for some reason she could not have explained. "And . . . and I'm very touched, Nigel, honestly I am."

"You're adorable," he told her, his hand still gently touching her cheek. "I want to marry you. I'm telling you that now, so that you'll know how serious I am about it. But I'll wait until you're more sure of yourself before I ask you for an answer."

"I. . . ." She went no further, shaking her head and remembering Lucifer's certainty that Nigel would ask her to marry him much sooner than she expected. She looked out across the darkening landscape and the impending storm and shivered. Even the elements, it seemed, were subject to his will, for surely that storm would break within the next hour or so.

CHAPTER SIX

It was the second thunderstorm in two days and Isobel felt that she was being unfairly tried as she listened to it rage outside. It had even passed through her mind, in a wild moment, that Lucifer had arranged for it to be so bad just so that he could laugh at her fear, then quickly dismissed the idea as not only idiotic but dangerously fanciful.

The tiny cottage shook with the fury of it as every crashing roll of thunder followed lightning flashes that ripped the sky into jagged pieces, reflected a million times in the rain that hissed and splashed through the leaves outside her windows. She was convinced it was much worse than the storm had been the previous night, although last night she had been at the house with Nigel and Mrs. Grayson for company and was better able to contain her fear.

If only this one had come earlier she would not have been alone, but now it was almost midnight and the people at Kanderby House would almost certainly be in bed. Only a coward like herself would have been afraid to go to bed and instead sit curled up as small as possible on the high-backed settee, her head buried in the pile of cushions, shaking like a leaf.

It was difficult to hear anything above the fury of the storm, even if she had not had her ears covered, but some faint insistent sound pierced even her defenses and blew, high and thin, on the blustering wind. Isobel raised her head and listened, only to bury it again when a deafening crash followed sharply on a vivid slash of white light almost immediately overhead.

A sullen rumbling respite followed and she lifted her head again, listening, sure now that she recognized the sound . . . a faint thin wail . . . almost like a baby crying. "Oh, poor little thing!" Compassion replaced her fear for the moment and she hurried to the front door and opened it, crying out when another mighty flash heralded a roll of thunder that seemed to shake the earth. Cold soaking rain slapped into her face as if it had been thrown from a pail and drenched her through even in the few seconds she stood there. It was impossible to see anything for the blinding downpour, but she shook her head, trying to clear her eyes and see the animal whose plight had called her out.

There was nothing . . . only the wind howling in the unrelieved darkness, split yet again by another flash of lightning as she struggled with the door, held back by the wind. "Isobel!" The cry made her pause, unsure if she had heard it, but before she could locate it, a tall, dark shape came toward her out of the darkness and ran into the hall, slamming the door shut and dripping onto the light tiles as he turned to face her.

"Lucifer!"

She stared at him, raindrops still clinging to her face and hair, her eyes wide and only half believing what they saw. He had a raincoat flung carelessly over his shoulders and his hair flopped wetly over his brow, the dark face streaming with water which he impatiently brushed away with a hand. Black eyes looked at her curiously for a moment before he grinned, and there was something so reassuring about the grin that she instinctively responded to it.

"I expected to see you with your head under the covers," he told her, and she started nervously at another almighty crash overhead.

"I have been," she admitted, her voice sounding horribly unsteady as she tried to ignore the noise outside.

"But you were at the door," he told her, and his eyes sparkled wickedly. "You didn't anticipate my coming, did you?"

"No, no, of course I didn't. How could I?"

He shrugged, still smiling. "Oh, I thought you might have joined the ranks of the all-knowing."

"Well, I haven't."

He dropped his wet raincoat over a chair in the tiny hall and Isobel led the way into the sitting room. "Then am I out of order asking why you were out on the doorstep getting wet, instead of in here where it's dry?"

She turned as she reached the settee where she had been sitting and frowned, remembering the faint plaintive sound that had drawn her from her hiding place to face the storm. "I . . . I thought I heard something out there. A . . . a cry or something, like a cat mewing."

"And your dear little soft heart made you brave the storm to rescue it."

She suspected sarcasm, but another crash of thunder startled her into wide-eyed fear and she put her hands to her mouth to stem the instinctive cry that threatened to emerge. "There . . . there *was* something out there," she told him, swallowing hard. "I couldn't leave it out there, whatever it was, not in this."

"Did you see anything?"

"No, you must have frightened it away, I suppose."

He grinned at her. "In other words it would rather face the storm than me, is that it?"

"I didn't mean that at all, and you know it," she told him. "The poor little creature must have been terrified with all that noise and you coming unexpectedly out of the darkness, so it just ran, I suppose." In the brief ensuing lull, she eyed him curiously. "What . . . what I don't understand is what you were doing out there."

"Coming home."

Isobel blinked uncertainly. "Coming home?"

He nodded, enjoying her curiosity. "Coming home from Vanessa's."

"Oh, I see."

He sat down, uninvited, on the settee, his long legs crossed one over the other, perfectly at ease and smiling as he read his own story into the mounded cushions at one end. "You don't, you know." He grinned up at her, annoyingly at ease while she was so uneasy. "Your brain's running in all the wrong directions."

Isobel frowned. "I only drew the conclusion you intended I should," she retorted. "I don't really care where you've been."

"Oh, you're a good little girl," he mocked, and Isobel flushed.

"I'm not a good little girl, I'm just not inquisitive, that's all." She looked at him, meeting his eyes and recognizing that welcome assurance still there. Then she smiled and made a grimace of reproach. "All right, I am inquisitive," she told him. "If you haven't been to see Vanessa for the . . . the obvious reason, why have you been?"

He looked as if he wondered what her reaction was going to be, his eyes curious. "I've been to a meeting."

Isobel blinked at the unexpectedness of it. "Oh."

"Oh." He mocked her surprise and laughed. "Or to be more precise, I've been to a gathering of fellow spirits."

"The Elgin Circle," she said, understanding at last.

He nodded, casting an eye at the storm raging outside. "We seem to have upset the weather, don't we?" he asked blandly.

"You. . . ." She looked at him uncertainly, the storm seeming louder and even more frightening suddenly, remembering her own hastily dismissed fancies earlier.

"It wasn't raining when we started," he informed her solemnly, "and now look at it . . . real witching weather. Mind you," he added with apparent seriousness, "you'd get pretty wet riding your broomstick in this, wouldn't you?"

"Oh, Lucifer, don't!" She sat down next to him on the settee, unable to do anything about the involuntary shudder that ran through her, or the way her hands trembled. "I . . . I hate this weather because it makes . . . makes such a fool of me, you don't have to try and do the same."

"I'm sorry, *bella mia*." He covered her trembling hands with his own, a gesture that did nothing to help still them, his eyes showing regret for having added to her fears. "I shouldn't tease you when you're so frightened."

"I . . . I know I'm silly about storms, but I can't help it, and I do try not to make too much of it when I'm not alone."

"Well, you're not alone now," he consoled her, his hands still holding hers, strong and comforting. "If you'd do something for me," he added with a smile, "I'd be grateful; will you?"

She nodded. "Of course, if I can."

He ran a hand through his wet hair. "If I could have a

towel for my head; it's pretty wet. Have you got one handy?"

"Oh yes, of course, I'll get one. I'm sorry, I should have thought of it myself." She fetched a towel from the bathroom, glad of something to occupy her mind, but hurried back to him as fast as she could, because the storm seemed so much worse when she was upstairs.

"Thanks." He rubbed his black head vigorously and the resultant tousle made him look reassuringly normal when he grinned at her a moment later. "If I'd had any sense I'd have driven straight here instead of walking, wouldn't I?"

"I . . . I suppose so." She jumped nervously when another crash cracked and rumbled overhead. To be honest she had scarcely realized what he said, but just the fact that he was there at all helped enormously. She glanced out of the blind, streaming window and shivered. "I say every time that I won't be frightened," she told him. "That I won't let it turn me into a shivering coward, but it always does."

He discarded the towel and combed his thick mop of hair into casual order. "I can see," he said. "You really are scared stiff, aren't you?"

She nodded miserably, her hands tightly clasped together on her lap. "I'm always scared stiff and I hate myself for it, but nothing makes any difference."

"Nothing?" he took her hands again as another crash sent shivers of fear all over her. "Having someone here helps, doesn't it?" He smiled at her wide-eyed look and squeezed her fingers tightly. "It's only like the 1812 Overture. Listen to it . . . the drums and cymbals crashing and

the electrician working overtime on the lighting effects."
She shook her head. "Oh well," he added, "I suppose it
appeals to my exaggerated sense of the dramatic."

"I . . . I think it's because it's so . . . so wild and uncontrollable that it frightens me so much."

He laughed, his eyes unbelievably gentle as he looked
at her. "Oh, *piccola*, must you have everything and everybody controlled and . . . and restrained? Isn't it rather
dull?"

"No, no, I don't think so at all," Isobel insisted, wishing her own emotions were under more control at the
moment. Her heart was hammering wildly at her ribs and
the pulse in her temple throbbed with more than fear of
the storm. "I like things and people I can understand."

The black eyes studied her face for a moment, then he
shook his head. "You disappoint me, *cara mia*. Don't you
ever feel like doing something less . . . less safe? Challenging something you've never faced before, like this
storm, for instance?"

"No . . . no, I don't." She raised her eyes again and
looked at him, almost appealingly. "And you despise me
for it, don't you?"

He shook his head, smiling, one hand reaching to touch
her cheek gently. "I shouldn't be here if I did," he told
her softly, and Isobel blinked uncertainly, deaf for the
first time to the noise outside, as she absorbed his full
meaning.

"You. . . ." It was too difficult to put into words, the
realization that came to her suddenly, and she could only
look at him wide-eyed, comprehending at last.

"I was parking the car," he told her, making light of it,

"and I suddenly thought to myself, poor little Isobel, all alone and the heavens opening up over her head, so here I am."

"You came because . . . because you thought I'd be afraid?"

"I knew you'd be afraid," he corrected her with a grin. "And I knew it was unlikely that Nigel would be here to hold your hand, so I thought I'd stand in for him."

"It . . . it was very kind of you, Lucifer, thank you."

His smile teased her outnf her solemn mood. "Oh, I'm always kind to children and animals."

"I'm not. . . ."

"I know, I know." A raised hand stemmed her protest. "But you did need company, didn't you?"

"Yes, yes, I did, and I'm very grateful to you for realizing it."

"Oh well, I suppose poor old Nigel couldn't really be expected to splash his way over here in all that plaster, could he?"

"No, of course not." She wished she knew how much of the rapid, anxious beating of her heart was due to her fear of the storm and how much to the knowledge that he had come to her because he knew she would be afraid and alone. "For one thing," she added, almost without thinking, "he doesn't know I'm such a coward about storms."

"He doesn't know?"

She shook her head, disliking the expression she glimpsed in his eyes.

"Well, well, well."

"I don't advertise the fact," she said. "I don't really know why I told you."

"Perhaps because confession is good for the soul," he

suggested lightly, "and you look upon me as your father confessor."

Isobel laughed shortly, looking at him from under her eyelashes. "I thought you drew the line at anything suggestive of a father figure," she said.

"I said father confessor," he pointed out with a grin. "There's a difference. The latter aren't always old men."

"They're not members of a . . . a heathen club either," Isobel retorted, "so you're not suitable for either role."

"How about big brother?" he suggested. "Then you can share me with Nigel." He laughed softly before she could reply. "Not that you inspire brotherly feelings in any red-blooded man," he added. "Even with rain on your nose, you're beautiful."

She brushed away the offending drops with a hand, just in case they existed. "I wouldn't know what to do with a brother," she told him. "I've never had one."

"An only child?" He made a sympathetic face. "Poor little kid, no wonder you look so soulful!"

"I'm not a poor little kid, Lucifer, and don't be so blessed condescending!"

"All right, all right." He held up his hands defensively. "But if I'm going to baby-sit for half the night, I expect the usual bonuses for the job. Where do you keep your coffee?"

"You're not baby-sitting," Isobel objected. "And I could have coped perfectly well on my own . . . I did last night."

An arched brow challenged her. "Do you want me to go?" he asked, and she looked at him for a moment, then shook her head.

"Good, then get me some coffee. And incidentally," he

added as she turned to go into the kitchen, "you weren't on your own last night. It was all over by the time you came flitting back to your little nest."

"How do you . . ."

"I saw you," he told her. "There was quite a bright moon after all the commotion was over and I spotted you as I got out of my car. As a matter of fact I nearly passed out on the spot, seeing you drifting through the shrubbery at that time of night . . . and me slightly the worse for wear."

"I didn't see you."

"You could have, I wasn't hiding, but I expect you were anxious to get home." He looked up at her, his eyes taunting. "You looked all fair and fairy-like in the moonlight," he added whimsically. "So much so, in fact, that I had an almost irresistible urge to hail you with 'Ill-met by moonlight, proud Titania,' only I thought you wouldn't appreciate it at that late hour."

"I wouldn't have," Isobel agreed.

"Don't you like Shakespeare?"

"Yes, as a matter of fact, I do, but not to the extent of playing Titania to your Oberon at eleven o'clock at night."

"Aaah! And I thought *A Midsummer Night's Dream* was rather appropriate too."

"In August?" She rose to her feet, smiling at her small victory.

"You little Philistine!" he called after her.

"I'll make us both some coffee," she told him as she disappeared into the kitchen, "it's no use trying to sleep while this goes on." She was forced to admit, however, that although the storm still raged outside she had never felt less afraid of one in her life and she thanked her stars for Lucifer's impulsive action and his consequent distraction, even if he was mostly teasing her.

"Can I help?" he offered, and she laughed.

"No, thanks, I can manage on my own."

"Don't you want me to hold your hand when the big bangs come?"

She ignored the jibe and switched on the kitchen light, taking things from cupboards almost automatically; cups and saucers, sugar and coffee. She put the kettle on to boil and got a tray from beside the dresser. It was when she straightened up with the tray in her hand that she saw the small, silent movement beside the table. Nothing really tangible, but a tiny dark shadow that, a second later, she was not even sure she'd seen, but she stood stiff and wary for a second or two. Then several things happened at once.

A long jagged flash split the black sky in two and an enormous crash of thunder set the spoons rattling in the saucers, at the same time a small black shape fled swiftly from beneath a chair and across the kitchen floor. Isobel's scream almost outdid the storm and she dropped the tray with a resounding crash on the tiled floor.

It was only a split second later that Lucifer came striding across the kitchen and barely more before she was tight in his arms, her heart hammering wildly as she clung to him. "It's all right, *carissima*, it's all right." The soft, deep voice was comfortingly close against her ear and a soothing hand held her head against his chest, shutting out everything but his warmth and strength.

How long she stayed like that, she had no idea, but the storm seemed suddenly to have receded and it was almost with reluctance that she raised her head and looked at him. "I'm ... I'm sorry," she said meekly.

The black eyes teased her, his arms still around her, but a little less tightly. "I told you you should have let me hold your hand," he said. "You see what happens when you're stubborn?"

"You were the one who said I should face up to a challenge," she reminded him, suddenly and inexplicably lightheaded. "And there was something . . . something moved down by the chair there."

"Something moved down by the chair," he echoed, and laughed. "You have a sense of the dramatic, too, *bella mia*."

She felt oddly fluttery and wary as she looked up at him. "Must you use Italian words?" she asked shortly, and he pulled her head back against his chest for a moment.

"Only when I get carried away," he told her softly. "I speak as much Italian as English, you know, and I don't see why you should object to my using both."

"I'm sorry." She raised her head again, looking slightly shamefaced at her outburst. "But I did see something, Lucifer, I swear I did."

"So you did," he agreed, and smiled at her puzzled frown. He walked over to the door into the sitting room and snapped his fingers. "Here! Come here!" Isobel watched him curiously as he bent and retrieved something just out of her view. "Here's your intruder," he told her. "The one you went out to rescue."

He held a huge black cat in his arms, its silky fur glistening in the light, slanted amber eyes half-closed in ecstasy as strong fingers caressed its chin.

"I knew I heard a cat out there," Isobel laughed, almost hysterical with relief. "He must have come in while I had the door open."

"*She* must have done," he corrected.

"He or she," Isobel remarked, "it gave me the fright of my life."

"Don't tell me you're scared of cats, too?" he said, and she shook her head.

"No, of course not."

"Of course not," he echoed, and grinned. "For a moment I thought it might have been your familiar."

"My . . . my familiar?"

He nodded, still smiling, his dark eyes taunting her wariness. "All witches have a familiar," he informed her, "and it's quite often a black cat. It's supposed to be her attendent spirit or demon, and this is the kind of night for them to be around, isn't it?"

"Must you?" Isobel complained. "You know that witchcraft jargon makes me jittery, and I have enough to contend with without you making it worse."

"Did you know that Isobel is a traditional name for witches?" he asked softly, and she looked at him for a moment uncomprehendingly. "It's true," he added when she looked like arguing. "Elizabeth, Betty, Isobel, Bella, Luebella, they're all witches' names, didn't you know?"

"Of course I didn't know," Isobel told him, eyeing the huge black cat with less favor now than she had done. "And . . . and I'm not sure I believe you, anyway."

He laughed again and rubbed the cat's chin. "I told you you were a little witch," he said. "A very pretty little witch."

"I most certainly am not!"

"Oh, but you are," he said softly, an expression in his eyes that she could not accurately interpret but which made her heart flutter restlessly against her ribs. "A witch is capable of casting spells," he went on, still in that same quiet, almost hypnotic voice, "and you can cast the most wonderful spells, *cara mia*; I know."

"Lucifer, stop it, please!"

He smiled, his long fingers still caressing the cat. "For a nonbeliever," he told her, "you certainly get involved, don't you? I've told you there's nothing to be afraid of, once you know about it, so take my word for it."

"I don't believe any of it," Isobel assured him, hoping she sounded more convinced than she felt. "It's a lot of rubbish."

"Oh no, not rubbish," he denied, "but perfectly explainable when you know how. Pyewacket here, for instance, isn't really a bewitched cat, but you were almost ready to believe she was, weren't you?"

"Pyewacket?"

"The witch's cat," he told her. "Another traditional name, like Isobel. Really she's only a common cat, although she's rather a beauty."

"She is a beauty," Isobel agreed.

"And black, too," he grinned, reminding her of the old superstition. "Lucky."

Isobel extended a hand to stroke the sleek black head and the cat struck, viciously and swiftly, claws extended and the amber eyes squinting maliciously. Isobel snatched back her hand, putting it instinctively to her mouth as the scratches stung sharply. "Not so lucky for me," she retorted. "Of all the ungrateful creatures!"

"Proving she's a female," Lucifer declared with

certainty. "She's jealous and she let you know it, didn't you, Pye?" The cat contentedly lifted its chin and purred loudly, its amber-colored eyes fixed warningly on Isobel.

"Since the admiration is obviously mutual," Isobel told him shortly, "you'd better take her with you."

"I don't want a cat," he said, putting the animal down on the floor where, still purring, it rubbed against his legs. "Anyway, it's got a good home of its own already." Isobel looked at him curiously. "It's Vanessa's," he explained.

"Oh, I see."

"Do you? I suppose you're now thinking that the cat scratched you on Vanessa's behalf, aren't you?" Her expression was sufficient confirmation, and he laughed, shaking his head slowly. "In fact it's simply because she's used to me and not you, so she lashed out. Easy."

"Oh, all right," Isobel agreed. "Anyway, I wish you'd take her with you when you go. I don't fancy having a vicious cat here all night."

"I will," he promised. "In the meantime, let me see those scratches." He took her hand in both his and looked at the bright red scores on the back of it. "I'd better put something on those before you go funny."

"I don't go funny," she objected, "and they're only surface scratches ... don't fuss."

"I'm not fussing, I'm using my common sense."

"You're being bossy."

"And you're being sassy again," he warned. "One of these days I shall do something about it."

"I wonder you don't put me to bed without any supper while you're about it," Isobel retorted. "I'm not a child, Lucifer, and I wish you'd stop treating me like one."

"You bury your head like a baby when it thunders," he taunted, and Isobel flushed indignantly.

"Oh, you horrible brute! You didn't have to use that against me; you know I'm ashamed of myself for being such a coward and you rub it in; it's not fair!"

"It serves you right for being cheeky! Now let me put something on those scratches. And for heaven's sake don't argue," he added impatiently. "You are the stubbornest little wretch ever born, I swear it."

She conceded him victory for the moment, and brought out disinfectant and cotton wool, watching as he gently bathed the scratches, keeping a wary eye on the cat as it watched the proceedings malevolently from the doorway. Sitting, some time later, drinking coffee with Lucifer in her tiny sitting room, she could not help wondering what Nigel would have said if he could have seen them, and decided he would in all probability have second thoughts about letting her work for Lucifer and also question her common sense where his brother was concerned.

CHAPTER SEVEN

"Lucifer says it belongs to Vanessa Law," Isobel told Nigel the following day when she was called upon, inevitably, to explain the scratches on her hand. "Its name is Pyewacket."

"Well, he'd know, certainly," Nigel said dryly. "He spends enough time up there."

"He spends most of his time working," Isobel retorted unthinkingly, and earned herself a frown of disapproval.

"Oh, I'm not denying he works hard all day," Nigel allowed, "but he also spends a good deal of time with Vanessa, and he'd certainly know her cat."

"The thing seemed to know him very well; she made no attempt to scratch him," Isobel said, rather rashly in the circumstances.

"I can believe it," Nigel remarked, a bit sourly, she thought. "Being a female she wouldn't, would she?"

He seemed not to have noticed anything untoward so far and she rather optimistically began to wonder if she might, by some miracle, get away with not telling him about Lucifer's visit last night, although it was a pretty vain hope one way or another. "Lucifer suggested she might have been jealous of another female," she told him, giving nothing else away.

"He could be right," Nigel agreed, "although I can't think why the thing should have been jealous of you in your own house. How did it come to be in your cottage anyway?" he added.

Isobel shrugged, seeing dangerous ground looming

large. "It must have run in when I opened the front door, I suppose. I heard it mewing outside and went to see what was wrong, but it was so dark and wet I couldn't see a thing out there. The first thing I knew it was there was when it ran out from under the kitchen table and nearly frightened the life out of me."

He frowned, still puzzled. "I can't understand why the wretched thing was out at all last night," he said. "Especially in that storm."

"Maybe it stays out at night," Isobel suggested, but he shook his head.

"No, it doesn't. It's coddled and pampered like a baby, that great brute, and it's certainly never out in the rain."

"Well, it was last night."

"Odd." He frowned over it. "Mind you, it's not very far coming across the fields for an animal. It may have escaped."

"Maybe it got out when Lucifer left Vanessa's," Isobel said, unthinkingly. "They arrived about the same time."

His expression told her that any chance she had ever had, however slender, of keeping Lucifer's visit a secret from him had just disappeared. She felt him watching her closely, although she preferred not to look at him at the moment, feeling rather as she had once or twice at Frome's when she had been reprimanded for some small carelessness.

"How do you know what time Luke arrived home?" he asked, and she hesitated. Only fractionally but long enough, she realized, to confirm his suspicions that she was keeping something from him.

"Well . . . well, as a matter of fact he came across and spoke to me." It was near enough to the truth and she could see that being honest was no more popular than she had anticipated.

"Spoke to you?" Suspicion glinted at her from his blue eyes and he regarded her sternly, as if she had been guilty of some dastardly crime. "I can't see why he needed to come anywhere near your cottage at that time of night and in that storm. Why did he, Isobel?"

"Oh, for heaven's sake, Nigel, does it matter?"

He frowned, unwilling to give even an inch, it seemed. "I think so," he said. "Unless of course you have any particular reason for not telling me."

Isobel looked up, getting more angry with him than she would have thought possible. "Of course I haven't," she told him, "and you shouldn't be so suspicious, it's not fair."

"Then tell me," he said shortly, and Isobel sighed resignedly.

"I . . . I opened the front door when I heard that wretched cat mewing outside," she told him reluctantly, "and . . . well, I suppose he saw the light and was curious. It was nearly midnight."

"All the more reason for not coming over, I'd have thought in the circumstances," he told her shortly. "But he couldn't possibly have seen your hall light from his driveway, Isobel; there's the main driveway and a couple of shrubberies between you."

Isobel sighed resignedly and looked down at her fingers, tracing the telltale scratches on the back of her left hand. "Maybe he felt like playing knight errant," she said lightly in an effort to lift the air of gloom that seemed to have enveloped him. "To be honest, Nigel, I was silly enough to tell Lucifer that thunderstorms frighten me to death and he . . . well, he came over to see if I was okay."

"You're frightened of thunderstorms?" He looked more disbelieving than sympathetic. "Why, for heaven's sake?"

"Oh, how do I know?" Isobel exclaimed. "I just am, that's all, I've been frightened of them ever since I was a child."

"You didn't tell me."

"I . . . I thought you might think I was stupid."

"But you told Luke. Does he think you're stupid?"

She lifted her head, her gray eyes thoughtful. "Rather surprisingly," she said, "he doesn't."

"And what was the object of his visit?" he asked. "Or perhaps I shouldn't ask in the circumstances."

"Of course you can ask," Isobel told him, determinedly offhand about it all. "His term was to hold my hand. Metaphorically, of course," she added hastily. "Actually it did help a lot just having someone there with me."

"If you'd let me know how you felt about storms," Nigel said reproachfully, "I could have held your hand, literally, not metaphorically. Why didn't you come over to the house and let me know?"

"Oh, Nigel, how could I? It was pouring with rain, and anyway I expect you were in bed by then, not being a coward like me. I can cope on my own fairly well when I have to."

"But you obviously can't," he argued, "and I don't like Luke taking things like that upon himself, not with you. He'd no right to come over to you. Damn him, why can't he run true to form?"

His vehemence startled her and she wondered how

much more angry he would have been if he had known about the moment of truth when she had dropped the tray and Lucifer had held her tight in his arms. "Isn't he running true to form?" she asked.

"Of course not. I've never known him care tuppence whether anyone's scared of a thing or not. He's no patience with fear as a rule; he's as hard as iron."

"He was very kind to me last night."

It was perhaps rubbing salt into the wound, but she felt bound to speak as she found, and Lucifer had been kind, and gentle, too, certainly not as hard as iron.

"Oh, damn him!" Frustration at his own forced inactivity welled up and almost choked him and Isobel believed that in that moment he really hated his brother.

"Nigel, please don't," she begged. "There's no need for you to feel that way about it. He came over because he knew I was frightened of the storm, that's all. He comforted me as he would have done a . . . a child. That's how he sees me, Nigel, as a child. He always treats me as one."

"A child!" He looked at her, his blue eyes dark with some expression she found it hard to recognize. "You're not a child, and he knows it."

"I am as far as Lucifer is concerned," she insisted. "Why, he even calls me a cheeky kid," she added in an effort to provide conviction, although she almost despaired of ever convincing him.

"He's got more nerve than anyone I know," he said darkly, "and I wish he'd marry Vanessa and get out of my way."

"Out of your way?" Isobel looked startled.

"Oh, you know what I mean." He looked so

disgruntled for a moment that she was unsure of the best way to deal with his mood. Then he suddenly looked up at her and scowled. "I suppose the truth is he gives me a real granddaddy of an inferiority complex," he confessed. "He's so smooth and unflappable, I loathe him for it."

"Oh, don't do that, he's your brother."

"I know," he sighed, "and that makes it worse in a way. If he wasn't I could hate him without feeling guilty about it." He took her hand in his and pressed his lips to her fingers. "I suppose I should be grateful to him for taking care of you last night," he said ruefully.

Isobel laughed, as much relieved as amused. "I could have coped without him, even if it does help to have company," she told him. "And I could well have done without his feline companion. She didn't like me at all."

"It's Vanessa's," he said shortly, "she wouldn't."

"It's a vicious great brute," Isobel remarked. "Although it was very fussy with Lucifer; it watched me with its big yellow eyes as if it suspected me of heaven knows what."

Nigel lifted her scratched hand and kissed its palm, an unusually sentimental gesture for him, although he had taken to such gestures lately. "I'm sorry I snapped at you, darling, but it's these damned legs and the heat. I feel so useless all the time." He leaned over and kissed her mouth. "But I'll personally strangle that ghastly animal if it hurts you again," he promised.

After the thunderstorms the weather seemed to improve again and it was warm and sunny without the oppressive humidity that had played havoc with tempers for the past few days. Isobel found it difficult to believe that she had been working for Lucifer for almost a month, although she seemed to have known him for much longer than that. He was not an easy man to know well, she thought, but he had such an easy way with him that made short acquaintance seem much longer.

She watched him now as he bent over a page of the almost indecipherable longhand she would be required to translate when he was satisfied with it, and frowned curiously. Nigel had said he wished Lucifer would marry Vanessa and settle down, but Isobel had her own ideas about that, although she had, wisely, so far said nothing to Nigel about them. In fact she could not really imagine Lucifer married to anyone at all, for, despite his extrovert manner, he had a strange air of remoteness about him at times.

He looked up suddenly and caught her watching him, smiling when she flushed bright pink and hastily looked down at her typing. "Why the interest, *piccola*?" he asked quietly, and Isobel shook her head without looking up.

"I was just taking a breather," she told him.

"You were watching me," he insisted. "I know it, I could sense you looking at me, that's why I looked up."

"You flatter yourself," she retorted, refusing to be inveigled into admitting it. "You just happen to sit in the window, that's all, and I was looking out at the sunshine, not at you."

"Liar," he said softly, and laughed when she looked up indignantly.

"I beg your pardon!"

"Granted," he obliged with another short laugh. He leaned his elbows on the desk and looked across at her, his eyes seeming to look right into her as they always did.

"But your attention was wandering, whether you were looking at me or not," he insisted, and she shrugged.

"Only temporarily," she said, and looked at him challengingly down her nose. "Are you going to sack me for laziness?"

"Not this time," he allowed, apparently serious. He studied her for a second or two, chin resting on steepled fingers. "Are you bored with your job?" he asked at last, and she looked startled.

"No. No, of course I'm not."

"I'm relieved to hear it."

She looked at him curiously. "What made you ask me that?"

He shrugged, smiling wryly. "Oh, I don't know, I just wondered, that's all."

"But why on earth should you wonder such a thing?" Isobel demanded. "I've given you no cause to think I'm bored, have I?"

"No." He studied her again for a second or two. "But girls of your age seem to change their jobs almost as often as they change their boy friends!"

"Well, in my case that's not very often, is it?" Isobel retorted, and he laughed.

"No, it isn't, I grant you that; not while you're more or less going steady, as they say, with Nigel, but I sometimes have the feeling that one of these days you'll tell Nigel where he gets off and disappear into the blue." His expression challenged her to deny it. "And I'd hate you to leave me in the lurch," he added.

Isobel looked at him unbelievingly for a moment. "I certainly wouldn't leave you without due notice," she told him, and he smiled.

"No, being a nicely trained girl, you wouldn't."

His slightly condescending air was beginning to annoy her. "Girls of my age, as you term it," she informed him loftily, "are no worse for changing their jobs than anyone else. We're just as hard-working and reliable as the rest, so you have no reason to be so blasted patronizing!"

"And you have no reason to swear, my girl. I don't like it."

"I wasn't swearing!" She looked indignant and not a little surprised at his tone. "For heaven's sake, I'm not a baby, I can say 'blasted' if I like without you going all righteous about it."

Repeating the word gave her a certain amount of pleasure when she saw him frown again. "I'm not going all righteous, as you call it, heaven forbid I ever should, but you're not the kind of girl who should swear at all, however mildly. It spoils the effect."

"Don't you approve of women being allowed a mild cuss?" she asked. "That's a bit of nasty sex discrimination, isn't it?"

"Not girls like you," he insisted.

Isobel could scarcely believe he was serious, and yet he appeared to be. The revelation of this unexpected streak of puritanism in him, of all people, gave her an elated feeling of having got the upper hand for once, and she would not have been human if she had not made the most of it.

"I'm sorry I offended your sensitive ear," she teased him, and saw a swift glitter of anger in his eyes which vanished almost immediately.

"Don't behave out of character, Isobel, it doesn't suit you."

Something—some intangible something in his voice and his eyes—encouraged her and she laughed, her gray eyes dancing mischievously at the idea of being able to shock him.

"*Si, papa!*"

Revenge was very sweet and she watched his dark face run through a gamut of expressions before he arose and came across to her. "Say that again, if you dare," he said softly, and she hastily lowered her eyes, finding the black gaze far too disconcerting close up, wondering if she had been too rash and he was genuinely angry with her. The unfamiliar excitement she felt, however, egged her on.

"I've been learning Italian," she told him defiantly and untruthfully.

"Oh no, you haven't," he argued. "Everyone knows that much Italian."

"Do they?"

He nodded, lifting her chin with one finger although she still refused to look at him. "If you want to learn Italian," he told her, "I'll teach you with pleasure, but if you call me that again I'll. . . ."

"You'll what?" she asked innocently, raising her eyes.

He said nothing for a moment; simply stood beside her, his eyes glistening with something she could only guess at, but which set her heart racing wildly and brought the color flooding to her cheeks. Then he bent over her, his strong hands cradling her face, holding her so that she could not escape him even had she wanted to, drawing her to her feet so that she stood close to him, and saw the dark, almost hungry look in his eyes before she closed her own.

His mouth was firm but unbelievably gentle as he kissed her, her head forced back against his fingers, holding her for so long that she felt her heart must stop.

Only it didn't; it tapped away anxiously at her ribs as if it sought to escape. She kept her eyes closed even after he released her, and his lips brushed warmly against her forehead before he moved away abruptly.

"Pack up and go home," he told her shortly, before she had time to recover, and she saw that he was already over by his own desk again and standing with his back to her, looking out of the window.

"But . . . but it's only. . . ."

"Go home, Isobel." She scarcely recognized the voice that spoke to her so shortly over one shoulder, and there was a tense stillness about him as if he was waiting for her to go; wanted her to go.

He did not even turn around when, several minutes later, she called out a tentative good night. "Good night," he answered briefly and without his customary casual wave to her as she moved toward the door. She felt suddenly and inexplicably sad as she looked back briefly at the tall, dark figure outlined against the sun-filled window.

Isobel's feelings were oddly mixed that evening as she sat with Nigel after dinner as usual. She could not have said whether she was glad or sorry that Lucifer had kissed her like that, although inevitably it would make her more self-conscious in his presence.

It was, she supposed, partly her fault that it had happened at all, but she had thought Nigel's assurance that she was not Lucifer's type of woman was a fact. It was too late when she realized the risk she was taking in teasing him. Also, she recognized ruefully, she had not imagined what her own response would be.

Preoccupied as she was, she appeared much quieter than usual and Nigel, almost inevitably, commented on it. "Is something wrong?" he asked, taking her hand, and she shook her head, smiling to reassure him.

"No, nothing's wrong, I'm just a bit tired, that's all."

"Has the slave driver been standing over you with the whip again?"

She shook her head again. "No, in fact he's been very good lately. Not that he's ever as bad as you make him sound," she added hastily.

"He let you off early enough tonight," he remarked, not challenging her on her last words as she half expected him to. "What came over him?"

She shrugged, making light of her early dismissal. She had certainly no intention of telling him of the outcome of her teasing Lucifer. "I don't know what came over him," she said. "Maybe he, too felt tired and thought he'd have an early evening for a change."

"Hmm. Or more likely he's seeing Vanessa."

"He didn't say so." She must surely have imagined that edge of resentment in her voice, she thought, but even so Nigel looked at her sharply.

"Does he usually confide in you about his off-duty plans?" he asked, and Isobel shook her head.

"Not always, but he sometimes says where he's going." She was thoughtfully quiet for a minute or two. "I expect he *is* seeing Vanessa," she said at last.

The blue eyes quizzed her briefly, then he half-smiled. "You don't like her, do you?"

The question was unexpected and Isobel looked startled for a moment. "I've never really had the opportunity to find out whether I do or not," she said. "A five-minute meeting in a hallway is hardly long enough to judge, is it? I don't imagine I'd take to her very easily," she added, and laughed. "Any more than she did to me."

"Ah, but I would say her dislike of you was quite understandable in the circumstances," Nigel told her. "After all, you work with Luke all day."

Isobel looked down at her hands. "She's jealous, you mean?"

He nodded. "Without a doubt, I should say. She's jealous of any woman who gets within smiling distance of Luke, and she wouldn't realize that she has nothing to worry about where you're concerned."

"No. No, of course not," Isobel agreed hastily, touching one finger to her lips almost unconsciously. "But I'm rather surprised they're still on speaking terms if she's as jealous as you say. After all, didn't you say he had quite a few women friends at various times?"

Nigel shrugged, as if dismissing something he had given up trying to understand. "Vanessa's the sort who never gives up," he said. "They've known each other about six years now and they've been on the brink of marrying for most of that time, as far as I can gather."

"You mean Vanessa *thinks* she's been on the brink of getting married," Isobel told him, rather rashly scornful of the other woman's optimism. "But if she's waiting for Lucifer I'm pretty certain she'll be unlucky. He isn't the marrying kind; he told me so."

Nigel looked at her closely, his blue eyes narrowed suspiciously. "You sound very sure about that," he told her. "How on earth can you know? What made him even mention the subject to you, of all people?"

Isobel laughed, a little uneasily now that she realized

how rash she had been. "Oh, it was just one of those things that crop up," she told him. "Actually he was teasing me about whether I would marry you or not."

He frowned. "Does it concern him?"

She shrugged. "I don't know. I never know what Lucifer's thinking, or very seldom anyway. But he was teasing me, as I say, and I retaliated by suggesting that he did something about himself before he started worrying about me. He told me he wasn't the marrying sort . . . and oddly enough I believed him."

"So do I," Nigel agreed, rather surprisingly.

Isobel raised her brows, curious to know his reasons. "You don't think he's the marrying kind either?"

He shrugged. "Well, he's shown no sign all these years of settling down with one woman for life. Maybe he isn't."

She smiled wryly, wondering if she was betraying too much interest and if he would notice it. "From what you say he's had plenty of choices over the years," she said. "So maybe he just hasn't found the right woman yet."

"Maybe . . . God knows he's had enough choices." He sounded as if he envied him. He was silent for a moment, then he frowned as if something puzzled him. "You know, it's odd, but I've always had the feeling about Luke that he's a bit of a loner despite his women."

"He's not an easy man to know," Isobel said softly, and Nigel nodded agreement.

"No, I suppose he isn't."

CHAPTER EIGHT

Isobel had an uneasy, fluttery feeling in her tummy when she thought about reporting for work next morning. She had even, during the early hours of the morning, wondered if Lucifer would send her packing altogether, playing safe in case anything similar happened again. She was not really surprised, however, when he greeted her in exactly the same way as he always did. He seemed to have forgotten their abrupt parting last night, a fact about which she was unsure whether to be relieved or disappointed.

He looked up with a wide grin when she walked, rather hesitantly, into the room. She could not have explained why she had dressed with such extra care that morning, only that she had felt some inexplicable urge to look a little different. Her hair was not simply drawn back and tied as it usually was, but lifted from her neck and falling into wispy softness that framed her face. The sleeveless white dress was one she had never previously worn and it flattered the pale gold tan she had acquired during the past few weeks, making her corn-gold hair look even lighter.

The grin, she noticed, was dismissed in favor of an appreciative smile when he saw her, and she wondered how she would cope with comments on her appearance if he made any.

"Good morning," she ventured warily, and he laughed softly, almost as if he knew exactly how she felt and was prepared to make the most of it.

"Good morning, *piccola*, it's a lovely day again."

"Lovely," Isobel echoed, and sat down at her desk, giving all her attention to uncovering her typewriter and folding the cover carefully.

He looked at her for a minute in silence. "Are you in a working mood today?" he asked, and she looked up, frowning curiously.

"As much as I usually am," she agreed. "Why?"

He smiled. "You look far too beautiful to sit behind a desk all day," he told her. The black eyes flicked upwards. "And I like your hair like that."

She fought against the wild hammering of her heart, to make her voice sound matter-of-fact. "Thank you."

She thought he was surprised at her apparent unconcern and went on with getting out the manuscript she was working on. "Why did you change it?"

The shrug she gave was careless and she only wished that her fingers would feel less trembly as they clumsily sorted the sheets of manuscript. "I like a change sometimes, and it's much cooler like this." She looked across at him, as blandly unconcerned as she could appear. "Are we going to be very busy today?"

He leaned his chin on one hand, the elbow resting on his desk, the black eyes watching her with a disconcerting steadiness. "That's entirely up to you," he informed her.

"Me? But. . . ."

"Whether *you're* busy or not," he explained. "I had an idea in the early hours," he went on, "but I'm not sure if you'll agree to it . . . not after last night."

It was most unfair of him to have brought that up without warning, for she knew she was blushing like a schoolgirl. "Last night," she declared, with deceptive airiness, "was a . . . a mere incident that meant nothing to anybody, and I refuse to let you embarrass me with it, Lucifer, so please don't try."

"You're blushing!" he told her, laughter in his eyes.

"Stop it, Lucifer!"

He tried to look suitably solemn. "But I like teasing you."

"I know you do," Isobel retorted. "It's a way of showing your masculine superiority . . . or so you think."

He laughed then, and Isobel restrained the impulse to throw something at him. "I don't think I'd better mention my idea after all," he told her. "Not in the circumstances. I don't suppose you'd come anyway."

"Come?" He had captured her interest as he knew he inevitably would. "Come where?"

"Out," he said. "I thought we could work until about ten o'clock and then sneak off." He laughed at her startled expression. "Strictly on business," he explained. "I have to see someone in Edgemorton about eleven and my bit of business won't take very long; then I thought we could have an early lunch."

"Oh." The invitation was so unexpected that it left her at a loss and very unsure what she should do. Certainly Nigel would not view the outing with much favor, but it would be nice to have lunch out for a change and if it was business then he surely could not say too much against it.

"Do . . . do you need me?" she asked, and he smiled.

"Of course I do."

"In my capacity as secretary, I mean," she explained, and he shook his head.

"No, but it doesn't make any difference, surely, does it?" He knew quite well it did, Isobel thought, but he was not going to admit it. "I like traveling in pretty company," he told her, "and I certainly don't like lunching alone, especially in a restaurant. Will you come with me?"

"Thank you, I'd like to."

"I thought you might," he said. "You don't go out very often, do you?" It sounded very much like criticism of Nigel, the way he said it, Isobel thought, and frowned.

"I don't really mind," she told him. "I'm quite happy going on as I am." She looked at him curiously. "Are you sure I won't be in the way while you're talking to your . . . your business friend?"

"No, of course you won't. I shall send you off to do some shopping or something equally extravagant, and pick you up when it's all over. Okay?" His eyes teased her. "You're not scared of walking around a strange town alone, are you?"

"No, of course not!" She raised bright indignant eyes to glare at him. "I've told you before, Lucifer, I'm not a baby, although you will insist on treating me like one. I'm a grown woman and perfectly capable of taking care of myself."

"Except in thunderstorms," he said softly, and Isobel looked at him reproachfully.

"That," she declared, "was a low blow."

"It was," he admitted. "*Scusa, signorina*, I should have known better."

"You should," she retorted. She remembered suddenly that considering she was being taken out for lunch, she was perhaps being rather ungracious and she smiled across at him. "I'm looking forward to my lunch out," she told him, placatingly, "thank you for thinking of me,

Lucifer." She eyed him for a moment, musingly. "You're very nice sometimes," she told him, and he looked doubtful.

"Nice?" he queried. "I'm not sure I can live that one down."

"Then don't try," Isobel told him, laughing at his expression.

It was a little after ten o'clock when he told her to finish the page she was working on and then pack up and, by a quarter past, they were ready to go. She glanced along the driveway briefly at Kanderby House as they went out to the car, wondering how Nigel was being occupied.

He chafed more and more lately at his enforced inactivity and she thought, yet again, how he would hate the idea of her going out with Lucifer, especially as it meant he would not see her at lunch time as he usually did.

As usual Lucifer correctly interpreted her hasty glance and shook his head as he saw her into the car. "No, you don't have to let Nigel know you're going out with me," he told her, and grinned at her inevitable look of surprise.

"You're reading my mind again," she accused. "I wish you wouldn't, it's most discomfiting."

"Only if you have a guilty conscience, surely," he said. "And you haven't, have you?"

"No more than anyone else," Isobel allowed. "But you're much too good at it, Lucifer, sometimes you . . . you bother me."

He stood looking down at her, his hands on the car door, leaning just above her and much too close for comfort when she remembered his similar stance last night.

"Why does it bother you, *bella mia*? I only guessed that you were thinking of Nigel because you looked up at the house. I've told you there's nothing magical about it. And let's face it," he added with a smile, "you're not very difficult to read."

"Oh!" She shrugged herself straight in her seat and turned a reproachful profile to him. "Just the same I should let Nigel know I'm going out, he might wonder what's happened to me if he doesn't see me at lunch-time."

"He already knows," he informed her, walking around the car and tucking his long legs under the steering wheel, smiling at her as he slammed the door shut. "I told him while you were out powdering your nose and getting ready to leave."

"Oh. Oh well, I suppose it's all right, then."

"Quite all right," he told her. "He wasn't very pleased of course, being Nigel, but he raised no worthwhile arguments, so I took it that we had his permission to go."

"You shouldn't tease him so," Isobel reproached him. "Especially when he's so unwell. Those legs of his worry him an awful lot in this hot weather."

"I know they do," he agreed, "but at least he knows it isn't permanent, and self-pity isn't going to help him or anyone else, is it?"

She looked at him reprovingly as they drove out through the gates and on to the road. "Sometimes," she told him, "I think Nigel's right about you . . . you *are* as hard as iron."

He laughed, completely undismayed by the criticism as usual. "Is that what he says?"

"He . . . he did once," she admitted, wondering if she had been too frank. Knowing him, it was possible that he would mention the fact to Nigel, even if it was only to laugh about it. "You . . . you won't tell him I told you, will you?" she asked.

"Don't worry," he told her cheerfully. "I hardly think that's the worst thing Nigel's ever said about me, anyway, and I won't tell him . . . unless I'm pressed, of course," he added, and she looked at him anxiously.

"Lucifer. . . ."

"Relax, *piccola*." He took a hand from the steering wheel and patted hers lying in her lap. "We're going to enjoy ourselves."

Edgemorton was bigger than Isobel remembered it from the only time she had been there before, and she had no difficulty in occupying her time in the variety of shops while Lucifer was busy. She was, as he had suggested, rather extravagant, but since she had been living in the little cottage at Kanderby House, her expenses had been negligible and she had never been on a real shopping spree, so she delighted in spending some of her accumulated wealth on two new dresses and some shoes.

She kept a careful eye on the time and managed to find her way back to their appointed meeting place almost exactly on time, blinking her surprse when she found Lucifer already there. Either his business must have taken less time than he had anticipated or else her watch was slow. He appeared not to mind the wait, however, for he smiled as he glanced at his watch when she joined him.

"I'm not late, am I?" she asked anxiously, and he shook his head.

"Right on time as usual," he told her. "It's all those years working for Nigel, I suppose; you're an inveterate clock-watcher."

"If I'm punctual you have no cause for complaint," she

declared, and he smiled, taking her arm as they started walking.

"I've no complaints at all," he told her. "Far from it." He glanced down at her packages and relieved her of the two larger ones. "I see you took me at my word," he said, "and were madly extravagant."

"I thought I might as well while I had the opportunity." She flicked him a brief look from under her lashes. "I was only following orders," she added.

"Does that mean I'm expected to foot the bill?"

"No, certainly not!" She looked quite scandalized at the idea. "I buy my own clothes; then there are no strings attached."

He regarded her curiously for a second or two while they made their way back to the parking lot. "You're an independent little devil, aren't you?" he said at last.

Isobel stuck out her chin, suspecting criticism. "I prefer it that way."

Surprisingly he said nothing for a minute or two, but the hand that held her arm hugged it close to him for a moment and he smiled. "We'll leave your shopping in the car," he told her, "and then go in search of lunch."

The smells that permeated the restaurant as they entered were delicious and Isobel was reminded how hungry she was. It was a big, well-appointed modern restaurant and gave the impression that only those in the upper income groups came to patronize it.

It was, Isobel thought, quite the most grand place she'd ever been taken to and she could not help but smile over the difference in taste between the two brothers. Nigel usually took her somewhere small and discreet, but quite cosy and with an excellent cuisine.

"I suppose," Lucifer said as they studied the menu, "being such a little one, you have an enormous appetite?"

"I can handle my share," Isobel informed him, "and I warn you I'm hungry. Do little girls always have big appetites?" she asked curiously a few minutes later, and he laughed.

"I don't really know," he confessed. "I've never lunched with one before."

"You're being patronizing again," she warned him. "I'm not that small. Anyway, good things come in small packages, so they say."

"Do they now?" His eyes danced wickedly as he leaned toward her across the table. "Are you good, Isobel?" he added softly and in such a way that she felt the color flood into her cheeks, laying such emphasis on the word that there was no doubt as to his meaning.

"I . . . I try to be." She wondered suddenly if he found her amusingly different from his more usual type of companion. The sophisticated thirties, as Nigel had called them.

He nodded slowly, sweeping her with one expressive glance that made her feel even more gauche. "Yes," he said softly. "Nigel wouldn't want to know you if you weren't."

"You make virtue sound like a vice," she told him, her hands clasped tightly together, resting on the table before her.

"I wasn't trying to," he denied quietly. "It's . . . just what it sounds . . . a virtue and it's part of you, *bella mia*, as much as your youth and beauty." His eyes swept over her again, this time with a more gentle look in them and he smiled. "You look very, very lovely in that white dress, it's most appropriate."

She thought he was serious, but she could never be quite sure with Lucifer and she looked at him uncertainly for a moment before shaking her head slowly, her eyes lowered while she spoke. "I . . . I wish I knew you better," she said, almost without realizing what she said, and his hands reached out for hers and covered them tightly, the strong fingers curling round hers like a vice.

"You wouldn't like what you found, *carissima*," he told her softly, while Isobel's heart beat a rapid and uneasy tattoo under her ribs.

He made no effort to explain this rather enigmatic remark, but dismissed the moment of solemnity with a determination that allowed no argument. It would be useless, she thought, to ever try to understand him.

They took their time over the meal because, as Lucifer said, they had no one to please but themselves, and Isobel enjoyed herself, chattering gaily, despite Lucifer's teasing that would, at any other time, have made her silent.

It was while they sat over their coffee at the end of the meal that she noticed a swift flick of surprise on Lucifer's face and a moment later he rose to his feet, smiling broadly, while Isobel looked around to see who was behind her. Her gaze clashed with the malevolent amber eyes of Vanessa Law and for one wild, unreasoning instant she felt fear. A sickening cold fear that clutched at her stomach like a tangible thing, so that she instinctively put a hand to cover it.

The thin gauntly striking face had little or no color even on such a warm day, and there was not a black hair out of place on the high-piled coiffure. Her dress, too, as it had been the first time Isobel saw her, was of some dark material that clung to her thin figure and looked most unsuitable for a hot summer's day, but at the same time made her conspicuous, even in a crowd. And that, Isobel thought a little uncharitably, was probably part of the exhibitionism that made up a good deal of Vanessa Law's character.

"Lucifer *dar*ling! I didn't expect to see you here." The rather harsh voice drew several curious eyes and Isobel felt a curl of embarrassment which Lucifer apparently did not share.

He smiled at the woman and raised a brow. "Hello, Vanessa, lunching alone?"

He looked behind her, seeking a companion, and Vanessa pursed her lips, inclining her head carelessly at a table some distance away where a short, stout man sat alone looking rather sheepish. "I'm with Freddy Gains," she said, "but I told him to wait for me at the table when I spotted you. He bores me silly," she confided, "but I thought you were busy, my darling."

Lucifer ignored the jibe and smiled at Isobel. "You've met Isobel, haven't you?" he asked politely, and Vanessa Law nodded shortly, no doubt reading her own interpretation into the question.

"I didn't realize you were coming into Edgemorton today," she told him, "and I certainly didn't know you'd be lunching here. Why didn't you let me know?"

"I never thought about it," Lucifer informed her blandly, and even Isobel felt a swift pang of pity for the look of hurt that showed briefly in the other woman's eyes. Lucifer could be horribly cruel when he felt like it. Either that or he was unaware of how Vanessa felt about him, and she could not believe that.

"Well, you should have," Vanessa scolded him. "You

know I love this place and you haven't taken me to lunch for ages."

He shrugged. "As you said," he told her, "I've been busy. Haven't I, Isobel?"

"Oh . . . oh yes, you have," Isobel agreed, not daring to add his first name in front of Vanessa Law.

"Busy with your wretched book, I suppose," Vanessa jeered, though she smiled when she said it. "You never let up, do you, darling?"

"Why should I?" Lucifer asked. "I enjoy work." The black eyes turned to Isobel and he smiled. "I enjoy my work very much, in fact."

To Isobel the meeting had gone on far too long and she could almost feel the malice that emanated from Vanessa Law, as she watched every move and word Lucifer made. Isobel shivered involuntarily, her lightheartedness quite gone, the clawing coldness in the pit of her stomach again when the amber eyes turned on her.

"I see you still employ Miss Hendrix," she said quietly, and Lucifer smiled.

"Of course," he agreed. "She's the best secretary I've ever had, and she's decorative too, what more can any man ask?"

"I wouldn't know, darling." The feline eyes looked up at him possessively. "When are you coming to see me again?" she asked. "It's weeks now since I saw anything of you."

The statement so surprised Isobel that she looked at the thin, dark face curiously. Surely Lucifer would not absent himself for so long from his usual haunts unless . . . unless he was seeing another woman. Having yet another affair. Her face hardened and she was surprised to find herself unwilling to accept the idea.

"I've been very busy," Lucifer repeated. "You know mine isn't a nine-to-five job, Van."

"Don't call me Van!" Her vehemence crackled sharply on Isobel's nerves, but the moment was shortlived and a second later she smiled reproachfully, a hand on his arm. "You know I don't like it," she told him.

Lucifer grinned unconcernedly. "I forgot," he said, obviously being untruthful. He looked across at the man seated at the other table waiting for Vanessa and raised an expressive brow. "Hadn't you better go and join Freddy?" he asked. "He looks as if he's about to die of the miseries."

"Lucifer. . . ."

"You don't want him to get up and leave you on your own do you?" he asked, and Vanessa was silent for a moment, seeing herself beaten, Isobel thought, but reluctant to recognize it.

"I'd better go," she said at last. The amber eyes turned on Isobel again and she held her gaze until Isobel shivered at the malice she saw there. "How's Nigel?" she asked meaningly.

"He's very much better, Mrs. Law." She knew she sounded stiffly formal, but her throat felt tight and dry and she wished only for that malicious gaze to be withdrawn.

"Shall we be hearing wedding bells soon?"

The question was so unexpected that Isobel could only stare at her for a moment or two and it was Lucifer who answered for her. "It's much too soon for wedding bells yet," he informed Vanessa with an air of certainty that surprised Isobel as much as it did Vanessa. "Isobel's far too much of a baby to be tied down to domesticity."

"Oh." Vanessa looked from one to the other, her eyes

looking genuinely puzzled, while Isobel, for some inexplicable reason, was obliged to smother an insane desire to laugh. "I rather thought it was more or less settled," Vanessa said.

Lucifer shook his head, his eyes wickedly dark. "Nothing's settled," he informed her profoundly, "until it happens."

The following silence could have been cut with a knife and Isobel wondered, somewhat dizzily, what would happen next. It was Vanessa who spoke, seeing the futility of further questioning. "I'd better be going," she said again, and Lucifer, taking her at her word, sat down to resume his leisurely lunch.

"Goodbye, Van."

He poured himself more coffee and Isobel watched the tall, thin gauntness of Vanessa Law move smoothly across the restaurant toward her neglected partner, unable to do anything about the unbidden sense of pity she felt for her.

She lowered her gaze when she turned and met Lucifer's black eyes watching her intently. "You don't have to, you know," he told her, and she shook her head slowly, knowing he had seen and recognized the momentary pity she felt for Vanessa.

"You're cruel and . . . and unfeeling," she told him in a voice that sounded a little breathless, "and I'd hate to be in love with you!"

CHAPTER NINE

Despite Nigel's complaints that he was not yet able to walk more than the length of the garden without discomfort and that he liked her to stay with him, Isobel often went for quite long walks alone and, in fact, quite enjoyed the solitude of the meadows that spread out around Kanderby House like a pattern of every shade of green and yellow. Sunday morning was her favorite time for walking and she loved to hear the distant summons of some hidden church bell as she made her way through the warm-smelling fields scattered thickly with buttercups and clover.

On previous Sunday walks she had noticed a beautiful old Cotswold stone house, tucked away behind a cluster of ancient elms and standing in an almost straight line, as the crow flies, behind Kanderby House. From the little she knew about architecture she estimated that it dated from Tudor times or perhaps even earlier, and it stood, mellowed and quiet, as if it basked in the hot sun. Enthusiastic mention of it had produced the information that it belonged to Vanessa Law and was part of the vast inheritance left to her by her late husband.

Learning that had discouraged Isobel from a vague idea she had had of one day walking right up to the old house and openly admiring it. She would never have dared do such a thing with Vanessa Law in occupation.

Seeing the house now, in the mellowness of summer, Isobel found it hard to picture it either as Vanessa Law's home or as the headquarters of a rather bizarre club that both she and Lucifer belonged to. Nothing looked less like a home for witchcraft, although she supposed that on a dark night and with a northeast wind howling across the open land around it, it could look quite alarmingly different. She wondered, too, how many and much more serious witching ceremonies the old house had seen within its walls than the mere curiosity of a group of inquiring minds.

Both Lucifer and Mrs. Grayson had assured her that as long as she kept a respectable distance from the house, no one would mind her walking in the fields, and she had done so on several occasions. She always gave the house a wide berth, although she was more than ever curious about it since she had learned to whom it belonged.

The tall slim chimneys of the house showed, softly yellow, against the blue sky and above the tops of the trees which were on slightly lower ground, and once again Isobel's curiosity was aroused. Just once she would love to go closer to it and really be able to see it, but the thought of perhaps being caught by Vanessa Law deterred her today as it always did.

The village of Green End itself lay in the opposite direction altogether, so that there was little likelihood of her meeting anyone else, and she walked slowly, enjoying the sun and the smell of the drying grass and clover. It was idyllic, she thought, almost too idyllic, for she could never quite decide what there was about the charming and beautiful countryside that gave her a feeling of unrest. It was almost as if she had strayed into some lovely, alien land and might at any moment come across the unexpected.

Adding to the sensation of unreality were seven tall,

roughly hewn stone pillars that seemed to grow out of the summery meadow, ugly and somehow menacing. She looked across at them warily as she usually did when she passed them, scolding herself for being ridiculously fanciful, but they always seemed ominous even in the bright sunshine. She remembered Nigel's reluctant and half-scornful explanation for their existance.

They were, he had informed her, supposed to be the seven witches of Greenwick, a village on the other side of the hill, and they had been magically turned into stone when they attempted to initiate the young sister of a good priest into their coven.

It was, of course, all utter nonsense and she had laughed when Nigel told her the story, but nevertheless she always kept a cautious eye on the huge yellow pillars of stone whenever she passed them, and wondered how they really came to be standing there, solid and gloomy, in that tranquil meadow.

She could never quite suppress the shiver that trickled icily along her spine, and she thought ruefully how Lucifer would have laughed at her and pointed out, yet again, how powerful psychology and autosuggestion could be.

She passed the seven witches and went on toward the promising shade of trees only a few yards ahead. It was so quiet and peaceful that the soft sound of voices immediately drew her attention, growing plainer as she walked on. There was, she decided, something vaguely familiar about both voices, although she could distinguish no actual words.

The very fact that there was someone else about, however, made her cautious and she decided to go no farther than the few extra steps that would bring her to the edge of the trees where they curved around as the thicket widened. Then she would turn around and go back before she was seen and perhaps accused of trespassing.

Knowing how sound carries in the open country, she had anticipated that the talkers would be some distance off yet, perhaps somewhere deeper in to the small wood, and hidden from her view. Coming upon them suddenly as she did, when she walked to the curving edge of the trees, she blinked in surprise, for there were two people so close that she felt sure they must have seen her.

Only the fact that they were so engrossed in their own affairs kept them from paying her more notice. Isobel recognized the man as Cal Ford, the artist who had sketched her portrait at the County Show, and there was certainly no mistaking the sleeky coiled black hair of Vanessa Law.

Obviously she had been riding, for a big bay mare stood waiting patiently nearby, but whether the meeting had been accidental or planned was debatable. Certainly it was not the sort of place one would normally expect to meet people except by arrangement, and Cal Ford had frankly admitted to being no country-lover.

Their actions, too, spoke of a rendezvous rather than an accidental meeting. The man, not so much taller than his companion, held her in his arms, the knuckles of his fingers showing bone-white as he held her tight, his mouth covering hers in a kiss that held them both silent for as long as it took Isobel to register the scene and then draw back hastily behind the trees again.

A low, blatantly seductive laugh reached her a moment later and the sound of the man's harsh, erratic breathing, reminding Isobel of Lucifer's half-scornful pity for the man's obvious infatuation for Vanessa. She wished she could turn and go, leave the intimate scene to the participants and forget she had ever seen them, but before she could move off the mare raised her sensitive nose to the wind and whinnied a warning.

There was nothing for it but to come out into the open; much better that than have Vanessa Law come over and find her there. Cal Ford's artistic eye at once recognized her and he looked both startled and wary.

"It's . . . it's Miss Henderson, isn't it?" he asked, now standing a restrained two feet away from his companion. "I remember seeing you with Lucifer Bennetti at the County Show."

"Hendrix, Mr. Ford, Isobel Hendrix," she corrected him, uneasily aware of Vanessa Law's strange catlike eyes fixed on her as she turned her head. "I'm sorry if I'm trespassing, Mrs. Law," she said, "but both Lucifer and Mrs. Grayson said it would be okay for me to walk in the fields as long as I didn't go too near the house."

"That was very generous of them," Vanessa drawled, her eyes suspicious. Wondering how much I saw, Isobel thought ruefully. "But I'd call this too near the house, wouldn't you?"

"I . . . I'm sorry." Isobel had scarcely expected a welcome, especially in the circumstances, but the sheer malice with which the other woman looked at her sent shivers down her spine.

"Then I suggest you go back where you came from," Vanessa told her.

"Yes. Yes, of course. I'm sorry, I didn't realize."

"Realize?" The voice was sharp and almost shrill, and

she was far more uneasy, Isobel thought, than she would have expected, until it occurred to her that Vanessa would certainly not want the scene she had just witnessed relayed to Lucifer.

"I . . . I mean I had no intention of intruding on your privacy."

"Then don't," Vanessa said shortly. "I'll inform Lucifer that I object to having every little girl he employs being given the free run of my land."

"But I had no . . ." Isobel began, and was waved to silence by a dismissing hand.

"Oh, spare me the excuses, for heaven's sake," Vanessa snapped, "and in future stay away from my property."

It wasn't just the land they stood on either, Isobel thought, that was included in that autocratic order, but if Vanessa's relationship with Lucifer was so precious to her why was she here with Cal Ford? Almost automatically she glanced at the artist where he stood, eyes downcast and half-ashamed of his silence.

Isobel shook her head slowly. "I certainly won't come onto your land again, Mrs. Law," she said. "Good morning." She looked again at Cal Ford. "Goodbye, Mr. Ford."

She turned around and would have walked off, but Vanessa had apparently read something more into her answer, and she called her back. "Miss Hendrix!" Isobel turned again, reluctantly, and met the slitted eyes that regarded her suspiciously. "Just don't get too ambitious," Vanessa told her, after a brief silence. "Lucifer Bennetti is far more than a silly girl like you can handle."

The crude, obvious warning made Isobel crawl with

embarrassment, but she lifted her chin, her cheeks flushed and angry, almost unconsciously noting Cal Ford's half-hearted attempt to stem any further abuse.

"I only have ambitions to be a good secretary, Mrs. Law," she informed her. "I leave anything else to you." She looked meaningly at the artist, miserably inadequate in the situation he found himself in, and Vanessa Law's strange eyes glittered angrily.

"I don't know how long you've been sneaking behind trees," she warned, "but if you're wise, you'll forget you've seen anything here this morning."

Isobel shook her head, anxious to be gone. "It doesn't concern me."

"You're right, it doesn't." She walked toward Isobel, who felt a sudden urgent desire to run as fast as she could away from there. "If you mention one word of what you've seen, or think you've seen, to Lucifer," she said quietly, her voice as hard and cold as steel, "you'll be sorry, Miss Hendrix, believe me, you'll be very, very sorry."

Isobel's nerves tingled warningly and she found it difficult to summon even enough courage to turn her back on the menace that looked at her from Vanessa Law's eyes. She began walking away, her chin high, even though her knees felt as weak as water and threatened to collapse under her at any minute.

It was cowardly and ridiculous to feel so afraid, she told herself, out here in the open with the sun shining warmly on her back, but that steady, malignant gaze had held more than a threat of physical danger and, at the moment, she could believe almost anything was possible.

The smooth silky black head and the strange,

disturbing amber-colored eyes were all too familiar in another enemy of hers, and for one crazy, incredible moment she could have believed that she was again face to face with a big, black, malicious-eyed cat, called Pyewacket, who sat contentedly enough in Lucifer's arms, but lashed out viciously when Isobel tried to make friends with her.

Isobel said nothing to Lucifer about her ignominious retreat from Vanessa's anger, but she did tell Nigel about it when they were alone that evening and sitting on the bench at the end of the garden.

Now free of strapping of any sort on his legs, but still needing a stick to help him walk, Nigel was getting about much better now, and had even been driven to his office in London once or twice. He had been annoyed because Isobel had refused to ask Lucifer for the time off to go with him, but it would not be right, she explained to him, to expect special privileges just because he was Lucifer's brother. It would not be very long now, she thought ruefully, before he asked her about moving back to Frome's and leaving her job with Lucifer, and she was determined to be firm about it.

"I never knew Vanessa had an interest in anyone else but Luke," he told her, when she mentioned Cal Ford. "Although I know he's been crazy about her for years. I was told so by a mutual acquaintance," he added, when he saw her curious frown. "Quite frankly, darling, you surprise me when you say that Vanessa was a willing partner."

"Can you imagine her being a partner at all if she

wasn't willing?" Isobel asked dryly. "I'm not sure whether I'm surprised or not, although I knew Cal Ford was what you call crazy about her."

"Did you?" He arched a curious brow. "You're very knowledgeable about such matters, considering. How do you know?"

Isobel shrugged. "Something Lucifer said when we saw Cal Ford at the County Show last month," she said. "Lucifer said he was a fool, but it wasn't so much what he said as the way he said it. I just got the impression that he knew the man was in love with Vanessa and he thought him a fool for it. Being Lucifer, of course," she added, "he didn't think twice about saying what he thought."

"No," Nigel agreed, "he wouldn't." He frowned over something else she had said, and looked at her with interest. "I didn't know you knew Cal Ford," he said.

"I met him at the show, as I said. I didn't imagine you knew him either, I thought he belonged to Lucifer's world, not yours."

"He does," Nigel agreed. "I met him once, though, and I thought he was rather an odd bird. What was he doing at the show? I thought he was strictly a town-dweller."

Isobel made a wry face. "As far as I could gather he was killing two birds with one stone," she told him. "He was working, doing sketches and selling them, and hoping to see Vanessa while he was there."

"Oh, I see. I've heard he's a very clever artist, though I've never seen any of his stuff." He smiled at her. "If I'd known he was going to be there and working, I'd have asked you to have had a drawing done of yourself."

"Oh, but he did. . . ." She bit her lip hastily, remembering too late who had both commissioned and kept the rather good sketch of her that Cal Ford had drawn.

Nigel's eyes narrowed suspiciously. "Did he do one, Isobel?"

There was no other way but to answer him truthfully, she realized, for if she denied it now he would almost surely ask Lucifer about it, and Lucifer, she felt sure, would have no qualms about admitting to possession of it.

"Yes, he did, actually," she said, not looking at him.

"And you didn't say anything about it," he accused.

She shrugged, hoping to make it appear far less important than he was bent on making it. "I didn't think it was worth special mention," she told him.

"Have you still got it?" She shook her head. "Why not? Wasn't it any good?"

"Oh yes, it was very good."

"Then why. . . ."

"It wasn't mine to keep," she said, a little impatiently, for she was tired of being questioned.

When she looked at him again, his eyes were a deep, dark blue in the evening light and it was difficult to judge what he was thinking, but there was a familiar warning tightness about his mouth. "I don't need more than one guess to know who has it," he told her, and she sighed.

"It was Lucifer's idea to have it done," she told him. "I think he felt sorry for Cal Ford one way and another, and he wanted to help."

Nigel's lip curled dubiously. "Charity isn't Luke's strong point that I know of," he said bluntly. "And if he wanted to help Cal Ford, he needn't have kept the drawing. Why did you let him, Isobel?"

She looked a little surprised at the question. "I had

very little option," she declared, truthfully enough. "You know what Lucifer's like, and anyway, he paid for it, so I couldn't very well lay claim to it."

"What I want to know," Nigel murmured darkly, "is why the hell he wanted it in the first place."

She pondered on that question herself for a moment or two. "I don't know," she admitted at last. "Maybe he just liked the picture."

"Or maybe he wanted it for some wretched trickery at that idiotic club of theirs."

Isobel looked briefly uneasy. "Oh no, Nigel, that's silly."

"Is it?" He shrugged. "They get up to some pretty silly things as far as I can gather, and I wouldn't put anything past him."

"Well. I'm quite sure he wouldn't use a perfectly harmless drawing of me to . . . to raise his devils or whatever it is they do. It's ridiculous!"

"I suppose so," he allowed grudgingly. "But I would like to know why he has it."

"Well, it was rather a good drawing," she said, and Nigel snorted his opinion of that idea.

"I've never known him as patron of the arts either," he remarked, and Isobel felt a flash of rising temper at his determined ill humor.

"Quite likely it's still rolled up into a tube the way he carried it home," she retorted. "And I really don't see why you're making so much fuss about a . . . a hasty sketch."

"It's his reason for having it that I'm questioning," Nigel insisted. "And I wasn't aware that I was making a fuss about it."

"Well, you are."

They were silent for several minutes, a brittle uneasy silence, then Nigel leaned over and took her hand in his, making her turn and face him. "If I'm fussing, darling, there's good reason for it," he told her, "but I didn't want to upset you. I'm sorry."

Isobel sighed. "Oh, I'm not upset, it isn't worth that, it just seemed a bit like making a mountain out of a mole-hill that's all."

He kissed her mouth, his eyes apologetic. "Well, anyway, I'm sorry." He put an arm round her shoulders and hugged her up close to him on the bench seat. "It won't be long now," he told her, "and I'll be back full time at the works and we can both get away from the . . . the rather dangerous atmosphere of this place."

"Oh, but it's lovely here," Isobel objected, and leaned away from him to look up into his eyes; suddenly feeling a strange uneasy beat in her heart. "And I'm not at all sure that I'm coming back to Frome's, Nigel."

He looked at her as if he found it impossible to believe he had heard her correctly. "But of course you will," he told her. "This arrangement was only temporary, you knew that."

"I didn't," she denied firmly. "You said nothing at all about it being temporary."

"But surely you understood that," he insisted. "It was only while I was here and I wanted you here with me."

"You didn't point that out to me or to Lucifer," she told him.

"Lucifer?" he asked, his eyes narrowing with suspicion. "What the hell has it got to do with Luke?"

"Everything I should think," Isobel retorted. "He

happens to be my employer and he pays me very well. Also," she added, "I happen to like my job."

"You . . . you mean you want to stay on?"

She nodded firmly.

"Even after I'm gone?"

"Yes. Oh, Nigel, be reasonable. I have a great deal to lose by leaving here."

"Including me," Nigel said gloomily.

"That's silly," Isobel told him shortly, "and you know it. It isn't as if this is the end of the world, it's only quite a short journey from London by car and you could see me every weekend, if you wanted to."

"You know I want to."

"Then why are you making so much fuss about my staying?" she asked reasonably. "After all, I only ever saw you about two or three evenings a week when I was in town, so if you come here each weekend I shall see you for actually longer than I did then, and I know Mrs. Grayson will be delighted to have you here more often."

"I know she will," he allowed, but he still had that discontented look that showed how much he disliked the idea of leaving her behind. "But I saw you all day as well," he said at last, insistently. "Isobel . . . please won't you reconsider? For my sake?"

She shook her head. "I . . . I told you, Nigel, that I need more time to think about . . . about what you asked me, and I think that being away from you for a bit will give me the chance I need to know how I really feel." She smiled at him wryly. "See how much I shall miss you when you're not here."

"I suppose you're right," he allowed grudgingly. "I did promise not to rush you, didn't I?"

"You did." She smiled at his sober face. "We'll both have more opportunity to find out whether absence really does make the heart grow fonder, or if it merely breeds indifference."

"It certainly won't breed indifference as far as I'm concerned," Nigel assured her confidently, and Isobel wished she could have been so certain.

CHAPTER TEN

It was several days after her rather eventful meeting with Vanessa that Isobel again got into difficulties with Vanessa Law's cat, Pyewacket, and yet again, it was Lucifer who came to her aid. It was while she was alone in the office, working on some rather worse than usual manuscript, that something caught her eye.

She glanced up, startled by the sudden movement, and saw the huge black cat standing on the sill by the open window. Its back was arched and the malevolent yellow eyes, so like its mistress's, watched her steadily and very disconcertingly. Lucifer was still not back from lunch or she would not have bothered herself, but would have left the cat's eviction to him; as it was she got up from her chair and approached it cautiously.

"Shoo!" she told it, clapping her hands together discouragingly. "Go away, you horrible great brute. Go home!"

Pyewacket looked at her, unmoved and quite unafraid, her smooth black back still arched threateningly. "Go away!" Isobel told her sharply, hoping to impress the animal with her sternness. "Go home!"

She reached out, meaning to use a bit of gentle persuasion, since verbal command seemed to be having no effect. She put her hands round the sleek, furry body and pushed gently toward the open window. "Go on," she instructed, "good kitty, go home. Go home, Pyewacket, or whatever your silly name is."

It was not to be as simple as that, however for the cat

resisted her efforts in no uncertain manner. It turned, spitting furiously, one paw raised to lash out with claws extended, drawing blood with one vicious rake down Isobel's right arm. She dropped the cat with a yell, instinctively putting the injured arm to her mouth while she stared at her assailant in momentary fear. "You vicious brute!" she told it, while it glared at her maliciously. "That's twice you've scratched me!"

Pyewacket stood her ground, her tail swishing back and forth in righteous anger, yellow eyes narrowed in warning against further liberties. Isobel stood for a moment, indecisive, then stubbornness made her determined not to let a mere cat have the last word, and she waved her hands and tried her original methods again. "Shoo!" she said firmly. "Shoo! Go home, you horrible, spiteful creature, go home to your mistress and . . . and scratch her."

She was so occupied with getting rid of her unwelcome visitor that she did not hear the door being opened, and it was not until she heard the laugh that greeted her uncharitable exhortation to the cat that she turned around realizing Lucifer was there. She looked a bit sheepish at being caught so openly hostile to Vanessa, and he smiled knowingly.

"Are you having trouble with Vanessa's Pye again?" he asked, and came across to the window, picking up the cat, who promptly became all soft and kittenish, closing her yellow eyes ecstatically when he rubbed her throat with his strong fingers.

"She hates me," Isobel told him, glaring at the cat resentfully, "and I've never done anything to harm her. She just doesn't like me, for some reason or other."

"She's just jealous, as I told you before," he said. "Aren't you, Pye?"

"But all soft and fussy with you," Isobel retorted, so indignantly that he laughed and pushed the cat unceremoniously out of the window.

"It sounds to me as if the dislike's mutual," he told her. "Don't you like cats?"

"I like cats," Isobel informed him, "but I'm not at all sure that that thing is just a common cat as you claim."

"Oh?" He gave Pyewacket a discouraging jab in the ribs when she attempted to come back through the open window, and Isobel looked vaguely uneasy.

"Oh, it's ridiculous, of course, and I know it is. The trouble is when she looks at me with those great, evil-looking yellow eyes I can believe she's anything from a . . . a wild animal to a reincarnated witch, which only goes to show how strong the power of persuasion is."

"Or how strong your imagination is," he teased. His laughter did little to pacify her, but at least he did something about the cat. He gave it a none too gentle shove and pushed her off the sill down onto the garden outside. "Go on, you prowling fusspot," he told the indignant Pyewacket, "go back where you belong!"

Isobel leaned forward in the window, watching the cat move off reluctantly along the drive. It turned once to look back at her with its yellow eyes narrowed and spiteful so that she drew back her head hastily. The scratches on her arm were much worse than before and ran from elbow to wrist, red and angry-looking.

Lucifer looked at them, tut-tutting impatiently, as if he considered it as much her fault as the cat's. "You just don't learn, do you?" he asked. "Come on through to the bathroom and I'll mop you up."

"There's no need to mop me up," Isobel told him shortly. "I'll survive with a hankie tied around it until it stops bleeding." She had never been through the rest of the cottage and somehow she shied nervously away from the idea now.

He made no effort to argue with her but simply put a hand firmly in the middle of her back and propelled her through the door and on into the hall, with no more cere-mony than he had shown when evicting her attacker.

"You," he informed her briefly as they went, "argue far too much . . . it's a distressing habit in the young. Beppo!" The last was yelled at his manservant who appeared with remarkable speed from the kitchen, his eyes curious, noting the marks on Isobel's arm.

"*Si, signore*?"

There followed a string of what was presumably instructions in, to Isobel, rapid and unintelligible Italian; then the man disappeared again to return a few minutes later with a first aid kit. He made what Isobel took to be an offer to help, but Lucifer dismissed it briefly and turned to her again.

"In here," he told her, and opened the door of a small but luxurious bathroom.

"I wish you wouldn't make so much fuss about it," Isobel protested. "I know it was my own fault, and you're right, I don't learn. Not where that wretched cat's concerned anyway, but I'm not mortally wounded."

"Why don't you stop talking for just a few minutes and sit down on that stool?" Lucifer asked, as if his patience was fast running out, and he opened the lid of the first aid kit, frowning over the contents.

"But I. . . ."

"Shush!"

"Lucifer, I'm not. . . ." She stopped when he drew a very deep breath and looked at her steadily for a moment before launching into a tirade of rapid Italian that lasted for several seconds, while Isobel sat and looked at him wide-eyed.

"Now sit down and shut up!" he told her.

She looked at him silently for a moment, then smiled mischievously. "*Si, P*. . . ." A warning glint in his eyes cut short the reply that had proved so provocative before and instead she giggled briefly before subsiding on to the stool.

"That's better," he approved, and bent over to look at her arm. He bathed it gently, although whatever he used on it stung sharply for a few seconds, while Isobel eyed him curiously.

"What did all that mean?" she asked after a minute or two.

He grinned at her ruefully. "I hope you never know," he told her. "I can safely cuss at you in Italian because I know you don't understand what I'm saying and therefore you don't know how uncomplimentary I'm being."

"I can guess," Isobel retorted, surveying her wounds. "You're not going to bandage it?" she added a few seconds later when he produced a roll of white cotton from the kit and proceeded to bind it around her arm with a dexterity that surprised her.

"Of course I am, to give that stuff a chance to work."

She surveyed the stark white wrapping with disfavor. "It looks as if I've broken it at least," she complained, and he shook his head slowly as he put the things back into the first aid kit.

"Stop complaining, you ungrateful little wretch," he told her, and grinned at her suddenly. "You and Nigel can compare notes now," he added, "and see who moans most."

Isobel looked at him indignantly for a second, then met the wicked glint in his eyes and almost inevitably smiled. "I'm sorry if I sound ungrateful," she said. "I'm not, really. Thank you for dressing my war wounds."

"You're welcome, but if I were you I'd give Pyewacket a wide berth in future; certainly don't attempt to pick her up again."

"I won't, don't worry," Isobel assured him fervently.

"Good. She's obviously chosen you as the object of her special hate and she'll probably swipe at you again if she gets the chance, so don't give it to her."

"Does she treat every female like that?" Isobel asked curiously, and Lucifer smiled, walking with her back to the office.

"Not every one," he said. "That's why I said she seems to have singled you out."

"Why?"

She looked at him suddenly more serious, some idiotic fear striking coldly at her heart as she recalled the awful similarity between Vanessa Law and the big black cat. Both of them appeared to hate her with equal intensity, and she had the uneasy feeling that it was for the same reason: Lucifer.

"Who knows?" he said, and shrugged. "Now forget

Pyewacket and Vanessa and let's get on with some more work, shall we?"

It was only as she rolled the first page of paper into her machine that she realized he had mentioned Vanessa and the cat in the same breath, almost as if he had followed her thoughts, and she shivered again at the coincidence.

It was later that day, after she had finished work, that Isobel sat with Nigel and tried to explain how her arm came to be so badly scratched. "It's not nearly as bad as it looks," she told him, when he exclaimed at the sight of it. "It's because Lucifer insisted on putting this wretched bandage on it that it looks so serious."

"It must be pretty bad," Nigel told her, "for Luke to have made so much fuss. He's not given to being over-concerned about anyone."

"Well, it isn't, I assure you," she said. "Underneath this bandage it's just a cat scratch, pure and simple."

"Pure and simple?" He questioned her meaning with one raised brow and she laughed, determined to have no more fuss made about it.

"Well, maybe it's a bit deep and it was rather messy because it bled a lot," she admitted, "but it really doesn't warrant so much fuss being made and it certainly doesn't warrant all this bandage wound around it."

"Have you something on it beside the bandage?" Nigel asked, as if he mistrusted his brother's ministrations.

She smiled. "Yes, I have. He used some horrible stuff that stung like fury and felt worse than Pyewacket's claws when he first applied it, although it's much better now. He's a very efficient doctor."

"He should be," Nigel retorted, as if he parted with the

information only reluctantly. "He did three years as a medical student and then changed his mind."

"Did he?" Isobel absorbed the new piece of information thoughtfully. "I wonder why."

"God knows," Nigel said impatiently. "He said something about not being cut out for it. Personally, I believe him."

"Oh, I don't know," Isobel mused, then hastily recalled herself, reproached by his frown of disapproval.

"That damned cat seems to follow you around," he told her. "You must have a fascination for it."

Isobel shook her head. "It's not me who's the attraction," she denied. "It's Lucifer, she's as crazy about him as her mistress is."

"Vanessa?" He raised a doubtful brow. "Is Vanessa crazy about him?" he asked, obviously doubting it.

"Very definitely."

"I'd have said she was more possessive than anything else." He seemed prepared to argue the point and she thought ruefully that another hot day had done nothing to improve his temper. "Although," he admitted, "she has to take a back seat every so often when he takes a fancy to someone else."

Isobel nodded, quite convinced she was right. "Oh, she very definitely is crazy about him," she assured him. "She's in love with him, Nigel, it's not just possessiveness; I've seen her face and the hurt look in her eyes when he's been thoughtless in what he says to her."

Nigel looked closely at her for a moment. "You seem to have been very observant," he remarked, and almost made it sound like a trait he disapproved of.

"Not really," Isobel denied. "I just happened to notice

the way she looked, that's all. I thought it was . . . well, rather out of character for her, but it showed, quite plainly, for just a second, once when they were talking."

"Hmm." He rubbed his chin, his eyes thoughtful. "That's quite a revelation."

"I thought so," Isobel said quietly. "Actually I felt quite sorry for her for a few seconds."

"It wouldn't be for very long, I can imagine," he said wryly.

She looked at him for a moment, curious and only half serious. "As a matter of fact," she said, watching his face to see what his reaction would be to the suggestion, "I wondered why, if she's so practised in the arts of witch-craft, she didn't concoct some weird brew that would ensure he stayed with her and didn't go wandering off after someone else all the time."

"Good grief!" Nigel exclaimed, in something akin to horror. "You're not seriously suggesting that she'd use a . . . a love potion or whatever it is they brew up, are you?"

"Why not?" Isobel asked defensively, and he stared at her for a moment, shaking his head slowly in disbelief.

"Because you surely don't believe in such things, Isobel, you're not so naïve."

"Of course I'm not," Isobel agreed with a smile, "but Vanessa Law's supposed to believe in it, isn't she?"

"Not believe in it, no," he denied. "They merely study the old witchcraft methods with the object of discovering how they were made to work; or appear to work, because obviously they didn't in fact, it was all psychological."

"So Lucifer says."

"Well, for once I agree with him." He looked at her

narrowly. "Don't you believe it's all psychological chi-canery?"

"Yes, I told you I believe, but I'm not at all sure that Vanessa does."

He was silent for a moment, as if the idea gave him food for thought, then he shook his head. "I find it hard to believe that a woman like Vanessa is that gullible," he remarked at last. "What makes you think she is?"

Isobel shrugged, not really prepared to put her mean-ing into words. "I don't know exactly," she said. "It's just . . . just the way she behaves generally. She even dresses the part. Those dark dresses and the high-piled black hair, which don't really suit her but which . . . well, give her an odd look, all weirdly exotic. You said your-self, she gives you the creeps."

"So she does," Nigel admitted, "but I hadn't gone very deeply into the reason for it." He was silent in thought again for a while, then he looked at her with eyes that had a curiously blank look, as if the full meaning of what she had said had only just penetrated. "Heavens!" he said, half under his breath, "it doesn't bear thinking about in this day and age."

"It's . . . it's nonsense, of course," Isobel said, a bit uncertainly for she was not at all sure that she had not raised some devil of her own by starting this conver-sation.

"Of course," he echoed, and was silent for so long that she felt sure he must be taking her seriously about Vanessa. After a while, however, he seemed determined to shake the idea and he shrugged his shoulders, leaning across to take her hand in his. "Oh well, I suppose she and Luke will sort out their own salvation one of these days," he said, and Isobel nodded absently. He smiled at her serious face and squeezed her hand. "You're very preoccupied tonight," he told her. "Is it your arm?"

"My arm?" She blinked for a moment. "Oh no, no, that's okay. Just a bit sore, that's all."

"And he didn't offer to give you any time off to recover, I suppose?"

Isobel smiled wryly at him. "Would you have done?" she asked. "For a cat scratch?"

He shook his head. "No, I suppose not," he admitted. "But if it isn't because your arm's hurting you, what's making you so thoughtful?"

She shrugged. "I didn't know I was." That wasn't quite true, in fact, for ever since she had left the cottage that afternoon there had been a strange sense of uneasiness troubling her that she could neither identify fully nor find a reason for.

"You've had an air of not-quite-with-me, all evening," he told her, and she smiled apologetically. "And I'm wondering if you'd tell me what was worrying you, even if you knew."

Isobel looked surprised at what sounded almost like an accusation. "Of course I'd tell you if I knew myself."

"Would you, darling?" He held on to her hand tightly. "Or would you run to Luke like you did when the prospect of a thunderstorm frightened you?"

She saw his reason at last and shook her head over it. "I didn't run to him," she reminded him quietly. "He ran to me, if you remember, and without my asking."

"Only because he knew you were frightened," Nigel insisted. "and you hadn't seen fit to tell me about your fear."

She sighed, not prepared to argue that subject again either. "Oh, please don't let's go into all that again," she begged. "I told you how it happened, Nigel, and it's ancient history now."

For a moment she thought he would carry it further, but then he smiled and kissed her fingers lightly. "I'm sorry, my darling."

Isobel shook her head. "There's no need to be," she told him, and laughed uncertainly. "I don't know; it seems to have been a funny sort of day altogether somehow. First that wretched cat scratched me and gave me the creeps, then when I. . . ." She hesitated, wondering if her vague, groundless fears would bring his scorn down on her head.

"When you?" he prompted.

She laughed, trying to make light of it. "It's really too stupid for words," she admitted, "but ever since I left my cottage to come over here, I've had the strangest feeling that . . . that something's going to happen."

"Something's going to happen?" It was obvious from the way he repeated her words that he had no conception of how she was feeling and she wished, though she would never dare have admitted it, that he had some of Lucifer's understanding of things that weren't always down to earth and easily explained.

She shrugged, trying to appear offhand about it. "Oh, you know what I mean," she told him. "People often say they feel all churned up inside, as if something's going to happen. It seldom does," she added optimistically.

"Of course it doesn't," he declared bluntly. "You're just letting the atmosphere of the place, and Vanessa's ghastly cat, get on your nerves, darling."

"I suppose so," Isobel allowed, not convinced.

Nigel looked at her sharply, disapproval plain on his good-looking face. "Well, I hope to heaven you're not going to start believing in that ridiculous hocus-pocus that Luke and Vanessa prattle about," he told her shortly. "I don't think I could stand it if you went mystic on me, too."

She flushed, angry because he was so lacking in understanding, and would not even pretend to humor her. "For heaven's sake," she told him, "there's nothing mystic about me. I just said I felt as if something was going to happen, that's all."

"Well, I hope you're wrong," he told her shortly. "Then you'll realize how silly the idea is."

Mrs. Grayon sat on the other side of the room. She never sat actually with them unless she was specifically brought into the conversation, but made herself as inconspicuous as possible while they spoke quietly together. At the moment, however, she seemed to sense that something was amiss between them and her head was raised, her blue eyes looking across at Isobel inquiringly, as if she realized her need for understanding.

"Is your arm very painful, Isobel?" she asked, and Isobel knew quite well that the question was only a way of admitting herself to the conversation.

"It's not too bad at all, Mrs. Grayson, thank you," she said, smiling her thanks.

"I know how it can be," the old lady said gently, but with a meaningful glance at her grandson. "With this hot weather an illness or a pain can seem so much worse and it can make one quite irritable at times, which is quite understandable."

Nigel glanced sharply from one to the other then made a droll face, that was partly apologetic. "I *am* being a bit of a so-and-so, I suppose," he admitted, and his grandmother smiled reassuringly.

"You did look rather edgy, dear," she told him mildly, "and I suspect you were taking it out on poor Isobel."

He leaned over and kissed Isobel gently beside her mouth. "I suppose I was doing that, too," he confessed, "but the idea of Isobel having mysterious feelings was too much for me to contemplate without objection."

Mrs. Grayson looked at Isobel inquiringly. "Are you having mysterious feelings, my dear?" she asked with a smile. "How very intriguing."

"Nigel's exaggerating," Isobel told her. "I merely said that I felt that . . . that something was going to happen. You know what I mean," she added, confident the old lady would be less impatient with her than Nigel had been. "It's nothing definite and most people feel like it at some time or other."

"I know exactly what you mean," Mrs. Grayson agreed. "I remember that's how Madge felt the day before Andy Frome was killed . . . Nigel's father, you know."

Isobel looked startled for a moment, especially when she saw the black frown with which Nigel greeted the information. "She felt . . . she felt something was going to happen?" she asked, uncertain if it would be wise to pursue the subject in view of Nigel's obvious dislike of it.

Mrs. Grayson nodded. "She told me the night before, just as she was going to bed, that she felt as if something unpleasant was going to happen, though, of course, like most people, she laughed about it, but I could tell it disturbed her." The old lady sighed deeply. "Of course what with Andy being in the profession he was, it was far more likely to become a fact than most people's intuitions are, and in this case it did. Poor Madge!"

Nigel looked at her narrow-eyed, as if he suspected her of making it up just to support Isobel. "I never knew about that," he told her, and the old lady smiled.

"I don't suppose you did, dear," she told him. "It isn't the kind of thing one tells one's children about, and especially the very practical little boy that you were." Her smile took the sting out of the words. "The very practical person you still are," she added. "I think after that, she was always afraid to admit to any such feeling again in case it came true as it did that time, but of course it was mere coincidence as it is with most people."

"Of course it's coincidence," Nigel retorted. "And I've never realized before that Madge was fanciful at all, quite the reverse, in fact."

"I don't think she is fanciful," Mrs. Grayson corrected him gently. "But it did frighten her a little, being such a traumatic experience for her. She was very much in love with your father, you know, dear," she added, as if that would be some comfort to him.

Nigel's facial expression when Isobel looked at him quite shocked her with its bitterness. "So much so," he said sharply, "that she married John Patterson after only fifteen months of being a widow."

Her grandmother shook her head reproachfully. "You mustn't judge so harshly, Nigel," she told him softly, regretting the bitterness as if it was directed at herself and not at her daughter. "Madge is a woman who needs a man to lean on, she never had my independent nature."

"Hmm." Isobel had the feeling that, had she not been there, he would have pursued the subject farther and not

in favor of his mother. She had not known that Madge
Frome had married again so soon after Nigel's father was
killed, or that Nigel felt so bitterly about his mother. He
had never revealed quite so much to her before, and she
wondered, briefly, if Lucifer's opinion of their mother
was as uncomplimentary as Nigel's was.

It was sheer disloyalty, she decided a few minutes later,
that gave her the idea that Lucifer would be much more
tolerant and less ready to condemn.

CHAPTER ELEVEN

It was quite late when Isobel left the house the following night and made her way along the gravel driveway and past the shrubbery to her cottage. The night was clear and cool after a warm day and the earth smelled loamy rich, tickling her nostrils and blending with the perfume of the late flowering roses that grew on the other side of the shrubbery.

A full, fat yellow moon sat in a starless sky and cast long black shadows that danced in front of her all along the driveway, her own shadow, tall and lean, leading her silently on. It was a beautiful night and yet she shivered involuntarily as she turned a corner and her elongated, silent other self moved swiftly around to her left as if trying to lure her from the path and into the rustling mass of rhododendrons and berberis.

She would, at almost any other time, probably have dismissed her own nervousness as sheer fancy, but all evening she had been edgy, plagued by that elusive feeling that something was about to happen. This time, however, she had said nothing to Nigel about it, thinking it rather unwise after his scornful reception of the same instinct last night.

A break in the shrubbery revealed the narrow path leading to her cottage and she breathed a sigh of relief, scolding herself a moment later for being so childishly imaginative. There were times when she viewed with some favor Nigel's wanting her to go back to London with him. At times the atmosphere of this place became almost unbearably overpowering and the full moon merely served to emphasize it.

It was ridiculous to believe in witches and witchcraft, or to think that Vanessa Law's Pyewacket was anything but a perfectly ordinary cat, but on nights like this and in this particular setting she could believe almost anything was possible. As Lucifer had so often told her, the success of witchcraft depended largely upon creating the right atmosphere and the right state of mind in the prospective victim, and at the moment both existed for her.

The little cottage appeared, small and squat, its square windows winking in the bright moonlight, and she pulled her front-door key from her purse as she walked toward it. She had opened the door and switched on the hall light when something caught her eye. It showed whitely in the long beam of light when she turned to close the door and she paused, the blood pounding heavily against her temple although there was nothing as yet to cause it.

How long she stood in the familiar comfort of the hall-way looking at it, pale against the rich brown loam beneath the rhododendrons, she had no idea, but she knew she must go and fetch it, whatever it was. It was only feet away and she ventured out at last, across the gravel path and looked down at the grotesque little image at her feet.

She bent and picked it up and, almost as quickly dropped it again when the cold clamminess of clay clung to her fingers. "Idiot!" she whispered scornfully to herself, and once again retrieved the ugly little figure from the ground, turning it over in her hands, although her instinct was still to throw it as far away as she could and wash her hands to get rid of its clammy coldness. She wondered how long it had lain there unnoticed, and a new kind of fear prickled her scalp; something which she could not yet identify for certain.

Surely if it had been there at lunchtime she would have seen it, or yesterday. If it had laid where it did now she would almost certainly have noticed it. Nevertheless she shivered again, looking at it with eyes wide in disbelief.

She carried it into the lighted hall and studied it more closely. It was several inches tall and the figure itself was crudely modeled from yellow clay: it was also quite obviously meant to be female. It had a face of sorts and a swath of blond hair crowned the hideous features. It took Isobel only seconds to realize who it was meant to represent.

"Oh no!" she shook her head slowly, a choking panic giving her voice a harsh timbre, and her fingers trembled when they touched the long, sharp pin that stuck up from the arm of the figure. Several long, deep scores ran the whole length of the clay arm and she instinctively put a hand to her own bandaged arm.

She stared at the grotesque effigy of herself with wide, blank eyes, her breathing shallow and erratic, as near to panic as she had ever been in her life. Sheer hatred must have gone into the making of it, and she had no hesitation in allotting the blame to Vanessa Law, for she could think of no one else who hated her enough to indulge in such a vicious and frightening practice.

She held the image at arm's length, her mind going swiftly back to Vanessa Law's warning only a few days previously. The flat yellow clay face with its crude features and the swath of blond hair that hung down over her hand and felt horribly real was, she felt, the outcome of that warning.

Her head still throbbed in panic and her heart hammered relentlessly at her ribs; then, before she realized what she was doing, she sped from the cottage and ran along the gravel driveway as fast as her legs would allow. She did not even pause to consider why she ran on, past Kanderby House, where Nigel's bedroom light still burned, and on to Lucifer's cottage. Nigel would never understand her fear; Lucifer was the only one who would both understand and explain. Nor did it occur to her that she was doing exactly what Vanessa Law had warned her against.

It was nearly midnight, but a light still burned in the hall of the lodge, and she ran straight up to the front door without hesitating, her breathing short and anguished as she rapped urgently on the solid wood. It was only seconds before the door was opened, although it seemed like an eternity to Isobel, and when Lucifer saw her face, he drew her quickly into the hall and closed the door before he uttered a word.

"Lucifer, I. . . ."

A strong arm encircled her shoulders. "Easy now, *cara mia,* easy." The quiet soothing voice was already helping to calm her and she strove to control her rapid, noisy breathing as he led her, unprotesting, into a room she had never seen before.

His manservant, the liquid-eyed Beppo, looked at her curiously when they came in, but a brief nod from Lucifer dismissed him and she was gently pushed down into an armchair. Lucifer crouched beside her, his black eyes curious but also more gentle and anxious than she had ever seen them. It was when he went to take her hands in his that he saw the effigy she still clutched tightly, and he took it from her unresisting fingers.

He frowned over it for a second or two. "Where did you get this?" he asked quietly.

Isobel swallowed hard. "It . . . it was lying on the garden opposite my cottage," she explained in a small trembly voice, and he nodded, turning the grotesque little figure around in his hand, then surprisingly he smiled.

"It doesn't do you justice, *bella mia.*"

"It . . . it is meant to be me, isn't it?" she asked, and he nodded.

"I should say it's meant to be you," he agreed calmly with another smile. "Although I wouldn't have recognized you, to be quite honest."

"Oh, Lucifer, don't!" she begged. "Please don't laugh at me."

He shook his head slowly and she realized that his smile was as gentle and understanding as the look in his eyes. "I'm not laughing at you, *piccola,*" he said softly.

"I . . . I know it's idiotic," she said, seeking to explain her fear. "I know it's . . . it's only superstition and I should have more sense than to take it seriously, but. . . ." She looked at him with her gray eyes already shining with tears and looking as vulnerable as a child's. "I'm . . . I'm frightened," she confessed.

"There's nothing to be frightened of," he told her quietly. "I've explained it all to you before, Isobel."

"I know. I . . . I was just being silly, I know that," she said, half fearing he might lose patience with her.

"Not silly, *bambinella,*" he argued gently, "just feminine, and no one minds that, least of all me."

"You didn't . . . didn't mind my coming here?"

176

He shrugged as he straightened up from beside her and, for a brief moment, the old devilment glittered in his eyes as he looked down at her. "Why should I mind?" he asked.

"It . . . it was just that I was so uncertain and . . . and so frightened."

He nodded, understanding, as she had known he would. "I know," he said. "These things are meant to frighten, *piccola*."

"It's . . . it's meant to make something happen, isn't it?" she asked, and he nodded.

"But it's all nonsense, of course," he told her, "and you're not frightened any more, are you?"

It was so difficult to meet his eyes and not feel childish and silly, so she kept her gaze lowered and deliberately looked again at the clay figure that now looked so much less ominous enclosed in his strong fingers. She shook her head. "Not . . . not so much," she said.

"You needed reassurance, is that it, *amante*?" She nodded. "And you thought I was the best one to come to?" It was obvious what he was carefully avoiding putting into words, and again Isobel nodded realizing for the first time that she had not even given Nigel a thought as she ran past the house.

"I . . . I knew you'd understand," she explained. "You know about these things, Lucifer."

He looked down at the figure with its long blond hair and half smiled. "Yes," he admitted quietly, "I know about these things." He left her side and walked over to sit in another armchair. "But you knew enough about them to be frightened, didn't you?"

"I know that making an effigy of someone and . . . and

marking it or sticking a pin into it where you want to do harm is supposed to bring that same injury to the person it represents." She watched how carelessly he held the effigy by one leg, in contrast to her own almost reverent handling of it.

He looked down at the thing again and laughed shortly. "It's meant to harm you," he agreed grimly, then looked across at her challengingly. "But mostly it's meant to frighten you . . . which it did. I did warn you what might happen, didn't I, *piccola*?" he added softly.

"That I might get involved in . . . in this witchcraft thing?" she asked, and he nodded. "Yes, you did, but I thought it all too farfetched to be true."

"And now you know it isn't, hmm?"

"It must have been. . . ." She stopped short, biting her lips, but he knew, as always, what she had been about to say and he smiled wryly as he said it for her.

"Vanessa," he said bluntly.

Isobel looked uneasy. "I . . . I couldn't think who else it could be," she confessed. She looked up then and frowned for a moment. "She hates me," she told him, "although I've never given her reason to."

He smiled softly, gazing at her with that slow, dark look that played havoc with her self-control. "You're very young and very beautiful," he said softly, "that's reason enough. Especially to a woman like Vanessa, who isn't overfond of her own sex anyway."

"But she has no reason," Isobel insisted, and stopped when he shook his head slowly.

"It's possibly my fault, Isobel, and I'm sorry."

"You're. . . ." She stared at him unbelievingly, both the admission and the apology taking her by surprise.

"I shouldn't have. . . ." Expressive hands lent meaning to the unspoken words and for a moment he seemed wholly Latin and much more dangerous. "I should have realized how young you were and how very, very vulnerable. It was selfish of me."

"Lucifer. . . ."

He raised a hand to silence her, a trace of the old uncaring insolence in his smile. "I should leave the *bambini* to Nigel and stay in my own league," he told her, "please see that I do in future, will you? Then Vanessa will leave you alone."

She was sufficiently recovered from her fright to translate and resent his reference to her as a baby and she flushed, lifting her chin, her eyes no longer tearful. "You don't need to keep referring to me as a . . . a baby," she told him, "and even if I was as old as the hills, Mrs. Law has nothing to fear from me in the way you're implying, as I've already told her."

"*Have* you?" His eyes glowed like coals in the yellow light, and Isobel resented what she suspected was admiration of childish pluck in defying the grownups. "No wonder Vanessa made your effigy," he added, and laughed.

"I saw her on Sunday morning with. . . ." She stopped short of actually betraying the confidence she had accidentally been admitted to, and lowered her eyes hastily before his compelling gaze.

"Cal Ford?" he guessed, and laughed again, while Isobel stared at him wide-eyed.

"*I* didn't tell you," she said, suddenly wary.

"I *know* you didn't." He grinned knowingly. "And I'll make sure Vanessa knows it wasn't you. You don't want any more dollies on your doorstep, do you?"

Isobel shook her head, reminded of the obscenely grotesque warning again. "I . . . I still don't see how she knew about my arm being scratched," she said slowly. "It couldn't have . . . she couldn't have. . . ." She could not entertain the idiotic suspicion that the effigy had been made before the cat's attack on her, but she looked at him appealingly, begging him to confirm that it *was* idiotic. "The arm of that . . . that thing is marked in exactly the same way as her cat marked my arm," she said.

He shook his head, holding the effigy where she could see it more plainly. "Not quite exactly," he told her quietly. "There's a significant difference, hadn't you noticed?"

She stared at it for a moment, her hand on her own injured arm, then her eyes widened. "Of course," she said. "It's . . . it's the left arm on that and it's my right arm that's injured. I didn't notice that." She shook her head. "Just the same, Lucifer, it's a coincidence. How did she knew about my arm?"

"Because I told her." She blinked at the blunt statement, and he smiled. "I warned her about keeping Pyewacket away from here, since she seems to have taken a dislike to you."

"Oh, I see."

"I told her you'd been badly scratched, but I didn't say which arm; she obviously took a chance and guessed wrongly, so you see she's not much of a witch, is she?"

"No, no, I suppose she isn't." She hesitated, cautious in case he laughed at her. "But it would have been different if the . . . the doll had been there before yesterday morning, wouldn't it?"

"It would," he agreed solemnly, "but it wasn't." He pulled the pin out of the clay arm and Isobel winced.

She looked down at her hands, silent for a moment, then she raised her eyes and met his black gaze. "It's . . . it's rather frightening when someone hates you so much they'll resort to that," she said, indicating the effigy with a nod of her head.

"Yes, I can imagine it must be." He smiled at her. "But now it's all been explained," he said, "and you know there's absolutely nothing to be frightened of, don't you?"

She nodded. "Yes, thank you. I . . . I'm sorry I came over here and behaved like a silly child, I shouldn't have been so selfish and troubled you at this time of night."

"Please!" He held up a protesting hand, and smiled. "You've been no trouble. I hadn't even thought of going to bed yet, although it's time I should." He stood up and smiled down at her. "But first I'd like to see you safely home."

"Oh no!" Isobel protested. "I wouldn't dream of letting you come out again tonight, I've been enough trouble and it's only a few yards. I'm quite over my heebie-jeebies now."

"Nevertheless," he insisted, putting a hand under her elbow, "I shall take you home. Come along."

She went, without further argument, partly because she thought that the garden with its shadows and whispering shrubs would be less disturbing if Lucifer was with her and partly, she admitted, because she wanted him to come with her simply for the pleasure of his company. The latter was something she recognized with some surprise and she wondered what Nigel would have said if he had known only a fraction of what had happened after she left him tonight.

The moon still shone, fat and yellow, only now it had, so it seemed to Isobel, a more benelovent look, and their two shadows fell together across the gravel driveway, intimately close, in silent company.

"It's a lovely night," Lucifer said, and she nodded.

"It is really," she allowed, "although I didn't think so earlier on when I was coming back from the house."

"You were nervous?"

Isobel nodded, and laughed, half ashamed to confess to such weakness. "I . . . I had a strange feeling that something was going to happen," she admitted, "like I did last night."

"Oh I see." The black eyes gleamed down at her in the moonlight. "You already had the heebie-jeebies before you found Vanessa's little toy?"

"In a way I suppose I had," she said. "Although I didn't say anything to Ni—" She stopped just short of making Nigel seem unsympathetic, but she should have known that he would see through anything as simple as that.

"Nigel doesn't believe in feelings," he guessed. "I know, he's strictly practical, that brother of mine, and it can give the quite wrong impression that he's insensitive."

"Oh, I know he isn't that," Isobel hastened to assure him. "But he laughed at my fears last night, so I decided to keep quiet tonight."

"Wise girl." She thought he looked a little disapproving as near as she could tell in the shifting shadows cast by the moon. "Doesn't he feel up to bringing you home yet?" he asked. "He could manage that far, surely."

"I suppose he could," Isobel agreed, "but I wouldn't let him. It isn't necessary for such a short distance."

His laugh sounded deep and soft and it vibrated against

her where he held her close to his side. "He doesn't use his imagination, that lad," he said. "I'd have thought a moonlight walk home in a setting like this was worth it, however short the distance."

Isobel smiled, despite the implied criticism of Nigel. "Nigel doesn't need an imagination," she told him. "As you said, he's strictly a practical man."

"And you don't mind?"

"I'm used to it." She had answered without thinking and she heard him laugh again.

"That, if I may say so," he informed her, "doesn't sound very complimentary."

"I didn't mean it to be complimentary or anything else other than a statement of fact," she said. "Nigel is a practical man and none the worse for it, I expect."

The cottage stood before them, cosy and reassuring, and she released her arm from his hold. "Your little gray home in the west," he quoted. "And no more spooky little dollies around as far as I can see."

She realized for the first time that she had left the cottage door open when she ran out to him, and she smiled ruefully. "They'd have had free access if there was," she said, and turned to face him. "Thank you, Lucifer."

He looked through the narrow opening into the lighted hall. "Shall I make sure Pyewacket hasn't decided to pay you another visit?" he asked.

Isobel shook her head, shining gold in the light from the hall. "She won't be here again at night, I shouldn't think," she told him. "Nigel says she doesn't usually go out at night."

"That's true." He grinned at her wickedly. "And I

must remember to stay in my own league, as I said earlier. No tricks to gain access to your maiden bower." He pushed the door wide for her and smiled down at her, his dark face very hard to read in the shadowy moonlight, even with the yellow light from the hall shining on one side of his face. Only his eyes glowed deeply and sent a brief, tingling shiver down her spine. "Good night, *piccola,* sleep tight."

She had half expected him to kiss her, however briefly, and when he didn't even attempt to she felt a swift twinge of disappointment. "Good night, Lucifer," she said, "and thank you again." She tiptoed and brushed her lips lightly against his chin. "Good night."

He looked at her for a breathless second or two in silence, then his arms swept her against him, so tightly she could hear and feel the strong steady beat of his heart, and her own pulses racing wildly when his mouth closed on hers and held her for so long that she felt it would never end.

"You make it very difficult for me to remember my vows," he whispered against her ear, while she clung to him tightly, her cheeks burning and a warm glow all over her body. "Now be a good little girl and go into your dear little house before I forget what a baby you are."

Isobel raised her head from his chest, her eyes huge and bright in the light, so lighthearted it seemed to affect her head and she laughed softly. "*Si, papa,*" she said demurely, and ran through the door quickly and closed it before he could voice his objections. She leaned against it for a second or two listening to the soft sound of his laughter as he walked away.

CHAPTER TWELVE

Lucifer, so it appeared, firmly intended keeping to his vow that he would, as he had termed it, stay in his own league. He treated Isobel with friendly politeness, but never once during the week or so that followed her panic-stricken visit to the lodge did he call her anything but a very proper Isobel. She had to admit that she missed the various Italian endearments he had regaled her with before. Perhaps, she thought, he cared about Vanessa Law's opinion more than he cared to admit.

Nigel, now increasingly mobile, demanded more and more of her free time and she knew that sooner or later he would almost inevitably repeat his wish that she should go back with him to Frome's when he returned on a full-time basis.

They had walked together toward the seat at the end of the garden overlooking the valley. With September already a day or two old, the evenings were drawing in and, even as early as this, the valley was too hazily dark to see anything other than the black bulk of the hills against the sky, although an old moon would soon lend a pallid light to the scene.

Now that he needed only one stick to help him walk Nigel could spare an arm to encircle her shoulders, hugging her close as they came to the seat and stood for a moment under the tall elm that shaded it on sunny days.

"You're very quiet," he told her, turning her around to face him and managing very well with his one free arm.

Isobel smiled. "Am I? I didn't realize."

"In fact," he informed her, peering down at her in the dusk, "you've been more than usually quiet for the past few days. There's nothing wrong, is there? I mean nothing to do with your job or . . . Luke?"

"No, of course not!"

"You're quite sure?"

"Quite sure," Isobel insisted. "I may be just a little quieter than usual, that's all, Nigel." She laughed softly, trying to see his face. "It's the autumn coming on, it always makes me feel rather sad somehow, though I can't think why it should."

He hugged her closer again and his lips brushed her brow gently. "I wish I could persuade you to come back with me to London, darling. I shall miss you terribly, you know."

"I think I shall miss you quite a lot, too," Isobel confessed, "but I shall see you at weekends, so it won't be too bad, will it?"

"Bad enough," Nigel retorted, "especially when the roads get snowed up in the winter. You know," he added, "I don't think you realize how bleak and inhospitable it can be here in the middle of winter."

Isobel laughed. "Oh, really, Nigel, anyone would think it was the North Pole instead of the west midlands! You do exaggerate so."

"Indeed I don't," he denied stoutly. "Don't forget I was brought up here, I know it better than you do. It's like the Antarctic when the weather's really bad."

"Does Lucifer go away in the winter?"

She could sense him looking at her curiously although she could no longer see him very clearly. "No, he doesn't. Why?"

Isobel shrugged. "Well, I just wondered, because he was more or less brought up in Italy according to you, so if he can stand the Cotswold winters, so can I."

He sighed his regret and sat down on the bench, easing her down beside him. "I'm fighting a losing battle, aren't I?" he asked, resignedly. "You'll never change your mind."

"I don't know about never," Isobel demurred. "I don't imagine for one minute that I shall spend the rest of my life here, but at the moment it suits me to stay, Nigel, and I shall. At least until Lucifer gives me the sack anyway," she added, and laughed at the unlikelihood of that happening.

He sighed again, holding her hand and squeezing it hard. "I wish I'd never even mentioned that wretched job to you, or you to Luke," he declared. "Things aren't working out at all as I planned they should."

"I'm sorry, Nigel."

"So am I," he retorted, his arm tightening on her shoulders. "Damn Luke, anyway, why can't he give you the sack, then you'd have to come back with me."

"That's very unkind and very selfish," Isobel told him.

"It's the way I feel." He sat for a moment silent and uncommunicative, then he turned her to face him and lifted her chin. "Isobel. Isobel, I know you've more or less made up your mind already about staying, but I must ask you again. Will you marry me?"

She was silent for several seconds, seeking the right words, knowing that whatever she said would be misinterpreted because he wanted to hear only one thing. "I . . . I can't, Nigel."

"Can't or won't?" Disappointment put a hard edge on

his voice and the arm that held her tightened possessively. "I love you, Isobel, and you can't say that I haven't known you long enough to be certain about that. As you reminded me yourself, it's four years now, and I've grown more and more certain in all that time. I want to marry you and I will eventually, no matter how long you procrastinate."

"I'm not procrastinating," she objected. "I just have to be certain I want to get married, and at the moment I'm sure I don't."

He sighed, resigned again. "All right, I accept your judgment, but I'll wait. I'll wait until you're old and gray if I have to, but nothing will ever change my mind."

She sought to lighten the somewhat tense atmosphere he had created, and laughed softly. "I'm very flattered," she told him, "but if I keep you waiting until I'm old and gray you'll probably have found someone else to marry long before then, and it will serve me right."

"Never," he vowed. "I'm not Luke, I'm a one-woman man."

Isobel smiled, wondering how Lucifer had managed yet again to get into their conversation. "I can't believe that," she said. "You must have taken out other women before me."

"Of course I have," he agreed. "I've taken out quite a few at various times, but that was before I met you and before I realized how I felt about you. When I say I'm a one-woman man, I mean I've never been really serious about anyone but you."

"Oh, I see." She was thoughtful for a while. "Does that mean that Lucifer is serious about more than one woman?" she asked, and Nigel frowned his dislike.

"How in heaven's name do I know when Luke's serious about his women?" he asked shortly. "I seldom see him and we certainly never discuss anything as intimate as that. Anyway," he added, "we're not discussing Luke, we're talking about you and me."

"We've already talked about you and me," Isobel said. "I'm staying on here, Nigel, for as long as the job lasts or until I get tired of it, depending on which happens first."

"Well, in that case I hope you soon get fed up," he declared, then got to his feet again, ready to walk back, his arm going around her waist.

They walked in silence for a while, then Isobel looked up at him, better able to see his face now that they were nearer the house. "You'll probably find there've been some changes when you get back," she told him. "Some new attractions, maybe. After all, you've been away almost six months."

"And I've been back once or twice lately," he reminded her. "There was nothing excitingly different that I noticed."

"No blonde dolly-birds?" Isobel teased.

"You know I don't fall for dolly-birds," he retorted, and Isobel laughed.

"Thank you. I have been referred to as one in my time, but if you say so. . . ."

He shook his head, taking her quite seriously it seemed. "Well, you're not," he said firmly. "I know you're young, but you're also clever enough to know that an excess of anything is laughable rather than attractive."

"Thank you."

"Oh, you know what I mean," he insisted. "Your dresses are just the right length and you always wear just the right amount of jewelry." He hugged her close and kissed her as they came across the lawn to the house. "In fact," he added, "you're utterly and completely adorable."

"You're in a flattering mood tonight," she smiled. Usually Nigel's compliments were few and far between and always rather restrained. It seemed almost as if, by changing his tactics, he was hoping to influence her to change her mind about going back with him.

"I'm not flattering you," he insisted. "I'm telling you the truth." He stopped them just short of the long rectangle of light that fell across the lawn from the open French windows. He turned her to face him, lifting her chin, his eyes a deep, dark blue in the diffused light. "I shall dream about you every night," he vowed earnestly, "and live only for weekends."

"And let your business suffer," she teased him. "I can't have you doing that, Nigel. I tell you what I'll do. I'll give you a life-size photograph of myself and then you can gaze at it as long as you like until you get tired of looking at me."

"Never!" He gathered her close to him in his one free arm, and his mouth on hers had an urgent, hungry appeal as he kissed her. "I'll never get tired of looking at you," he vowed, and held her close, his face resting on the softness of her hair. "But I will have a picture of you, my darling," he told her. "A big one so that I can gaze at you as often as I like." They stood like that for several minutes and only the soft, secret sounds of the autumn night broke the silence, surrounding them like a dark shawl. "Darling."

"Hmm?"

"There's something I'd rather have. Better than a photograph."

Isobel raised her head and looked up at him curiously. "What's that?"

He brushed his lips against her forehead and she thought there was a curious, slightly malicious smile touching his mouth. "The drawing that Cal Ford did of you."

"But I haven't got it, Nigel, you know that."

She wished she was more sure, suddenly, of the fate of the sketch that Lucifer had had done of her and she wondered, too, if Nigel had asked for it with any ulterior motive in mind. "I know you haven't got it," he agreed, "but you could get it for me."

"From Lucifer?"

"You said he'd kept it," he pointed out. "I expect he's still got it."

Isobel traced a line down from his collar to the top button on his jacket, her eyes following its progress. "Then why can't you ask him for it?" she asked.

"Because I think you'd stand more chance of succeeding than I would," he told her bluntly. "He'd never part with it if he thought I wanted it."

"Oh, I'm sure he would," Isobel argued, ignoring his frown at her defense of Lucifer. "He's not petty like that, Nigel. If you really want the drawing, I'm sure he'd let you have it."

"You won't ask him for me?"

She shook her head. "I'd rather not."

"Okay." He kissed her again before resuming their stroll. "I'll ask him myself, but he won't let me have it, you'll see. I know my big brother much better than you do, my darling, and he won't let me have it."

Nigel's opportunity to ask for the drawing he wanted so much came on the following Sunday when Lucifer was lunching at the house again. He waited until they were at the coffee stage and then broached the subject, rather abruptly, since he hated asking Lucifer for anything, and his brother looked at him in silence for a moment or two, his black eyes curious.

"I don't quite see why you want a drawing," he told him. "You've got the original, haven't you?"

"Only at weekends after next week," Nigel told him shortly. "I'd like the drawing to hang in my apartment. I'll pay you what you paid Cal Ford for it," he added hastily, as if the financial aspect of it was the reason for Lucifer's hesitation.

"If you had it at all," Lucifer told him quietly, "I wouldn't dream of taking anything for it."

Nigel pounced on the betraying 'if,' his brows already drawn into a frown, ready to argue. "*If* I had it," he said. "I suppose that means you're refusing to part with it?"

Isobel, watching Lucifer's dark, expressive face, thought his mouth tightened fractionally, but he smiled a moment later and shrugged in that peculiar way that Nigel despised so much. "It was a roll of paper I slung into the back of the car on the day of the show," he told his brother. "Heaven alone knows where it is now."

Isobel felt a strangely hurt feeling at his casual dismissal of it, while Nigel positively glowered at him. "Do you mean to say you've lost it?" he accused, and Lucifer shrugged again.

"Something like that, old sport. Sorry and all that."

"You careless devil!" Nigel hated losing anything he had set his heart on.

Isobel still watched Lucifer, puzzled by something in his manner. "You know me," he shrugged.

"Isobel says it was a good one, too," Nigel complained, and Lucifer nodded, his black eyes lowered in uncharacteristic reticence while his long fingers played with the spoon in his saucer. "It was a good one," he agreed quietly.

"And you had to go and lose it."

Lucifer looked up then, a small, shadowy frown between his black brows for Nigel's pettiness. "You're making an awful fuss about a bit of paper with a sketch on it," he told him shortly. "Instead you should be thanking your stars it isn't the original you've lost. Your trouble is, Nigel, you never know when you're well off."

Nigel looked at him in surprise for a moment, then he too, shrugged resignedly. "I suppose I am lucky," he allowed. "I shall be able to come and see Isobel every weekend; but I had set my heart on having that drawing."

Lucifer smiled wryly. "Losing something you've set your heart on is supposed to be good for your immortal soul," he said softly, and Isobel could not quite understand why he looked at her when he said it.

Mrs. Grayson had said nothing during the exchange between them; now she refilled Lucifer's coffee cup and smiled at him in a way that confirmed Isobel's suspicions. There was something going on between Lucifer and his grandmother that they were not going to mention, and it was surprising that Nigel did not notice it, too. Had he been aware of it he would have said something. Perhaps, she thought in a flash of inspiration, Lucifer had destroyed the drawing and Mrs. Grayson knew it, but they would not let Nigel know.

"As Lucifer says, dear," Mrs. Grayson told Nigel, "you still have Isobel, and she's far prettier than any drawing, I'm sure."

"Of course she is." Nigel leaned across and squeezed Isobel's hand. "If only I could persuade her to come back with me and marry me!"

His grandmother smiled tolerantly. "Never try to rush a woman into marriage, Nigel," she told him. "It can lead to so many regrets later on, and Isobel's very young."

"Isobel's twenty-two," Nigel told her bluntly. "Almost the same age as Madge was when she married my father."

"Your mother already had a divorce behind her then," the old lady sighed, "and a little boy to worry about. Let Isobel enjoy her freedom while she can, dear; she'll know her own mind one of these days." She smiled at Isobel, her blue eyes strangely appealing. "Won't you, Isobel dear?"

"I'll know," Isobel agreed, hoping she would when the time came. "And I'm in no hurry to settle down yet."

On the following Monday morning Lucifer had said he must go into Greenlaw to see someone urgently, but he made no offer this time to take her with him, and she stayed at her typewriter, felling rather cross and disappointed.

It was during the morning that she saw her empty coffee cup still standing on her desk and decided to return it. Usually Beppo, Lucifer's man, had collected the coffee cups by now, but she supposed he had simply forgotten it this morning.

Welcoming a break from her typing, she left the office and found the cottage oddly silent, as if there was no one else there but herself, and she stood for a moment outside the kitchen door. "Hello!" she called. "Is anyone here?" It was possible, she supposed, that Lucifer had taken Beppo with him to do some shopping or some other chore, but a moment later the kitchen door opened and the man's dark, soulful-looking eyes looked at her curiously.

"*Si, signorina?*"

"Oh! There you are." She offered him the empty cup with a smile. "You forgot to collect the empties," she told him, and then realized suddenly that she had no idea at all if he spoke any English. She had heard Lucifer speak to him only in Italian.

Whether he understood or not he smiled his understanding and bobbed his black head in thanks. "*Grazie, signorina, grazie.*" He darted back into the kitchen and left Isobel with a crazy desire to laugh because he reminded her of the little man in a weather-house, the way he had popped in and out so quickly.

She turned and started back through the small hall, past the room where Lucifer had brought her on the night she had been so panic-stricken about that horrible effigy of herself. There was another door, too, on the other side of the hallway, a bedroom, judging by what she could see through the narrow opening where it stood ajar.

She would have walked on and into the office again, but something caught her eye and stopped her dead in her tracks, her eyes wide and unbelieving. It was such a big bedroom that it must be Lucifer's and facing her, right opposite the door, was the drawing he had denied knowing the fate of.

A wary finger pushed the door just a fraction wider and she stared at the framed drawing. The sharp black charcoal lines stood out on the white background, her own features clear and unmistakable and she found herself smiling, a small secret smile that acknowledged the fact that Nigel must never know about this.

She dared not linger too long for fear the manservant came out of the kitchen suddenly and caught her there, so she pulled the door to, as it was before, and almost tiptoed back to the office and her neglected typewriter.

The following morning, Isobel frankly admitted that she would have given much to have relations as they had been before Lucifer's self-imposed formality. She would have liked to tease him about the drawing, although he would probably not take kindly to her wandering about his home while he was away. Anyway, she shrugged, he was far too formal and polite these days to allow her to indulge in anything like their former lighthearted banter.

She found him already in the office when she came in, slightly early, his black head bent busily over a pile of work, and he did not even look up when she came in.

"Good morning." She was determined not to be ignored.

His head lifted briefly, and the black eyes smiled a friendly greeting. "Good morning, Isobel."

Still a very formal "Isobel," she noted wryly, and only briefly polite. She put her coat on its hanger and put purse and gloves tidily in a drawer before uncovering her typewriter.

"Are we going to be busy today?" she asked, and he again glanced up.

"Not too bad, I hope," he told her. "As you can see, I've made an early start."

"I did notice," she remarked, unable to resist the jibe. "It's most unusual, isn't it?"

For a moment the familiar imp of devilment glittered at her from across the room, and he half smiled. "I'll treat that with the contempt it deserves," he told her. "Now will you please get on with your own work and leave me to get on with mine?"

"Of course. I'm sorry."

There was verbal silence for a moment or two while Isobel pounded away on her typewriter, then he looked up suddenly, sighed, and put down his pen. "Okay," he said, "I'm sorry if I was rude, now will you stop trying to wreck that poor innocent machinery?"

"I didn't know I was. The typewriter's never bothered you before."

The black eyes regarded her for a second or two, then he laughed, the first time he had done anything so informal for far too long, and she looked at him hopefully. "The typewriter doesn't bother me now," he told her, "it's your treatment of it that I'm complaining about. I can feel you being self-righteous even from here."

"I was not being self-righteous," she denied. "I just don't like having my nose bitten off for no good reason, that's all."

"It's a very nice little nose." His voice was soft and low and her spine tingled warningly at the sound of it.

She did not look at him but down at the paper guide that she flicked up and down with one finger, very tempted again to mention the drawing she had inadvertently discovered. "Lucifer."

"Hmm?" He was still watching her, she knew, although she refused to look at him.

"That drawing . . . the one Cal Ford did of me at the show."

"What about it?"

Her heistation was only brief. "Have you really lost it?"

His chin rested on one hand, the elbow propped on his desk, black eyes regarding her steadily. "Are you calling me a liar?" he asked softly, and she shook her head hastily, wishing now she had not mentioned it. He was far too astute and far too good at reading her mind, and it was just possible he would tumble to the fact that she'd seen the drawing. Then she would be required to explain how she came to see it.

"Of course I'm not calling you a liar," she denied. "It's just that Nigel was so sure you wouldn't let him have it and you seemed—" she raised her eyes at last and looked at him briefly "—evasive," she decided at last, and saw him frown.

He looked down at the work in front of him again, a closed look on his face that was strange to her, and which she recognized meant he was not going to say any more on the subject.

"It seems rather a lot of fuss to make about a small sketch that's only worth a few shillings," he said quietly. "Now can we please get on with some work?"

"Yes, of course. I'm sorry." She felt it rather an anticlimax and she rolled another piece of paper into her machine with fingers that shook. "Actually," she said as offhandedly as she knew how, "I've been wondering if I should take Nigel's advice and do as he wants me to. Go back to London with him," she added to make sure there was no mistake, and felt a small flutter of satisfaction at the momentary shocked look she saw on his face.

He was silent for quite a long time, his whole attention apparently concentrated on the pen he was twirling between his fingers. "It might be a good idea," he told her at last, and Isobel stared at him.

"I . . . I beg your pardon?"

His attention was still on the twirling pen and he did not raise his eyes. "I was agreeing with you," he said quietly.

"You . . . you mean you're telling me to go? You're dismissing me?"

She could scarcely believe she had understood him correctly, but when he looked up at last he was nodding. "Not in so many words," he said, "but I'll take your notice to leave as from today if you like, and then you can leave when Nigel goes next week."

Isobel had never in all her life felt so utterly dazed and lifeless. Even her fingers were suddenly stiff as she flicked the paper guide automatically, her eyes blank and darkly gray with that hot, prickly feeling at the back of them as if she would cry at any moment.

"I . . . I'm sorry if I haven't been very efficient," she managed at last, in a voice that sounded horribly choked. "I thought you were quite satisfied with my work."

"Oh, I am," he assured her. "If you needed a reference I'd give you an excellent one without any hesitation."

"Then why . . ." she began, and a moment later bit her lip as the answer became only too clear to her. Of course, she should have known that Vanessa Law would probably issue an ultimatum which he could no longer ignore if he wanted to continue their association. "It doesn't matter, of course," she told him. "I think I understand."

For a moment the black eyes held hers steadily and her blood raced through her veins, making her head throb, then he shook his head and hid his gaze again. "I doubt if you do," he said softly.

"I . . . I leave a week today?" It was staggering how suddenly cold and empty she felt.

"You can leave on Friday," he said, "then you can go back with Nigel on Sunday."

"Thank you."

It sounded oddly stiff and formal and he glanced up curiously. "What for?"

"For . . . for not making me work a month's notice."

He laughed shortly. "I'm not giving you a month's notice either," he reminded her dryly.

"Will . . . will you be able to get someone else so quickly? To finish the last chapters," she added hastily, and he shrugged, still not looking at her. "Oh, we'll get those done by the end of this week," he said, and the familiar 'we' almost shattered her self-control.

"Yes . . . yes, of course."

She stared at the blank page in her machine, and gave herself a mental shake. It was no use allowing the suddenness of it to make her miserable, and at least Nigel would be pleased. She would, she thought, probably marry him quite soon and settle down, for suddenly she saw the prospect of life as a secretary far less attractive. Office routine and business letters would never have the same appeal again after typing Lucifer's manuscripts.

"After that," he said unexpectedly, "I'm off to Italy for a couple of months for a break."

"Oh! Oh, I see. I didn't realize that." Somehow it helped a bit to know that he would be away for quite a while after she left and that her dismissal had another reason than Vanessa Law's jealousy behind it.

"I haven't seen my father for quite some time now," he told her, "and I rather miss Italy when I stay away too long."

She hoped she sounded only casually interested, and that her voice wouldn't shake too much. "I expect you do," she said. "It's very beautiful, isn't it?"

The black eyes sought hers, but she refused to meet them. "Beautiful," he said softly. "You've never been there?"

"No."

"You should, you'd love it."

Her laugh, she knew, sounded breathless and rather forced as she pushed the carriage along and was ready to start work again. "Maybe we'll spend our honeymoon there," she told him, and almost felt the silence that followed.

"Maybe," he said at last, and she thought there was sadness in the way he said it, so that she raised her eyes swiftly to look at him, and as hastily lowered them again.

CHAPTER THIRTEEN

Nigel stared at her blankly for a moment when Isobel told him about her sudden change of plan. "He must be out of his mind," he said. His reaction was not at all what she expected; in fact he seemed rather more outraged than pleased that she was coming with him after all.

"But isn't this what you wanted?" she said. "It was only the other day that you were urging me to come with you."

"I was also urging you to marry me," Nigel retorted, "but quite frankly I didn't expect either thing to happen." He eyed her for a few moments speculatively. "I suppose it's too much to hope that that could materialize out of the blue as well, isn't it?" he asked hopefully.

Isobel smiled slowly. "I'm afraid it is," she said. "I have rather a lot on my mind at the moment." She sat thoughtfully quiet for a while, then looked up at him curiously. "Did you know that Lucifer's going to Italy?" she asked.

"Is he? It's the first I've heard of it," he said. "Gran doesn't know either, I'm sure, or she'd have said something."

"He says he needs the break."

"Oh, nonsense," Nigel snorted. "He's as tough as old boots. He never needs a break, and I doubt very much if Papa Bennetti will extend much of a welcome in the circumstances."

Isobel pursed her lips. "You mean the young wife?" she asked, and Nigel nodded, a malicious smile on his face.

"The beautiful young Contessa," he said. "She's too young by all accounts for it to be safe to have Luke around in the place."

"Is she so much younger than her husband?"

Nigel laughed. "She's only about thirty, according to Gran, and that's several years younger than Luke, let alone his father."

"I see." She thought about it for a while. "He . . . he seems to be a man who likes younger women, doesn't he? Didn't you say your mother was young when she married him?"

"She was seventeen and he was thirty," Nigel said, his opinion of the arrangement evident in his voice. "No wonder it didn't last."

"Oh, I don't think that's a likely reason for a marriage to break up," Isobel argued, without thinking of the consequences for the moment. "Quite a few well-known people have married women much younger than themselves and it seems to work perfectly well."

Nigel eyed her dubiously, obviously not liking her opinion. "I'll take your word for it," he told her shortly. "I've never studied the statistics."

Time had never passed so quickly as the last week at Kanderby Lodge did, and Isobel found it more and more difficult each day to adjust to the idea of leaving not only her job with Lucifer, but also her little cottage in the garden. Even the weather seemed to have turned sympathetically gloomy and huge, dark clouds sat ominously on the hills, threatening rain or worse.

Lucifer remained quietly polite, even aloof by comparison with his former manner and Isobel told herself she should be glad to be leaving tomorrow. Only

Nigel seemed really pleased that she was leaving, although he was still a bit annoyed that Lucifer had had the temerity to dismiss her so abruptly.

On her last evening, she thought, Lucifer might perhaps be a little regretful because she was leaving; he might even offer to take her to dinner as a sort of farewell present, but she was rather shattered to discover that he was leaving early to go out for the evening.

She was still busy typing the last pages of the manuscript and he paused by her desk on his way out. "I don't suppose I shall see you again," he told her, his black eyes almost hidden under lowered lids as he towered above her. "Unless," he added with a wry smile, "I meet you one of these days as my sister-in-law."

Isobel swallowed hard on the lump that rose in her throat and threatened to choke her words, or at least make her voice horribly husky and trembly. "It's . . . it's possible," she said. "Nigel's very persistent."

"He's a good man, Isobel."

"I know." At one time, she thought, she would have been surprised at both the words and the seriousness with which he said them; now she merely accepted that he knew his brother possibly better than anyone did, and was far more fond of him than he would have anyone believe.

He extended a hand and she put her own into it after only a brief hesitation. "*Addio, bella mia,*" he said softly, and raised her fingers to his lips. "*Piccola.*"

"Lucifer. . . ." She looked up, but he was gone, and for several minutes she sat quite still and alone in the big room, her vision blurred by the big, warm tears that trembled on her lashes and rolled slowly down her cheeks.

Isobel went to her cottage quite early that night. She had

no desire to be in anyone's company and, as she told Nigel, she had to pack and be ready to leave on Sunday. In reality she wanted to be alone, to think and to sort out the thoughts that tumbled chaotically over each other until her head spun with them.

The air was sultry, heavy with a threatening storm, and it was pitch dark once she had reached the gravel path where the light from the house porch was hidden by the shrubbery, but she scarcely noticed. She knew her way along that piece of driveway blindfolded and needed no lights.

A faint distant rumble distracted her briefly and she winced nervously, shivering at the prospect of a storm before the night had ended. A thunderstorm was all she needed right now, she thought ruefully, and immediately remembered the last time there had been a thunderstorm.

It seemed incredible that it was barely a month ago that she had crouched like a coward on the settee in the tiny sitting room, hiding her head from the storm, but drawn to the door by the plaintive mewing of Vanessa Law's cat. Not only the cat had found its way into the cottage that night, but Lucifer as well, and she shook her head impatiently as she hurried down the last few feet of path to her cottage. Lucifer was a thing of the past and it was no use getting maudlin about things that were best forgotten.

She finished her packing in a very short time, and wandered back into the sitting room and sat down, shivering in a sudden chill as a distant rumble growled over the hills in warning.

It would not be easy to get accustomed again to rooms in London after having her own cottage, nor would the air smell as sweet through the open windows. She got up again, made restless by the storm as well as her own uneasy spirit. She opened the window wider and admitted the first heavy drops of rain that plopped onto her hand that held the catch, cool and big as coins, rattling like small pebbles on the leaves of the shrubs.

Beyond the trees and bushes she glimpsed the first searing flash of lightning in the distant sky and felt the inevitable grip of fear in the pit of her stomach. It was still early enough for her to go back across to the house if she chose to, and sit in the company of Nigel and Mrs. Grayson until the storm was over, but somehow she still preferred to be alone.

She made coffee and found a magazine to read, and by the time she was having a second cup the storm was much closer and Nigel had still not come across to her. It had been rather a vain hope that he would, and she was even unsure if she wanted him to come, but it would have been a welcome gesture of understanding.

Just after eleven o'clock the little cottage was shaking with the fury of the storm and by some miracle she had managed not to hide her head in the cushions. She felt her knees trembling as she got to her feet, and gasped aloud when the streaming windows were suddenly and brilliantly lit by a vivid slash of light that crackled and cracked, and for a brief second illuminated the pathway and the shining wet shrubs outside.

Tense and holding her breath in fear, she waited for the roll of thunder to follow, but not only for that. In that split second of illumination she had seen something move against the shining wet background of leaves, some dark shape that vanished when darkness fell again.

The shuddering roar of thunder and some other sound, barely heard above the racket, sounded almost as one as she swiftly put her hands to her ears, then lowered them slowly when the thunder died and left the other sharper sound still rat-tatting impatiently on her door.

For a moment her legs refused to carry her even that short distance, and then suddenly, some heart-stopping skip of elation ran through her body and she found herself running to the door. The knob at first behaved clumsily in her fingers and she wrestled with it impatiently, then at last it opened and she flung the door wide to admit the man on the step.

His wet black hair flopped over his forehead and his jacket was soaked across the shoulders, the dark face glistening in the light of the hall. Isobel closed the door carefully behind him and followed him into the sitting room, her heart hammering unbearably against her ribs and the blood singing through her veins until her whole body glowed with it.

He turned when he reached the fireplace, and looked at her. "I couldn't leave you alone in this," he said, and Isobel felt the tears blind her for a second before they rolled warmly down her cheeks.

"I . . . I'm glad you came." It sounded so ridiculously formal saying it like that, but he knew how much she meant it and his arms reached out for her, pulling her close against the dampness of his coat.

His lips brushed gently against her forehead and he laughed softly above her head. "Did you use your powers of witchcraft to lure me here?" he asked.

"Yes." She snuggled closer to him as an angry roar

shook the cottage. "I called up the storm devils and told them to bring you to me."

He held her away from him, his black eyes glowing like coals in the yellow light, and Isobel felt the pulse in her temple racing wildly as she looked up at him. "I have no right here, *carissima*." He was suddenly very serious, and she feared he might have second thoughts and leave again, so that she clung to him tightly, her huge eyes wide and anxious. "I have no right here at all. If Nigel had been here I'd have turned back and never seen you again, but he wasn't."

She shook her head. "He didn't come," she said. "I thought he might, now that he knows I don't like storms, but he didn't come."

He looked at her for a while in silence, then a hand gently touched her face, and she leaned her cheek against it. "You're very beautiful," he said softly, "and very, very young."

Isobel shook her head, her eyes shining darkly gray, quite sure of her own feelings now. "I'm old enough to know my own mind," she told him, and he smiled.

"Are you, *carissima?*"

"Quite old enough," she insisted firmly, and he pulled her close again and kissed her mouth lightly. "I've been quite sure how I felt ever since I—" She stopped short and he raised a curious brow at her.

"When?" he asked quietly. "Ever since you saw that drawing of yourself in my bedroom?" He laughed when she stared at him wide-eyed.

"How on earth did you know about that?" she asked.

"Easy." His eyes teased her gently. "Firstly Beppo saw

you walking away from the open door, and secondly I knew you'd been up to something when you asked me so pointedly about having lost the drawing."

"Oh, you. . . ." She pouted her mouth at him reproachfully.

He was serious again suddenly, looking at her in a way that made her heart do crazy things. "Saying goodbye to you was the hardest thing I ever did in my life," he told her. "But I should have kept to my vow and gone away without seeing you again. It would have been easier."

She stared up at him. "You . . . you're not going now?"

He sighed. "I should, *bella mia*. I'm not a very desirable character, you know."

"You are to me!" She held on to him tightly. "I don't care how many . . . how many girlfriends you've had in the past." It sounded rather childishly prissy put like that and she was not at all surprised when he smiled the old familiar smile, mocking her reticence.

"Oh, you do make it sound so very polite, my darling," he told her, and she looked at him reproachfully.

"Lucifer, will you stop treating me like a child?" she said firmly. "I'm not a child, you know."

He said nothing, but pulled her so close to him that she could feel his heartbeat as plainly as her own, and his mouth was warm and strong, and as gentle as she remembered it from what seemed like a lifetime ago. Then he put her from him, shaking his head slowly. "Oh, Isobel, *bella mia*, you can so easily make me forget what I should do." His hands caressed her cheeks softly, the black eyes unbelievably gentle as he looked down at her. "I swore I wouldn't let this happen, and now. . . ." He shrugged lightly. "I told myself there were so many reasons why I had no right to love you, and that I'm old enough not to reform easily."

"Do you want to reform?" she asked softly, and he nodded.

"I think I do, *cara mia*. For you I'd try very hard."

Isobel lifted her face and kissed the firm strong mouth gently. "Don't change too much, darling Lucifer," she said.

She understood nothing of the soft, lyrical words that were whispered softly against her ear, but their meaning was plain enough and she raised her head at last to smile up at him. "You must teach me Italian," she told him, "then I can understand all those beautiful words you say."

"Of course I shall teach you." He kissed her mouth, and her throat, closing her eyes with the gentle pressure of his lips before he held her against him tightly. "It would never do if the Contessa Bennetti couldn't speak at least some of her husband's language, would it?"

"Contessa?" She looked up again hastily. "Oh, yes, of course. I'd forgotten about you being your father's only son." She considered the idea for a moment, uncertain suddenly of her own capabilities as a countess. "Oh, Lucifer, suppose. . . ."

"Suppose you say you'll marry me?" he said, kissing the tip of her nose. "I love you, God help me, but I shall probably hate myself in the morning for being so selfish as to ask you to marry me, so please say you will before you have second thoughts too. Will you marry me, *piccola?*"

"Of course I will," Isobel told him calmly. "I love you."

He looked down at her, at the huge, shiny gray eyes and the slightly disheveled golden head that barely reached his chest. "You're a witch," he informed her solemnly. "A pretty little gray-eyed witch, and you brew such powerful magic that I never really had a chance." Strong gentle fingers lifted her face to him and as he kissed her again, neither of them noticed that the storm overhead had passed them by.

WITHOUT ANY AMAZEMENT

Without
Any
Amazement

Margaret Malcolm

Marriage to Jonathan was her grandmother's dying wish; it never occurred to Jacynth to disobey.

She was unaware that her ne'er-do-well father was still alive. Only a husband could keep him from gaining control of her inheritance, and Jonathan had promised to fulfill that role. Not surprising then that neither of them was aware of the other's feelings—their true reasons for going through with the marriage.

Faced with Jacynth's youthful innocence, Jonathan vowed, "I'll never willingly do anything to hurt you." But in a way it was Jonathan's kindness that hurt her most, for when his old girlfriend, Cynthia, reentered his life, what Jacynth really needed was the assurance of his love!

CHAPTER ONE

In the great four-poster bed Christina Allardyce lay dying. And she was dying as she had lived—courageously and rather impatiently.

The impatience showed now, for the frail, ivory-hued fingers were fidgeting restlessly as they lay on the smooth coverlet. She had always been one to do things for herself; now she was dependent on others. And they were slow, so slow! And there was so much need for speed.

Outside, under her window, the traffic of Bath flowed by in a dignified stream, but at last she heard the sound she had been waiting for—the sound of a car being brought to a standstill. She half raised her head to listen. Yes, there was a subdued knock on the beautifully proportioned Regency door, and her brows nipped in a frown. They were so long in answering it. Had they heard? Jonathan was thinking of her, of course, but he should have knocked loudly so that they were sure to hear.

Now there was a little flurry in the hall below. Then the firm footsteps of a man on the stairs and a gentle knock at the door. Jonathan came in.

She could not see him very clearly, but that did not matter; she knew so very well what he looked like. Tall and firm-fleshed, always in perfect condition, golden fair hair that became bleached in the sunshine, and a mouth that could be hard and grim—but not always. As he bent over her she saw the tenderness there and felt the strength of the fingers that closed around hers.

"I knew you would come!" she whispered.

He kissed her softly.

"I was in New York when I received your message. I flew back."

"Bless you," she murmured tremulously. "Bless you!" And then, anxiously, impatiently, "Jonathan, it's time. More than time for you to keep your promise."

"Yes," he said reflectively. "Yes—"

"Jonathan!" She raised herself on one elbow, hardly realizing the effort it cost in her anxiety. "Jonathan, you're not going to fail me?"

"No," he said shortly. "I promised. But it's sooner than I'd anticipated. It troubles me."

"For yourself?" she asked swiftly, sinking back on her pillows.

"A little perhaps," he admitted. "But mainly for Jacynth. She's so very young. . . ."

"Nearly eighteen. I'd been a mother for three months at her age." The faded blue eyes were imploring. "Besides, it's because she's so young that it's all the more important. You know that!"

"Has Tim been worrying you lately?" he asked sharply.

"No. That's why I'm afraid." The restless movement of the fingers began again. "Don't you see, he knows that he can afford to be patient! He knows that I'm old and must die soon. That will be the time for him to claim Jacynth! But, until then, he only stands to lose the allowance I make to him to keep him away from her. Only I stand between her and the wastrel who broke her mother's heart, and I . . . am dying!"

His clasp of her hand tightened comfortingly.

"You haven't told her?" he asked, apparently abandoning all thought of argument.

"No, since you wished it that way." A little pause. Then, imploringly, questioningly, "Jonathan?"

"Yes, I'll go at once and get her. I will be as quick as I can. But even when she comes, it will be a day or two before we can get married, you know."

"No!" She fumbled under her pillow. "Here—an Archbishop's license—anywhere, any time!"

"Now, how in the world did you get hold of that?" he demanded in amazement. "They're not come by every day of the week!"

She smiled mischievously, provocatively, she who had known what it was to twist men around her little finger, and momentarily, he saw the ghost of a vanished beauty.

"Never mind, never mind! It's here. Jonathan, Jonathan, go. Please go!"

Twenty minutes after he had arrived at the house he was on his way again. He headed east, the setting sun at his back, the dusk slowly gathering about him until at last he had to switch on his lights.

His mind was full of his mission, yet no one watching his set, grim face, could have guessed what doubts or uncertainties were passing through it.

The dormitory was in darkness and there was no sound. But the silence was not because anyone was asleep. The six neat white beds were empty and the owners of five of them were huddled around the open window.

"She's been an awful long time," someone whispered uneasily. "We shouldn't have let her!"

"Huh, *let* her!" said another voice, muted but scornful. "You try to stop Jacynth from doing anything once she's made up her mind!"

"Anyway, things always turn out all right for Jacynth." An envious whisper this. "She'll do it all right. And anyhow, she isn't due back yet. Five minutes to get down to the river, ten minutes to swim across, five minutes to find her book, and then she's got to come—Oh!"

Suddenly the light was switched on and the five girls, consternation written clearly on every feature, turned to face the woman who stood framed in the doorway.

She looked the group over. Anyone less preoccupied than the guilty five might have noticed her anxiety.

"Where is Jacynth?" she asked sharply.

"She's . . . she's gone down to the river," someone faltered. "She's swimming across it to get a book she left there this afternoon."

The schoolmistress sighed.

"I suppose someone dared her," she said resignedly. "Really, you ought to know better by now! Jacynth always take a dare, no matter how foolish it is!"

"But we didn't, Miss Alsop, really we didn't! We told her that she ought not to—"

"Worse still," Miss Alsop said crisply. "How long was she supposed to be?"

"Any time now, Miss Alsop." And then, hesitatingly, the girl added, "Miss Alsop, please, I think if you put the light out she'd come in quicker. I mean, she knows we wouldn't have it on—"

"Yes, well, when she comes in, tell her to dress, bring

her hat and coat and come straight down to the head-mistress's study." Miss Alsop switched out the light and shut the door.

"Golly!" said a horrified voice in the darkness, "Jacynth's done it this time. Bet you what you like we shan't see her in the morning! They'll sack her—in the middle of the night, too!"

When she entered the room Jonathan's heart seemed to turn over. He had said that she was young, but in the shapeless simplicity of the school uniform she looked like an absolute child.

He stood up and held out his hand.

"Do you remember me, Jacynth?" he asked pleasantly, anxious to put her at ease.

But his thoughtfulness was unnecessary. Jacynth had all the confidence of a child whom life has never rebuffed.

"Yes, of course, Mr. Branksome," she said, putting her hand in his. "I met you a year ago at Gran's. She told me that if she had had the arranging of things my mother would have married your father."

He smiled faintly. That was so like Christina Allardyce!

"Your grandmother sent me to you tonight."

"Did she?" Jacynth said cheerfully. "That was nice of her. You're a bit late, though. We go to bed awfully early here, you know."

The headmistress stood up. She disliked the feeling of being ignored in her own study, and besides, she believed that when bad news had to be broken it was best to face up to it as quickly as possible.

"Jacynth, Mr. Branksome is not here to pay you a social call. He has a definite reason. He has news for you—"

Jonathan stopped her with an imperative gesture.

"If you please, Miss Prentice, I would prefer to tell Jacynth myself. And if you will allow me to trespass still further on your good nature. . . ." His eyes turned significantly to the door, and with the dignity of dethroned royalty the headmistress swept out of the room and closed the door gently behind her.

"I say, that was one in the eye for the head! I can't think how you did it!" Jacynth said admiringly. "What *have* you come for, Mr. Branksome?"

He took her hand in his and drew her toward him.

"Jacynth, it's bad news," he said gently.

He saw her dark eyes widen and the color drain out of her little pointed face.

"Gran?" she said sharply. "She's ill?"

"Very ill." His arm was around her shrinking shoulders now. "So ill that you must come to her at once, Jacynth."

He felt the sudden rigidity of the young, supple body, heard the quick, whistling breath. Then she gently released herself.

"Can we go at once, please?" she asked, making a gallant attempt to keep her voice steady.

"Immediately," he said, opening the study door.

In the hall, a few feet away from the door, stood the headmistress with a small tray in her hands.

She glanced quickly from one set face to the other and silently applauded the self-control that both showed. Not unexpected in the man, perhaps, but surprising in a child so warmhearted and reckless as Jacynth.

"I've brought you some hot cocoa and sandwiches," she said practically. "You must have them before you start your journey, Jacynth."

"No thank you, Miss Prentice," Jacynth said hurriedly. "We haven't time!"

Miss Prentice glanced at Jonathan, and he nodded ever so slightly.

"Drink up the cocoa, Jacynth," he said quietly, and without another word of protest she obeyed him. "If we might have the sandwiches wrapped up to take with us?" he suggested.

He's clever, thought the headmistress. *He knows just how far he can impose his will, and he refuses to go further than that, so he probably has a reputation for always getting his own way! I wonder who he is, just what he is in Jacynth's life?*

But no one was likely to answer that question just then, and she saw them to the car with mixed emotions: anxiety for what the child would find at the end of her journey, reassurance in the thought of the man who would doubtless stand by her.

She sat very still and silent beside him, and once Jonathan thought that she was sleeping. But when he stole a glance at her he saw that her eyes were wide open and fixed unseeingly on the road ahead. He would have given a lot to have been able to say something that would comfort her, but what was there to say? It was her first meeting with death and it was coming to the one person who had been her security and background. No, there was nothing to say, and he believed that she preferred it that way. Once or twice he saw that her eyes were on the speedometer and knew that all she wanted from him was speed.

Yet after they had been traveling for a little more than an hour he stopped. Instantly she looked up at him, alert, apprehensive.

"No, there's nothing wrong with the car," he said reassuringly. "It's just that you must eat those sandwiches now."

"Oh, Mr. Branksome, please!" She shook his arm impatiently. "What does it matter if I am a little bit hungry? We must hurry. You said so!"

"Listen, child," he said gently. "It will take you perhaps five minutes to eat them. They may make all the difference between your being a comfort to your grandmother and fainting all over the place. Eat them up, for her sake!"

Perhaps she sensed the inflexibility of will that underlay the gentleness, or perhaps she realized that it would save time if she argued no more. Whichever it was, she obediently opened the packet and took out a sandwich.

"You, too," she insisted; and, though he had never felt less like eating in his life, he took one as well.

When the little meal was over he said quietly, "Now you're to relax. I don't suppose you'll sleep, but you can at least rest. And you're to have this blanket over you...."

He tucked it around her, and in the dim light of the little overhead lamp he saw that her eyes were fixed wonderingly on him.

"You're being very kind," she said wistfully. "Are you always like this to everybody? Or is it just because you're sorry for me?"

He laughed rather shortly.

"There are a lot of people who would tell you that I'm hard and heartless!" he replied grimly.

She slipped her hand out from the folds of the rug and touched his face very lightly with the tips of her fingers.

"But I know they're wrong," she said softly.

For a moment he was silent, but a telltale muscle twitched at the corner of his mouth.

"At least you can be sure of this," he said, surprised at his earnestness, "I will never willingly do anything to hurt you!"

"I know," she said contentedly and closed her eyes.

He switched out the light, and a second later they were on their way again.

Jacynth slowly descended the stairs, and Jonathan, waiting below, knew that Christina had told her. Something in her manner and bearing told him unmistakably.

He came to meet her at the foot of the stairs and she stopped on the second stair up, so that she was as tall as he and their eyes were on a level.

"Grandmother says you want to . . . marry me," she said breathlessly. "Is that true?"

"Quite true," he said.

"But why?" she wanted to know, her dark eyes searching his face. "Why, you don't really know me at all!"

"Come into the living room," he suggested. "We can talk things over better there."

But when they had reached the room, he was not so sure that he had been wise. Though he had always been fond of Christina Allardyce, and much as he had admired her quick, mercurial temperament he had always found her house oppressive. The heavy, expensive furniture spoke of security and the ability to indulge one's whims that money brings. But it was neither comfortable nor, to his way of thinking, in very good taste. With a sudden flash of sympathy, he wondered if the daughter who had been the apple of Christina's eye and who had run away from all this magnificence had felt that way too. Had it seemed to her that these possessions had tried to impress her with their importance and their value until she could bear them no longer? He could not even guess the answer, but at least he was quite sure that they made little impression on the girl standing before him with her hands linked behind her back.

"Why do you want to marry me?" she repeated. "It can't be, of course, because you love me."

She was quite right, but somehow the directness of the statement disconcerted him.

"Why not?" he asked curtly.

"You've seen me twice," she said briefly. "Once, last year, I'd just come in from playing tennis on a windy day. My face was shiny and red and my hair was in a tangle. Now—" scornfully she drew attention to the prim navy blue skirt and white blouse of the school uniform "—this. It isn't exactly glamorous, is it?"

In spite of himself, his mouth twitched.

"Very well, we'll agree then that it isn't love," he said. "But there are other reasons why people—" He stopped.

He couldn't go on with it. This child, with her clear trusting eyes, made all the logic he had brought to bear when he had first decided that he would marry her sound cynical and unpleasant. He might have told her that what so often passed for love was something that did not and could not, in the nature of things, last, and so it was better to start without the beguilement of it. Better, rather, to build on the firm, solid base of mutual liking and respect. Something like that. But he couldn't say it.

He caught her by the shoulders.

"Child, put it out of your head," he said almost roughly. "I do have a reason, of course. But you must not be influenced either by that or by the fact that your grandmother had a sentimental desire to see you married to the son of the man she wanted your mother to marry. You ought never to have been asked—"

In the depths of the dark eyes something stirred.

"You mean, it would be a reckless thing for me to do?" she interrupted softly.

"Exactly!" he said with something approaching relief in his tone. "You're too young—"

"No," she said very clearly, "I don't think I am. Of course, I haven't had very long in which to think it over, but I would quite like to marry you."

She looked up fearlessly at him, and involuntarily Jonathan stepped back a pace. Just what he had expected her attitude would be when she heard of their plans he had hardly imagined. Perhaps Christina had somehow or other implied that she was a sweet, docile child and he had accepted that. But now . . . there was something in the upturned face that he could not read, and it both intrigued and startled him.

"But why?" he demanded, as gauche and ill at ease as a boy in his teens.

The long lashes flicked down over the pale cheeks.

"Does it matter so long as—to me—it seems a good reason?" she asked.

"But you know nothing whatever about me," he

blurted out, and a sudden dimple flashed into her cheek.
"Nor you about me," she retorted. "It will be . . . rather
fun finding out, don't you think?"

A knock at the front door interrupted them and
momentarily Jacynth's hand flew to her throat.

"That's the vicar," she said breathlessly. "Grandmother told me that he was coming. Mr. Branksome,
please, please say you'll marry me! Gran wants it so
and . . . and after all, these days, if it doesn't work out. . . .
Oh, say you will!"

The absurdity of the situation struck him anew. He had
thought he might have to persuade her. Now, she was
beseeching him to do the very thing he had planned to do.
For a moment they stood gazing intently at one another.

"Very well," he said.

A sudden light flickered in her eyes, flamed momentarily and was gone.

"Thank you," she said demurely. "I'll tell Gran."

It was all over. He had stood beside the big bed waiting
for his bride. There was at least that amount of conven-
tion about this strange wedding. The vicar was quite
unperturbed by the strangeness of the situation, and the
nurse and the housekeeper who were to be the witnesses
were a little fluttered and excited. Then Jacynth had come
quietly in, and involuntarily he had caught his breath.

Only a few minutes ago when she had left him, she had
been wearing the plain school uniform. Now, in every
particular, she was dressed as a bride. Her long white silk
skirts swept the floor, her dark head, covered with a filmy
veil and crowned with orange blossom, was slightly bent.
In her hands she carried a bouquet. Afterward, he could

never remember what flowers it was made of because he suddenly noticed the tips of her little satin shoes and was reminded of a verse about another girl who was getting married:

> Her feet beneath her petticoat
> Like little mice stole in and out,
> As if they feared the light;
> But oh! she dances such a way,
> No sun upon an Easter-day
> Is half so fine a sight.

Was Jacynth like that, too? Lighthearted and carefree? He did not know. He heard the echo of her voice, "It will be rather fun, finding out. . . ."

"Now, if you're ready, Mr. Branksome," said the vicar.

It was a brief, reverent service. His voice and Jacynth's made their responses. Someone slipped a ring into his hand—he had forgotten about that, but evidently Christina had remembered it. . . .

"I now pronounce you man and wife. . . ."

He had a feeling of anticlimax and an imperishable memory of the peace and tranquility on Christina's ivory-white face.

Two hours later she had died so quietly that no one could have said where sleep ended and death took its place.

Jacynth had not cried. Nor had death frightened her. She stood with her hand in Jonathan's looking down at the quiet face and said softly, "She looks so happy. I'm glad, so glad we did what she wanted."

All that was hours ago. In the interval they had had an odd, picniclike meal, which appeared to be all that the staff could produce, and although Jacynth had not eaten very much, he had been relieved to see how composed she was in circumstances that might have tried many a woman older than she.

After the meal, he had told her that he, as Christina's executor, must begin to go through her papers. He asked if she would like to help him.

"They concern you, you know," he reminded her. "Because all that was your grandmother's is now yours."

"Yes, I suppose so," she said, not in a way that suggested any eagerness to assume possession, but rather a realization that because Gran had loved her so much it was the natural thing for her to have all Gran's treasures. "But if you don't mind, I think I'd like to go to bed. I didn't really get much sleep last night, you know."

He looked at her more closely and saw the smudged black rings under her eyes, the pinched whiteness of her little face, and realized for the first time the conscious restraint that she was imposing on herself.

"Yes, I think that would be a very good idea," he agreed. "Ask the nurse for some aspirin before you go."

"Oh, I won't need that," she said quickly. "I'm so tired—you must be as well, Mr. Branksome. Must you do the papers tonight?"

"I'm afraid so," he said regretfully. "You see, I've only just returned from New York. And I must get back to Liverpool to discuss the business I did there with my partner as soon as possible."

"I see." She stifled a yawn and laughed shamefacedly. "I *am* tired," she repeated apologetically.

When she had gone he went into the room that Frederic Allardyce had used as his study and library. The big, bare desk was equipped with a vast, silver-cornered blotter and an ornate silver inkwell. He cleared both carefully away before fumbling in his pocket for two small keys Christina had entrusted him with just that morning. One the key to the old-fashioned safe, which, he thought, a good burglar could probably open in a few minutes. The other belonged to the safety deposit box where all Christina's jewelry had reposed for many years. That, too, was Jacynth's now.

He opened the safe, stiff with disuse, and peered inside. Everything was very neatly arranged and, remembering Christina's instructions, he put his hand unhesitatingly on the two papers he needed most urgently—Christina's own will and a copy of her husband's, since much of his property had been disposed of not only for Christina's lifetime but after. An astute man, Frederic Allardyce who, having come by his money the hard way, saw no reason why others should have a too free handling of it.

Yet even so, to Christina's way of thinking, there was a flaw in his will . . . and a vital one at that.

Jonathan knew the story of the Allardyce family as well as if it had been his own. For he had no mother, and during his boyhood much of his spare time had been spent at the Allardyce home.

Isobel, Jacynth's mother, had been their only child. He could conjure up her picture now, though he had only been about ten at the time. But Isobel was not the sort of woman one easily forgot.

Tall, slim, graceful, and so intensely *alive*, she had been the sunshine of the grim, dignified house. And there was nothing that they would not have done for her, until she began to want something that they honestly believed to be bad for her to have—freedom to marry graceless Tim Furnival, a gambler, as lacking in a sense of responsibility as a man could be, and utterly irresponsible. They explained why they said "No," and she appeared to accept the decision. But she grew thin and sad and stopped singing about the house. But she was young and they believed that she would get over it in time, so they tried to distract her, and she was very sweet and gentle. Until a day came when she could bear it no longer. She ran away to Tim and for a while they heard regularly from her. They must forgive her, she loved Tim so much she simply couldn't bear not to be with him. She was so happy. . . .

So they wrote, full of love, forgiving her. But they had not enclosed the check that Tim had hoped would come.

And then she stopped writing. For nearly a year their letters went unanswered—she and Tim were in Madrid now, though heaven knew why except that he was the restless type who had neither the need nor liking for a settled home. Then Tim wrote to say that she was dead. She had died when her little girl was born . . . perhaps because she had no longer any desire to live. For even in that short time Tim had deteriorated. Or so it seemed to the prejudiced eyes of his wife's parents.

But deterioration or not, he still had his wits about him. They wanted him to give them little Jacynth and, knowing their man, they offered him a large sum of money in exchange for the complete legal surrender of the child. But that he would not do. He would let them take charge of her, let them bring her up, but legally he would remain her guardian. And in the end they had to agree because he had the whip hand. But Frederic Allardyce had not made his way in a hard world for nothing. Instead of the lump sum, he would pay Tim a quarterly allowance, so long as he never came near the child. The day he did that the money would stop. Of course, they might have made a fight of it and have proved him an unfit person to have charge of Jacynth, but after all, Tim was her natural parent, and courts are notoriously reluctant to take a child from its parents' care without very good and sufficient reason. Besides, Tim had charm. He would have been a dangerous opponent.

So, though they took little Jacynth home with them, fear remained in their hearts. But she never knew. They never spoke of her father to her, so she had concluded vaguely that he, as well as her mother, was dead.

The years went on and Tim kept his word. Every three months the allowance was paid into a London bank and sooner or later they received a businesslike receipt from him, rarely from the same place twice running. Tim was evidently as footloose and fancy-free as ever. And so, gradually, their fears had subsided. Evidently Tim realized on which side his bread was buttered and preferred the security of a settled income to the inconvenience that a growing child would be to a man of his roving habits.

But then another fear had developed. Frederic Allardyce developed heart trouble. He knew that the end might come any day, and he set to work to plan for the security of the child they loved so dearly.

His money—and there was a lot of it—must be tied up in such a way that when it came to Jacynth, if, as might well happen, she was under age at the time, Tim could not touch it.

He must find someone he could trust, acquaint him with the truth and give him the power to protect Jacynth. And who was more suitable than the man who had wanted to marry Isobel and whom they had so hoped would be their son-in-law, Andrew Branksome?

He had been a widower with a little son—Jonathan—when he had met Isobel, and he had fallen in love with her as deeply as if it had been the first adoring love of his life. But Isobel, much as she liked him, had not been able to love him, and he had never found anyone to take her place. Of course, Andrew agreed. To him Isobel's little girl had been at once a painful reminder of the past and a beloved solace. He could be trusted to follow out Frederic's instructions to the letter.

So, for her lifetime, Christina was to have the free use of his income, but the capital she could not touch. And at her death Andrew would continue those payments indefinitely to Tim. But they overlooked only one thing. There is no guarantee to the length of human life. Eighteen months after Frederic died, Andrew was involved in an accident that cost him his life.

There was nothing that Christina could do. Frederic's will stood, of course, but some other guardian would have to be appointed, and once there was no one to tell tales on him, Tim could make out a pretty story that might result in his handling the Allardyce money . . . and gambling it all away.

Jacynth was sixteen at the time—not quite a child, yet certainly not a woman. Yet to Christina's shrewd, loving eyes was the promise of a splendid and lovable womanhood. In a few years' time any man would be proud to have her as his wife. And, once she was married, her husband would be her guardian, not her father. It only remained to find the right man. And once more Christina turned to the Branksome family, to Jonathan, Andrew's son, whom she had known most of his life.

Jonathan thought now of that incredible interview. At first he had given an unequivocal refusal, but Christina had persisted, and at length he had given her the promise she had wanted—mainly because at that time it simply didn't matter very much to him what the future held. Besides, there were advantages—though it was not the financial ones that she pointed out to him; she was too clever for that. And he had kept his promise. Jacynth was his wife, and he had every intention of seeing to it that she and not her wastrel father had the benefit of the money.

He laid the two wills down. He had already spoken to the Allardyce solicitor, who would be coming the following day. Next, he found Tim's receipts, and for a moment he held them in his hand, weighing them up thoughtfully. If it were possible, he intended that Jacynth should never learn that her father was alive. So it followed that she must never see these receipts. Should he burn them? No, he decided against that. They had a certain value. Supposing Tim did try to get in touch with Jacynth? Brutal though it would be, he must make it clear to her what sort of man he was, and these receipts would help. But he would transfer them to his office safe or possibly to his bank. Yes, that would be better. There was little else in the safe of any immediate interest. Details of investments—but he already had a copy of that, anyhow. A few papers of family interest. . . . He was just returning everything to the safe when a little sound made him turn.

Jacynth was standing in the doorway. She was wearing her plain school dressing gown and her feet were bare.

He went over to her quickly, for she was shaking from head to foot.

"What is it, Jacynth?" he asked gently, putting a steadying arm around her.

"I'm so tired," she muttered. "But I can't sleep!"

It wasn't surprising, of course. As she had said, she had had very little sleep, and, besides, the day had been crowded with incident. Without a word he half led, half carried her to the big leather couch and switched on the electric heater. Then he went to the little side table, on which whisky and soda had been left for him, and poured out a fairly stiff shot.

"I want you to take this, even though you may not like it," he said, taking it to her. "Sip it very slowly."

With a little grimace of distaste she did as she was told, and he could see that the warmth of the spirit was gradually stealing over her. But even so there was still that imploring look in her eyes, and suddenly he realized that she needed more than physical warmth. She needed comforting, and only the reassuring contact of another person could give her that. He sat down beside her, his arm around her shoulders, and instantly she snuggled, childlike, up against him.

"It isn't that I'm afraid or anything silly like that," she confided shakily. "But. . . ."

"I know," he said softly.

There was a silence, and he guessed that she was

turning over the experiences of the day in her mind, reassured by his nearness. Gradually he felt her relax. The liquor and the warmth were doing their work, and soon, he thought, she would sleep. Yet he was reluctant to suggest that she go back to her room. Very gently he drew her down into his arms, and like a sleepy child she automatically accepted the greater comfort the new position provided and lifted her bare feet up onto the couch. There was a blanket lying over the back of it, and he contrived to arrange it over her without disturbing her. Then he sat very still, and quite soon he had his reward. Her heavy lids dropped, the hand that held the lapel of his coat relaxed and slipped to her own gently rising breast. Jacynth was asleep.

For a long time Jonathan sat staring at the electric heater, hardly conscious of thought, mesmerized by the bright bars. Then suddenly he was wide awake.

A slight movement of Jacynth's hand, the glitter of something bright—the wedding ring that someone else had bought for him to put there.

This was his wedding night! He glanced down at the tranquil, trusting face pillowed against him. And surely, an odder marriage night no man had ever spent!

CHAPTER TWO

It was about a week after Christina Allardyce's death that Jonathan asked Jacynth to come to the study so that he could explain everything to her about the estate.

It had been a strange interlude in normal life for both of them. After that one outburst, Jacynth had appeared to regain control of herself. But it had completely changed the relationship between them. Just what the new one was either of them would have been hard put to say. The nearest to it that Jonathan could get was the instinctive trust in him that Jacynth had apparently had, now seemed to be based on a more solid foundation. Consequently she now regarded him as part of her life. Which was just as well, he thought rather grimly, seeing that he was her husband.

There were times when he wondered whether she realized in the least the implications of that fact and, if not, just what the future held for them. If he tried to analyze it, he would have decided that the undoubted affection that she was beginning to show him was rather more like that of a niece for a young and favorite uncle than anything else. There were times when he was glad of that, and others when he was not so sure what he felt.

As she came into the study, where he had already put in a good hour's work immediately after breakfast, he suddenly realized that something would have to be done about her clothes. You couldn't have a married woman going about looking like a schoolgirl; he wondered just how he would manage to tell her that without hurting her feelings, then came to the conclusion that it might not be so difficult. After all, most children like dressing up to look older than they are. It was a shock to realize that that was how he wanted her to look.

"Sit down," he said cheerfully, and then, as she sat down obediently in the big easy chair he indicated, one leg tucked under her, he added in rather a surprised way, "Why, you've done your hair differently, haven't you?"

Jacynth felt the swift color stain her cheeks and wished she could overcome that trick of blushing. He must think her such an awful kid!

"Yes, do you like it?" she asked hurriedly.

He considered thoughtfully before he answered. Until now her hair had been parted simply in the center and tied in a ponytail. Now, she had done something to the hair at the back; he was too inexpert to know just what, but the effect was vaguely Grecian, and he realized that she could not have chosen a better style. Not only did it show the pretty, girlish nape of her neck, but it seemed to reveal her profile in greater detail, and he realized for the first time just how faultlessly classic it was, and yet how charmingly warm and feminine.

"Yes," he said slowly, "I like it very much. Don't ever have your hair cut short, will you?"

She flicked a quick, startled look at him that reminded him how careful he had to be. It was the first compliment he had ever paid her and the first time that he had even so much as implied that in the future either of them would be affected by the actions of the other.

He turned deliberately to the papers before him.

"Now, about your inheritance. I don't know whether you know that my father was to have been your guardian?"

"No," Jacynth said faintly, "I didn't know. Is that why

you have to look after things for me now? I mean, did you inherit the job from him?"

"No, the law doesn't work that way." He paused to wonder if it would have been better if it had. It would have meant that this amazing marriage of theirs had been unnecessary. "Actually, that's one of the reasons why your grandmother wanted you to . . . marry me." He spoke slowly, choosing his words carefully. "You see, neither she nor your grandfather had thought of the possibility of father dying so soon, and consequently made no alternative arrangements. That being so—"

"I know," Jacynth said eagerly. "I would have been a ward in Chancery, wouldn't I? Like Bleak House. I wouldn't have liked that much. It would be very impersonal, wouldn't it?"

"I suppose it would," he agreed, realizing thankfully that she was unconsciously helping him out more than he had dared to hope. "But, on the other hand, because your grandfather had disposed of his estate not only for your grandmother's lifetime, but after as well, it did not lie in her power to make any other arrangements. The only way out was for you to be married at the time of her death. Since that was with her approval, and also, no doubt because your grandfather had had sufficiently high an opinion of my family to trust his money to father, I'm regarded as the natural guardian of your money until you're of age."

"Well, that seems fair enough," Jacynth said judicially. "I think it was a jolly good way out. And I must say I think it was very nice of you to agree. I don't suppose you would have thought of marrying me if Grandmother hadn't suggested it, would you?"

"Possibly not," he agreed. "On the other hand, you're more than likely to come across people who would tell you that I would have been a fool to refuse."

She looked up sharply.

"Why?" she asked blankly.

His mouth twitched wryly.

"Because you're a very wealthy young woman," he said slowly, his eyes fixed with more than usual intentness on her.

For a moment the implication of the words did not seem to penetrate, and then, suddenly, she jumped to her feet, her cheeks crimson.

"Oh!" she blurted out. "How can you say such a beastly thing! You wouldn't . . . you know you wouldn't do a thing like that!"

He nodded.

"No, I wouldn't," he agreed deliberately. "And just this once I'm going to tell you so. But not again. That's the sort of thing that loses in conviction by constant repetition. So remember, if ever anybody suggests such a thing, you know it isn't true."

She nodded gravely.

"I'm glad you told me," she said. "But I would have known without!"

He was rather touched at her confidence in him, but having made his point, he went on to explain in greater detail just what she had inherited, and she listened with an intent seriousness that rather surprised him. It was, he thought, surely rather unusual in a girl who had, up till now, shouldered no responsibilities and known few burdens of any sort.

When he had told her all that was necessary for her

to know, she sat silent for a few minutes and then said almost timidly, "I wonder if you would mind if I asked you a few questions about yourself?"

"Go ahead," he said cheerfully.

She hesitated for a moment, and then asked, "Are you rich?"

He considered for a moment.

"That depends on how you look at things," he said at length. "I haven't as big a capital as you have, but I earn enough a year for my income to be slightly more than yours will be."

"I expect you're glad, aren't you?"

He looked at her curiously.

"Why?" he asked.

"Oh—" she made a vague movement of her hands "—I think most men like to have more money than their wives, don't they?"

"Perhaps they do," he admitted, amused at her instinctive psychology. "Any other questions?"

"Oh yes. Where do you live and what do you do?"

"Well, my office is in Liverpool. And I'm an exporter."

"What of?" Jacynth asked with evident interest.

"Oh, anything, everything." And then, seeing her puzzled face, he went on, "There are quite a lot of manufacturing firms in this country that don't have their own representatives in the countries where they want to sell their goods. So they tell me what they have, and I link them up with people in other countries who want those things."

"I see," she said. "I've often wondered how things like that happened. And do you live in Liverpool?"

"No, though I sometimes spend an odd night or two there during the week if I am very busy. But my home is actually near Conway."

Jacynth shut her eyes and thought for a moment.

"Yes, I know. Along the top edge of Wales. Near Llandudno. Isn't it?"

"Yes, that's right," he said, absurdly pleased at her knowledge. "How did you know? Have you been there?"

"No, but I like maps," she said unexpectedly. "I like trying to decide what places look like from what they look like on maps."

"And are you often right?" he asked.

"Sometimes. Only no matter how good your guess, there are always surprises."

"Well, I hope in this case that they will be pleasant ones," he said cheerfully. "Any more questions?"

"Isn't it rather a long way to live away from Liverpool?" she asked. "Doesn't it take you a long time to get there?"

"It's something over fifty miles," he said. "Yes, I suppose it is rather a long way, but I think it's worth it." A note of warmth crept into his voice, and it was impossible for Jacynth not to realize that he loved his home. "Anything else?"

"No, I don't think so," she said slowly. "Except . . . you'd better look after this, hadn't you?" And drawing off the narrow platinum wedding ring from her finger she laid it in his hand.

He stood staring at it.

"But why?" he asked, completely taken aback at her matter-of-factness.

"They won't let me wear it," she said simply.

"Who won't let you wear it?" he demanded.

"Why, at school, I mean. We're not allowed to wear any jewelry—except a wrist watch."

"But. . . ." He was too astonished to remember to be tactful. "You didn't think you were going back to school, did you?"

"Aren't I?" For a moment her eyes were wide with astonishment. Then her look gave way to michievous delight. "Oh, what fun! I hadn't thought of that! No, I suppose it would be rather difficult, because, of course, they would have to call me 'Mrs.' Though that might be fun, in some ways. . . ," she added thoughtfully.

"Don't you think it might be more fun to go back on Prize Day or whatever they call it and present the prizes?" he suggested. Her face crinkled with delight.

"You do think of marvelous things, Mr. Branksome!" she said warmly.

"Don't call me Mr. Branksome!" he said, with sudden irritation. "Don't you realize I'm your husband?"

"Well, wives used to call their husbands 'Mr.,' " she reminded him. "Jane Eyre did."

"Well, you're not Jane Eyre and I'm not Mr. Rochester."

"He had an insane wife," she said thoughtfully. "I don't suppose you have a secret life like that, have you?"

"No, I haven't," he said shortly. "And in future will you please call me by my Christian name?"

"Jonathan, Jonathan, Jonathan," she said experimentally. "Yes, I think I can manage that. It's nice. I'm glad your name isn't Claude or Percival or something like that. I think having a name like that must affect anyone's character. Well—" she looked at him inquiringly. "—if that's all. . . ?"

"Yes, except that I must go up to Liverpool the day after tomorrow. Would you like to come with me or follow on later?"

"Come with you," she said promptly. "Then I can get some new clothes. I mean, a wedding ring and a school tunic don't go awfully well together, do they?"

"No, they don't," he agreed.

She gave him a casual, friendly nod of farewell and left him. Jonathan stroked his chin thoughtfully with his thumb and finger.

What an extraordinary mixture she was! At one minute a feckless, mischievous child. At another, hardly a woman and yet capable of those flashes of insight that were completely lacking in some women he had known—one in particular.

For a moment he was lost in thoughts of the past. Then, with an impatient shrug, he sat down at the desk again and packed up the papers into his briefcase.

It was the first really long drive that Jacynth had ever experienced and she enjoyed every moment of it. To Jonathan it was something of a novelty to have as a companion someone who was at the same time so inexperienced and so appreciative. Nor, to his relief, did she show any signs of gushing or chattering of her delight at the constantly changing scene. In fact, the greater her appreciation, the more silent she became. Now and then she would silently raise a hand as if to point out something that particularly appealed to her, and once or twice he heard a swift, almost awestricken intake of her breath. Just once she spoke in a way that expressed what she was feeling more than the most lavish of eulogies.

"Could we stop just for a minute?" she asked, and when, after gazing her fill, she said softly, "Thank you!" he was more touched than he cared to admit.

He was surprised, too. But then she was a surprising girl: so young and yet so tranquil and reposeful. The thought made him realize the magnitude of the task he had undertaken, and without putting it into so many words, he vowed that her trust in him would never be betrayed—no matter how difficult that might prove to be.

"I'm sorry that we have to make the drive as quickly as this," he began. "I'd have liked to show you some of the towns we'll pass through. But I really am in a hurry, so we have no choice. I promise you, though, that one of these days we'll stop and look just as often and long as you like, and there is one thing at least that we can do today. We'll stop at Gloucester for lunch at an old coaching inn. I think you'll like it."

"It sounds lovely," she said warmly, then added, "Are we going straight through to your home?"

"No, we'll spend the night in Liverpool—I called last night and made the reservations. Then, tomorrow I shall have to spend most of my time in the office and we'll go home in the evening. Do you think you will be able to entertain yourself while I'm busy?"

"Oh yes," she said tranquilly. "I shall explore, and if you'll give me some money, I'll buy some clothes. I can't go on wearing my school ones."

Jonathan smothered a chuckle. Surely no bride was ever less embarrassed at asking her new husband for money! But then, of course, she knew that she had a lot of money of her own, even though the delays of the law would make it impossible for it to be touched at present.

He frowned suddenly, partly because he had suddenly realized how difficult it was for a husband to give a rich wife a present and partly in surprise at the knowledge that it mattered to him that it should be so.

"All right," he said indifferently. "Don't buy too much, though, until you have a taste of life at Crellie and know what you want. By the way, do you have an evening dress?"

"A short one that I had at school," she said with a little grimace. "But it's short—I think you'd call it a party dress. And, of course, my wedding dress. Do you know, Jonathan, Gran had that made so that the sleeves come out without any bother and you can do things to the neck, and it's an evening dress in about five minutes. I think she thought of everything," she said in an altered, wistful voice.

He glanced down at her briefly.

I wonder, he said to himself.

They drove in silence to Gloucester, and Jacynth wasn't sure if she had annoyed him in some way or whether he just liked being silent at times. She did herself, she knew, but then some people thought you were being sulky if you didn't talk. She would have to find out how Jonathan felt about that sort of thing. Because it was equally irritating to have people chattering if you didn't want them to or being silent when you felt like conversation, and she didn't want to annoy him. He was being so very sweet and considerate, she told herself, that it was the most natural thing in the world that she should want to please him.

She was disappointed at Gloucester. She thought it was rather a drab, dreary town, and when Jonathan turned down a perfectly ordinary street lined with stores and paused for the traffic to clear she looked at him in surprise.

"Wait a minute," he said, evidently reading her thoughts. "Gloucester has grown since the inn was built!"

He turned in through a narrow, almost unnoticed gap between two modern shops and Jacynth gave a little gasp.

Suddenly they were in a different world. The car was running over a cobbled courtyard, and when Jonathan stopped it, Jacynth jumped out eagerly.

The inn was built on all four sides of the yard; the passage they had come through was, she saw, actually a short tunnel. It was very old and the heavy timbers looked as if they were good for as long again as they had been there. A gallery ran around the upper floor, making a covered way on the ground floor, so that one could get from one side of the inn to the other without crossing the yard.

"Well?" Jonathan asked.

She turned to him eagerly.

"Oh, Jonathan, it's wonderful! I had no idea such places still existed! And isn't it funny, although it's so old, a car doesn't seem out of place here and neither do I!"

He looked down approvingly at her.

"I've noticed that myself," he agreed. "I think it's because it's so old—fifteenth century—that nothing surprises it any longer. After all, it has seen a lot of changes."

Lunch was an unqualified success.

They were both in a contented frame of mind when they got back into the car, and for the rest of the journey their conversation was desultory and more superficial.

They reached Birkenhead about six o'clock and, after paying the toll, Jonathan drove the car down into the Mersey Tunnel. He had done the trip so often that it had not occurred to him to prepare Jacynth for its advent and, after a few minutes, he was surprised to hear her say rather shakily, "Does this . . . go on for long?"

He glanced down at her and saw that her face was white and sick-looking.

"I'm sorry," she gulped. "It's silly . . . but tunnels . . . anything underground. . . ."

"I'm sorry," he said anxiously. "I should have warned you. I'm afraid we must go through now, but we have a pretty clear way ahead—I'll make it as quick as I can. Shut your eyes and clasp your hands in your lap. I don't know why, but I know that helps."

Obediently she did as she was told, and to her relief she found that the feeling of nausea was gradually going.

At last Jonathan said reassuringly, "Daylight ahead!" and she opened her eyes to find that they were running up the slope into the open street. Unconsciously she breathed a little sigh of relief. Five minutes later they were being shown to their rooms in the rather massively built hotel.

When the luggage had been brought up and the porter dismissed, Jonathan went over and stood beside Jacynth as she stared out of the window.

"Not very pretty, is it?" he said, putting an arm around her shoulders. "Never mind, wait until you get home! And in the meantime, how about a bath, a rest for half an hour, and then dinner and a dance before bedtime?"

"Oh, I don't think I want to rest," she said, but Jonathan led her through the communicating door to her room.

"I promise not to be the stern husband too often, but just this time I'm giving you orders."

He saw the very slight stiffening of the soft lips—how sweet and pale unrouged lips were, he thought. Fragrant, like petal flowers . . . and then he realized that she was too young, too near to the discipline of school life to appreciate the time-worn jest.

"Please, Jacynth," he said coaxingly, and her lips curved to an appreciative smile. Evidently she was not too young to appreciate—and relish—the fact that she had made him change his tactics.

"Very well, Jonathan," she said demurely. "And you?"

"Oh, I have a little business to attend to," he said lightly. "Nothing much. Just to claim a package from the manager that I had left here today."

"Oh!" Jacynth said without very much interest. "I say, Jonathan, before you go, could you unbutton me down the back? It means I have to tie myself in knots if I do it myself."

"Well, keep your hair out of the way," he said, and bent to the task. "Why you women don't do up at the front like men do— Stand still, child, it's me who has to look at them, not you! There you are! Don't I get paid for that?"

"Your pleasure at doing it for me should be sufficient reward," she said demurely, and just for a second their eyes met before, rather precipitately, she vanished into the bathroom.

There was a thoughtful expression on Jonathan's face as he ran downstairs. It was odd how, just as each time he had decided that Jacynth was just a child, something happened to make him less sure. There had been more than a hint of coquetry in that last remark of hers.

Jacynth stood in front of the long mirror. She was wearing the quickly altered wedding dress and the result was rather surprising. With its long sleeves and cleverly filled in neck it had been demure in the extreme. Now, with the sleeves removed and the neckline lower, it contrived to look both youthful and sophisticated. She saw a self that she had never seen before—and a rather startling self. The effect of the long dress was, of course, to make her look taller and most satisfyingly slim.

"Golly, and ten days ago I was playing basketball!" she thought, awestricken. She calculated rapidly, "They'll be breaking up tomorrow and having a cocoa party in the dorm after lights out tonight!" she chuckled contentedly. "While I shall be having dinner . . . and dancing!"

She leaned forward, frowning a little. If only she had some makeup! Well, that was one of the things she would buy tomorrow. She pinched her lips vigorously and brought a brighter color to them. It improved her immensely, but of course the effect quickly faded.

She shrugged her shoulders resignedly and was just going to turn away from the mirror when Jonathan spoke. He had come in without her noticing and stood now directly behind her.

"Open your mouth and shut your eyes and see what the king will send you!" he chanted. "At least, you needn't open your mouth. . . ."

Obediently she shut her eyes and felt something cool

touch her neck and the warmth of his fingers at the nape of her neck.

"There!" he said triumphantly. "Now you can look!"

She opened her eyes and uttered a little gasp of delight.

He had fastened a string of flawless, perfectly matched pearls around her neck, and it was, she quickly recognized, the finishing touch to her appearance.

Her shining eyes met his in the glass.

"Oh, Jonathan!" she said, almost in tears. Then, suddenly, impetuously, she turned and put her slim young arms around his neck. Involuntarily his arms closed around her as her warm, soft lips were pressed against his.

Then, very gently, he released himself and held her at arms' length.

"That was a very sweet 'thank you,' " he said rather unsteadily. "But we mustn't crush your finery."

Jacynth's arms dropped to her side and her dark lashes fluttered to her cheeks.

"No, Jonathan," she said meekly. But for the moment, at least, her pleasure had faded.

Her spirits rose quickly enough when they went downstairs together. Evidently the dance had already begun, for they could hear the music faintly.

"Oh, Jonathan, must we have dinner?" she pleaded. "It seems such a waste of time, and I'm not really hungry."

"Well, I am," he insisted. "And when I'm hungry I dance badly, all over my partner's feet. You wouldn't like that, would you?"

She giggled appreciatively.

"I suppose I am hungry really," she admitted. "Only dance music always makes me tingle all over."

They were interrupted by the arrival of the waiter with the menu, and by the time he had gone with the order Jacynth had thought of something else.

"I say, can you figure out how people dining at a perfectly marvelous place like this can possibly look as glum as that couple over on your right."

He glanced casually in the direction she indicated.

"You're right, they are pretty glum," he agreed. "Perhaps they're too used to it to appreciate it any more. Or else they are bored with themselves . . . or each other."

"I can't understand anybody being bored," Jacynth said vigorously. "What I'm afraid of is that there won't be time in life to do all the things that I want to!"

"One of these days you must make a list of them," he said idly. "But tell me some now."

"Well, I want to go for a long journey in a boat and another in an airplane," she said, puckering up her forehead in an effort to oblige him. "And I would like to have a walled garden full of roses, lots of colored satin shoes, and two babies."

"You've got it all planned," he said in a strangled sort of a voice.

"Of course. I decided when I was twelve," she said matter-of-factly. "Do you mind?"

"I can't say I've given the matter very much thought," he said carefully.

"No, I don't suppose you have," she said tolerantly. "Men don't, you know. Still, in principle, don't you think that married people ought to have a family?"

"Yes, I suppose I do," he agreed, undecided whether to be shocked, relieved, or merely amused.

"Yes, one of each—a boy and a girl. Oh, here comes our waiter. He's rather like the Frog Footman, isn't he?

252

Do you think when we go you could give him rather a large tip, Jonathan? I'd love to see if he can smile!"

"I'll try to remember," he promised, considerably relieved at the change of topic. He saw to it that for the rest of the meal conversation was strictly commonplace, and, after waiting patiently while Jacynth ate an additional ice cream, he led the way to the ballroom.

Jacynth looked around her and drew a deep breath of appreciation and satisfaction.

"What's the time, Jonathan?" she asked.

He glanced down at his watch.

"Half past nine," he told her.

"Oh! The juniors will all be in bed and the seniors will by tidying up their sitting room. Then bed for them as well!"

Then, with another of her disconcerting changes, she melted into Jonathan's arms and danced with the poise and inspiration that one would have expected, perhaps, from a woman five years her senior, but certainly not from a schoolgirl.

She inspired Jonathan. Every movement of her slim, supple young body followed his lead to perfection. He was hardly conscious of any individual movement. They drifted in perfect accord and unison, silently, needing no words.

The music ended and he led her by the hand to the edge of the floor.

"Do you know you're the most perfect dancer I've ever met?" he said sincerely, and saw her flush with pleasure.

"Oh, it was mostly you," she said hurriedly. "I felt so safe and my feet felt sure. . . ."

"Well, don't let's waste time," he urged. "The music is beginning again."

Half a dozen times they danced together. The music was sweet and provocative and so, however unconsciously, was the girl Jonathan held in his arms. He could smell the faint perfume of her hair, feel the warmth of her soft body against his. . . .

The music stopped, the band played the National Anthem very firmly to intimate that they had really finished, and Jacynth and Jonathan left the ballroom with their fingers linked.

They walked into the lounge, the music still echoing in their ears. Suddenly they were startled by a sudden exclamation from a woman they were passing.

Quickly, and yet with an oddly smooth movement, she rose from the chair she was sitting in—a tall, pale, blond woman, exquisitely groomed.

She laid her hand detainingly on Jonathan's arm.

"Why, Johnny darling! This is marvelous. Of all people, fancy seeing you!"

CHAPTER THREE

The words were commonplace enough, but to Jacynth's startled ears the richness of the voice, combined with the obvious pleasure in the tone, gave them a tremendous significance.

Unconsciously her hold of Jonathan's hand tightened and she took another step forward. But Jonathan had come to a halt, and she had no choice but to do the same.

"Cynthia!" He sounded both surprised and, yes, there was some other emotion in his tone, but just what it was Jacynth was too inexperienced to know for certain. But at least she knew that it was something that seemed to envelop the three of them in an atmosphere of tension. "This is certainly unexpected! I thought you had no use whatever for the provinces."

She shrugged her slim white shoulders and made a little *moue* of distaste.

"Nor have I. London, Paris, and New York for me every time. But beggars can't be choosers, you know! Times have changed since we last met!"

Jacynth was conscious of an odd feeling that she might not really be there, for neither Jonathan nor this woman seemed to be aware of her presence. When she came to know Cynthia Grant better she was to find that that was the effect she had on most women, since her own sex bored her unutterably, though she was not above making use of a member of it if it suited her.

"Yes," Jonathan said thoughtfully, "they have, haven't they? You've got married . . . and so have I! Jacynth, I would like you to meet the wife of an old friend of mine, Mrs. Howard Grant. Cynthia, my wife."

Cynthia was startled and could not hide it. Her blue eyes widened as she glanced from Jonathan to Jacynth and back again. Johnny Branksome, whom she had regarded as her own special property—married! It was incredible. And it was not very complimentary, either. Her eyes narrowed and her lips curved to a smile.

"But how marvelous!" she said warmly. "I do wish you both every happiness." She turned entirely to Jacynth and put a slim finger under her chin. "You lovely, lovely child! Jonathan, what a lucky man you are!"

"Yes, I think I am," he agreed, pulling Jacynth's arm through his. "And now, if you'll excuse us—"

"Oh no, you can't go yet!" she protested gaily. "I must drink to your health. Come along, just one. . . ."

For a moment Jacynth saw that her eyes and Jonathan's met—no, clashed would be a better word. It made one think of the sharp kiss of fencing foils; it was Cynthia who challenged, Jonathan who stood on guard. Suddenly she felt that she could not bear to see Jonathan capitulate.

"Yes, let's," she said quickly. "I'm awfully thirsty."

Jonathan shrugged his shoulders.

"Why not?" he said, lightly snapping his fingers for the waiter. Then, as they sat down at the little table, he asked, "Is Howard with you?"

"Oh yes, but he turned in long ago," she said, and sighed wistfully. "Actually, it's on his account that we're here. I . . . I ought not to worry you on your honeymoon, but we're afraid one of his lungs is tubercular, and our local doctor thought he ought to see a specialist and have an X ray."

"Oh, poor old chap!" Jonathan exclaimed, with very evident concern. He leaned forward toward Cynthia, his face serious.

"When does he get the verdict?"

"Tomorrow," she said briefly.

I'm being a beast! Jacynth thought. *Just because I don't like her is no reason why I should imagine she's insincere and hard and unsympathetic. And yet I don't believe she cares a pin about her husband. I believe she's just pretending so that she gets Jonathan's sympathy and his attention.*

Something seemed to stir in Jacynth that she had never been conscious of before.

"You must be very anxious," she said softly.

The blue eyes flashed a rapier glance at her, and Jacynth felt a sudden stab of fear.

Cynthia smiled and sighed.

"Yes, I am," she said wistfully. "Only I've had to train myself not to give way, for Howard's sake. And it's become second nature. But it doesn't mean that I'm callous, you know!"

There was only the faintest tinge of reproach in her voice, but it was sufficient. The color flamed into Jacynth's cheeks and her not very vast store of self-confidence vanished, leaving her feeling like a gauche and disconcerted schoolgirl. She had tried in what had seemed a very subtle way to make this woman include her in the conversation, and all she had done was to give her an opportunity of making her look small.

"But never mind about us!" Cynthia insisted. "After all, there's quite a good chance that it's a false alarm. And besides, I want to know all about you two people.

How does it come about that your old friends were not invited to your wedding, Johnny?"

"Because it was a very quiet one, and for family reasons, a little earlier than we had anticipated," Jonathan said easily.

Cythia laughed and clapped her hands.

"Oh, Johnny, you always did say that your wedding wouldn't be a peep show, didn't you?" she said delightedly. "Do you remember the Handson-Betts wedding? You were best man and I was the maid of honor, and we had so many rehearsals that we practically wore a track up the aisle."

Jonathan laughed.

"Yes, I believe we'd still be at it if Mrs. Betts hadn't insisted on walking backward up the aisle to see what the effect was, so that she tripped up over a hassock and came a most undignified purler."

"I met Jerry Handson the other day," Cynthia remarked reminiscently. "He's become terribly fat! He and Irene are living in Cornwall now."

The conversation flowed on. Jacynth told herself fiercely that when two old friends met after a long interval it was the most natural thing in the world that most of their talk should be of the past. Nor was there anything in what Cynthia recalled to which the most thin-skinned of wives could object. But it was a past Jacynth had played no part in, and so of necessity she had to sit silent and resentful.

Of course, the real reason I don't like her is that I'm jealous, Jacynth thought miserably.

Cautiously she examined Cynthia from the top of her exquisitely dressed head to the tips of her slender, sandaled feet. Not a hair was out of place; her black gown, obviously chosen to set off her dazzlingly fair skin, was as uncreased and fresh as if she had only that moment put it on. Jacynth, in an agony of self-torment, forgot the charm of the picture that had looked back at her from her mirror such a short time before, and only remembered her uncontrollable curls and the place in the hem of her skirt where she had caught her heel and ripped a few stitches undone. Nor did it occur to her that Cynthia might be feeling a consuming envy for the girl who, she guessed, was about ten years her junior; though at the same time she might be despising her for her lack of finesse.

But then Cynthia had always been contradictory: she'd always wanted to have her cake and eat it, too.

One of a big family of girls with a father who said quite bluntly that their faces must be their fortunes, since he had no intention of wasting his money on securing husbands for them, she had decided early that she must marry a rich man.

And then, as far as she could love anyone except her own lovely self, she had fallen in love with Johnny Branksome. And Johnny had been completely crazy about her. But in those days he had been comparatively poor. So it was obviously impossible for her to marry him. Still, there was no need to tell him that at once. Time enough for that when the rich suitor appeared, and in the meantime it was an idyllic summer and Johnny was very much in love. No one else had ever satisfied her longing for adulation and flattery as he did.

And then Howard Grant, whom Johnny had known from his schoolboy days, had come to stay with him. And Howard was rich—very rich.

If she had dared, she would have married him for his money and tried to persuade Johnny that there was no reason he should not be her lover. But she had the wit to know that such a thing was not possible. Johnny had odd notions about loyalty to his friend, and so she did not even dare to let him guess that the only attraction that Howard—a heavily built, rather clumsy young man—had for her was his money. She told Johnny that she hated herself for hurting him, but it was Howard that she loved.

Johnny had been distraught. Even now she smiled when she thought of his impassioned appeals. But at length he had realized that she meant what she said, and went away.

It hurt to let him go—hurt her vanity that he could go, though that was somewhat consoled by his insistence that if he could not marry her he would not marry any other woman.

She had married Howard eight years ago, and much had happened since then. Howard's flourishing business had failed, while Jonathan had prospered, and when it was all over Howard was a poor man and Jonathan a rich one. The irony of it!

And in the interval she and Jonathan had never met. Chance, perhaps. Or intention on his part? For she knew that he still kept up a desultory correspondence with Howard, which convinced her that Howard had been too slow to realize that there had been anything deeper than friendship between his wife and his friend. But Johnny had always been something special in her life.

And now, when she met him again, there was not one, but two, barriers between them. Howard, and this lovely, half-fledged child whom Jonathan had so astonishingly married.

Johnny was on his guard. She sensed that immediately. Was it because he was so much in love with his wife that he preferred to leave the past alone? Or because, even now, he was afraid of his own passion for her? Whichever it was, it had not been difficult to put him at his ease and reassure him.

But the girl was a different matter. She was jealous, of course. But there was something more to it than that. She had sensed, known, guessed—whichever it was—in the first five minutes that Cynthia had no use now for her husband.

Yes, that might be dangerous. She had made a mistake in not realizing from the first that she must gain the girl's friendship, but the announcement of the marriage had been too much of a shock, and she had foolishly surrendered to the desire to hit out. Well, it was too late to worry about that, and, in any case, just how much it mattered would depend on the influence that Jacynth had with Jonathan. It might, of course, be a lot, although, surely there was something odd about this marriage? She could not put her finger on it, but she was convinced that it was there. . . .

Anyhow, the thing that mattered was that at a moment when life seemed unbearably and excruciatingly dull she had not only met Jonathan again, but had a means of gaining his sympathy and kindness. She must be careful, play her cards well. Rather amusing, too, to think that Howard himself was her strongest card.

Suddenly Jacynth stood up.

"I'm dreadfully sorry, Jonathan," she said rather breathlessly, "but I'm so tired. I simply must go to bed. Will you give me the key of the room?"

Grudgingly, Cynthia gave her full marks for that. No suggestion of the possessive wife, no attempt to drag him away from his old friend. But inevitably Jonathan glanced at his watch, and, of course, it was very late.

"Heavens above, no wonder!" he exclaimed. He, too, stood up and Cynthia had no choice but to do the same thing. "It's been delightful to see you again, Cynthia, after all this time. Give Howard my greetings. I expect we'll see him at breakfast?"

"Yes, of course," Cynthia agreed. "And, Johnny, if you could do something to cheer him up a bit. . . ?"

"Of course!" he agreed warmly. He held her hand a little longer, Jacynth felt, than was necessary. "And keep your chin up, Cynthia. After all, even if the result of the X ray is positive, no one actually dies of that illness nowadays."

"I know," she smiled, but her lip trembled ever so slightly. "But sometimes one is almost afraid to hope. Bless you, Johnny; you don't know how much you've done for me!" She put a hand up to her eyes and hurried away as if she could not trust herself to speak. Jonathan watched her go and then turned to Jacynth.

"Just about asleep on your feet, aren't you?" he said self-reproachfully. "I think I'd better carry you up, hadn't I, child?"

She would have given anything to have felt the warm security of his arms, but not because he was thinking of her as a tired child.

"No, thank you," she said distantly. "I can manage by myself."

She saw that her tone surprised him, and for a second she felt that she must put her arms around his neck and tell him that she was just silly and tired and he mustn't be hurt. But no woman, however immature, can throw herself into the arms of a man who has never made love to her, even if he is her husband.

She turned away and made for the stairs, her eyes stinging with tears. Their lovely, lovely evening, all spoiled because of that beastly woman! And Jonathan had said that it was delightful to have met her again, and they had laughed and talked and he had forgotten all about his wife.

She stumbled, blind and unseeing, as the tears slid down her cheeks. She felt Jonathan's arm around her shoulder steadying her, but it was intolerable now.

"No," she said fiercely. "No!"

He took it away instantly.

"As you wish," he said indifferently.

Jacynth dreamed that she heard a door shut, and she immediately awakened to wonder if, after all, it had not been the sound itself that had disturbed her.

She slipped out of bed and ran into the next room. Jonathan was not there, and except for the rumpled bed covers there was no sign that anybody had been there. For a moment sheer unreasoning panic shook her. Suppose Jonathan was so angry with her for the way she had behaved last night that he had gone away and left her! Then common sense told her that she was being silly, but all the same it was a comfort to see that his suitcase, although packed, was still standing there, although she had not seen it at first.

What had probably happened was that he had decided

not to disturb her until the last minute as she was still asleep, and so he had gone down to breakfast alone.

She wondered whether Cynthia would be down there as well, but decided that she was hardly the sort of woman who would get up early. Probably her idea of breakfast, Jacynth thought scornfully, would be a piece of toast and a cup of coffee, if you could call that breakfast.

But either way, whether she was there or not, it seemed a good idea to hurry with dressing and go down to join Jonathan.

She decided to not take a bath, but in spite of the need for speed she hesitated over her choice of clothes. They were all so childish, but they were all she had. She chose green pants and sweater; after all, people wore those at any age.

Five minutes later she ran downstairs to the dining room, but on the threshold she paused. Jonathan was at their table, and he was sharing it with a big, heavily built man who was sitting with his back to the door.

Quite suddenly she lost her nerve. Until now she had found it the easiest thing in the world to talk to Jonathan, sure of his sympathy and understanding. Now, without any warning, she felt that he was a stranger, and her heart beat suffocatingly. She had almost decided to go back to her room and phone room service for breakfast when Jonathan looked up and saw her, and there was no retreat.

As she walked slowly toward them the two men stood up. Jonathan's face showed neither pleasure nor annoyance at her sudden appearance, and his voice was just as noncommittal when he said, "I was afraid the door slamming would wake you up. Jacynth, this is an old and a very dear friend of mine, Howard Grant. Howard, my wife."

As Jacynth lifted her eyes to the stranger's face her heart contracted with pity. Whatever the X ray might reveal, Howard Grant had a conviction amounting to certain knowledge that the verdict would be unfavorable. His face was drawn and gray, but not for an instant did it occur to Jacynth to feel that he was cowardly. You didn't think that of a man who could put his own feelings into the background as he smiled at his friend's wife and made her so charmingly welcome.

Jacynth took no longer to decide that she liked him tremendously than she had done to discover the reverse about his wife.

And I don't care how little use she has for breakfast, she ought to be here making him feel loved and looked after, she thought angrily. Forgetting the feeling of self-consciousness that the sight of Jonathan had produced, she set herself to entertain Howard.

"Yes, porridge, please," she told the waiter. "And everything else you can think of afterward. You know," she said earnestly to Howard, "I've only just left school and I have a lot of catching up to do. They always starve one at school."

"I know," he agreed sympathetically, amused and delighted at her utter naturalness and simplicity. Surprised a little, too. Somehow or other, Cynthia had given him a totally different idea of the child. "That is, when they don't actually poison you. Remember the way we used to tell the days of the week by what we had to eat, Jonathan?"

"Sunday, roast beef. Monday, cold meat. Tuesday, hash." Jonathan ticked off on his fingers. "Wednesday, stew. Thursday, mince. Friday, fish. Saturday, sausages. And always potatoes—gray ones and wet cabbage or hard peas."

"The peas and the cabbage are still just the same," Jacynth said reflectively. "But you were spoiled! Meat five times a week! We had at least two vegetarian days and no second helpings!"

"You poor child!" Howard said feelingly. "Here, have some toast to keep you going!"

"Thank you, I will," Jacynth said gratefully.

It was a cheerful meal, in spite of the shadow that was hanging over Howard and in spite of the fact that Jonathan was rather quiet. He seemed content only to take part in the conversation when directly addressed, and once or twice Jacynth stole a glance at him. That he was preoccupied was obvious. And his thoughts were not too pleasant. All the same, once, when she caught his eye, he nodded very slightly and smiled encouragingly, which made her redouble her efforts to amuse Howard.

At length he rose.

"I'm afraid I'll have to leave you now," he said regretfully. "And just in case I don't happen to see you again. . . ." He smiled and held out his hand to Jacynth, but instead of shaking hers he lifted it to his lips. "Bless you, Jacynth!" he said softly, and then, with a nod to Jonathan, turned and walked slowly out of the room.

Their eyes followed him and then, involuntarily, they both sighed and looked at one another.

"Thank you," Jonathan said quietly, and Jacynth did not need an explanation.

"Oh, but he's so nice!" she said, and Jonathan smiled.

"So are you," he said lightly, and for a second laid his hand over hers.

Miraculously, all was well in Jacynth's little world.

She went to the door of the hotel with him when he left, chattering nineteen to the dozen. Suddenly she paused.

"Oh, Jonathan, some money!" she reminded him.

He laughed and drew out his wallet.

"You women!" he commented and pulled out some notes. "Twenty pounds in five-pound notes and five in one pounds. How will that do?"

"Lovely!" She took the notes and caressed them with fingers that he suddenly noticed were beautifully slim and well formed. "I've never had any five-pound ones before! They're almost too nice to spend!"

"A very proper way of regarding them!" he said lightly, and was gone.

Jacynth turned and walked slowly into the lounge, still holding the notes in her hand. She only just avoided colliding with Cynthia, who was coming out.

"Good morning!" she said politely.

Cynthia nodded carelessly, and then her eyes fell on the notes.

"Lucky girl!" she said in a tone that one might have used to a small child exhibiting a Christmas present. But there was a sting to come. "Isn't it lovely having a nice rich husband?"

To her annoyance, Jacynth felt the color rising to her cheeks.

"It happens to be my own," she blurted out. "Jonathan is my guardian as well as my husband."

Cynthia raised her eyebrows as if she were faintly amused at Jacynth's annoyance and the frankness into which it had betrayed her.

"How interesting!" she drawled. Too late Jacynth realized how much wiser she would have been just to say, "Yes, isn't it?" to what had really been a piece of calculated rudeness and so have left Cynthia guessing. But she had, in fact, never met anyone like Cynthia before, and that put her at a considerable disadvantage. You never knew quite what she would say next.

But apparently Cynthia had lost interest in the topic.

She yawned expressively.

"Heavens, how I hate this early-morning rising!" she said petulantly. "Though I suppose you are one of those people who don't find it difficult to get up early and enjoy a hearty breakfast?"

"I think it's the best meal of the day," Jacynth said, her self-confidence oddly restored by the fact that she had been right in her guess that Cynthia thought the reverse. "I had a lovely one this morning, with Jonathan and your husband. Porridge and bacon and eggs and honey and toast—lovely!"

"How amazing!" Cynthia said in a tone that quite clearly implied "How revolting and childish!"

It was on the tip of Jacynth's tongue to make a sharp retort, and then the memory of Howard's weary, patient face rose before her mind's eye and she bit it back. For Cynthia's feelings she did not care a rap, but Howard needed their friendship, Jonathan's and hers. And if the price of achieving it was being civil to his wife, then it had to be paid, however difficult it might be.

"I expect I am a bit of a pig," she admitted cheerfully. "So it's lucky for me I'm too young to have to worry about my figure."

To her surprise, Cynthia flushed angrily and turned sharply on her heel.

Now what on earth. . . ? Jacynth wondered at the woman's reaction and suddenly covered her mouth with her fingers. *Golly, I bet she thought I was insinuating that she did have to worry! I would go and say a thing like that when all the time I meant to be polite!* Jacynth wondered if it would be any good to explain. No, it would only make things worse and, in any case, she'd never believe her.

Deciding ruefully that there was nothing she could do to rectify matters, she went upstairs to dress for going out.

The shopping was a great success. Methodically Jacynth inspected all the likely shops, decided which one she thought looked nicest and took the assistant completely into her confidence.

"So you see," she finished, "I want to look a bit more grown-up, but not as if I'm a little girl trying to look grown-up. That sounds a bit complicated." She smiled disarmingly and won the salesgirl's heart completely.

As a result, she emerged from the shop flushed and triumphant, carrying a box that contained an attractive afternoon dress of a tawny red shade, and a long dress in deep turquoise.

"That's all the money I have," she said regretfully.

"Oh, well," the girl said cheerfully, "I expect you can get some more out of your husband, can't you?"

Jacynth felt the smile fade from her lips. First Cynthia, now this girl. Why did they both assume that she had married Jonathan for what she could get out of him? And yet, if anybody had asked her just why she had married him, what would she have said?

She walked back to the hotel rather pensively and found that Jonathan had looked in for a moment and, finding that she was out, had left a note for her.

"Afraid I can't get back for lunch so don't wait for me. I ought to be through by about half past four. If you can be ready by then we shall be home in time for dinner.

Love,
Jonathan."

She read it through a second time up in her room, and a little smile touched the corners of her mouth. This was the first letter that she had ever had from Jonathan, and though it could hardly be called a love letter, it was oddly satisfying. She folded it up again carefully and put it into an inner recess of her handbag. Then she considered what she should do. She could either have lunch in the hotel or she could have it out somewhere else. Finally she decided on the latter course because it would mean it was far less likely that she would meet the Grants. And without Jonathan there, and with the possibility that Howard had bad news, she did not feel that she could cope with the situation. It would be all right if Howard were on his own, but to see them together, to see Cynthia's complete indifference to his need for comfort, would be intolerable.

So she found a cheerful restaurant not very far away

and was easily back and waiting for Jonathan with her cases packed by the time he arrived.

"All ready?" he asked, and then, as his eyes fell on the neatly piled luggage, "Good girl! You're a model for your sex. Far too many women simply don't know what it means to be punctual. Come on, let's get going. I don't mind telling you I'm simply itching to get home—it's been the best part of two months since I went to New York, you know!" He slipped an arm through hers and was just remarking, "I'll send the porter up," when another thought occurred to him. "Have you seen anything of the Grants?" he asked.

"No, I had lunch out," Jacynth said guiltily. "I suppose I shouldn't have gone—"

"Silly infant, no reason at all why you shouldn't. I'll call the desk and ask if they can run them to earth."

A few minutes later he put down the telephone receiver, and Jacynth saw the anxiety on his face.

"They checked out just before lunch."

Jacynth looked at him in consternation.

"Does that mean. . . ?" she asked falteringly.

He shrugged his shoulders.

"I don't know. What do you think?"

"I think if I were him and . . . and it was tuberculosis I'd want to . . . hide at first. You'd have to get used to the idea before you could bear sympathy."

He looked at her without speaking for a moment. Then he said softly, "You've been given understanding beyond your years, my dear! Well, there's nothing that we can do. At least, not immediately. But I shall write to Howard. I took care to get his address. We've rather drifted apart since his marriage. But now. . . ." He shook his head and sighed, and Jacynth realized that, in spite of his pleasure at meeting Cynthia again, all his thoughts now were for his male friend.

"Come!" he said shortly.

"I'm afraid it means the tunnel again," he said regretfully when they were in the car, but Jacynth assured him that, this time, it wouldn't be so bad. All the same, she did not enjoy it, and she was thankful when they were out into the open again.

She enjoyed every moment of the drive, particularly as for a large part of it they were within sight of the sea.

"Of course, I've been to the seaside on holidays," she confided to Jonathan. "But I've never lived with it. Oh, Jonathan, I am glad you don't live in a town! I know people say that there's more life in a town, but I don't think so. At least, it isn't the sort of life that I want to live!"

"What sort of life do you want to live?" Jonathan asked. He sounded interested, but he did not take his eyes from the road until he realized that Jacynth was slow in answering him. It surprised him, for he had begun to expect a certain impulsiveness about her conversation, and now she was obviously thinking hard before she replied.

"I don't quite know," she said slowly. "I think perhaps I have to find out just what I want. But I do know one thing. . . ."

"Yes?" he said encouragingly.

"I don't want always to know what's going to happen. I want the feeling that, just around the corner, anything might be waiting."

"Good or bad?" he asked, and she shrugged.

"Good *and* bad. You can't have one without the other,
And nothing would be perfect if you had nothing less with
which to compare it. Oh, look, Jonathan!"

He had made the trip hundreds of times before, but
now, seeing it through her eyes, it all seemed fresh and
new.

"I have a couple of boats in the bay," he told her
eagerly. "Sail, of course. One is just a little dinghy that I
can manage on my own. The other takes three of us to
handle it. Do you know anything about sailing?"

"Not a thing," Jacynth said regretfully. "But I'd love
to. Will you teach me?"

He smiled down at her, and Jacynth suddenly felt her
heart begin to race.

"Yes, I'll teach you—everything that you want to
learn!"

It was not a very pretty house—and to Jacynth her first
glimpse of it was disappointing. But it was solid, and what
it lacked in outward appearance it made up for in the
comfort inside and the glorious view that most of the
windows afforded.

Crellie House was built on a little bluff that ran out
into the sea, so that one had almost the sense of being on
a small island.

Jacynth ran from one window to the other.

"Oh, Jonathan, Jonathan!" she said excitedly. "Why
didn't you tell me it was like this?"

"I wanted you to fall in love with it without any
boosting from me," he said, obviously pleased at her
delight. "You really like it?"

"I think it's the most wonderful place in the world,"

she said unhesitatingly. "I don't see how anybody could be anything but happy here!"

He did not reply for a moment, and when he did speak it was simply to say, "I'll slip down and tell Mrs. Evans to serve dinner in twenty minutes. Will that do?"

"Lovely," Jacynth said, making up her mind on the instant that she would put on the tawny red dress.

Over the pleasant little dinner in a room made cheerful with a log fire Jacynth suddenly said, "I say, Jonathan, need you go to work for a day or two? I want you to show me things."

He looked at her thoughtfully for a moment. The red dress was a good choice, he thought. It seemed to bring a brighter color to her cheeks and lips and to enhance the darkness of her hair and eyes.

"I see no reason at all why I shouldn't stay," he said deliberately.

He took her sailing the very next day. Quarters were somewhat cramped in the little dinghy, but she soon learned to duck at the right moment and to shift her weight when he told her to.

It was a perfect day with just enough wind to send them cutting along through the blue green water as if, Jacynth said delightedly, they were a bird that was just going to take off.

"It's the next best thing to flying!" she said ecstatically. "Not flying in a plane—that must be too noisy to be really enjoyable. But flying with one's own wings. Jonathan, have you ever been out in a storm—a bad one?"

"Bad enough," he said grimly. "I didn't think I'd make

harbor. It was my own fault, too. The day was bright and I didn't bother keeping an eye on it. The first thing I knew I'd shipped more water than I could conveniently dispose of, and there was every prospect of more to come. And there was a deuce of a wind—for a while I wasn't sure whether the sail was going to be torn off or whether I'd turn turtle."

"But you didn't!" she said exultantly. "You made it?"

"Yes," he said slowly, looking at her rather intently. "I made it."

She sat forward, her chin propped up on her clenched fist.

"I'd have loved that!" she said seriously. "I wish I'd been with you!"

"You would most likely have been scared stiff," he said lightly, but she shook her head vigorously.

"Because it was dangerous?" she asked. "No, I don't think so. I think I like things to be dangerous and to take a chance on them. That night you came for me at the school, I'd left a book on the other side of the river and they dared me to go and get it—and I did, you know. I always take a dare!"

It seemed to Jonathan that a warning bell was ringing in his head.

Tim Furnival, a gambler if ever there was one.

Jacynth, his daughter.

The same blood. The same characteristics?

He could not guess. But suddenly he wondered if Christina Allardyce had known. Whether there had been, not one, but two reasons why she had wanted him to marry Jacynth.

To protect her from her father and . . . to protect her from herself.

CHAPTER FOUR

Three days later Jonathan reluctantly decided that his brief holiday must end. They had been halcyon days spent mostly in the little dinghy. Immediately after breakfast they would go down to the anchorage with a generous pile of sandwiches provided by Mrs. Evans, a bottle of beer for Jonathan and one of lemonade for Jacynth.

There always seemed to be someone lounging about who would push them out, and then Jacynth would give a little crow of delight. She adored that silent gliding movement, and she was, as Jonathan had already realized, completely fearless. Realizing that, he took the safest course and began at once to teach her to handle the boat. She took to it instinctively, and Jonathan, in spite of the apprehensions that her contempt of danger had already roused in him, could not help but be proud of his pupil. All the same, he issued a stern edict.

"You're doing very well," he told her. "But all the same, you're not to go out in her alone until I say you can. Understand?"

"Oh, Jonathan!" she pouted reproachfully.

"In that outfit"—she was wearing blue jeans and an open-necked scarlet shirt—"you look about fourteen," he commented. "But don't you behave that way. Either you give me your word that you won't go out on your own, or I treat you like a child and have the sail and the oars locked up. Which is it to be?"

"I promise," she said reluctantly, but not, he was glad to see, sulkily. "All the same, what am I to do, Jonathan?"

"Do?" he echoed. "Surely there's plenty to do?"

Jacynth moved her slim shoulders restlessly.

"Yes, I expect there is," she agreed. "Only I don't know what it is. You see, at school they arrange almost every moment of the day for you. I suppose it does keep one out of mischief. But it also means that when you have time on your hands you just don't know what to do with it."

"Yes, I suppose so," he admitted. "But there were holidays. What did you do with yourself then?"

"Well, Gran was a darling, but naturally, she wasn't terrifically modern in her outlook," Jacynth said so seriously that the words were robbed of any air of unpleasant patronage. "She thought that even on holidays I ought to have a set task every day— needlework or housework or cooking. She said that it was the proper training for a girl in her day, and she didn't see that things were different now, and that if more girls knew how to run their homes there would be fewer divorces."

"Something in that," Jonathan commented. "What else did you do?"

"Oh," she said vaguely, "we were invited out to afternoon teas and sometimes we went to concerts. And in the evening we played a game of some sort or else I played the piano to Gran."

"Do you like that—the piano, I mean?" he asked.

"I love music," she said. "But I get impatient with myself because I'm just not clever enough to do it justice. And I don't think I ever shall be. But I make an awfully good audience. And that's something, isn't it?"

"It is indeed," he agreed, and then he added hesitatingly, "Did you never go about with people of your own age?"

"Hardly ever. You see, most of Gran's friends were her own age, and so their children had grown up and often gone away. You do miss rather a lot when you don't have parents, you know. Because, if you have, their friends' children are likely to be one's own age, and that must be fun, don't you think?"

There was an unconsciously wistful note in her voice, and Jonathan remembered his own younger days, when, with a lively, happy pack of youngsters who all lived nearby, he had surely had the most delightful childhood that anyone could have had. And regretfully he knew that nothing could make up for that loss now. One changed so, and what seemed utterly desirable at one age failed entirely to charm one at a later one. Jacynth would find that, too. She would never be able to recapture the charm that those past days should have held. After a little silence Jacynth said wistfully, "So would you like me to help Mrs. Evans, or what?"

That seemed to amuse him. He threw back his head and laughed so that the brown skin of his throat stood out, she thought, like a cameo against the white of the little lug sail, only, of course, the colors were reversed.

"Heavens, my dear, Mrs. Evans has kept house for me for years! She has her own way of doing things, and only the meekest and mildest of the village girls can put up with her ways. You could hardly work under her orders, could you? And I very much wonder if she would work under yours or anyone else's!"

Jacynth thought that that was very probable, but it did not stop her from thinking that, none the less, a little supervision might do even Mrs. Evans good. Jonathan probably did not notice the little trifles that made all the difference between a house that is well run and a house

that is not, but she had. Even in the short time that she
had lived at Crellie House she had realized that the rooms
were turned out without any regard to the convenience of
the master or mistress of the house, and several quite
reasonable little requests she had made had received no
attention. She wondered whether she ought to point that
out to Jonathan, but decided that it was better not to.
After all, what would happen if she did? Either he would
shrug his shoulders and say it wasn't worth bothering
about—Gran always said that a man would put up with
anything rather than have his peace disturbed—or he
would say that something must be done about it. And he
might speak to Mrs. Evans himself. That would never do,
because Mrs. Evans would be sure to resent a new wife
who made complaints.

Jonathan interrupted her thoughts.

"Aren't there things that you've always longed to do
and never had time or never been able to do?"

Jacynth looked away, her eyes brooding over the blue,
gently ruffled water.

"Yes," she said slowly, "yes. . . ."

There had always been one dream. To be a part of a
family. When she was very little she had pretended that
brothers and sisters shared the big, lonely nursery. But
that had not been sufficient when she grew up. Just once
or twice Gran had let her stay with friends she had made
at school. And she had seen what the real thing meant.
Squabbles, naturally, but a lot of fun and a completeness
that she had never known existed. With a family you
could do things, plan things, and yet be completely
independent of outsiders. And they seemed to have a sort
of secret language of their own: they would understand

each other sometimes without speaking, simply because they were the family and looked at things from the same point of view. So she had made up her mind then and there that as soon as she could she would get married and have babies. The girl of a few days ago had told Jonathan that. The girl of today found that she was tongue-tied and silent.

"Well?" he asked.

She turned and smiled at him.

"I'll tell you something I would like to do," she said lightly. "I'd just like to hunt through the attics and see what there is in all those trunks and cases. May I?"

He laughed at the absurdity of it.

"You won't find any hidden treasure there, I'm afraid," he said. "Or are you still worried that there might be the first Mrs. Rochester-Branksome up there?"

A faint shadow fell across her face, or so it seemed to him. And yet what could there have been in what he had said to put it there?

She shook her head without answering his question.

"But may I?" she persisted.

He shrugged his shoulders a little impatiently.

"Yes, of course, if you want to," he said shortly. What a whimsical, inquisitive child she was.

And yet a child who had had no proper childhood. An odd mixture.

The next morning it was on the tip of Jacynth's tongue to ask Jonathan if she couldn't go with him, but it was obviously a silly thing to suggest. After all, what was there for her to do during the long hours that he was at his office? She could not go shopping all the time. And besides, even if she went with him today, the same situation would have to be faced again tomorrow. So one might as well take the plunge. She waved Jonathan off at the gate and then came slowly back. She glanced at the clock. It was still only half past eight. Jonathan had made an early start as, so he told her, he always did, and the day stretched interminably before her.

She went into the rather heavily furnished drawing room, lifted the lid of the piano, and struck a few tentative chords. They echoed forlornly in the empty room and, like so many pianos near the sea, it had a rather tinny sound. With a sigh, she closed it again and went on a tour of inspection around the room. Someone in Jonathan's family must have traveled abroad quite a lot, she thought. There were so many obviously foreign little trophies scattered about. Rather sweet, some of them, she thought. A two-inch-long rabbit made of clear crystal stood on a small ebony base with little depressions to match its feet. She picked up the little thing and rubbed its smooth coldness against her cheek. And that was the moment that Mrs. Evans chose to knock and come in.

Hastily, Jacynth put the little rabbit down, but not before Mrs. Evans had seen her playing with it.

"She must think I'm quite silly," Jacynth thought uncomfortably. "Yes, Mrs. Evans?" she asked aloud.

"I was just wanting to know what your plans are for the day, madam," Mrs. Evans said stiffly. She was a tall, heavyset woman and she made Jacynth feel absurdly insignificant.

"Plans?" Jacynth asked uncomprehendingly.

"Will you be lunching in?" Mrs. Evans elaborated. "And will you be entertaining at all?"

She doesn't like me, Jacynth thought unhappily. *She's waiting until Jonathan is out of the way. I mustn't let her see I'm next door to afraid of her.*

"Yes, I shall be lunching in," she said firmly. "And as to entertaining, I think not, unless Mr. Branksome telephones to say that he's bringing anyone here."

She had not the least expectation that he would, but it put the responsibility comfortably onto Jonathan's shoulders.

"It's very inconvenient, not knowing until the last moment," Mrs. Evans grumbled.

"Yes?" Jacynth said quietly. "Then, if Mr. Branksome does call to say he's bringing anyone, I'd better say that it's not convenient to you?"

"Oh, I didn't mean that, madam," Mrs. Evans was obviously taken aback. "I'm sure I—" Fortunately, the doorbell rang, and with a muttered apology she retreated.

Well, that didn't do any good, Jacynth thought regretfully. *It isn't fair! If I'd just taken it sitting down she'd have despised me, and yet, because I scored the last point, she's going to bear malice!* She ran a hand through her curls and shook her head, wondering if she ought to tell Jonathan when he came home.

After lunch she went down to the anchorage and gazed wistfully at the dinghy bobbing at her mooring. If only Jonathan had not made her promise—

"Nice little craft, isn't she?" a man's voice said behind her, and she turned. He was not one of the men that she had seen about there before, but, in spite of being a stranger, Jacynth answered him unhesitatingly.

"Yes, she is, isn't she?" she agreed. "I was just wishing my . . . Jonathan hadn't told me not to go out in her alone."

"And I," he said deliberately, "was just wondering if I could find out to whom she belonged and borrow her for an hour or so."

They stared at one another like conspirators, and then the two pairs of eyes, both so dark, glinted mischievously.

"Let's!" Jacynth said; then her conscience suddenly got the better of her. "I say, you do know how, don't you?"

He laughed, and something about his laugh made Jacynth sure it was something he didn't often do.

"Four generations of us in the navy, lass," he told her. "You sort of pick things up, you know!"

None the less, Jacynth kept an anxious eye on him for the first ten minutes. Then she relaxed with a little sigh. Even to the eyes of a beginner such as she was herself, it was perfectly evident that her new friend knew just what he was doing. He saw her relax, and he grinned disarmingly at her.

"I told you it would be all right," he reminded her. "Big brother Jonathan himself couldn't do better, now could he?"

"He's not—" she began, and stopped. For some reason or other she did not want, at that moment, to tell him that she was married, and yet instantly her conscience pricked her for not doing so. But evidently he had not heard what she had said, for he began to speak again.

"What's your name?" he asked idly.

"Jacynth." She added slowly, "Jacynth Branksome." It was the first time that she had said it, and it sounded strange and unfamiliar.

"Quite nice," he said. "Though rather a mouthful for a snippet like you! Mine's Mick Lavery. I'm down here for a month. Doctor's orders."

"Oh, have you been ill?" she asked sympathetically.

"In a way," he said vaguely, cursing himself for having mentioned the doctor at all. After all, what right had he to worry this happy kid with his troubles. Ill? Yes, very ill. Sick in mind and sick at heart.

The fourth generation of his family to join the navy, he had found it no hardship to follow in their footsteps; the sea had been in his blood as it had been in theirs. And then, after four years, the blow fell. He succumbed to a severe attack of glandular fever, and a few months later was passed unfit and invalided out of the navy.

So here he was, with the knowledge that the one career he was suited for was denied him. Side by side with that knowledge was the realization that he had no heart for the future that a kindly uncle had offered him in his firm of textile manufacturers.

A failure all around. That was Mick Lavery, he thought bitterly. It was what he had been thinking when he had been staring out at the blue sea and the craggy headland. And then, suddenly, his eye had been caught by the sight of the little *Firefly* bobbing at her anchor, and an almost overwhelming longing to get into her and get clear of all humanity—good, bad, and indifferent. And here, by great good luck, he was. Not quite alone, it was true. But you could hardly count a kid like this. Heaven knew, of course, what she'd grow into, but at the present those big eyes of hers were full of candor and innocence. She had a fresh, bubbling laugh, too, that made him think of a bubbling, chuckling little mountain stream sparkling in the sunshine.

Jacynth, stealing surreptitious glances at him, wondered what had been wrong with him. She could see the brooding shadow in his eyes, and, just as Howard had made an appeal to a quality in her that she would probably have laughed to hear described as maternal, so did this boy. Of course, he wasn't really a boy, she admitted quickly. But something about him made her feel years older than he was, although, in fact, he must be some five or six years her senior.

He saw that she was looking at him and they smiled involuntarily at one another.

Jacynth made a comprehensive little gesture of the hands.

"It's good, isn't it?" she said with a lilt in her voice that found an answering, throbbing note in him.

"Yes," he agreed. "If only one could go on like this forever. . . ."

"Oh no," she said gravely. "That would spoil it!"

"Oh?" he said with equal seriousness. "Why?"

She looked at him wonderingly. How funny that he didn't know that!

"Because, if you can do something all the time, if all your wishes are fulfilled, then there's nothing to look forward to, and no time to turn things over in your mind and realize how lovely they were and will be again."

"So you think all pleasure is either a matter of anticipation or retrospect?" he asked. "Jam yesterday, jam tomorrow, but never jam today? Isn't that rather cynical?"

"Oh no!" she said, and he realized that she was quite genuinely shocked. "But pleasure, real pleasure, has to be more than just physical. You have to feel it with your inside you. And you can't always do that at the time because you—well, I, anyway, just gobble when things are actually happening. And then, afterward, I think them over again like a cow chewing her cud," she added reflectively.

Mick shouted with laughter.

"Oh, you priceless infant!" he said delightedly. "You're as good as a tonic!"

Jacynth felt rather perplexed.

"Have I said anything funny?" she asked with a little assumption of dignity that pulled him up with a jerk.

"It was the contrast between the real depths of your philosophy and your final simile," he explained apologetically.

"I know. That's what they say at school," she sighed. "Last term, in an essay, I wrote that—no, perhaps I'd better not tell you," she finished hurriedly. "But it was quite awful!" she sighed. "The worst of it is, I can see that now. But at the time, it seemed just right!"

"Never mind," he said consolingly. "It's something that you *can* see it now. You're growing up at a terrific rate!"

"But I am grown up," Jacynth protested. "I'm married!"

There, it was out and now she realized why it was that she had hesitated before. He simply didn't believe it! He gave a little derisive snort and said, "Tell that to the marines!"

"But I am, truly," she insisted, holding out her left hand with its slender circlet.

He stared at it unbelievingly for a moment and then lifted his eyes to her face.

"Good lord!" he said softly. "Good lord!" And then, as if he could not help himself, he added, "And are you very much in love?"

He saw the delicate color rise to her soft cheeks and an expression come into her eyes that made him feel as if he had blundered into some holy of holies. Impulsively he leaned forward and touched her hand.

"You sweet kid!" he said softly.

Startled, she looked at him quickly. But what she saw in his face evidently reassured her, for she smiled tremulously.

But she was rather quiet for the rest of the trip, and when they came ashore again he said, with something of an air of finality in his tone, "That was marvelous. Thanks for letting me come!"

Jacynth took his outstretched hand, but she looked a little troubled.

"But if you enjoyed it, you'll come again, won't you?" she asked.

For a moment he hesitated. It had startled him quite a bit to hear that she was married, and yet at the same time it had roused something tender and protective in him. What worried him was whether, if their friendship continued, that something might develop into anything that might harm Jacynth. It would be very easy to fall in love with her. Then he made up his mind. All right, suppose he did? Why should it hurt her? He'd take darn good care she never knew it and, anyhow, there was little chance that she had room in her thoughts for any other man than her husband. That adorable blush had told him that.

"I'd love to come," he said frankly, and she smiled happily up at him.

She ran up the slope to the house, but actually there was plenty of time. Jonathan was not due for another hour or so, and she filled it in by having a bath, in the middle of which she suddenly realized that now, for the first time in her life, she could have baths more or less any time she liked instead of having to fit in with other people's arrangements. She tipped in an extra handful of bath salts, and as she splashed she sang happily at the top of her voice.

She was still singing when she came out of the bathroom in her rather skimpy school dressing gown and almost crashed into Jonathan who had just reached the top of the stairs.

"Hello!" he greeted her. "You sound on top of the world, young woman!"

"I am!" she said happily, and then, suddenly conscious of her appearance, she added, "I'm sorry I look like such a ticket, but I must have spent more time in the bath than I meant to."

"Well, I'm a bit early, anyhow," he said indulgently. "I have a present for you!"

"Have you?" she said eagerly. "But it isn't my birthday."

He laughed.

"Haven't I heard of unbirthday presents somewhere?" he suggested. "Anyway, here it is." He put his hand into his pocket and pulled out a small leather case from which he took a ring.

"Give me your hand," he said.

Obediently she held out her slim hand with its trim little pink nails, and he slipped the ring into position.

"There!" he said triumphantly. "Rather belated, but I hope none the less acceptable!"

"Oh, Jonathan!" she breathed. "It's lovely! Sapphire and diamonds! But you've given me so much! First the pearls and now this! Jonathan—" she looked up a little wistfully at him "—do you like giving me things?"

He took her slim hand in his and held it on his open palm.

"I suppose I do," he admitted. "Particularly when my

288

gift is enhanced by being worn on a very lovely hand!" He bent and kissed it very gently.

Jacynth's breath quickened.

"I wish there was something I could give you," she said rather breathlessly.

But apparently Jonathan did not hear. His eyes were on a letter lying on the table.

"When did this come?" he asked, slitting it open.

"Oh, I'm sorry," she said quickly. "I brought it up without thinking. I suppose because I always used to hurry Gran's letters up to her as soon as they came—"

But Jonathan was not listening. He was already deep in his letter, and from his expression it was not very pleasant reading. Once she saw him wince and she waited in silent anxiety.

At last he finished it. For a moment he stood irresolute. Then he handed it to her.

"It's from Howard," he said. "You'd better read it."

It was very brief—a brevity that told under what a strain the writer had been.

"It isn't quite as bad as I had feared," Howard wrote. "But bad enough. The doctor tells me that there's just a spot of trouble—something that he believes can be cured, but which would become worse if neglected. His prescription is a long sea trip or else to spend as much time as possible out at sea. Well, you know how I'm placed. These days, I have to work for my living and that's probably a damn good thing for me. But I haven't been working long enough for the firm to give me six months' leave with pay—and even if they did, it wouldn't run to any long sea trips. So, old man, I'm going to cadge off you. Do you have a cottage or a shack nearby where we could put up, and will you let me have the run of your boats? Don't think I don't know what a devil of a lot I'm asking—particularly as you're still practically on your honeymoon—but, Jonathan, it's important to me—and there's Cynthia. . . ."

Jacynth folded up the letter with fingers that shook a little. Everybody seemed to be in trouble these days.

"Well?" Jonathan demanded.

"You can't let him down, Jonathan," she whispered. She saw from the relief in his eyes that she had said the right thing.

"Bless you," he said gratefully. "But you do realize they'll have to live here? There just isn't a cottage or anything else available."

"They?" Jacynth said blankly. "You mean Cynthia will have to come as well?"

"Of course," he said rather shortly. "What other arrangements could we make?"

He seemed about to add something else, but apparently changed his mind.

"Well?" he asked again.

Jacynth swallowed a lump in her throat. She had felt so happy and so secure and now, quite suddenly, all that had gone. She was afraid and she would have given anything to be able to tell Jonathan that. But how could she?

He would want to know why and that would mean confessing that she loved him.

And it was so obviously a love for which he had no use.

CHAPTER FIVE

Within a few days everything was arranged. Howard would need a week or so to get his affairs settled and then he and Cynthia would come to Crellie House.

When Jonathan told Jacynth during breakfast that they were definitely coming, she listened gravely, and when he had finished she said diffidently, "Will you tell Mrs. Evans or shall I?"

"Oh, I will," he said carelessly. "She'll be pleased."

"Will she?" Jacynth said doubtfully. It hardly seemed likely to her that Mrs. Evans would welcome the additional work that two guests would make. "Why?"

"Oh, she used to know Cynthia in the old days," he said casually. "In fact, Cynthia was by way of being a favorite of hers. She had a way of getting around her that was the envy of all the rest of us."

"I see," Jacynth said fidgeting restlessly with her teaspoon. "Does she . . . does Cynthia like sailing? Will she go out with Howard a lot?" She had had that question on the tip of her tongue ever since the question of the Grants' coming was first discussed between them. It was, she realized, going to be very difficult to continue her friendship with Mick Lavery when they came, and she wished with all her heart that she had told Jonathan about it immediately after her first meeting with him. Just why she had not she would have found it difficult to explain. It wasn't, she knew, because there was anything wrong about it or that she was ashamed of the friendship. And yet it was just that very fact that made it all so difficult.

She had felt an instant, warm affection for Mick, and yet it was a totally different feeling from what she felt for Jonathan. It didn't cause her any tearing, aching heartburn, for one thing. It was placid and happy and very comfortable.

A psychologist could have told her that one was the love of a woman for a man; the other, the complete passionless love of a young girl for a good friend. Only a girl of Jacynth's age, and possibly only one of her peculiar upbringing, could have experienced the two emotions simultaneously. And only such a girl would have been aware of the gossamer delicacy and innocence of her feeling for Mick and combined with it a fear lest any breath of cynicism should tarnish its freshness.

"Cynthia? Sail? My dear girl, I very much doubt if we'll be able to persuade her to come out at all!" he said, as if Cynthia's attitude was one that aroused a feeling of amused toleration in him. "As a matter of fact, I was rather relying on you to go with him while I'm away. It would do him good to have company, and it will mean that you can get out when you otherwise couldn't."

"Yes," she said hesitatingly, rolling a crumb of bread into a ball between her finger and thumb. Now was the time to tell him—tell him that Howard wasn't the only person who needed the curative pleasure of sea and wind. He was in a mood to have understood; sympathy with Howard would have helped him to understand her sympathy for Mick.

But he glanced down at his watch, gave an exclamation, and rose to his feet.

"I must get a move on!" he said briskly. And then, as he passed her and saw what she was doing with her bread,

292

he said, "You are a messy infant, aren't you?" he said, ruffling her curls. And the moment was past.

She heard him call to Mrs. Evans, heard her exclamation—yes, she certainly did sound pleased—and with a sigh, went out to join them. Not, of course, that it really mattered whether she was there or not. The house had been run for years without her help, and actually it was natural enough that Jonathan should not feel it necessary to alter things. Yet if she had had a real job of her own, felt that she was necessary to Jonathan, if only for the creature comforts. . . .

She saw him off in rather a sober frame of mind and retraced her steps to the dining room. Mrs. Evans was already clearing off the breakfast things and she was very evidently in a good temper.

"It will be just like old times having Miss Cynthia here again," she volunteered. "Always in and out of the house, she used to be—not this one, of course. But the old house, Mr. Jonathan's parents' home. I was first housemaid then. Until old Mrs. Briggs died. Then I was housekeeper in her place and I stayed there until the old home was broken up. Then I came to look after Mr. Jonathan."

"I see," Jacynth said thoughtfully. It suddenly occurred to her that, except for the Grants, Mrs. Evans was probably the only person she was likely to meet who would be able to tell her what Jonathan was like in those days. Like every other woman in love she wanted to know all about him in the days before she knew him. But somehow or other she could not frame the question, and evidently Mrs. Evans took exception to her silence. She had, as Jacynth had guessed, all the strong emotions of the Welsh: her likes and dislikes were so vigorous as to warrant the stronger terms of loves and hatreds and, from the moment she had heard that Jonathan was bringing home a bride acquired in that unexpected, underhand way, she had resented the newcomer. Jacynth's extreme youth had been the last straw.

"Of course, in those days we all thought they would get married—Miss Cynthia and Mr. Jonathan," she said, her beady eyes bright with malice. "Always together they were, and so devoted! It came as a great surprise to everybody when she married this gentleman. I shall be interested to see him; he must be a fine gentleman for her to prefer him to Mr. Jonathan. And a lucky one, too. I don't suppose for a moment that Mr. Jonathan would do so much for him as he is, but for Miss Cynthia's sake!"

"Mr. Grant is very nice indeed," Jacynth said quietly. "He's also a very old friend of Mr. Jonathan's. They were at school together."

Mrs. Evans scowled. She knew both facts perfectly well, but she had not known that Jacynth did, and in her twisted, roundabout way she debited another black mark against her because of it.

Jacynth went slowly upstairs. She had somehow or other formed the habit of staying in the house during the morning, less because there was anything that she had to do than because rather forlornly she tried to pretend that there was. This morning she decided that she would pay her deferred visit to the attics. There were two of them, one looking toward the sea, the other, smaller and darker, facing inland. But that seemed more exciting. The bigger room was mainly full of discarded furniture, both too old and too new to be of much interest, being of that vague, indeterminate period usually called Victorian, but actually extending into the newer century. Inspection having proved that none of the drawers or cupboards contained anything, she went to the smaller room, which was full of boxes and trunks and a few mysterious bundles.

Haphazardly she opened one box and laughed. Of all things, it was full of rubber overshoes in the last stages of ruin and two or three decorator's paint brushes stiff with paint. If they were all going to be like that, it wasn't going to be much fun.

But the next one proved more interesting. It was full of letters, and after a moment's hesitation Jacynth picked one up. She looked at the date, and somehow or other the fact that it was written nearly 100 years ago seemed to make it almost as impersonal as a history book and to rob her reading of it of any suggestion of eavesdropping.

It was a charming little bread-and-butter letter from a girl who signed herself, "Your dutiful granddaughter, Chloe."

She read it through, smiled at the excitement a croquet party had evidently caused and scented a possible romance in an artless reference to the curate. She wondered if anything had come of that. Probably not. Curates were notoriously short of money, and in those days marriages were arranged. She laid the letter down hurriedly. So they were today, sometimes, too. One listened to older people saying that they knew best. Did they, always?

She soon grew tired of the letters. Most of them were prosy and contained countless allusions to people she had never heard of. She shut the lid of the box and went on to the next. Clothes in that. But not very exciting ones. The clothes of an elderly lady who had been reluctant to part with a single stitch, no matter how worn.

Some crocheted bedspreads and heavily embroidered cushion covers—more praiseworthy for the patience that the maker had shown than for the artistic result achieved. Another contained an odd collection of brass candlesticks—some of them quite interesting, she thought—rather ugly vases, and two very large fruit bowls.

As she closed the last lid she almost decided that she would leave it at that. Then, standing by itself, she saw a wooden box with the name "Jonathan E. Branksome" painted on it in big black letters. She smiled. Obviously Jonathan's tuck-box. She must ask him one day what the "E" stood for. She opened it and looked with interest at the contents. Old exercise books. Old textbooks. The remains of a chemistry set and two or three school caps. She sat down on the floor and lifted the top layer out, opening an exercise book at random. It was a very youthful attempt, judging by the writing, and Jacynth smiled again. Inky scribble, smudgy fingerprints. "Very bad," was the red-penciled comment at the end. Absurdly, Jacynth's heart felt suddenly lighter. The thought of Jonathan as a grubby, careless little boy was oddly endearing . . . and still more oddly reassuring. She laid the book down and her hand fell on a small bundle of letters. Perhaps because the other letters had been so impersonal, she did not realize that to look at these was a very different matter. She spread the first one out and caught her breath.

"I must see you, darling," it said imperatively. "It's been so dull while you've been away. I'll be at our own special tree at eight o'clock. Your Cynthia."

She laid it down, her hand shaking. Now, of course, she knew that she ought not to read any more. They were private letters and she had no right; but she had to know. Cynthia, very evidently, had believed herself in love with Jonathan. But what about Jonathan? Had he cared too? Actually, there was little in the notes. Mostly they were to make appointments or to apologize for not having kept an appointment—there seemed to be an increasing number of these. And then a torn sheet in a different handwriting—Jonathan's. Short, terse sentences, almost incoherent some of them. He had just heard that she was engaged to Howard. He couldn't believe it. Good old Howard, the best of fellows. "But," he said imploringly, "it's always been you and me. Tell me it's a mistake—just idle gossip, and that you're going to wait for me. I shall be a success, Cynthia; how could I help it when you're the prize—"

She had read enough! Hastily she thrust them back, well down to the side, so that, if he went to the box, Jonathan would not realize that she had seen them.

So it was true. Jonathan had been in love with Cynthia. Probably, as Mrs. Evans had hinted, he still was.

"Then why, why did he marry me?" she moaned, her head down on the dusty top of the box. "He didn't have to. Even Gran couldn't have made him! He said he had a reason, but whatever it was he ought not to have married anyone else if he still loved her! And now she's coming here. . . ." Suddenly an idea occurred to her and she sat up. Jonathan was poor and Howard was rich. So she married Howard. Now he was poor and Jonathan was rich! What was Cynthia going to do about the situation?

Quickly she jumped to her feet and ran downstairs as if something evil haunted the attics; to her it seemed as if it did.

She was vaguely conscious of Mrs. Evan's voice pursuing her, but she did not stop to listen. She must get out of the house. . . .

She almost ran down to the little anchorage. Mick was there, comfortably at ease in the sun and talking spasmodically to another idler—a stranger, Jacynth realized.

As soon as he saw her, Mick jumped to his feet.

"Hello!" he began, and then in an altered voice, he said, "Here, what's the matter? Aren't you well?"

She caught his arm with hands that gripped almost painfully.

"Mick, take me out in the boat," she begged imperatively. "I've go to go out."

He said nothing, realizing that, whatever was the matter, Jacynth was in no condition to tell him. He sketched a casual salute to the man to whom he had been talking and drew the *Firefly* alongside.

"Hop in," he said.

A few seconds and they were under way, but still Jacynth made no attempt to tell him what was the matter, and his rather heavy brows met in a frown. If someone had been unkind to her—that husband she seemed half-afraid of. . . . It was a good half hour before she gave a little sigh and seemed to relax. He leaned forward and touched her hand.

"Tell?" he invited.

Her fingers twisted nervously.

"I expect I'm just being silly—" she began, and

stopped. More than anything else in the world she longed to take someone sympathetic into her confidence and share the burden of her problem. But something stopped her. She wasn't just a child now who could run to a grownup if she tumbled down and hurt herself. She was a married woman who owed a loyalty to her husband, and besides, her own pride wouldn't let her admit that she was hurt. She sighed. So this was what growing up meant! And one had always imagined that it meant perfect freedom and the ability to cope quite confidently with any problem that might arise. "Mick, if I could tell anyone, I'd tell you," she said earnestly. "But this is something I have to work out for myself."

He looked at her thoughtfully.

"Sure?" he asked.

"Quite sure, Mick," she said gently, smiling at him reassuringly.

"Well, all right," he said, reluctantly accepting her decision. "But you do know that it would give me intense pleasure to paste anybody who's upset you? Any time, anywhere. At your service."

Jacynth suddenly laughed. The idea of anybody pasting the exquisite Cynthia seemed really funny. If only one could deal with such a subtle personality as straightforwardly as that!

"I wonder!" she said lightly. "Perhaps, instead, you might fall in love with her!"

So it was another woman, Mick thought. Well, that was so much information. It let her husband out, too, unless, of course. . . . He scowled at the idea and forced it to the back of his mind. But not before he had said casually, "Well, perhaps it might solve your problem at that!" He saw, with a feeling of guilt, that she started irrepressibly. So he'd got uncomfortably near the bull's eye!

She shivered, and he used this as an excuse to take her back to shore. The man Mick had been talking to when she came down was still there, and for a moment she lingered in conversation with him.

He was rather a peculiar personality, she thought. Weather-beaten and wearing the casual flannels and sports coat that any man from a duke to a dustman might wear. But he wore them with an air, and somehow he possessed an aura of experience and shrewdness that she found intriguing, because it was combined with complete naturalness and simplicity of manner.

He was, she learned, living at the small local inn, and from his expression it was clear that he didn't think too much of it. In his opinion, Mrs. Williams was the world's worst cook.

"And having eaten all over both hemispheres above and below the equator," he said, "I've a good many cooks with whom to compare her. Yes, she's quite the worst. On the other hand, she sings like an angel, and her name is Blodwyn. So I forgive her much. I've always wanted to know someone named Blodwyn. It sounds like a bit of history popping up out of the past, doesn't it?"

Jacynth agreed that it did, and there was a little smile on her face as she went slowly back to Crellie House. But, as she came in sight of the house, her smile vanished abruptly and she gave a little exclamation of distress.

The car was standing outside the house, and from the road she could see that Jonathan was watching her from a window. With her heart beating she hurried into the house and went straight to him.

"I didn't know that you were coming home early!"

"Evidently," he said curtly. "Otherwise, no doubt, you would have been more careful."

She colored guiltily because he so obviously thought she had disobeyed him.

"But I haven't been out alone in her," she protested, realizing that he must have seen the boat out from the house.

"So I saw," he said coldly. "But does that make matters any better? Doesn't it strike you as being in questionable taste that you should go off for hours at a time with a man who's a stranger to me without even asking whether I have any objection to having my boat handled by a bungling amateur?"

"He isn't that," Jacynth said quickly. "He's been in the navy. He's taught me a lot."

"That doesn't alter the fact that in the short time you have been here you've already started the local gossips talking—" he began, then stopped short. "I'm sorry, I shouldn't have said that."

"No, I don't think that you should have," she said rather unsteadily. "After all, I can't be so young that I haven't the sense to know whether a thing is silly and dangerous, yet, at the same time, so grown-up that my behavior is cause for scandal of the sort you mean."

"I'm not so sure . . ." he began, shrugging his shoulders hopelessly. "We're not getting anywhere. Can't you see—"

"Look, Jonathan, I can see that it would have been wiser for me to have told you in one way. But I knew that this was the way you would take it. So, because I knew that it was really quite all right, I didn't tell you! Can't you understand?" she asked desperately.

He looked at her sharply.

"You knew. What makes you say that?"

She made a little gesture of perplexity.

"I don't quite know. . . . I think it was because you just forbade me to go out in the *Firefly*. If you'd just said, 'Please don't. . . .'" Her voice trailed away inconclusively. What was the use? He really did think of her just as a child, and it wasn't any use pretending anything else. She swallowed convulsively.

There was a silence and she stole a glance at him. His face was masklike, and she could not tell whether she had made any impression on him or not. Then he gave a little sigh. When he spoke again his voice was so gentle that it made Jacynth start.

"You're quite right, Jacynth; I should have trusted you," he said. "Will you accept my assurance that, in future, I shall?"

"Oh, Jonathan!" Her face lit up immediately. "You can! Honestly, I won't let you down!"

"Nor I you, Jacynth," he said soberly, and held out his hand.

She laid hers in it, and then, still holding on, she asked impulsively, "Jonathan, may I tell you about Mick?"

"Of course," he said, then added hurriedly, "That is, if you really want to."

"I do . . . now," she said frankly. "Jonathan, do you remember how, at breakfasttime at that hotel, you could *feel* Howard needing something? Something we both tried to give him?"

"I remember," he said, giving her hand a little squeeze.

"Well, Mick is the same as that," she said earnestly. "I can't quite explain because I don't know anything more than that he's been ill. But I know he gets away from something when he's in the *Firefly*. And I think," she added, looking at him clear-eyed, "that my being there helps. Not," she said flushing, "that he's in love with me, because he isn't. I think it must be rather like having a brother." She searched his face to see if he understood and gave a little sigh of relief at what she saw there.

"And, Jonathan," she went on more confidently, "I have the feeling that he needs to tell somebody what's wrong, but it won't be me. It will have to be someone older and wiser than he is. Somebody who's been through it as well. You say Cynthia doesn't like sailing. Well, I think if Howard and Mick got to know one another they might help each other. . . ."

Jonathan looked down at her thoughtfully.

"Yes, you may be right," he said reflectively. "And, in the meantime, if you want to go out with your friend, well, do!"

"Oh, Jonathan!" She was fairly sparkling now. "I do wish I'd told you right from the beginning! I was stupid to think that you wouldn't understand!"

"Not so stupid," he said ruefully. "And now what about coming over to Conway with me? I want to see about the *Gadabout*. She's been in for an overhaul, and I had a phone message today to say that she's ready. We can use her on weekends when I'm home. With Howard and Mick, I can handle her. Run upstairs and get a coat in case we're late."

Jacynth ran blithely upstairs. The shadow had gone; she and Jonathan were friends again. What if he had been in love with Cynthia years ago? One could fall out of love as well as in, and was it too much to imagine that Jonathan's anger at her being out with Mick had had its roots in jealousy, even though he might not recognize it as that?

As they went out to the car she slipped her hand confidently in his, and a pair of dark eyes that watched them from behind a curtain snapped angrily at the sight.

"So you've managed to pull the wool over his eyes this time!" muttered the housekeeper. "But don't think you'll be so successful every time, my lady! Not if I can help it!"

Jonathan met the Grants in Liverpool the following Friday evening and brought them down with him. Jacynth did her best to make her welcome to Cynthia sound cordial and sincere, but at least that to Howard was genuine enough. He responded with a grave smile that was infinitely touching to Jacynth and brought tears to her eyes.

Cynthia seemed in the highest of spirits, and when Mrs. Evans appeared to help with the lighter luggage she greeted her effusively.

"Why, Evans, you remember me, don't you?" she asked, vivaciously putting an arm around the rather forbidding figure. "I'm Cynthia Howes—at least, I was—and I used to plague the life out of you years ago!"

"That you did, Miss Cynthia," Mrs. Evans said delightedly, flashing a glance of triumph at Jacynth. "A regular handful in those days, you were indeed! I never knew what you would be doing next!"

"I still am," Cynthia said gaily. "And you still won't! Now, take me up to my room. I feel absolutely blown to bits!"

"Yes, of course, ma'am, this way." Mrs. Evans swept up the stairs completely ignoring Jacynth, who stood awkwardly at the foot wondering whether she should follow or not. She felt a light touch on her arm and turned to find Howard smiling at her.

"You know, what I want more than anything else in the world is a drink," he told her confidentially. "Do you think you can do anything about it?"

"Oh, yes!" She flashed a quick glance of gratitude at him, realizing that he was fully aware of the predicament Cynthia and Mrs. Evans had forced her into and was annoyed about it. He, at least, was determined that she not be pushed into the background.

When Cynthia came down she found a happy little group sitting in deck chairs in the garden, eagerly discussing the prospects of the weather on the following day.

"Well, I put my faith in our local prophet," Jonathan insisted. "For one thing, his Christian name is Elijah and, for another, I've never found him wrong yet! He says, mist in the morning, clear by lunch, and not more than a ladylike breeze the rest of the day. So I vote we have an early lunch and go straight off in the boat immediately after. How about it?"

"Not for me!" Cynthia chimed in, shuddering delicately. "The mere thought of it makes me feel ill! Has Jonathan coerced you into going with him?" she asked Jacynth patronizingly. "You mustn't let his enthusiasm run away with you, you know!"

"I don't," Jacynth said serenely. "If I had my way, I'd spend all day and every day out."

Cynthia sank into a chair and smiled lazily.

"My dear, how marvelously robust and enthusiastic!" she murmured, closing her eyes.

"Tired, Cynthia?" Howard asked gently, and instantly her blue eyes snapped open.

"My dear, how tactless you are!" she drawled the words, but somehow or other they made Jacynth wince.

She glanced at Jonathan to see his reactions, but either he had not heard or he chose to pretend that he had not, for his face was completely expressionless.

"Don't you know that to ask a woman if she is tired is the equivalent of telling her that she looks like a worn-out old hag!"

"Sorry," Howard muttered, and there was an awkward little silence. Then Jonathan rose lazily to his feet.

"I'm going down to see if Lavery is there," he said casually to Jacynth. "Coming? I have to ask him yet if he'd like to come with us tomorrow."

"Yes, I'll come," Jacynth said eagerly. "That is, if. . . ." She looked inquiringly at the Grants.

"I'll stay here," Howard said quietly. "It's peaceful, and I think I'm rather tired."

"In that case, I'll leave you to rest," Cynthia said promptly. "I'll come with you two, if I may."

"Of course," Jonathan said, and Jacynth dug her hands down into the pockets of the little jacket she was wearing. This was how it was going to be now! Never on their own, never with a chance of getting to know one another.

Mick was down there, staring out to sea, but he stood up when he saw them approaching.

There was a little pause, and then Jacynth said rather breathlessly, "Mick, this is my husband, Jonathan. Jonathan, this is Mick. . . ."

The two men looked at one another guardedly, measuring each other up, and Cynthia, a little behind the group, looked from one of them to the other.

How odd! she thought. *Jonathan has lived here for years, Jacynth a week or so. And yet she's introducing them!*

306

She herself was included in the introduction, but she took no part in the conversation that followed. It was far more interesting to watch . . . and draw conclusions.

Quite a decent-looking boy, she thought. Just a bit grim, perhaps—then suddenly her eyes widened.

Jacynth was talking animatedly and confidently. She was describing something to Jonathan, and Mick was watching her. Standing where she was, Cynthia could see his face clearly, and it told her something that interested her very much indeed.

Just what Jacynth's feelings toward the boy were she had no idea, but she was as sure as she had been of anything in her life that he was head over heels in love with her.

And that might be a very useful piece of knowledge.

CHAPTER SIX

Afterward, looking back, it seemed to Jacynth that the first weekend that the *Gadabout* was in commission was the most wonderful that she had ever known up till then.

For one thing, even her experience on the *Firefly* had not prepared her for the thrill of sailing in this exquisitely proportioned yacht with its incredibly slender mast and wide expanse of sail. Jonathan and Howard had worked together before, and it was soon evident that Mick had had sufficient experience to be able to pass, even in their critical eyes. The fact that the *Gadabout* had a tiny cabin and what Jacynth, in her ignorance, referred to as a kitchen, until severely reprimanded as being a landlubber and not knowing a galley when she saw it, added to her delight. It seemed to give the yacht an entrancing air of permanence, and yet, at the same time, to work in her was just glorified play. Jacynth "kept house" with the serious absorption of a child. It was hers, her very own, with no Mrs. Evans to rob her of the thrill that many women feel when preparing meals for the menfolk.

And at one and the same time the men took her for granted and yet paid her a subtle deference that was sweet, heady wine to Jacynth.

More than once Jacynth would feel Jonathan's eyes on her and would look up to find that she was right. They would smile at one another—an easy, comradely smile that yet held the magic of a joy shared. Once, he laid his hand on her warm brown arm and said, "Happy?" At which she nodded and smiled because her heart was too full for words. He seemed to hesitate for a moment, his hand gently caressing her arm, and then he said, as if it had just come into his head, "Jacynth, about the house in Bath. You do realize that we won't be able to live there?"

"No, I suppose we won't," she said, unperturbed by the introduction of such a mundane subject because of the realization that in his mind he was planning for a future that they were to share. "I suppose it ought to be sold. It doesn't seem fair that it should stand empty when there's such a shortage of housing."

"That's how I feel about it," he agreed. "As a matter of fact, Barrows, the solicitor, tells me that he has already been approached by several people. Of course, the alternative is that we could rent it out."

"You mean, so that it would still be mine?" she asked, and he nodded. She thoughtfully considered possibilities. "Jonathan, I hope you don't think it's hard and rather nasty of me, but, although I know it's a lovely house, I've never felt fond of it. Does that sound silly?" she added anxiously.

"Not a bit," he said roundly. "There are some houses that, in themselves, seem to be friendly and some that don't. Though, in this case, I have an idea that the trouble was the furniture more than the house itself. It's too heavy and there's too much of it. I've always felt overpowered by it, as if a rather pompous, self-righteous guardian was keeping an eye on me."

Jacynth gave a delightful little chuckle that caught the ears of the other two men and caused them to exchange a smile.

"Yes, I think you're right," she agreed. "Then, we'll sell the furniture as well?"

"Unless there's anything you would like to have up here?" he suggested.

Jacynth pursed her lips.

"Yes, just a few things. There's a portrait of Mother when she was a very young girl. It's in the study."

"I know the one," he agreed. "It's artistically a gem, quite apart from anything else. What else?"

"All the crystal?" she suggested. "Glasses and decanters and things. And there's a little desk of Mother's. . . . But really, Jonathan, I don't know everything that's there. You see, Gran loved to keep things under her own thumb as much as she could. So you mustn't really rely on me to know what there is that we would be silly to get rid of."

"No, I see," he said thoughtfully. "Well, look here, Jacynth, why not go down there and run through everything? It would be the safest thing to do."

"With you?" she asked quickly.

"No, I'm afraid I can't manage it," he said regretfully. "But would you mind being there alone? Actually, you wouldn't be, because the housekeeper—what's her name?"

"Miss Probyn," she said soberly.

"Yes, well, she's still there. So you'd have her to help you. . . ."

"Yes, all right, I'll do that, then," Jacynth said, and then she added abruptly, "Do you think Cynthia would come with me?"

Her eyes avoided his face, but she sensed his surprise.

"Cynthia? What made you think of that?" There was a sharp note in his voice that made her wince.

"Oh, I just thought it would be company," she said

lamely, feeling rather mean and guilty, because she knew quite well that it was because, however uncongenial her company might be, it would be better than knowing that she and Jonathan. . . .

"You could ask her," he said doubtfully. "But the trouble is, it would be rather difficult for her to refuse, even if she didn't want to go, wouldn't it? I mean, I'm awfully anxious that there should not be any suggestion of there being strings attached to our offer to have them here. Do you see what I mean?"

"Yes, I hadn't thought of that," she said in a small voice. "All right, I'll go on my own, then, Jonathan. Will you write and tell Miss Probyn?"

He nodded absently and left her to lend the other two men a hand.

They arrived back in the early evening, tired, hungry, and happy. Just for a moment, after they had come ashore, they stood in a little knot talking, and then, with an impetuosity unusual in him, Jonathan asked Mick if he would come up to the house for the evening. Mick looked doubtful and glanced at Jacynth.

"That would be delightful," she said pleasantly, and Mick no longer hesitated.

"Well, if you're quite sure I won't be a nuisance," he said gratefully. "I'll just drop in at the hotel and change. Be up in about half an hour. Would that do?"

"Splendidly," Jonathan said, then he and the other two strolled up to the house.

Just for a moment Mick watched them go with an expression on his face that the man watching him found inscrutable and puzzling.

"Had a good day, son?" he asked casually.

Mick turned and smiled.

"Hello, Mr. Farrow! Yes, wonderful. That boat's a beauty, and what those two chaps don't know about her isn't worth knowing!"

"Decent of them to ask you," Farrow suggested tentatively.

"Very," Mick said shortly.

"Very attractive girl, too," Farrow pursued. "Pretty name, too."

"Actually, I've never heard it before," Mick said, suddenly feeling guilty at his curtness to this agreeable old loafer, whose only fault was his inclination to talk too much.

"No? I have . . . once," Farrow said reflectively. He sighed. "Well, I must say I envied you today. Perfect for sailing."

"Are you keen on it?" Mick asked, fairly sure of the reply. He had long since summed Farrow up as a man who would turn his hand to anything, but who would soon tire when the novelty wore off.

Farrow smiled as if he read the younger man's thoughts.

"I've sailed in my time, among other things," he said laconically.

Mick smiled.

"Well, I must get going. I'm due up there in half an hour, and I want to get a bath in if I can. . . ."

Farrow waved a negligent hand, and to his amusement, Mick felt as if he were being dismissed by royalty.

Cynthia was sitting on the lawn under a huge spreading conifer. She was wearing a pale green dress, and she looked the picture of cool perfection. Jacynth immediately felt grubby and uncouth beside her and rather hated herself for being sure that that was just what the other woman meant her to feel.

Cynthia sprang up when she saw them and came toward them.

"Did you have a good time?" she called out. As they came level with her she slipped one cool arm through Howard's and the other through Jonathan's. "Was there enough wind? It's been very stuffy ashore."

"It's been wonderful," Howard said, looking down at her fair head with eyes that were both tender and puzzled. "I wish you'd been with us."

She sighed.

"Yes, I wish I wasn't so silly about the water, but I always feel squeamish, so it isn't much good coming, is it?"

"No, but I always feel mean to be enjoying myself when you're not," he said rather boyishly, and Jacynth's heart warmed to him. He *was* nice. If only Cynthia would realize it.

"Oh, but you mustn't feel like that," she said quickly. "After all, it's what we're here for, and if I'm a bit bored. . . ." She sighed and made a little gesture to indicate her own acceptance of the situation.

I wish she meant it, Jacynth thought uncomfortably. But she was sure all Cynthia was trying to do was make her feel she ought to stay at home and keep her company. Or make Jonathan think that she ought to . . . which was worse!

Upstairs, she glanced through her dresses with a disparaging eye. She had nothing as delicately charming as the dress that Cynthia was wearing, nor yet, so subtly sophisticated. Involuntarily she sighed, and then, brightening, decided that while she was in Bath she would buy some things.

Finally, she chose a rather severely cut, white linen dress. It made an attractive contrast to her sunburned skin, and its severity was mitigated by a cherry-colored belt and a ribbon of the same color for her hair. White, wedge-heeled sandals—she had bought those surreptitiously because Gran would not have approved, and this was the first time that she had worn them—finished the picture. She came slowly downstairs and found Cynthia waiting.

"I hope you don't mind," Cynthia began immediately, "but Jonathan tells me that young Lavery is coming up for the evening, and I've told Evans that there'll be one more for dinner. I'm afraid she wasn't too pleased, but—"

"Oh, rubbish!" Howard said cheerfully from behind her. "Evans was always inclined to make a fuss if she got the chance. Besides, when she's feeding four—five with herself—what's one more?" he added, with true masculine belief that somehow or other a miracle would be performed.

Cynthia's lips tightened and she shrugged her shoulders.

"You don't realize how difficult it is," she murmured, and Jacynth knew that it was she who was supposed to feel guilty. But after their lovely day she was in no mood to do that.

"We must send Jonathan out to placate her," she said lightly. "It was he who issued the invitation. Jonathan," she said as he joined them, "Cynthia says Mrs. Evans is annoyed because Mick is coming. She likes to have plenty of warning, you know."

"Well, she can jolly well like," Jonathan said casually. "This is our home, and if we can't invite guests without consulting the housekeeper. . . . Anyway, she can open an extra tin or two—"

Howard laughed.

"There you are!" he scoffed. "Simple! You women don't understand the rudiments of housekeeping! I told you there was no need to butter her up like you did, Cynthia."

Two lines appeared between Cynthia's shapely brows. She was prevented from saying anything by Mick's arrival, but in the subsequent cheerful babble during the dispensation of drinks she said anxiously to Jonathan, "Jonathan, I hope you don't think it was officious of me to try to coax Mrs. Evans into a better temper. But, you know, I do feel that if there's anything that I can do to . . . oil the wheels, so to speak, I ought to, because, after all, we are so much in your debt. It seems the least I can do."

"That's delightful of you, Cynthia," Jacynth heard him respond smilingly. "I appreciate your thoughtfulness very much. But I don't want you to feel obliged to do anything, you know. I'd like to feel that it's a holiday for you as well as for Howard. . . ."

She smiled wistfully.

"That's so like you, Jonathan," she said softly. "But you know, I've had to be a busy woman for a good many years past and I've got out of the habit of sitting with idle hands. It's rather boring, in fact!"

"I'm afraid you *have* been bored!" he said regretfully, and Cynthia smiled and shrugged.

During dinner it was very difficult to keep Cynthia in the conversation. Every now and again one of the others would realize that because she had not shared the day with them she was out of it, and would do their best to include her; but she gave monosyllabic replies and then lapsed into silence, a faint, wistful smile on her lips.

There was only one way to deal with it. Sailing as a topic of conversation had to be dropped, and to four people who were very full of a day whose joys they were tasting over again in retrospect it was not very easy. They all became rather silent.

After coffee, which they had out in the garden, they seemed somehow or other to split up into two groups. Jacynth and Howard in deck chairs with Mick sprawled on the grass, Cynthia and Jonathan in two other chairs that were just a sufficient distance from the others to make them a little separate entity. Cynthia seemed to have changed her mood. She was chattering away animatedly and was evidently amusing, for more than once Jonathan laughed aloud. He, too, seemed to be exerting himself to be entertaining, and from the little that drifted across it was evident that they were recalling past days. Jacynth did her best to be sensible. After all, they were old friends. Then Cynthia glanced in her direction, and in her eyes Jacynth saw unmistakably both triumph and amusement. She was deliberately monopolizing Jonathan's attention . . . proving to Jacynth that she could.

Jacynth set her teeth and sat a little more erect in her

chair. In a rather high-pitched, excited voice that she hardly recognized as her own, she began to talk to Mick, joking with him, teasing him, spurring him on to reply in kind. Cynthia would not have the satisfaction of knowing that she had succeeded in hurting her.

Howard was very quiet. But for the fact that there was a deep groove between his eyebrows as if his thoughts were none too pleasant, one would have thought that he was asleep. Then, without opening his eyes, he called out, "Jonathan!"

"M'm?" Jonathan turned immediately.

"I've got a nerve to suggest this, old man," Howard went on apologetically, "but do you think there's a chance that when you go back on Monday we could find a substitute for you so that we could still take the *Gadabout* out? I mean, the point is, the farther I can go out, the better. . . ."

"But of course," said Jonathan. "I want you to have her. I was going to have a word with you about that. What about me calling the yard and seeing if they can send along a man?"

"Well. . . ." Howard hesitated. "Yes, that would do, of course. But it's an unnecessary expense, isn't it? I mean, we can get just as much work out of young Mick here, and he thinks you're doing him a favor!"

"True enough!" Jonathan agreed. "But it isn't always possible to come across the right type. I haven't seen anyone else about—"

"I say!" Mick said, sitting up suddenly. "There's a fellow down at the pub—he seems to know a bit about sailing. Told me so this afternoon. He might do."

"What sort of a fellow?" Jonathan inquired with interest.

"Oh, I'd say he's a ne'er-do-well . . . but rather a charming one."

Howard laughed.

"They so often are! Yes, I think I saw the chap you mean. He was around when we came ashore this evening, wasn't he? Middle-aged fellow with very shrewd eyes?"

"That's him," Mick agreed. "Name of Farrow, so he says. I imagine it's more than likely not his own."

"Well. . . ." Jonathan hesitated. He was as broad-minded as the next, but somehow or other he felt oddly reluctant to have anything to do with this man.

Howard, mistaking his hesitation for concern that the man might have been bragging beyond his true capabilities, said suddenly, "Look here, why not have him out tomorrow? Then you can see for yourself. If he's any good, we can extend the invitation. If not, we can drop him."

And because it seemed unreasonable to do anything else Jonathan agreed.

They started off early the next morning and Cynthia watched them go with a smile. On the whole she was very well satisfied with the way things were going. Last night she had ample proof that Jacynth's pride reacted in a very normal and, to Cynthia, useful way. Cynthia had monopolized Jonathan, knowing that, as her host, he had no choice but to be polite. And Jacynth's reaction had been to turn to Mick. Unimportant as the incident was in itself, it showed her clearly how one could deal with the silly chit that Jonathan had been fool enough to marry.

It was not, to Jacynth, quite such a good day as the previous one, because to her sensitive perception the atmosphere was strained by the antagonism that Jonathan felt for Tom Farrow. Yet she had to admit that she herself could not understand his feelings. To begin with, Mr. Farrow was showing himself to be quite competent, and for another, his manner both toward her and the men was just what it should be. He was neither assertive nor inclined to shirk his fair share of work. Actually, she herself felt an odd liking for him, and more than once she found herself catching his eye and sharing a joke. His conversation was interesting, although today he seemed to have lost his inclination to monopolize the conversation and, instead, went to considerable pains to bring Jacynth out. Actually, that brought a little frown to Jonathan's forehead, although Jacynth did not notice that. She was trying to persuade Farrow to tell her how he'd acquired a long, wide scar that went from wrist to elbow in a wide, jagged line. But he shook his head.

"It happened when I was pretty young, and if I hadn't been a complete fool it wouldn't be there," he told her. "So let's leave it at that, shall we?" And Jacynth had no choice but to drop the subject.

At the end of the day Jonathan explained the situation and asked Farrow if he would like to accompany Howard and Mick during the week.

The older man looked thoughtful for a moment and then said, "Thanks, I'd like to—but do you mind if I make a condition?"

"Go ahead," Jonathan said rather coolly.

"Just this," Farrow said casually. "Any time you prefer my room to my company, you say so without beating about the bush. Agreed?"

"Certainly," Jonathan said, wondering why this piece

of tactfulness did not increase his liking for the man. "Tomorrow at the same time, then, Howard?"

"Suits me," his friend responded laconically.

Jacynth did not enjoy her visit to Bath. For one thing, it was like stepping back into a different life that was yet so familiar that at times she had to glance down at the two rings on her left hand to convince herself that she did not now really belong here. But the house seemed more overpowering than it ever had before, and Miss Probyn, a spinster of uncertain age, was still inclined to address her as Miss Jacynth and tell her when to go to bed.

She arranged with a local mover to pack everything she wanted under Miss Probyn's eagle eye, and the remainder Jonathan would arrange to have sold.

And then, with some relief, she set out for home. Probably it was because she was so eager to get home that it seemed such a tedious journey and the wait at Bristol, where she had to change trains, seemed interminable. Still, Jonathan was to meet her at Chester, so that saved her another transfer. As the train ran into the station she poked her head out of the window in an effort to see Jonathan. At first she thought that he was not there, but then she spotted him and almost fell out of the train in her eagerness to meet him.

"Hey, don't break your neck!" he greeted her, his eyes smiling and welcoming.

"Oh, Jonathan, I'm so glad to be home!" she said, holding tightly onto his hand. "I began to wonder if it was all a dream."

He took her case from her and drew her arm through his.

"No, it's real all right," he said reassuringly, and Jacynth gave his arm a little squeeze.

In the car she settled down with a sigh.

"I like cars better than trains," she said with childish satisfaction, and he laughed.

"If I ever think you're getting discontented I shall send you away on a train journey," he teased. "Thank you for giving me the hint!"

She laughed happily and said, without it being the effort that she had thought it would be, "How is everybody?"

"Fine," he said, and then added thoughtfully, "I think you were right about our two invalids. They seem to be doing each other a world of good, and I think they're both putting on weight, which they wouldn't be doing if they weren't mentally and physically fitter."

"No, I suppose not," Jacynth agreed. "And Cynthia? I hope she hasn't been too . . . bored?"

"I don't think so," he said. "She seems to be much more contented and happy."

"Oh?" Jacynth said, trying to keep the sharp note out of her voice. "Why is that?"

"Well, she's taken on various jobs about the house," he explained. "I didn't want her to, but it seems to make her feel more comfortable—less in our debt. And Mrs. Evans doesn't seem to mind."

"That's fortunate," Jacynth said tonelessly. "Of course, she's very fond of Cynthia."

"Yes," Jonathan said shortly, and Jacynth had the feeling she had said the wrong thing. Perhaps he did not want to be reminded—by her at least—of those other, earlier days when Cynthia had been such a constant visitor.

They were rather silent for the rest of the journey home, and once Jonathan turned and looked at her.

"Tired?" he asked.

"A little," she said, more because it explained her silence than because it was particularly true.

"Never mind, we'll be home soon now," he consoled. "And Cynthia promised to see that tea was waiting when we got there!"

So it was not surprising, when they arrived, to find that a dainty and appetizing meal was laid in a shady spot of the garden.

Nor did it surprise Jacynth when Cynthia came toward them, welcoming her as if she was a guest in her own home and Cynthia was its mistress.

It was just what she had anticipated. She glanced at Jonathan.

He was smiling as if he saw nothing strange in the situation.

CHAPTER SEVEN

Once Jonathan had loved Cynthia. Did he still? That was the question that was never long out of Jacynth's mind. And sometimes she thought "Yes" and sometimes "No."

If only Jonathan's attitude toward her were at all lover-like, that would have told her, but it never was. He was always kind and friendly and attentive, but that was all.

But that, she would tell herself hurriedly, though it meant he was not in love with her, did not of necessity mean that he was in love with Cynthia. And besides, Jonathan was too fine and straight to have asked a woman that he loved to come as a guest to his house now that he and she were married to other people. On the other hand, he hadn't really had much choice. Howard's appeal to him for help was one he could not refuse, and inevitably Cynthia came as well. So it seemed there was no positive answer.

Nor did Cynthia's attitude really help. That she was doing everything possible to appear attractive in Jonathan's eyes was obvious enough, but that might mean one of two things as well. Either that she knew he had got over the old infatuation and was trying to rekindle it, or that he had not and she was trying to tempt him into yielding to it.

And if it's that, poor Jacynth thought, *then I must forget all about whether it hurts my pride or not and help him to stick it out. Because however much he may love*

*her, he is married to me, and I think he'd hate himself if
he were to let me down. . . .*

And then, forlornly, she wondered why he did marry
her.

That was a question to which she found no answer
whatever.

She ticked off her slender fingers. It wasn't because he
loved her; it wasn't for her money; it wasn't because—
She colored rosily and jumped to her feet. There was no
answer, she told herself hurriedly. Except perhaps—to
help him forget Cynthia? She wondered. It could be. . . .
She turned it over musingly and suddenly squared her
shoulders. "I'll take a chance it is!" she declared, unconscious that she had spoken aloud.

The thought that it was for Jonathan's sake that she
was going to join battle with Cynthia seemed to give her
both confidence and clear-sightedness. Nor did it strike
her as odd that she, a girl, and a young one at that, should
want to protect Jonathan.

But he was a man, and men had a totally different way
of fighting, she thought wisely, though she would have
been puzzled to find how she knew that. There was only
one way of fighting Cynthia, and that was by using the
same weapons that she did, only better. And only another
woman could do that.

To begin with, she decided, she must find some good
reason for not going out so much in the *Gadabout* during
the week. But how could she do that? Just to say that she
felt guilty at leaving Cynthia to work while she played
was not good enough. It would simply give Cynthia the
opportunity of posing as a generous martyr—Jacynth had

reached the point where she did not mince words in her own mind—and it would sound ungracious to insist.

No, she must find something to do that she could assert convincingly mattered more than sailing. It proved not too difficult. The house she would leave to Cynthia, all the more so because she was quite sure that really and truly Cynthia did not like housework. But there was still the garden.

There was, of course, the daily gardener, but he was an old man—that same Elijah whom Jonathan had so extolled as a weather prophet—and not in the least averse to having assistance.

And if it so happened—as it so often did—that Jacynth was working at that part of the garden where Jonathan always stopped the car when he came home, *just* at the time he was due, whose business was it but hers? But it completely spoiled the effect of Cynthia's dainty waiting tea-table when Jacynth would enthusiastically drag him off to see what she had done that day.

But it was injudicious of Cynthia to refer to it as she did—sharply, as if Jacynth was a child, and in front of Jonathan at that.

Jonathan looked up sharply, aware of the tenseness in the air—indeed, no one could miss it—but before he had time to speak Jacynth gave a little exclamation of distress.

"Oh, Cynthia, how naughty of me!" she said self-reproachfully. "That comes of being too enthusiastic! I hadn't realized what fun gardening is—but that's no excuse. I must punish myself for it! Look, I'll stop gardening early and *I'll* get the tea. I've felt guilty all along about your doing it. And let me pour out now! Yes,

I insist. You must be tired; go and talk to Jonathan and let me do the work."

Was it chance, Cynthia asked herself. Yes, of course it must be! A girl of that age hadn't the sophistication required to compel other people to do as she wanted without leaving them a loophole, and all without being in the least bit unpleasant. And yet surely it could not have been all luck?

Whichever it was, she found herself an onlooker while Jacynth assumed her proper place behind her own teapot and looked after the needs of her husband and her guest with assiduity. Jonathan found Cynthia's replies to his attempts at conversation both brief and not particularly appropriate.

Afterward, when Jacynth said very seriously to him, "I feel dreadfully guilty that we've let Cynthia do too much," he could only agree, and from then on Jacynth did a little less gardening and was always ready to help get the tea.

It gave her confidence, just as it made Cynthia lose some of hers.

In fact, Cynthia found herself in a mood that was unusual for her—one of absolute recklessness, of determination to bring things to a head, no matter what the consequences.

Jonathan had been quite right in thinking that the two men whom he had described as "our invalids" had both benefitted, not only from all their long days at sea, but also from each other's companionship.

A month after his arrival, Howard went up to Liverpool to see his doctor, and the report on his condition was most encouraging. Nor was anyone more delighted than Mick, for Howard, kind, warmhearted man that he was, was wonderful to be around in his present mood. One felt refreshed just by being in his company. Jonathan, too, was a decent chap, although he took a bit more knowing, and Mick knew quite well that he and Jonathan would always hold a little in reserve from one another.

But lately something had been bothering Mick. Something that he wanted to talk over with someone who was wiser, more experienced than he—something that was beginning to get on his nerves.

There were times when he thought of going away, and yet he knew that was no solution. This had to be thrashed out. Because, after all, he might be wrong. There might be no more foundation to his perplexities than the sickness of his own brain. That was not a very pleasant thought. Though, in the circumstances, he admitted that even that was better than that it should be the truth. One way, only he suffered. The other—he gritted his teeth—God knew what unhappiness might come to little Jacynth. That was what made it so unbearable—it was also the reason why he could not go away. He must stand by in case she ever needed him.

She was thinner than she had been, he thought, and more serious, although, when he had challenged her about that, she had laughed and shaken her head.

"It was just baby fat," she insisted. "It always goes, if you're lucky, at my age."

"How old are you, Jacynth?" he asked suddenly, and she looked at him with troubled eyes.

"Nearly eighteen," she said reluctantly. "In fact, it will be my birthday on Saturday!"

"Then you have to celebrate it in style!" he insisted. "What about it, Jacynth? Why not throw a party?"

"Oh!" She turned it over in her mind and a slow little smile dawned in her eyes. "Yes, that would be fun! I'll ask Jonathan. . . ."

"What would you like for a birthday present, Jacynth?" he asked idly. "A purse that never empties, a cloak to make you invisible, or three wishes?"

"Oh, three wishes!" she said promptly; then, in spite of the triviality of the conversation, she grew suddenly serious. "No, perhaps I'd better not. It would be so easy to wish something that might turn out the wrong way."

He looked at her thoughtfully. There *was* something worrying her—something that frightened her.

"That sounds as if they would be very serious, important wishes," he said lightly, determined to give her a chance of confiding in him if she wanted to. "I suppose merely an ordinary blundering mortal without any magic at his disposal couldn't do anything to help?"

"Oh, but there isn't anything!" she insisted a little too quickly. "Really, Mick!"

"I'm glad," he said, simply because there was nothing else to say, unconvinced though he was.

She went slowly back to the house, turning over several plans in her mind. Actually, the way she would have liked to celebrate her birthday would have been to spend the day on the *Gadabout*, but that would mean leaving Cynthia out, which obviously was hardly the thing to do. But at least, she decided, any official celebrations could be left until the evening, otherwise it would mean that Howard would have to stay ashore earlier in the day than usual, and clearly that must not be.

She had made up her mind that she would not mention it until she and Jonathan were alone some time, but in fact it was Jonathan himself who brought the subject up at dinnertime.

"Jacynth, don't you have a birthday coming up soon?" he asked suddenly. "I have the impression that it's sometime about now."

Cynthia gave a little cry.

"Have you, Jacynth?" she asked. "What fun! I'm afraid I've reached the age where I try to forget birthdays, but of course it's different for you. What is it? Your eighteenth? Nineteenth?"

"Eighteenth," Jacynth said slowly. "Next Saturday."

Cynthia clapped her hands.

"Then you must have a party!" she declared. "And you must let me do all the planning, and then it will be a real surprise to you. Jonathan"—she turned to him vivacious and eager—"you and I must put our heads together and think up something really good. . . ."

"Unless, of course, Jacynth would rather make her own plans," Howard said quietly.

"Oh, would you, Jacynth?" Cynthia asked, the sparkle dying out. "Yes, of course you would! I didn't think, I'm afraid. You must forgive me for interfering. Truly, I was only thinking of making it more fun for you, but if you'd rather. . . ."

"I'm sure Jacynth loves surprises, don't you?" Jonathan asked quietly. Quite unmistakably, he was telling her that she must accept Cynthia's offer . . . or at least that he wanted her to. And what else was there for her to do now? If she refused Cynthia's offer it made her sound childish and ungracious in Jonathan's eyes. Oh, if only he

could see . . . or did he see and did he think that nothing
else mattered except what Cynthia wanted?

Well, at least she would not give Cynthia the pleasure
of knowing just how resentful and troubled she was.

"It's very sweet of you, Cynthia," she said steadily.
"Thank you very much indeed."

But, even as she spoke, she knew that her party was
spoiled already.

About one thing Jacynth was gently determined. She
would choose her own guests. And she would have them
limited in number.

"I want just friends," she exclaimed to Jonathan. "And
at present I don't know so many people here that there
can be a lot of them."

To her relief he agreed to that, although Cynthia
shrugged her shoulders helplessly as if to tell them that it
would not be her fault if the whole thing was a failure.

"We four," Jacynth said, counting off the numbers on
her fingers. "And Mick and Mr. Farrow."

"He'll hardly shine in society, I'm afraid," Cynthia
said cuttingly, and Jacynth laughed.

"He'll probably arrive wearing some frightful old
clothes," she admitted. "But then it isn't for his clothes I
want him. He's—rather a dear," she smiled beseechingly
at Jonathan, and he smiled and nodded in reply.

"Your party," he said, "Go on."

She wrinkled her forehead.

"That's six, isn't it—and far more men than women. Is
there anyone you would like to come, Jonathan?"

"How about some of your old schoolfriends?" he
suggested.

For a moment she did not reply. The girls she had worked and played with—the school itself—how far away all that life seemed! She wondered what had happened to them. Whether they had carried out the plans that all of them had made, herself included. They all seemed so childish now—things like persuading indulgent parents into buying sports cars for them or making the maximum number of boyfriends. As from a great height she seemed to be looking down indulgently on them and pitying them for their immaturity.

"Yes, I think that would be a good idea," she said slowly. "Of course, it's rather short notice, but there were two. . . ."

"Well, write and see what they say or, better still, telephone if you have their numbers."

"Yes, I think so," she got up from the chair. "I'll see about it now."

She put through the two calls and explained the situation. It meant, too, that she had to tell them about her marriage, and she listened in silence to their exclamations and rhapsodies.

"Darling, the most romantic thing I've ever heard!" Lois Bland said. "And we thought that night you vanished that you had been expelled. I suppose you're frightfully in love?"

"Tremendously," Jacynth said emphatically.

Helen Trent took it rather differently.

"Well, of course, my dear, it is romantic—don't think I don't realize that," she drawled. "But frankly, I think a girl is very silly to throw herself away on the first man that crooks his little finger at her. I do so feel I'd like to pick and choose."

Jacynth laughed as she had always done at Helen's pseudo-sophistication, and wondered just how Cynthia and she would react to one another.

However, whatever might be the two girls' reaction to her marriage, they both accepted the invitation eagerly.

She took the invitation to Tom Farrow herself, because she was more than half-afraid that he would find some excuse not to come—he had not previously been asked up to the house, and she had thought more than once that his feelings had been hurt by the fact.

"Eighteen?" he looked at her quizzically. "Not been married very long then, have you?"

"About five weeks," she said primly.

He laid his hand over her brown one.

"Offended?" he asked, his mouth twisted wryly.

Jacynth sighed.

"No, not really. But I don't think it's a very easy age to be," she replied obliquely.

"No," he agreed. "I don't suppose it is. Halfway betweenish?"

She nodded and his grip tightened a little.

"Bound to be, you know," he said consolingly. "Where brook and river meet. It's not just that you're peculiar."

"I know," she said quickly. "Only . . . I guess different people have different problems, don't they?"

"Sure to," he agreed. "Still, it's not much use worrying, you know. Life's something of a gamble."

She looked at him wistfully.

"Yes, I know. I used to think that was rather fun—not knowing what's round the corner, taking a chance. . . ."

"It *is* fun," he insisted, watching her intently.

"Yes." She did not sound very sure. "But don't you

think that, even so, there are some things you want to be firm and sure—reliable?"

"Basic things?" he suggested. "Yes, I suppose most people feel that. Lavery does, you know. That's what's the matter with him. People's beastliness has sickened him. That's why you and the others do him so much good."

"Oh!" She turned it over in her mind. "Poor Mick! It's rather a responsibility for us, isn't it? I mean, if we let him down. . . ."

"*You* won't," he said.

"I'll try not to," she said. "And about the invitation . . . you will come, Mr. Farrow?"

He looked at her thoughtfully and nodded.

"Thank you, I'd like to," he said, and Jacynth was satisfied, because, although the words were conventional, there was a convincing sincerity in his tone.

Lois and Helen arrived the evening before Jacynth's birthday. Jonathan and she met them at Lime Street and drove them down, and it seemed to Jonathan that they didn't stop chattering in all the fifty-odd miles.

"Heavens!" he said a little later to Jacynth. "What an escape I've had! Suppose you'd been a chatterbox like that." He looked at her thoughtfully. "As a matter of fact, you're rather a silent person, aren't you?"

"People aren't all the same just because they are about the same age," she said demurely. "Besides, living with Gran made a difference, you know."

He put his hand under her chin and turned it up.

"Yes, I'm afraid so," he said regretfully. "But you ought not to miss your girlhood, Jacynth. Play with your friends while they are here and be young with them."

Her long, silky lashes drooped over her cheeks.

"I don't think one can go back like that," she said gravely. "I remember one of our teachers telling us that there were things that she had wanted to do in her teens that she wasn't able to do until she was in her thirties. And by that time, she didn't get any fun out of them because they were things that were so much younger than she was."

He was silent for a moment. Then, releasing her and turning away, he said, "But you're not in your thirties! You're the same age as they are! Don't be ashamed to do the things that are natural at eighteen. And don't imagine that the only good times, the only miracles, are in the future. They're not!"

"It isn't possible to live in the past, and you tell me not to try to live in the future," she said wistfully. "That means one should make the best of the present? Live for the day and take things as they come?"

"I suppose so. Yes," he said thoughtfully. "After all, what else can one do? One never knows what's round the corner."

"That's what I—" Jacynth began eagerly, then stopped. After all, what was the good of repeating to Jonathan the things that she said to Mr. Farrow? They were the sort of things that just didn't count if you had to ask for them; they had to be given freely.

Fortunately, Jonathan did not seem to have heard her, and with a little sigh that was half relief and half regret she went downstairs to her guests.

Jacynth's birthday dawned fair and bright. She slipped out of bed and regarded herself gravely in the mirror feeling that the fact she had actually reached her birthday ought to make some noticeable difference in her appearance. But, rather disappointingly, she looked the same as usual except, perhaps, her eyes. There was a hopefulness in them she herself could not explain, but which was nonetheless a fact.

She had elected to have her presents at breakfast time, so there was nothing to delay her preparations for the day. Nonetheless, it was some time before she turned on the water for her bath, and by then she had to hurry through it in order to be down to breakfast in time. Even so, she was last into the room.

A little chorus of good wishes greeted her, and she sat down at her place with a flushed, happy face. "I hope you don't mind," Cynthia said. "But we've helped ourselves."

That meant, of course, that she had taken advantage of Jacynth's being late and had appropriated the role of hostess to herself.

"Of course," Jacynth said blithely. "Pour me out some coffee, there's a dear, and I can begin opening presents."

So, while Cynthia, looking none too pleased, did as she was asked, Jacynth began to untie strings.

"Oh, darling, *cut* them!" Lois implored. "I know they're not mine, but I'm terribly impatient to see what you've got."

Jacynth paid no heed. Like a child, she was still reveling in the joys of anticipation, and those last few seconds before she actually knew what she had been given were especially precious.

By chance, she happened on Jonathan's present first. The wrappings off, she held a cedarwood box in her hands, and when she lifted the lid she uttered a little gasp of pleasure. On a white quilted cushion lay a high tortoiseshell comb carved so that it had the fineness of lace. Its upper edge was lined with pearls, and in a smaller box beside the comb she found a pair of earrings made of seed pearls fashioned into tassels.

"Oh, Jonathan!" she breathed, her eyes bright with delight. "How shall I thank you?"

"How about the way you thanked me for the pearls?" he suggested, evidently pleased at her reception of his gift.

She flushed a little, but got up immediately and, rather shy because of her audience, kissed him lightly on the cheek.

"Thank you *very* much," she said softly, completely oblivious to the fact that her two schoolmates had exchanged glances and lifted significant eyebrows.

Mick's gift was a very small transistor radio, obviously intended for use in either of the boats. The two girls had clubbed together and given her an evening bag, while the Grants had chosen a gold watch on a thick double cord that she swiftly fastened around her wrist.

"Everything's lovely," she said ecstatically.

"You've still one more," Helen said, and Jacynth, conscious that for some inexplicable reason she had deliberately left that one until last, picked it up and slowly undid it.

She could feel whatever it was move slinkily under her fingers as she unwrapped its tissue-paper covering. And when it was uncovered, she could understand why. She held up a supple silver belt in her hand made up of innumerable tiny sections each linked to the next with a little chain. At the front was a silver buckle, and both belt and buckle had tiny figures and scenes wrought on it in raised work.

"Indian," Howard commented with interest. "And a nice piece of work at that! Who's it from, Jacynth?"

"Mr. Farrow," Jacynth said absently. "There's a note."

She read it through, and then handed it to Jonathan. It was quite short.

My Dear Jacynth,
    This belonged to my wife, and I shall be very proud if you will accept it and wear it.
                                    Yours,
                                        T. Farrow

Jonathan put it down and held out his hand.

"May I see the belt?" he asked, in a tone so odd that Jacynth looked slightly startled as she complied.

"What is it, Jonathan?" she asked anxiously.

"Nothing. Just . . . I thought I'd seen it before, but of course, I haven't."

He restored it to her and dropped the subject, but several times during the day Jacynth caught herself fingering it and wondering. . . .

Tom Farrow turned up with Mick at seven o'clock. To everyone's surprise Tom as well as Mick wore an irreproachable dinner jacket suit. He was perfectly well aware of the surprise that he had caused and his dark eyes snapped with amusement. He was, in fact, an outstandingly handsome man, dressed so, and both Helen and Lois admitted frankly that they had fallen in love with him on sight.

To everybody's amusement, the two girls hung around

him all the evening and later, when Jonathan switched on the fairy lamps that had been threaded through the trees, they took turns dancing with him until he declared that they were dangerous young women and for safety's sake he was going to sit out with the pair of them.

Those three, Jacynth thought a little enviously, were having more fun than anyone else. Mick, a little out of it it seemed to her, did his best to entertain Cynthia, but with little success. She was in a wistful, withdrawn mood and only answered him in mollables until, at last, he decided she did not want to talk and turned to Howard.

Jonathan, too, was very quiet, and Jacynth found herself making conventional conversation as if he were a stranger.

Then Mick put on another record and they danced again. Jacynth, in Jonathan's arms, was too much enthralled to hear what anyone else was saying, which was perhaps just as well, for Helen, in her clear young voice, was not being too discreet.

"Quite frankly, I'm off this marriage business," she told Tom in all seriousness. "I mean, look what it's done to Jacynth!"

"Well, what has it done?" he asked, maneuvering her cleverly out of Cynthia's hearing.

"Well, if you'd *known* her!" Helen said emphatically. "At school she was always on top of the world. If ever there was a lark going she was in the thick of it. And reckless! She'd take on anything. A born gambler. Sorry, I'm a foul dancer, aren't I? Did I hurt your toes?"

"My fault," he said mechanically. "Well, perhaps if she was that, it's as well she's changed. Gambling's a fool's game."

"Well, yes," she agreed judicially. "Of course, that's true. But she's so dull—oh, a perfect darling, of course. But I simply couldn't imagine her shinnying up the school flagpole and putting a . . . well, something on top of it now, could you?"

"Did she do that?" he asked, his eyes twinkling. "So did I—" He stopped and cleared his throat. "Perhaps it's just as well she doesn't do that sort of thing now that she's married."

"There you are!" Helen said dramatically. "It all comes back to that. If that's what growing up and getting married means, well, I'm for a career, that's all."

Yet, for all the quietness of which her friend complained, Jacynth enjoyed her evening. All day long she had felt that it was too good to be true, that there was a catch somewhere, and that sooner or later something would happen to spoil it all. But as time wore on and nothing happened she became more and more at ease, more high-spirited than she had been for a long time, and, by the time she had danced an inspired Irish jig with Tom, Helen had nothing to complain of.

It was late when they saw their guests off, and as they left Jonathan slipped his arm through hers.

"Happy, little girl?" he asked gently. And when she nodded, shiny-eyed, he said, "You look very lovely tonight," and set a seal on her happiness.

Suddenly he stood still.

"I've left the lights on in the garden," he said. "I won't be a minute."

She went slowly upstairs and, throwing her window wide, she stood there gazing dreamily at the moon, and time passed.

With a start, she realized that it was a long time since she had come up and that there was still no sign of Jonathan.

Of course, it was nothing, but a little stab of fear shot through her, and, without stopping to think what she was doing, she ran downstairs again and out into the garden. She peered into the dim shadows that the trees cast and then went slowly around by the shrubbery to the lawn where they had danced. But she stopped before she reached it, her hand over her lips to stifle a cry she could not entirely suppress.

Only a few yards away from her stood Jonathan and Cynthia. They were talking earnestly, and Cynthia's face, upturned in the moonlight, was white and ethereal. Then, as she watched, Cynthia put her arms around Jonathan's neck, and his hands gripped her arms.

With her breath coming in short, racking sobs, Jacynth ran back to the house and the sanctuary of her room.

CHAPTER EIGHT

Two days later Helen and Lois left, and though it was rather a relief to Jacynth to be without their constant chatter, nonetheless their presence had meant that she could make a pretense of high spirits that were a more adequate mask for her wounded pride than anything else could have been.

"And I won't be miserable," she told herself fiercely. "I'll be young and irresponsible and carefree—after all, why not? It's what Jonathan himself said he wanted me to be. And if he doesn't like it—well, he can—" Suddenly her lips twisted and she buried her face in her pillow. The thought was courageous enough, but it was not enough to counteract the cold ache in her breast.

She had so believed in Jonathan—so trusted him. And he had done this to her! It hurt so much it simply couldn't be borne.

But it had to be. They told you that time would cure anything. But not this . . . not this!

And the worst of it was she was so helpless. There was nothing she could do. Jonathan had decided for himself, and all her hopes that he would turn to her for help and comfort were shattered.

"If only I could get away," she thought, and sat up erect.

Well, why not? She had plenty of money, and they said that travel was part of one's education. She would tell him that she was bored and that if she hadn't married him Gran had promised her a world trip.

But none of her arguments made any impression on Jonathan.

"I'm afraid not," he said, as if he really hardly bothered to listen to what she was saying. "It wouldn't be at all suitable."

"Why not?" she asked indignantly.

He looked at her dispassionately.

"Because you're very young and very pretty, and the world can be a very dangerous place. No, be a good girl and wait until next spring. Then I'll take you to both North and South America. How will that do?"

Jacynth did not answer his question. Instead she said jerkily, "What about the Grants? Will they still be here?"

Jonathan picked up a letter that lay by his plate.

"I imagine not. Howard was telling me the other day that, if all goes well, in a month or so he will be looking out for some job or other that will allow him to live in the open."

"Oh!" Jacynth said, her heart giving a little leap. "Will Cynthia be going with him?"

"I presume so." He spoke absently, his eyes on his letter.

Apparently he considered the subject closed, for he stuffed the letter into his pocket and pushed back his chair.

"Yes, but Jonathan," she protested, "I must do something. I can't stand it here—"

She bit her lip, angry with herself for betraying her feelings to him. He was looking at her in a surprised way.

"But I thought you loved it here," he said.

How could she explain to him that it was the most lovable place she had ever seen—if one were happy. But that otherwise the very beauty of it all just made everything seem even worse than it was.

"I do," she said hesitantly, "in a way, but. . . ."

"Yes, I imagine the place does seem dull now that Lois and Helen have gone," he said in a relieved voice as if he were glad to have found an explanation of her boredom. "We must have them up again. In the meantime, aren't there any girls of your own age around here? There must be somewhere. You could play with them."

How he dwelt on her youth! How little he understood! If only he would treat her as an equal, tell her the truth about himself and Cynthia instead of treating her as a child, and moreover, a child not even nominally his wife.

Jonathan glanced down at his watch.

"I'll have to go," he said, with what sounded to her very much like relief in his voice. Suddenly, he laid his hand on her shoulder. "Jacynth, things are worrying me a bit just now. Be a dear and. . . ." He finished the sentence with a smile, but what he meant was clear enough, and involuntarily she smiled in return.

And then the smile vanished. Cynthia swept into the room, obviously dressed for town.

"I was so afraid I'd be late!" she said triumphantly. "Is it all right, Jonathan?"

"Yes, of course," he said slowly. "Jacynth." He turned to her, but she drew back.

"I mustn't keep you," she said breathlessly, and with a shrug, he followed Cynthia to the waiting car.

Jacynth stood a little way back from the window, watching them and biting her lip. Then she realized that she was not alone. Howard had come into the room and was standing a little behind her, watching, as she was.

"Oh, Howard!" she burst out uncontrollably. "Don't you hate Cynthia's going anywhere without you?"

He looked at her curiously for a moment, then he shook his head.

"I might, if I didn't think that it was one of the deadliest of sins for love to be possessive," he said quietly.

For a moment her eyes wavered. Then they dropped from his and she turned to the breakfast table.

"I'm afraid the coffee may be a bit cold," she said hurriedly.

"Never mind. Serves me right for coming down late," he said cheerfully. "What shall we do today?"

"What is there to do?" she asked moodily. "Oh, Howard, I wish I had a job—anything—so long as it was so important that if I didn't do it something would go bust!"

He looked at her speculatively without answering, and she laughed in a shamefaced way.

"I'm being silly," she said repentantly. "Of course, we'll go out and thoroughly enjoy ourselves. It's only that I'm—" She cut herself off and hurried out of the room. Howard, left alone, pushed his plate irritably aside and leaned his arms on the table edge.

Poor child, she had given herself away so completely. And there was nothing he could do about it. The knowledge that he must wait a while before he even thought of looking for a job, however ideal it might be, gnawed at his conscience as if it were due to a fault of his own.

"We should never have come!" he muttered. "I should

have known. Oh, my God, isn't there any way out for any of us?"

Never before in her life had Jacynth known what moodiness was, but now by turns she would feel the need for long solitary rambles, and then, as abruptly, the solitude would get on her nerves, forcing her to seek as much company as possible. Only she knew that it needed a tremendous effort to keep up appearances at all, and the inevitable strain began to show in her face, so that more than one of her friends saw it and felt anxious.

"Of course, if I had any courage I'd go to Jonathan and have it out with him," she told herself miserably. "But that might make mountains out of molehills. Perhaps he doesn't really love her—perhaps it was just the past and the present getting mixed up for a moment." It was not very convincing, and the small amount of comfort that it brought faded as the days went on and Jonathan still remained preoccupied and even morose.

She wondered if having to look after her affairs was proving troublesome, and when she noticed an envelope bearing the name of her solicitors in his pile of mail one morning she watched carefully to see his expression as he read the letter. There was an enclosure secured to the corner of it, and although she could not see what it was from where she was sitting, it was obvious that it was causing Jonathan considerable annoyance. His face grew grim and his lips set in a thin, forbidding line, and when she tentatively said "Jonathan?" he started violently and hastily folded the letter.

"Is there . . . is there anything the matter?" she asked, a little breathlessly. "Is it difficult to settle Gran's estate?"

"Oh!" He glanced down at the envelope still lying on

the table. "No, it's nothing to do with that. As a matter of fact, I asked them to attend to some business of mine, and this is their answer."

"Oh, I see," she said, realizing, for all her lack of experience, that it somehow sounded very unconvincing. She waited to see if he offered any more explanation, but he put the letter in his pocket without another word and went out of the room.

Feeling far more troubled than the incident should really warrant, Jacynth went slowly down to the anchorage. Mick was down there already, swabbing out the *Firefly*, since it had rained a little during the night. He looked up immediately he heard her footstep and paused in his job.

"Hello!" he said, leaning on the handle of the mop and surveying her critically. "What's the matter with you? You look as if you have all the cares of the world on your shoulders."

Her laugh was rather forced.

"What nonsense!" she disclaimed, trying to sound completely carefree. "One can't be laughing all the time, you know!"

"No, but—" he stepped ashore and stood looking down at her "—there's a difference in being quiet when you're happy and being quiet when you're not. Jacynth—" he took her hand in his "—I'm awfully worried about you. I know it's no business of mine, but you're one of the people that matter to me. I couldn't bear it if you got mixed up in anything—" He stopped short, and Jacynth noted anxiously the sudden nervous little twitch in the corner of his mouth that had almost ceased during the past weeks.

"Mick, dear," she said gently, "nobody ever gets

through life without finding difficulties now and again,
and one of my difficulties is that I've sort of jumped from
being a schoolgirl into being a married woman. I haven't
had much experience of life, you see, and I have a lot to
learn. So sometimes it isn't surprising if I'm . . . puzzled.
But that doesn't mean that there is anything truly wrong.
Do you see?"

He looked at her for a minute without answering, and
again she saw that nervous little twitch. Nor, when he
spoke, did he answer her directly. Instead, in a low,
hurried voice he said, "Jacynth, you know I'd do
anything in the world to help you, don't you?"

She looked up at him, her clear eyes wide and startled.

"Why, Mick . . ." she began uncertainly.

But at that moment there was a sound behind her, and
they both turned to see Jonathan standing there. There
was a peculiar expression on his face, but his voice was
perfectly normal as he said, "Have you seen Farrow
about this morning?"

"He's still up at the pub," Mick said, turning back to
the *Firefly*. "Said something about making a phone call."

"Thanks," Jonathan said briefly and turned on his
heel.

Jacynth's eyes followed him.

"I thought he'd gone to Liverpool," she said rather
anxiously.

"Well," Mick said rather ambiguously, "does it really
matter?"

"No," Jacynth said a little uncertainly, "I suppose it
doesn't."

"Well then, stop worrying about nothing," he said
sensibly, "and come out in the *Firefly* for an hour or so.

Grant won't be down until then; he's—good lord, how odd! He's waiting for a phone call as well. What a busy lot they all are. And we're the only ones who know what to do with a heavenly morning. Come on!"

Still, for a moment, she hesitated, and then her heart gave a little leap. Mick really wanted her company. She was—he had just said so—one of the people that mattered to him.

"Why not?" she said blithely, letting him help her into the *Firefly*.

From above Jonathan had turned and was watching the little scene being enacted below. Then Mick pushed off, and Jonathan continued his walk to the little pub with a face absolutely devoid of expression.

Farrow was sitting in the sun idly scraping out the bowl of his pipe. He glanced up as Jonathan approached and sketched a casual salute.

"Lovely morning!" he commented.

Jonathan did not reply. He stood looking down at the older man, his hands in his pockets, his eyes narrowed.

"If you have some time, I'd like to have a talk with you," he said slowly.

Farrow nodded imperturbably.

"Go ahead," he said.

Jonathan took the solicitor's letter from his pocket and unfastened the enclosure. It was a small snapshot, which he handed to Farrow.

"That's a photograph of Jacynth's father, Tim Furnival. It's also a photograph of you, *Mr. Farrow*!"

Farrow took it from him.

"Yes," he said reflectively as he studied it. "Taken just

before I married her mother. What a handsome young devil I was in those days! No wonder—" he checked himself.

"No wonder you persuaded a sweet, innocent girl like Isobel Allardyce to dance to your tune," Jonathan finished.

Tim Furnival raised his grizzled brows.

"That's one way of putting it, of course," he admitted. "There are others."

"Quite!" Jonathan said curtly. "Some people might go as far as saying that, even to a man as footloose and fancy-free as you appear to have been, it was worth while exchanging your freedom for Isobel's money!"

Furnival's face twitched with amusement.

"You know, Branksome, one might almost think that you were deliberately trying to provoke me," he taunted.

Jonathan's nostrils flared, but he kept a tight hold of himself.

"Not at all," he said coolly. "I merely want to make it perfectly clear to you that I know the facts of the case inside out and that I'm not susceptible to your charm, if it still exists."

"We'll not argue about that," Furnival said lightly. He rasped his hand over his chin as he regarded Jonathan thoughtfully. "Lord, man, now I can see why the old lady chose you to marry Jacynth! You're as prim and prudish and unimaginative as she and the old man were! And that," he added unexpectedly, "is the real reason why Isobel ran away with me, if you want to know. And until she died at Jacynth's birth, poor lass, she had the time of her life with me. Why, d'you know one of the last things she said to me?" Suddenly he checked himself and shook his head. "No, that was for my ears. *You'd* never understand."

"Do you mean to say . . ." Jonathan began, a sudden vision appearing of the conventionally elegant house in Bath with its overpowering furniture, and Christina's overpowering disposition.

"I don't mean to say anything," Furnival said coolly. "You began this conversation. You'd better do the talking."

"I will," Jonathan said curtly. "It can be said fairly briefly. The terms of your agreement with the Allardyces were that they would pay you an allowance so long as you didn't get in touch with Jacynth. You've broken that agreement and your allowance is forfeit. However, if you will go—"

"Just a minute." Furnival lifted a hand. "You've not got it quite right. My agreement is with the Allardyces, not with you."

"Haven't you rather agreed to a continuation of it by accepting the instalment you received a week or so back?" Jonathan suggested grimly. He had expected a fight and, by heavens, there was going to be one.

"Ah, yes," Furnival said blandly. "But have you not heard yet from your solicitor—or rather, Jacynth's— that, acting on my instructions, *my* solicitor wrote asking why it had been sent to me and returned the check?" check?"

"No, I certainly haven't," Jonathan said skeptically.

"You will," Furnival said placidly. "In the meantime there's another point. Since you speak of my agreement with the Allardyces, it might have been as well if you had mastered the terms of it more accurately. What I agreed to was not that I should never see my daughter, but that I should never make myself known to her. There's a difference, you know."

Jonathan scowled angrily. Tricky devil!

"I see," he said ironically. "And you now feel, for some reason or other, that you're in a position to dictate new terms of agreement?"

"Oh yes," he replied simply, "I am. You see, I'm not taking that allowance any more."

"You're not. . . ." Jonathan stared at him in astonishment. "But I was under the impression that you'd lived on it all these years."

Tim Furnival shrugged his shoulders.

"I'm hardly responsible for your impressions," he pointed out.

"But if you didn't need it, why have you taken it?" Jonathan asked.

Tim laughed shortly.

"I'll tell you," he said rather grimly. "First of all can you imagine what a man feels like when his wife dies giving birth to his child? No, of course you can't. He feels like a murderer." He stood up and strode impatiently up and down until, apparently, he had managed to control his feelings a little. "That was how I felt when the Allardyces came—raw and bleeding and with every nerve quivering. If they'd shown a grain of sympathy. . . . But no, they made no bones about it. They hadn't come to see if I would let them have the child. They had come, so they told me, to take the child. And before I had time to say a word they began to talk about making me an allowance if I would agree."

"They evidently knew you pretty well." Jonathan's voice was dry. "After all, you did take it."

"Yes, I took it," Tim agreed. "I wonder, have you ever been told to your face that you're an utter rotter? It doesn't always make you determined to show what a fine fellow you are. It may have exactly the reverse effect! It had with me, in the mood that I was then. I haggled with them and put up the price. That gave me a certain amount of satisfaction. I knew I had the whip hand and I dictated my terms!" Seeing the distaste written on Jonathan's face he paused. "Not impressed?" he inquired cynically.

"Hardly. After all, she was your child. You practically sold her."

For a moment Furnival looked at him curiously.

"I was a fool ever to try to explain," he admitted. "Still, I may as well finish. How could I keep an infant with me? You know perfectly well that I've always lived by my wits—well, who doesn't? But my methods were more direct, maybe. At least I knew she'd be safe with them."

"In spite of the fact that you blame them for making Isobel unhappy?" Jonathan laughed. "That'll hardly do, Furnival!"

"No! Aren't you forgetting that I would never permit them to adopt her? At any moment I could have taken her from them—"

"That I very much doubt. If they'd contested it, no court in the world would have given you the custody of her, or her money." Jonathan told him.

"No? Then why was the old lady so anxious to get her married to you?"

"So that there was no chance of your living off Jacynth," Jonathan said grimly.

"Exactly! And would she have done that if there hadn't been a good chance of my being accepted as Jacynth's guardian?" he demanded.

Jonathan was silent. He knew only too well that was true. It had been Christina Allardyce's constant fear. He himself had said he thought she exaggerated that fear, but now he was not so sure.

Furnival laughed.

"It's very awkward, isn't it?" he suggested. "We're like a couple of duellers with sword-points at each other's throat. If either of us lunges, he may kill the other, but at the cost of his own life as well. It's rather amusing in a way."

"I see nothing amusing in it," Jonathan told him grimly.

"But then your sense of humor is not your strongest point, is it?" Tim suggested aggravatingly. "I've noticed that before. Anyhow, we can sum it up like this: you're under the impression that I'm going to do my damnedest to get on Jacynth's right side and then make a much better thing out of it than the allowance? And you're determined that I shall do nothing of the kind?"

"You appreciate my feelings exactly," Jonathan agreed dryly.

"And, of course," Tim went on softly, "the reason is easily apparent. You don't intend that anybody but you shall have the handling of her money, do you?"

"Exactly." The word cut like a knife, and even Tim, though he himself had suggested as much, started at its vigor.

"You're a cool one, I must say," he said slowly.

"Perhaps it's as well. We know just where we stand now. Now I'll tell you what I propose. Just so long as Jacynth is happy I'll keep out of the picture, except as a casual friend. But, by heavens, Branksome, if she isn't . . . and, I might tell you, I'm none too sure about it at that."

"What makes you say that?" Jonathan asked sharply.

Tim raised his brows.

"I've got eyes, haven't I?" he pointed out. "Well?"

Jonathan's lip curled. "I prefer to put it another way," he said coolly. "I won't tell her about the allowance you had from the Allardyces—on condition that you don't tell her you're her father."

Tim turned it over in his mind, his bright eyes on Jonathan's face. Suddenly he laughed.

"I told you we're at each other's mercy," he pointed out. "All right, I'll agree."

"Good!" Jonathan said briefly, then turned away.

Tim let him take a few strides and then he called him back.

"Well?"

"I was wondering—for what reason does Jacynth think you married her?" Tim said reflectively.

He thought that Jonathan would hit him. For a long moment they stared at each other in silence—a silence that could be felt. Then, without a word, Jonathan turned again and strode off.

Tim's lips pursed in a soundless whistle. He had thought that he was too much of a man of the world for any odd manifestation of human nature to startle him. But Jonathan had succeeded in doing it. Tim had read in his eyes a secret that Jonathan had believed nobody so much as guessed at.

CHAPTER NINE

The weather, which until then had been clear and golden, broke with no more warning than an ominous gathering of clouds one afternoon.

"There'll be a thunderstorm before nightfall," Jonathan predicted. "I think I'll go down and see that the boats are hauled up and covered. They've got standing orders down there to see to it in case of need, but I'd sooner make sure for myself."

"I'll come with you," Cynthia said quickly. "It's stifling in the house. I could do with a breath of air."

Jacynth said nothing. What was there to say? On the face of it there was no reason on earth why Cynthia should not go down with Jonathan. Besides, what could she say that would not produce an amused laugh from Cynthia or an ironical jibe at her unsophisticated conventionality? Either would simply serve to make her look foolish in Jonathan's eyes. So she set her lips firmly and somberly watched them start off.

The first heavy drops were already falling as she turned away from the window, and with a sinking heart she realized just what the rain was going to mean. Inevitably she and Cynthia would be thrown into one another's company, and surely that would produce a crisis. Up to the present she had robbed Cynthia of the satisfaction of knowing for sure whether her regaining Jonathan's love mattered in the slightest to his wife. But at close quarters it was going to be a different matter. How could one hide the fact that one's heart was breaking?

For three days the rain never ceased to fall, and during that time, with one excuse and another, Jacynth managed to spend as little time as possible in Cynthia's company. But on the fourth day she found it difficult to avoid her.

It almost looked as if Cynthia was deliberately seeking her out, when suddenly she said to Jacynth with a sigh, "Dear Jonathan, he's his own worst enemy, isn't he?"

Jacynth stiffened defensively. "In what way?" she asked as coolly as she could.

Cynthia shrugged her shoulders.

"He finds it so difficult to say no when anyone asks him to do anything for them," she said sweetly.

"Who had you in mind?" Jacynth said, refusing to listen to the panicky beating of her heart. Something in Cynthia's manner or voice told her unmistakably that there was no avoiding the issue now.

"Oh . . . at the moment? That Farrow man!"

"I don't see. . . ." Jacynth said incautiously.

Cynthia sighed.

"My dear, there's so much that you don't see!" she said, with an impatience that Jacynth was convinced was all part of her plan. "You really ought to make an effort—for Jonathan's sake. It must be very trying for a man of his intelligence—" She broke off abruptly. "But of course, I ought not to say that, ought I? I'm sorry. But as for Farrow, isn't it obvious to you that he's cadging off Jonathan? Obviously he's a 'won't work,' but admittedly he has charm. Jonathan's softhearted enough to fall for his line. Someone really ought to warn him."

For a moment Jacynth was silent. She knew perfectly well that everything that Cynthia was saying was barbed and double-edged. She clenched her hands together, hardly aware that her nails were cutting into the flesh, and with the deep, shuddering breath of a swimmer plunging into a cold sea she said steadily, "Cynthia, why do you think Jonathan married me?"

Cynthia's eyes widened a little. She had, she admitted to herself, underestimated the chit. She might not have much wit, but she had courage. Then, mentally, Cynthia shrugged her shoulders. Well, what if she had? Couldn't she, Cynthia, match it—yes, and beat it—with a recklessness born of boredom and a determination to let nothing stand in the way of getting what she wanted?

"My dear," she drawled lazily, "you're the one that should be able to answer that."

"Yes," Jacynth said deliberately. "Put that way, it doesn't seem to concern you very much, does it? But if I put it differently. . . . If Jonathan loves you, why did he marry me?"

It was out! She had played, not the highest card that she held, but one that must serve to make Cynthia show the strength of her own hand. And Jacynth knew that she held a master card—in certain circumstances. She held her breath, waiting for Cynthia's answer.

Cynthia shrugged her shoulders.

"Surely the most obvious suggestion is—for your money!" she said tartly, not relishing Jacynth's outspokenness. For Cynthia the hint, the half-spoken word, the innuendo were preferable weapons.

Jacynth laughed softly, triumphantly.

"Jonathan said someone would be sure to say that!" she said. "And he told me that it wasn't true. He gave me his word."

Cynthia smiled, though there was nothing humorous in the twist of her lips.

"Clever, clever Jonathan!" she said softly.

"What do you mean?" Jacynth said sharply, completely taken aback by Cynthia's reaction and, because of her surprise, betrayed into exposing her vulnerability.

"Just . . . clever Jonathan. Oh, my dear girl, don't you see, he thought of everything. He saw the wisdom of getting his word in first. Could anything prove more utterly how right I am?"

For a moment Jacynth did not reply. She was staring at Cynthia with both amazement and disgust written clearly on her face.

"You love him—and yet you can believe he would do a beastly, calculating thing like that?" she said wonderingly.

Cynthia laughed triumphantly.

"A woman will excuse any fault in a man, if she loves him!"

"No!" Jacynth said with sudden passion. "You don't know what it means to love anybody but yourself. What you mean is that you would forgive a man anything—if he loved you enough. But if ever he stopped loving you, you'd do everything in your power to hurt him!"

Cynthia looked at her with something like respect in her eyes.

"Clever girl! You're really beginning to grow up, aren't you?"

She rose to her feet and stretched lazily, yawning as she did so.

"Really, the day hasn't been as boring as I thought it was going to be," she said carelessly.

As Jacynth watched her stroll out of the room, confident, beautiful, utterly self-centered, she suddenly buried her face in her hands. She had gambled . . . and she had lost. All that was left was the choice of waiting until Jonathan told her that their marriage was a mistake or of telling him that she herself knew it was.

The weather improved, although not sufficiently for them to take either of the boats out. Sudden squalls of rain would blot everything out, and the early mornings and evenings were often misty and damp.

However, there were bright intervals, and Jacynth took the opportunity they afforded to go out on long, solitary tramps. She sought no company, partly because she did not want to have to talk and partly because she knew that she was not looking well and did not want to answer questions about her appearance. All the same, it was inevitable that sooner or later she would meet someone she knew, and that someone chanced to be Mick. He loomed up suddenly in a way that suggested he had been hanging about on the off-chance of encountering her, and although his greeting sounded cheery, the cheer in it was not very convincing.

He fell into step beside her and Jacynth accepted his presence fatalistically. One could hardly tell a friend that he was just not wanted, but Mick was quick to see that she was far from being her normal, happy self.

However, to Jacynth's relief, he had the tact not to refer to the fact, and they talked small generalities in fits and starts until, suddenly, Mick's self-control snapped.

"Jacynth, you're looking rotten," he said bluntly. "What's the matter?"

It was no good saying "Nothing," because he just wouldn't believe it. Having to find some sort of an explanation, she said rather unconvincingly, "It's being shut indoors," she fenced. "One soon loses sunburn, you know."

She knew that he was not convinced, but he made no more effort to press her for an explanation. But even more disconcertingly he suddenly said, "Several times I've made up my mind to come and see you. Then I thought perhaps I'd better wait for an invitation. But it didn't come."

"Oh, Mick!" She looked distressed. "I'm sorry! But things have been a bit difficult—"

"Between you . . . and Jonathan?" he asked swiftly. "He's said he'd rather I didn't come?"

"Oh no!" she said quickly. "Nothing like that. . . ." But her voice trailed away unconvincingly. It was true that Jonathan had not specifically said he did not want Mick to visit the house, but surely it was rather odd that he had not suggested that he should come, since they had all spent so much time together.

She went home in rather a thoughtful mood and found that Jonathan had come home a little earlier than usual, and that, rather amazingly, they had the house to themselves.

They shared a rather silent tea, and then, suddenly, Jacynth said bluntly, "Jonathan, I think we should ask Mick to dinner soon. I think he's a bit hurt that we haven't done so already."

"Oh?" Jonathan said lightly. "That's a pity, but look here, Jacynth, don't think I'm being unpleasant, but I'm not sure it isn't a mistake to become too friendly with holiday folk. After all, one knows very little about them. . . ."

It sounded lame and evidently Jonathan realized it, for he changed the subject abruptly.

"The weather looks as if it might improve tomorrow," he said, and Jacynth though unhappily how ill at ease he was with her now. Perhaps that was not unnatural in the circumstances. Perhaps he was finding it difficult to know how to come to the point. How to tell her that even the slight bond of their marriage that was really no marriage was too much.

Some people would say that I can't love him very much or else I would make it easy for him, she thought desperately. *But I can't—I can't—not yet, anyhow.*

"Will we be able to sail?" she asked with perfectly genuine eagerness.

"I doubt it," he said shortly, and Jacynth had the feeling that she had said the wrong thing, although it was difficult to see why. "I suppose you're finding it difficult to get through the days?"

"Well. . . ." She shrugged her shoulders.

Jonathan looked at her reflectively and sighed.

"It's odd," he said slowly. "Somehow or other, I had the impression that you were the sort of person that would always find something to do to keep from being bored."

"It's been the weather," she told him evasively. "Now that it's improving, I think tomorrow I'll go to the fair. Did you know there's one a mile or two away? I love fairs, don't you? Which do you think are more fun, dodgems or roundabouts?"

"Neither," Jonathan said shortly. "I think they're inventions of the devil. Jacynth?"

"Yes, Jonathan?"

He stirred restlessly in his chair.

"Will you do me a favor?" he asked. And then, before she had time to answer, he went on, "Would you mind very much putting it off until either Howard or I can be with you? He's coming up to town with me tomorrow, by the way."

"Why, Jonathan?" she asked gravely.

"Because there are usually some pretty rough types at these places and . . . you're not unattractive, Jacynth!" His smiled suggested his awareness of the absurdity of the understatement. But the compliment brought no comfort to Jacynth. After all, people didn't love you just because they thought you were pretty.

"Well," she said slowly, "I don't suppose it would be much fun alone, anyway."

Early the next morning Mick phoned. He sounded depressed and the conversation between them was halting and lame.

Suddenly he said, "I say, Jacynth, did you know there was a fair a few miles off?" he asked diffidently.

"Yes, I knew," she said slowly, realizing what was coming.

"Well, what about it?" he asked hopefully.

"Oh, Mick," she began, distressfully hating to refuse him yet equally disliking the thought of going against Jonathan's wishes.

"Never mind. It was just an idea," he said quickly. "It's quite all right."

"Mick . . ." she began, and paused. After all, what harm was there in going? Jonathan's objection had been to going alone. Well, with Mick there she would be perfectly safe. They would both enjoy it, and, after all, she hadn't promised in so many words. "Mick, I'll come!"

"Oh, good!" she could tell from Mick's tone that his spirits had rocketed. "I'll be right over."

"No, Mick, wait a minute—" she said, but he had already hung up.

She stood there for a moment after she had replaced the receiver wondering whether, after all, she ought not to call him back and tell him that she oughtn't to go with him. Indeed, her hand was already stretched out to lift the receiver again when Cynthia, lounging up against the door drawled, "Well, of course, you know best. But if you're not too stupid to take a word of warning from someone who knows Jonathan a lot better than you do, you're a fool. I know I wouldn't disobey him if I were in your shoes."

"How did you—?" Jacynth began and stopped. What did it matter how Cynthia knew that Jonathan didn't want her to go to the fair? That was a minor detail. What really mattered was that Cynthia was taunting her with her own lack of decision. It hadn't, of course, been difficult for her to pick that up. The way she had spoken to Mick, the fact that she had lingered by the telephone, her expression. . . .

So Cynthia thought she was afraid of Jonathan. That she didn't dare. . . .

"Don't talk nonsense, Cynthia," she said coldly. "Of course I shall go. And if I'm not in by the time Jonathan comes home, please tell him where I am."

Without waiting for Cynthia's answer, she ran upstairs for her coat.

With eyes that glinted with triumph, Cynthia watched her move out of sight. What an innocent Jacynth was.

Almost as soon as they had arrived at the fairground, Jacynth knew that she was going to be incredibly bored. It frightened her a little because, not so very long ago, she had regarded such entertainment—particularly if indulged in illicitly—as the height of enjoyment.

"I must be growing up," she thought rather dismally. "How awful if it means losing one's taste for things that used to be such fun. At least," she added honestly, "it wouldn't matter at all, of course, if there were other things to take it's place; but there aren't!"

Perhaps that was the reason it all seemed so dull . . . or perhaps it was that Mick was the wrong man. If only Jonathan had been with her!

"I say, are you bored?" Mick asked anxiously. "Because, if you are, we can leave, you know."

"No, no, of course not, Mick," she said quickly, hearing the disappointment. "Let's have a go on the dodgems. That's always fun! And then I bet I'll beat you on the rifle range. Come on!"

She goaded herself into a semblance of high spirits and evidently it deceived Mick, for he, too, showed every sign of enjoyment.

How odd! Jacynth thought wonderingly. *He's years older than I am, and he's had experiences such as I've never dreamed of.* She felt years older than he and much more experienced. She wondered when she might decently ask to go home without hurting his feelings.

Actually, it was Mick who suddenly seemed to tire of

the entertainment. He slipped his arm through Jacynth's and said abruptly, "I've had enough. How about you? Shall we go home?"

"Yes, let's," she said faintly and let him guide her to the parking lot.

Actually, the distance between the fairground and home was nearer to five miles than the one or two that Jacynth had calculated. And before they had gone more than a mile or so Mick suddenly uttered an exclamation and pulled up at the side of the road.

"What's the matter?" Jacynth asked, with the quick alarm of ignorance.

"Got my foot flat down on the gas, and she was hardly doing more than a crawl," he said as he got out and lifted the hood.

Jacynth watched him fiddling with the car's complicated interior, and then, to her relief, he closed it down again and climbed back in.

"Something wrong with the jet," he explained. "A bit of grit, I expect."

"Have you fixed it?" she asked anxiously, suddenly realizing that daylight was slowly fading.

"Hope so," he said as he let in the clutch.

For a few moments his hopes seemed justified, and then, without warning, the car gave a few gasping pants and came to a halt.

"Damn!" Mick said angrily, jumping out again.

A few minutes later he gave his verdict.

"Sorry, Jacynth; we've had it," he said. "It's a garage job. I'm awfully sorry."

"Oh, Mick, it isn't your fault!" But in spite of her desire not to appear to blame him, it was impossible to keep a note of anxiety out of her voice. "What shall we do?"

For a moment he hesitated.

"The deuce of it is . . ." he began. "You see, Jacynth, if it were a sedan, I could lock it up, walk back with you and find a garage that would come out and tow her in. But she's wide open, and it would be the easiest thing in the world for anyone to release the brake, hitch her to another car, and vanish with her."

"Well, it isn't necessary for both of us to stay. I'll walk back and tell a garage to come out to you," Jacynth said practically.

"Would you?" Mick asked eagerly. "You wouldn't be frightened? It's getting dark."

"Of course I won't be," Jacynth said staunchly, sliding out of her seat. "I just keep straight on, don't I?"

"Yes, absolutely straight. You are a brick, Jacynth. Most girls would have been as mad as the dickens!"

"That would be silly," Jacynth said, not having the hardness of heart necessary to tell him that anything would be better than just waiting here when every nerve in her body ached to be home.

She set off briskly, whistling gaily while she was within hearing of Mick. But then that little bit of gallant defiance broke down. It was a lonely, desolate road and the dusk seemed to hang about her like stifling curtains. Once or twice she heard a sound, and though common sense told her that it was nothing more than some little wild beast or grazing cattle, her heart seemed to turn over. It *might* have been a footstep.

With her hands clenched in her pockets, she forced herself to keep to a steady, swinging gait, and at last, with a little gasp of relief, she saw lights.

A few moments later, she had reached the garage. It was closed, but fortunately the owner lived next door to it, and he agreed to go out at once, though he grumbled at having to do it and muttered something about it being a dog's life.

The last bit of the way home was uphill, and Jacynth dragged herself wearily up it, wondering just what was going to happen when she reached the house. Jonathan would be home by now; he would be angry.

Suddenly she was dazzled by approaching headlights, and the car pulled up just short of her. Jonathan jumped out and came toward her.

"Jacynth, where the devil have you been?" he demanded angrily.

Involuntarily, she had swayed toward him when she had seen who it was, but now she held herself erect.

"To the fair, with Mick!" she said defiantly.

"He might at least have had the decency to bring you home!" said Jonathan sharply.

"He couldn't help it—the car broke down . . ." Jacynth began and swayed again. Instantly Jonathan put out an arm to steady her, but because she so longed for the comfort of his arms she drew herself away from this mechanical gesture of help.

"You'd better get in the car," Jonathan said, as if he had not noticed her movement, and in silence he drove her back to the house.

"Go into my study," he said shortly, and Jacynth was too cold and tired to protest.

There was a log fire burning, and she sank down on the rug in front of it, grateful for the warmth.

"Drink this," Jonathan said curtly, handing her a glass.

She sipped it cautiously and made a face.

"Ugh, it's horrid! I'd rather not."

"Drink it!" he ordered, and Jacynth found herself meekly drinking the fiery stuff.

"That should warm you," Jonathan commented as he took the glass.

"It has," Jacynth admitted. She began to make trifling conversation, because a glance at Jonathan's face had told her that he was really angry—just as Cynthia had said he would be. "What was it?"

"Brandy," he said.

"Oh!" Jacynth said with attempted lightness. "I've never had it before. I simply can't imagine how people can drink it for pleasure."

Her voice trailed away to silence and she began to pick at a thread on her skirt.

"If you're feeling better, I'd like to thrash this business out here and now," Jonathan said grimly. "Are you all right?"

"Yes," Jacynth said in a very small voice. "Quite all right."

"Very well, then. I'd like you, if you don't mind, to tell me just why you went to the fair—after having promised me you wouldn't."

"I didn't promise," Jacynth said quickly. "I only said I supposed it wouldn't be much fun alone."

"That was implying that you would not go," Jonathan said inexorably. "You know perfectly well that I accepted it as a promise. And yet, the minute my back was turned, you went!"

"But not alone," she said quickly. "Mick was with me. I was quite safe—"

"Were you?" he asked ironically. "I hardly call a

three- or four-mile walk after dark very safe. People are apt to jump to very definite conclusions if they meet a young girl out by herself in such circumstances."

"What nonsense!" Jacynth said angrily. "Besides, it was quite an accident."

"That's beside the point, and you know it!" he said angrily. "Well, at least I know one thing now. You're not to be trusted."

She jumped to her feet, her face flaming, her fists clenched.

"How dare you say things like that! How dare you!" she stormed.

"Because they're true," he said stonily.

"They're not!" she contradicted. "But if they were, isn't it your fault? You stop me doing everything I want to! You never let me be happy. Oh"—the bitterness in her heart suddenly welled over—"why did you marry me if it was only to make me miserable?"

The minute the words were out she regretted them. For what answer could he give that would satisfy her? He could not tell her that it was because he loved her, and there was nothing else that would do.

But Jonathan did not answer her. Instead he put a question to her.

"Suppose, instead, you tell me why you married me?" he suggested.

Just for a moment she hesitated. Suppose she told him the truth! Suppose she explained that it had seemed the most natural thing in the world to do, that instinct had guided her, and that she had grown to love him so that it felt as if she must always have done so.

Then she looked at his hard, angry face, and all the pain he had made her suffer, all the indignities Cynthia had put upon her, suddenly shut out every other feeling.

"Because you told me I ought not to!" she said recklessly. "Don't you remember you told me I ought never to have been asked to do it? That it would be reckless folly? Well, you shouldn't have said that to me. My father was a gambler and I'm his daughter. I always take a dare."

He was so silent that for a moment she was frightened.

Then, heavily, he said, "That was all? There was no other reason?"

"No!" she said defiantly. "No other reason at all. So now you know!"

"Yes, I know," he agreed.

"So it's all your fault," she went on hurriedly. "And you've got to let me go. You must, Jonathan! I can't stand it any more. It was all wrong. A marriage ought to mean something more than this. You know that!"

"I know," he agreed.

"Then, you'll let me go?" She hardly knew what she was saying; only knew that anything—even never seeing Jonathan again—was better than this torment of seeing him, being with him yet never sharing his life because he loved another woman.

"No!" Jonathan gritted the word out. "I'll not let you go. You've given your word and you'll stand by it!"

She stared at him incredulously.

"But you can't do that!"

"I can and I shall," he said stonily.

"Then I shall . . . just go! And you can't stop me!"

"No?" he asked grimly. "Don't be too sure of that. Haven't you forgotten something?"

"What?" she demanded, her heart thudding fearfully.

"That I have absolute control of your money, and by heaven, I mean to keep it," he told her.

CHAPTER TEN

The next morning, almost to her relief, Jacynth woke up with a headache so bad that there was no question of getting up until it was at least a little better.

She called Jonathan into her room and asked him to tell Mrs. Evans to bring her up a cup of tea, but to her surprise Jonathan himself brought it, together with a couple of aspirins.

She sipped the refreshing drink languidly, and Jonathan stood by to take the cup from her when she had finished. She wished he wouldn't, for she knew that she was on the brink of tears, and to have given way to them in front of him would have been the last humiliation.

Even after she had finished it he still stayed there. With an effort she lifted her heavy lids and looked at him questioningly.

"I'm sorry your head's so bad," he said awkwardly.

Jacynth's heart contracted. Deep down ·he was so essentially kind and decent; the desire to hurt him had long since died.

"It's all right," she said, hardly understanding the closeness of the link between love and something that had been very much like hatred.

But even as she spoke her eyes closed again, and after a moment's hesitation, he tiptoed out of the room.

But Jacynth could not sleep. Her brain was too active, the problems she had to solve too urgent.

It was all such a tangle. After all, Cynthia had been right. Jonathan had married her for her money. He had all but admitted it in saying that he meant to keep absolute control of her money. She had not believed that it could be true, and even now it seemed odd that a man as rich as Jonathan should hanker after more to the extent of marrying a girl he neither knew nor loved to get it. Except, of course, that he had told her he hadn't as big a capital as she had, but his income was a little more than hers. Perhaps it was capital he wanted. Men wanted such funny things.

But that didn't explain Gran's anxiety that they should get married. Nor could she believe that Gran, whatever her reasons had been, would have urged her to marry a man who only wanted her money. No, Gran was shrewd and she must have been satisfied. Of course, she hadn't known about Cynthia.

There was no solution, no way out. One just went in circles like a mouse in its wheel.

Mercifully, she began to feel drowsy, and for an hour or so she slept deeply. When she awoke the headache was gone, although it had left a weariness that showed in her heavy eyes.

She refreshed herself with a warm bath and then dressed slowly and apathetically. After all, what did it matter how she looked? There was nobody to care.

She went slowly downstairs, and to her relief no one was about. But a letter was lying on her little desk. It bore no stamp, so evidently it had been delivered by hand, although she did not recognize the writing.

She slit it open mechanically and glanced at the signature. It was from Mick.

Dear Little Jacynth,
It will probably come as rather a surprise to you that

I have decided to accept the offer my uncle made some time ago to go into his factory. You see, there's really no reason on earth why I shouldn't—and quite a few reasons why I should.

Bless you for everything you've done to help me with your spontaneous friendship and your kind little heart. I'm afraid sometimes it's made trouble for you, hasn't it? If it has, that will be all over now that I'm going away.

I won't forget you, Jacynth, ever. But I shall never seek you out. Perhaps you can understand why. Only promise me that if ever you are in trouble you will tell me, because I shall be completely at your command always. The address at the head of this note will always find me. I'm leaving this morning.

> Yours,
> Mick.

With fingers that shook she folded Mick's letter very tenderly, and after a moment's thought she put it in the folds of the little diary she always kept.

Slowly she sat down.

So that was Mick's secret. He loved her. Of course, he had not said so in so many words, but could any woman mistake the true meaning of what he had written?

"How funny," she said shakily, unaware she was speaking aloud, "to long for one man's love and be unable to win it, and yet to have another that just doesn't count that way head over heels in love with one!"

She brooded over the contrariness of life, and then, without any conscious effort on her part, an idea came to her.

Here was a way out! She didn't love Mick, but she

liked him very much, and there would be such comfort in being loved. If she went to him, would that solve all her problems? And Jonathan's?

"I don't know, I don't know!" she muttered, passing her hand over her forehead. Suddenly she jumped to her feet. Through the window she had seen Cynthia approaching the house. Somehow or other she must avoid meeting her. She must get things worked out alone—now.

Quickly she made her plan. It was quite simple. As Cynthia reached the front door she herself would slip out of the long window into the garden. By the time Cynthia was in the house she would be out of sight.

It was the work of a second to put the plan into action, and as far as Cynthia was concerned it worked perfectly. But she had hardly made it beyond the gates of the house when she encountered Howard.

"Hello, where are you off to?" he asked pleasantly. And then, looking at her closely, he added, "Headache better?"

"Almost," she said hurriedly. "I thought a little sail might clear it altogether."

"You don't mean you're taking the *Firefly* out—on your own, do you?" he asked.

"Yes, why not?" she said defiantly.

He shrugged his shoulders.

"Well, you know the way Jonathan feels about it," he began.

Jacynth stopped walking and turned to him.

"Howard," she said imploringly, "haven't you ever come to a place in your life where you simply have to be alone to think things out?"

He looked at her sharply.

"Yes, most people get there sooner or later," he admitted. "But you—"

"Yes, me!" she said defiantly. "Howard, I must go, please!"

"Well. . . ." He hesitated. "Look here, Jacynth, let me come with you. I swear I won't talk to you. I understand too well how you feel for that."

"Howard, if there was somebody I could tolerate, it would be you," she said desperately. "I know. You do understand. But I must be alone."

"All right," he said suddenly. "Only, Jacynth, swear you won't do anything reckless. . . . I mean, there's always more than one way out of a problem, if one is patient."

She smiled wryly at him.

"Is there, Howard?" she said wistfully. "I don't know . . . perhaps you're right. Anyhow, I won't do anything desperate, I promise you that."

He nodded, thankful at least for that assurance. But after he had watched her move out of sight down the narrow path he found that her restlessness had conveyed itself to him. He was not in the mood for company. He had no desire to go back to the house.

He hesitated for a moment and then, with a shrug, set off cross-country to seek solitude among the hills.

Jacynth had been mistaken in thinking that she had been out of sight before Cynthia had had a chance of seeing her go. Actually, she had not been able to find her key in her purse, and so she had still been on the porch as Jacynth had stolen across the grass. Some instinct had made her draw back still closer in the shelter of the porch, and then, as Jacynth passed through the gate, her forehead was suddenly creased in a frown. Where on earth was the girl going on a cool day like this without a coat?

Curiosity rather than concern for Jacynth prompted her to run down the short path to see which way she had turned.

To the right. That meant that she was going down to those boring boats.

And then Howard had appeared from nowhere, and the two were walking together. Cynthia shrugged her shoulders. What if they were? She was certainly not jealous.

Slowly she turned back to the house and saw that her path was blocked by the old gardener to whom Jonathan had referred as the local weather prophet—Elijah or Elisha something.

"None of you people are going out in the little boats today, I do hope?" he inquired, peering shortsightedly at her.

"I really couldn't say," she said indifferently. And then, as she was turning away, she suddenly stopped. "Why?" she asked in a totally different voice.

"Because it's dangerous," he said in the singsong local accent that got on her nerves.

Cynthia's heart seemed to miss a beat.

"But it's a lovely day!" she pointed out, and indeed, it was. As clear and golden as all those that had gone before the weather had broken.

"So it seems to you," he said with irritating conviction. "But not to me. It is true, I tell you. Before two hours are gone there will be a mist. And by nightfall there will be a proper fog. I am telling you!"

"Rubbish!" Cynthia said uneasily. He was an annoying old man, but after all, Jonathan believed in him.

She turned and hurried to the road. If she was quick she would catch them, because it always took a certain amount of time to get ready.

Reaching the top of the little path that ran steeply down to the bay, she paused. Yes, there they were. Jacynth in her thin dress and Howard in his disreputable old mac and that ridiculous tweed hat she could not persuade him to abandon.

She opened her mouth to shout to them . . . but no sound came. Slowly she lifted her hand and pressed clenched knuckles against her mouth.

If she didn't call . . . if they went . . . and the old man had been right. . . .

"No!" she whispered breathlessly. "No. I must tell them. Of course I must!"

And yet, if she didn't, who would know? She could say that she had shouted and they had not heard and that before she could reach them they had started off.

With horrified, staring eyes she watched them make the necessary preparations. She tried to move, but she felt as if she had turned to stone.

They pushed off, a little breeze filled the sail, and they slipped out to sea.

Suddenly Cynthia seemed to come to life.

"Come back!" she screamed. "Come back. . . ."

But they were too far away now to hear.

All the strength seemed to leave her, and abruptly she sat down on the short, damp grass, shivering as if she had a fever.

It was nonsense! She told herself that a dozen times over. The day was as glorious as ever. The old idiot had simply been showing off. After all, all these weather prophets made mistakes sometimes. She had been a fool to worry.

And yet she could not relax. Restlessly she wandered from one room to another, trying to shut from her mind the picture of the little boat putting out.

She sought Mrs. Evans's company simply for the sake of having someone to talk to, but the woman was in a bad mood and answered her curtly.

The house seemed to stifle her, and she went out into the garden. One didn't feel so shut in there. But—she gave a little shiver—it wasn't as warm as she had thought. She glanced up at the sun and stifled a little cry. It wasn't as bright as it had been. A filmy mist seemed to be gathering about it. A dampness hung in the air.

"No!" she said desperately. "No, it can't be. It mustn't be!"

But now there was no doubt about it. Elijah had been right. With every passing moment the mist thickened. It pressed about the house and it made Cynthia feel as if she were a prisoner, shut off from everybody else.

It seemed hours before she heard the sound of a car crawling cautiously up to the approach to the house, but even then the relief at the thought of human companionship was completely lost at the realization that it must be Jonathan—Jonathan, who would be certain to ask questions.

He came in evidently chilled to the bone and made for the fire.

"Heavens, it's cold!" he said, rubbing his hands to restore circulation.

Cynthia said nothing. She stood staring at him with widely distended eyes, frightened as she had never been frightened in her life before.

"How's Jacynth?" he asked next.

Cynthia ran her tongue over her dry lips.

"She's . . . better," she said jerkily. "She . . . went out."

He turned sharply, his face full of startled amazement.

"Went out in this?" he said incredulously. "She must be mad!"

"No. Before it came," she managed.

He frowned in his perplexity.

"Did she say where she was going?" he asked.

She shook her head.

"No," she said with something like relief. That, at least, was true. But surely Jonathan's next question would force her to tell the truth.

But for some reason or other it did not occur to him to think that she might have gone out in one of the boats. She started as he said suddenly, "She had a letter this morning. One of the boys from the inn brought it up. Where is it?"

She laughed hysterically.

"Jonathan!" she said, with something of her habitual self-possession. "How should I know? I'm not Jacynth's keeper."

He gave her a quick, questioning look, but evidently her face did not betray her. Without a word he went up to

Jacynth's room and looked about. There was no sign of the letter there. Then he came down to the study.

For a moment he stood irresolutely in front of her little desk, and then, overcoming the feeling of revulsion that the thought of prying into her private affairs roused, he tried to lift the lid. The scowl on his face deepened as he discovered that it was locked.

With a little exclamation of impatience, he took out his own bunch of keys and tried them in the lock. By chance one of them fitted and he lifted the lid.

At first, in spite of its tidiness, he could not see anything in the nature of a letter. Then he picked up the little diary and out it fell. He put the book down and opened the letter with hands that shook so much that the words blurred before his eyes.

He read what Mick had written and his face went white. To him it seemed that there could be no doubt where Jacynth was. Last night she had begged him to let her go, and he had refused. Now, because this unprincipled young hound had offered her what seemed like a sanctuary, she had rushed off to him.

And he, Jonathan, was to blame. He had promised to care for her and cherish her, and instead he had subjected her to all sorts of difficulties and bewilderments—not intentionally, he could comfort himself with that, if comfort it was—but to his dying day he knew that he would blame himself for this mad folly of hers.

Suddenly he started. What was he doing wasting time here? He must go after her and bring her back. Make her understand, if one could make such a child understand, that this was no way out of their problems.

He hurried downstairs and found Cynthia waiting for

him. Her whole manner suggested an uneasiness that matched his own, yet when she put a sympathetic hand on his arm he found himself shaking it off.

"Jonathan, where are you going?" she asked shrilly as he opened the front door. The mist poured into the hall as he turned and said briefly, "To bring Jacynth back, of course!"

"But Jonathan!" she wailed, then was silent. A desperate hope filled her. Perhaps, after all, they had returned in time. Perhaps they had gone for a walk.

But that was silly. If they had realized that the mist was threatening enough to make them turn back, then the obvious thing would have been to come straight to the house, not go for a walk.

And yet she had been convinced that Jonathan had had some definite destination in mind; there was a purposefulness about him.

She wandered back to the living room and sat there like a woman of stone. Now there was neither hope nor fear in her heart. Only a feeling of numbness so complete that she wondered if she would ever feel any emotion again.

Time dragged on. She was quite alone. Mrs. Evans had gone down to the village to see a friend and had evidently decided not to venture back until the weather improved.

Then from nowhere, it seemed, came the sudden sound of quick footfalls. Someone was coming up the path. A man. It must be Jonathan.

She heard the key turn in the lock and forced herself to go to the door. Then, as her eyes fell on the man who had let himself in, she screamed.

"Howard!"

He shook himself like a dog.

"Lord, I've had a time finding my way back," he said. "Twice I almost gave up— Here, what's the matter? You look like you've just seen a ghost."

"Howard!" She was shaking his arm desperately. "Jacynth! Where's Jacynth? You were together."

"No, I left her. She went out in the *Firefly*. My God, do you mean to say she isn't back?"

She shook her head, her fingers pressed to her mouth.

"But . . . but I saw you start," she whimpered.

"No, she went alone. She didn't want anybody with her."

"No!" she said stubbornly. "I saw you both in the boat!" She caught hold of his arm again. "Howard, don't play with me. Tell me where Jacynth is! Don't torment me any more."

He looked down at her wonderingly.

"Torment you?" he said uncomprehendingly. "You speak as if it was your fault that she went out."

"No!" she said breathlessly. "No, why should it be?"

"I don't know," he said. "Unless you knew that this mist was coming up."

"Don't be absurd," she said hysterically. "How could I know? I'm no weather prophet!"

"No, but old Elijah is. I suppose you didn't see him? He didn't warn you?"

His voice trailed away, and husband and wife stared in horrified silence at one another.

"He did tell you," he said positively. "And you started to come after us to warn us. And then you suddenly realized—"

Suddenly he caught her shoulder in a fierce grip and

forced her face up so that there was nothing she could hide from him,

"You realized that here was a chance you had been longing for," he whispered. "A chance to get rid of Jacynth . . . and me, for always!"

CHAPTER ELEVEN

As the sound of Howard's voice died away, something happened to Cynthia that had never happened before. She saw herself as she really was.

Perhaps few people are really honest even to themselves about their failings, but Cynthia more than most had consistently refused to admit that she could ever be in the wrong. Somehow or other, she would contrive to lay the fault at the others' doors, particularly if it was something that touched her personal vanity.

It meant so much to Cynthia that it should never be hurt. And it was not very difficult. After all, she cared little for the opinion of other women—anything unpleasant they might say about her was instantly dismissed as due to their jealousy.

And men? Well, she was very beautiful and she could be very gracious. And so she had never been without her admirers. Admiration, the sense of her own power—these had been heady incense to a girl who had been self-centered from her childhood days. In time they began to be the only things that mattered. And yet, oddly enough, it was just because of his steady devotion that she had grown to despise Howard. "He's always *there*," she had told herself impatiently. "Always under my feet like a dog that wants you to take it out for a walk."

It never occurred to her that the other men who admired her were constantly changing. Perhaps she did not notice it, finding a thrill in each new conquest, each triumph of her beauty. In her own mind, those who faded from her circle went because she dismissed them. It did not enter her head to doubt but that she lived forever in their hearts, and that she had only to crook her little finger for them to come running . . . until she had met Jonathan again on the very day of his marriage.

Even now, she could remember the fury in her heart as she had seen them come out of the ballroom, their fingers linked, their eyes dreaming. . . .

Suddenly she heard Howard speaking, and she listened with a queer, detached intensity.

"You've hated Jacynth from the day you met her," he was saying inexorably. "Not because she was Jacynth, nor even because Jonathan had married her. But because he loved her and had forgotten all about you."

"It isn't true," she muttered, but there was no conviction in her voice.

"It is true and you know it," Howard insisted. "Oh, I'll grant you that it was because of you that Jonathan had remained unmarried for so long. But don't flatter yourself it was because he had an undying love for you! You killed that yourself the day he found out that you'd married me for my money."

"*You* told him that!" she said, her breath coming in short, hard sobs.

"I?" Howard laughed curtly. "Heaven knows, a man who'll marry a woman who only wants his money has little enough self-respect. But, at least, he doesn't go advertising the fact!"

Suddenly she realized the full implication of what he was saying.

"You knew?" she said incredulously. "And yet you married me! Why?"

He shrugged his shoulders.

"I think you know the answer to that well enough."

Of course she did! Always she had known that he loved her with an intensity that was completely beyond her comprehension . . . or desire. Perhaps it was just because she had always known it was beyond her achievement that she had so resented it in him. But now?

Unconsciously, she had spoken the last two words aloud and Howard looked at her reflectively. His usually good-natured face was grim and hard. She would never know it, but in his heart he was blaming himself that things had ever come to such a pass. Knowing her weakness, he should have been her strength. But he had been afraid. Even now, he could remember that desperate agony that had almost killed him when he discovered that she didn't love him. How had he known? He hardly knew. Little things at first, though she had been very clever. And for one flaming moment his whole manhood had risen in revolt at the indignity she would put on him. Then he had known that he could not put her out of his life. Perhaps, he told himself, after they were married it would be different. He would teach her to love him. But that had been just so much self-deception. She had never learned to love anybody but herself. And he had let things slide because he was afraid of losing her. But now. . . .

"Yesterday, I went to see a man Jonathan introduced me to," he said quietly. "He has offered me a job in Canada, and I've accepted. I shall be leaving in two or three weeks."

Vaguely, in the back of her mind was a growing amazement at the revelation of something in Howard that she had never known was there. A sureness of himself, a strength. . . . But there was something else that mattered even more than that just now.

"What about me?" she whispered.

He might, in the old days, have grasped too eagerly at the wisp of hope that her words offered. But those days of weakness were over. Never again must she think that she could play with his heart just as she chose.

"If Jacynth comes back, you'll come with me," he said sternly.

"And suppose I won't?" Cynthia said with a flash of her old disdain.

He did not attempt to touch her, but suddenly she could feel the intensity of his eyes. They held a message that would forever be burned into her consciousness.

"You will come with me," he said very positively, "because you can't help yourself. You can't do without me."

"Why can't . . . I . . . do . . . without you?" she whispered, her lips dry with suspense.

He smiled crookedly. The smile of a man who has at last learned his own strength and who yet can be tender and pitiful.

"Because I'm the only man you're ever likely to meet who knows you as you are and yet still loves you," he said quietly.

And Cynthia's eyes dropped. Humility was a new experience for her, and perhaps she hardly even yet recognized it in herself. But gratitude for the devotion that she had so long despised surged into her heart. A gratitude that was shot with fear.

"And supposing she doesn't come back?" she faltered.

"You will still come with me," he told her grimly, and she shuddered at the bleak chill in his eyes.

Inland, the mist and fog were not so intense, or else Jonathan could not have found his way along the unfamiliar road that lay between his house and the address Mick had given Jacynth. As it was, the thirty-odd miles took him almost two hours.

Nor were his thoughts comfortable companions.

"Your fault!" they hammered ceaselessly. "Only yourself to thank! You knew you'd no right to take advantage of her ignorance. Yes, you warned her! But what was that? You should have remembered what a warning means to a child like that. Just incitement to recklessness! She told you so herself, and you knew as she told you that you should let her go. And yet you told her you wouldn't! Told her you'd hold her by her very dependence on you! What sort of a love is it that would hold a girl against her will— Oh, my God, and yet to let her go!" Unconsciously his hands gripped the wheel with desperate tightness and his foot pressed down on the accelerator.

"You've got to let her go!" insisted that inner, torturing consciousness.

"But not like this!" he insisted. "This time she must realize what she's doing first."

"And you think she'll listen to you?" jibed the other self.

"She must! I'll tell her."

"What will you tell her? What is there that she wants to hear from you?"

His chin set stubbornly.

"At least I can try," and the mocking voice ceased to trouble him.

But the journey seemed endless.

The house at which Mick was staying was set back from the road, and the first time he passed it he failed to recognize the gravel drive as anything but a narrow lane. Then he realized what he had done and went back, forcing himself to be patient, creeping slowly along until he found what he was looking for.

The house was brightly lit and Jonathan's imperative knock was answered immediately.

"I must see Mr. Lavery at once," he said to the man who opened the door.

"Well?" the other man looked at Jonathan. "What do you want? I'm Mr. Lavery."

Jonathan passed his hand over his forehead. His nerves were strained almost beyond endurance and this confusion was more than he could cope with.

"Not . . . you," he muttered.

"Uncle Mat, I think this concerns me, not you." Mick had come quietly downstairs and joined them. "This is Mr. Branksome whom I recently met. D'you mind if we go into the study?"

"By all means, my boy," the older man said pleasantly. He followed the two men with his eyes and then shrugged his shoulders.

"There's something the matter, isn't there?" Mick asked as soon as he had closed the door. "What is it?"

The veins on Jonathan's forehead stood out like cords.

"You've got a nerve!" he said furiously. "As if you didn't know! Where is she? Come on, you can't get away with this, you know!"

"Where's who?" Mick demanded. It was the question that an innocent man might ask, but there was fear in his eyes.

"Where's Jacynth?" he demanded. "What have you done with her? Come on, man, you've given yourself away now! You didn't think I'd get here so soon, did you, and you're scared."

"If I am, it's because you're obviously half out of your

senses," Mick retorted. "What have you driven that poor child into doing now?"

"She's here," Jonathan insisted.

"She's not. I wish to heaven she were," Mick said grimly. "Look, if you like, you can search the house, but I give you my word, she's not here."

"She's not. . . ." Jonathan stared at him blankly. "Then, where. . . ?"

"I don't know. You'd better tell me everything that's happened," Mick said anxiously. Then he saw how ill the other man was looking and he took him by the arm and led him to a chair. "Here, you're all in. Wait, I'll get a drink."

"Never mind," Jonathan muttered, but nonetheless he took the glass that Mick put in his hand and drank from it gratefully.

"Now then?" Mick urged.

"She went out during the morning and she hasn't come back. I found your letter—"

Mick turned away. "You'd better know the truth," he said in a strained voice. "Last night, when I got back to the pub, Furnival was waiting for me."

"Furnival?" Jonathan said quickly, and Mick nodded.

"Yes, he told me. He had to because, naturally, I resented a mere acquaintance sticking a finger into my affairs. But when I knew, I had to listen. He said that, because I loved Jacynth, I must do the decent thing. I'd better get out. I said I was damned if I would, seeing that you were singeing your wings at Cynthia's candle and sooner or later Jacynth would need a friend."

"What!" Jonathan leaped from his chair. "You young hound! Cynthia means no more to me than—"

"All right, Furnival convinced me of that." A faint smile twisted his lips. "Oddly enough, it was because he obviously didn't like you very much. He said, 'Look here, Mick, I'd cheerfully punch him. You've got to accept it from me that he loves her, incredible though it seems.'"

Jonathan sank back into the chair and shaded his eyes with his hands.

"That's true enough," he admitted. "But not the other. I only wish it were!"

"It is," Mick said grimly. "You ought to believe *me* because it doesn't give me much pleasure to admit it."

"Then why hasn't she—?" Jonathan began, then stopped. "Did she think I was still in love with Cynthia?"

"It certainly isn't Cynthia's fault if she doesn't believe it," Mick insisted.

There was a little silence. Then Jonathan sighed.

"What a fool I've been!" he said with a quietness that robbed the words of any pretentiousness, "I realize now. . . . Cynthia hinted . . . made me think . . . you and Jacynth. . . ."

"She would," Mick said bitterly. For a second the two men stared at one another. Then Mick said softly, "Poor old Howard!"

Jonathan nodded, sick at heart, even in the middle of his own anxiety, for his old friend.

"I thought things over most of the night," Mick went on with his story. "And this morning I decided that he was right. So I packed up my things, wrote that note to Jacynth, and came straight here."

"And you haven't seen her since last night?" Jonathan asked.

"No."

"Then where in the world—?" Jonathan began, but he was interrupted by the telephone.

Mick answered it quickly and held it out to Jonathan.

"For you. It's Howard," he said.

"Yes?" Jonathan asked in a voice that he hardly recognized as his own. "Yes, Howard?"

For a moment or two he listened in silence, his face draining of blood.

Then he said in a staccato voice, "What have you done? The police? That's not much good, is it? Oh, I see. Yes, a broadcast from the B.B.C. Thanks, Howard. I'll be right back."

"Well?" Mick demanded.

Jonathan laid the receiver with exaggerated tenderness into its cradle.

"Jacynth—and Furnival—are out in the *Firefly*," he said tonelessly. "They're sending out a radio in the hopes that some ship or lighthouse may spot them, but—"

He broke off and after a moment's hesitation Mick laid his hand on Jonathan's arm.

"I'll drive you back," he said gruffly. "You're in no state to drive yourself."

For a moment Jonathan felt that he could not stand the presence of another person, least of all this man. Then he experienced a sudden revulsion of feeling.

"Thanks," he said.

Howard was waiting for them when they reached Crellie House, although, to their relief, there was no sign of Cynthia.

"No more news?" Jonathan asked, and Howard shook his head.

"Not yet, old chap," he said gently.

Then, as if by mutual consent, he and Mick stood back to let Jonathan wander where he would alone.

And, as if he had been drawn by a magnet, Jonathan went straight to the study in which Jacynth's little desk stood.

He sat down before the desk and opened the top. There was the little book in the same place he had thrown it. He picked it up, and for a time, sat with it in his hand. Then, with an effort, he opened it at random and read the words that Jacynth had written in her unformed, schoolgirl scrawl.

"I've been trying to think when it was that I first knew I really loved Jonathan," she had written. "It seems as if I always must have done. I think I didn't so much fall in love as *grow* into love."

So it was true! But even over this he had been blind, thinking her a child, when all the time. . . .

He began to read on a little further.

"I wonder what made me think that just loving somebody was enough? It isn't, of course. One has to be clever as well. At least, when there are people like Cynthia about. And I'm afraid I'm not clever enough. And she can't, simply can't, give him as much as I can because she doesn't really love him—not the way that makes you feel that you *ache* to make somebody happy. She will never love anybody more than she does herself."

And then, on the morning of that very day:

"I don't know. Perhaps what I have to do to make Jonathan happy is to get right out of his life. I thought that I was doing the right thing by trying to fight for him, but I'm not so sure now. After all, it doesn't really matter what the person is like that you love. It's the loving them that matters. And if Jonathan loves Cynthia, then she's the one that can make him happy."

"I've got to think things out—alone—"

He laid the book down and read those last words again and again.

She loved him—enough to want his happiness before her own. She had gone out in the little *Firefly* alone—

No, but she hadn't been alone. Tim Furnival, the man he had despised and mistrusted, was with her. Surely, whatever sort of man he was, he would stand between her and any desperate act on her part, but that was not the only danger that beset her. What might not happen in that blanket of fog? There were rocks they might drift onto, a ship, blindfolded, might cut down on them.

He buried his face in his hands. Had this miracle been given to him only to be snatched away again?

No, he wouldn't believe that! There was, there must be hope.

Deliberately, he lifted a pencil from the rack and added something to the diary.

"Come back to me, my little love, come back."

The telephone rang.

CHAPTER TWELVE

Far, far away there was a voice. It was very insistent—so insistent that it hurt to listen to it. So Jacynth tried to shut it out. But the voice kept on, and in the end, she listened because, perhaps, that would satisfy it and it would be quiet.

"Jacynth, Jacynth, listen to me! It's Jonathan, my darling."

"Jonathan, Jonathan," repeated another voice, high and monotonous that was speaking inside her head. And then, wonderingly, it asked, "Who is Jonathan?"

"Jonathan—your husband who loves you! Come back, Jacynth, I can't live without you." The voice broke.

"Come back?" It seemed to Jacynth as if there was a fight going on inside her aching head. Whoever it was that had that high, monotonous voice didn't want to be turned out. And it would be so much easier not to try to turn it out—just to drift.

"No, let me . . . sleep."

"Not yet." The outside voice was more insistent than ever. "Not until you open your eyes and tell me you won't go away— Oh, my God, doctor, can't she hear me? Isn't there anything?"

"Jonathan!" It was her own voice, very weak, almost timid; as if she could not really believe that he was there. She put out her hand blindly, gropingly, and instantly it was caught and held in a warm, comforting grasp. She could feel the warmth of his breath on her cheek.

"Listen, Jacynth," he was saying. "There's nothing to

be frightened of. You've been very ill, but now you can get better if only you'll try. And you must get better!"

"Must I?" she asked weakly. "Why?"

"Because I love you." His voice shook with suppressed passion. "Because I can't live without you."

"Can't you? Are you sure?" she asked wistfully. Of course, if that were true, she must get better. It would be silly not to.

"Quite sure." His voice was steady now.

"Say it again," she whispered.

He bent so close that his lips were touching hers.

"I love you, I love you."

She gave a little sigh and seemed to creep closer to him as she had done on their strange wedding night when she had come to him for comfort.

Her convalescence was very slow. Those who were caring for her sensed her reluctance to think about what had happened or to ask any questions. She seemed content just to live in the present, accepting Jonathan's devotion gently and gratefully, yet never demanding it, never offering any evidence of love for him.

It troubled Jonathan, for it seemed to him that not only was she making no progress but she had no desire to do so.

"Sometimes it seems to me as if she's living in a dreamworld," he told the doctor, "as if she isn't really here at all."

The doctor looked at him thoughtfully. He had had sufficient experience with people and their peculiarities to have realized, long since, that somehow or other his patient and this anxious husband had drifted apart, but he was firmly of the opinion that there were few occasions when the interference of an outsider helped, and he did not think that this was one of the few.

"You must remember that she's had a tremendous shock," he said discreetly. "Mental as well as physical. It's bound to take time for her to feel that she can really take up life with both hands again; you'll have to be tremendously patient. It doesn't do in such cases to try to force things."

No, that was probably true, Jonathan realized. But it made his heart ache to see this wistful little shadow of a girl and then to remember what she had been so few months before when he had married her. And who could be blamed for the change except himself? That being so, he ought to be thankful, he told himself, that she did not turn from him altogether. At least she was friendly, but as the days went by he wondered how he could possibly have been persuaded that she loved him. Then, still more tormentingly, there were times when he was convinced that she had loved him and he had killed her love. These were the times when he clung desperately to the memory of the time when she had been so desperately ill and only the repetition of the words "I love you" had soothed her.

The weeks crept past and November had come before Jacynth was able to come downstairs. Jonathan carried her down one day, and she lay on the couch watching the flames dance up the chimney as if that was all the entertainment she wanted. He saw her once or twice glance at the door as if she were half expecting someone to come in, and at last, wondering anxiously whether he was doing the right thing, he said, "Howard and Cynthia aren't here now, you know."

Her eyes came back to him in a sharp, startled way that convinced him he had read her thoughts.

"Oh, aren't they?" she said nervously.

"No." He chose his words carefully. "They flew to Canada two weeks ago. I think they'll be happy—*both* of them."

"I hope so," she said quietly, and though she changed the subject almost immediately, he had the impression that he had been right to tell her.

Her progress seemed to be quicker after that, and soon she was allowed to walk about a little.

He came in one day and found the door of the room in which he had left her open and Jacynth herself not there.

"Here, Jonathan. In the study!"

He caught his breath. There was something in her voice—a lilt, a joyfulness. He hurried in and saw that she was standing by her little desk and that in her hand was her diary.

"Jacynth—" he began, but she interrupted him.

"Oh, Jonathan, Jonathan, why didn't you tell me!" she asked, half laughing, half crying. "It is true, it isn't just a dream—"

"A dream?" he said wonderingly, and she held out the diary for him to see the words that he had penciled there. Instantly his arms went around her. "But you know it's true!" he insisted. "I told you again and again when you were ill!"

"I thought I'd only dreamed it," she sighed. "Tell me again, Jonathan!"

But instead he held her to him, and there was no need for mere words.

Then, at length, he held her from him.

"You'll get cold in here," he said unsteadily. "Come back into the lounge."

But when they were there, she refused to lie down again.

"I don't want you to let go of me," she confessed, with a complete lack of self-consciousness that sent his pulses throbbing.

For a time words seemed completely unnecessary, and then, her cheek pressed against his, she said, "Jonathan, will you tell me about . . . everything now?"

He looked down into her flushed, happy face.

"Are you sure?" he asked doubtfully. "Perhaps it would be better to wait."

She turned her face against his shoulder.

"No . . . because, really, I know. Father . . . is dead, isn't he?"

He held her more closely to him.

"Yes. He died about two days after you were rescued, and the last thing he said to me was that it was a better way of going out than he had conceived possible. You see, he had bad heart trouble. It was only a matter of time, and he felt that to have been of service to you, after all these years. . . ."

He felt a scalding drop fall onto his hand, and waited until she said unsteadily, "Go on."

"He left you his love," Jonathan said softly, thinking gratefully of that brief opportunity he and Tim Furnival had had of getting to know one another.

"He left me more than that," Jacynth said softly. "He gave me faith in the future. He told me about you. He said that he was too big a rotter himself not to know the other sort when he met them, and you were one of them.

And he said that, no matter how much appearances were against it—you loved me as much as I loved you. And then he said, 'Though *he's* little cause to believe that, heaven knows! Rather odd, isn't it, when *you* know it's true? Had you realized how easy it is for people to misunderstand one another?' And then I knew I had to come back—to give us both another chance."

"And yet you tried to slip away," he said, his lips against her temple.

"I was so tired," she said a little forlornly. "And besides, when you want a thing to be true so much that it hurts wanting it, you can't believe it is true very easily. It seems such a miracle. And Cynthia. . . ."

Her voice drifted away into silence.

"Cynthia," he said reflectively. "How curious it seems now that I ever let her influence my life—oh, not because I still love her. That finished when I realized that she had married Howard for his money. But because of that, I lost all my faith in love—or in myself, more accurately. That was why I planned to marry a girl purely as a practical, businesslike arrangement."

"But why, Jonathan?" she whispered, holding her breath. The question that had troubled her for so long.

"Because a wealthy man has a way of wanting a son to whom to pass on his wealth," he said deliberately.

"But you . . . you didn't . . ." she faltered.

His arm tightened around her.

"What I hadn't taken into my calculations was the possibility that I might fall in love with you almost as soon as I'd met you."

"Oh, Jonathan!" she said delightedly. "Did you? But why didn't you tell me?"

He looked at her ruefully.

"I wish I had," he admitted. "But don't you see, I had no idea that you cared in the least for me, and so I wanted you to learn to love me before—"

"But I did," she said indignantly. "All the time! It just happened."

He laughed and kissed her and Jacynth sighed contentedly. Suddenly she sat up.

"But my birthday night, when you went to put the lights out . . . you and Cynthia. . . ."

He put his hands on her shoulders and turned her around so that she faced him.

"So you saw that," he said slowly. "My poor baby! And of course you thought— Darling, listen. Remember I told you I'd tell you *once* that I wasn't marrying you for your money?"

She nodded, flushing a little as she remembered how easily Cynthia had persuaded her that that was nothing but a clever lie.

"Well, just this once, we'll talk about Cynthia. Then we'll forget her. By the time she married Howard, I'd precious few illusions about her. But then she was my friend's wife. For his sake I kept out of the way lest I should give her away. You see, I hoped—after all, Howard is such a decent chap. I thought she *must* care for him sooner or later. And then, when we met that night, I just didn't stop to think about her at all. All I thought of was Howard needing help. What I didn't realize was that she would never forgive me for that."

"Oh!" Jacynth said sharply. Why, that was just what she had told Cynthia. If ever a man stopped caring for her she would try to injure him, and Cynthia had not realized that *was* just how she had felt toward Jonathan. "No, never mind. I'll tell you afterward. Go on."

"That night she was still out in the garden. She told me—" He stood up abruptly and stood staring down into the fire. "Never mind exactly what she said—perhaps you can guess. It was the most hideous moment I've ever experienced. I was pretty brutal. At the time, I was rather relieved at the way she took it. She started to cry and said that she must have been mad and that, of course, the last thing she wanted to do was to hurt Howard."

"Did you tell her that you loved me?" Jacynth asked, and he nodded. "Jonathan," she went on anxiously, "when you told me they'd gone to Canada, you said that you thought they would both be happy. Why?"

He wrinkled his forehead in an effort to clarify his ideas.

"I'm not quite sure. There's a difference, somewhere, in both of them, as if he had his self-respect back and she . . . as if she were very grateful. I've wondered—" He stopped and shook his head. Elijah had told him some garbled story about telling the fair lady that there was going to be a fog, but he had not been able to make head nor tail of it and somehow or other he didn't feel he wanted to.

"I think, deep down, Cynthia has always loved him— Oh, not what *we* call love," he hastened to add. "But there was something."

Jacynth nodded.

"I do hope you're right," she said. "I'm so happy that I want everybody else to be the same."

Jonathan sat down beside her again and began to play with the rings that were still rather large for her thin fingers.

"Those, Mrs. Branksome, are very praiseworthy sentiments," he said gravely. "And I echo them whole-heartedly. But at the moment, I'm far more interested in making some plans for two other people."

"Oh, are you?" she asked, her eyes mischievous and provocative as she laid her head back on a silk cushion and looked up at him. "And what might they be? Do you think I would be interested to hear them?"

"I hope so," he said, drawing her to him. "Because what I had in mind was the fact that we haven't had a honeymoon yet and I think we deserve one. Only then again this is hardly the time of year for honeymoons. So perhaps we might postpone it until the spring. What do you think?"

"I think—" she began, then stopped. "Jonathan," she resumed pensively, "isn't it a honeymoon if you don't go away?"

"Well," he said judicially. "It's the usual thing to do."

"Then let's be unusual," she said. "Let's have a honeymoon at home—here."

He put a finger under her chin and turned her face up to his.

"Honest?" he asked, his eyes searching hers.

"Honest!" she confirmed.

He drew her close to him, and with a lightness that served only to reveal the depth of his feelings more clearly, he said, "Have I ever mentioned the fact to you, Mrs. Branksome, that I love you?"

She screwed up her face as if in deep thought.

"I believe you did mention it," she admitted. "But I'd like to hear about it again. . . ."

STORM OVER MANDARGI

STORM
OVER
MANDARGI

Margaret Way

Toni had no regrets about coming to Mandargi. She'd left her city job and a lukewarm romance to join her brother at the cattle station he managed. Then she met its owner, Damon Nyland.

She'd heard so much about him, so resented his life of advantage and power, that she'd determined one thing: she would never throw herself at the "great man" as so many other women had done.

It was especially galling that, from their meeting when he practically saved her life, she should have to feel grateful. For when it came right down to it, Toni found herself just as vulnerable to Damon's considerable charm as any other woman!

CHAPTER ONE

It was the quality of the silence that made her nervous and uneasy: more acute than could be imagined, a silence as eerie as an empty vault and twice as ominous. Even the birds and reptiles had withdrawn to shelter conveying their own message of warning. *Something* was going to happen as it always did in the tropics. There were no kind, easy seasons in the Gulf. The dry was too dry and the wet was too wet, heralded by sudden violent wind and rain storms, terrific storm centers that built up over the isolated stations.

Today, none of the usual happy chatter, the soft singing and rhythmic hand-clapping issued from the kitchen. Tikka and Leila, the two young aboriginal women, were nervous, lacing Toni's own senses with a peculiar tension. There was no magic powerful enough to ward off the hot winds of trouble, they told her, their dark eyes pools of foreboding. Soon the Big Wind would come, led by Pippi-munni, the Lightning Woman, the messenger of the Sky Country.

Toni shrugged off the effects of that harrowing tale. There was no question, the foreboding stillness and the mythology *got* to you. She eased herself out of the bamboo armchair and walked into the comparative cool of the wide, deep porch. Its ten-foot shelter ran around two sides of the ninety-year-old bungalow, protecting it from the heat and the heavy onslaughts of monsoonal rain. Banks of flame-colored lilies, speckled with crimson, ran the full length of the front porch, their brilliance unbearable in the supercharged air.

Toni leaned her head against the crisscrossed white hardwood pillar, looking out over the large, rambling garden. Another day in the wilderness! The lonely bush, a bitter-sweet isolation; yet it had its own peculiar magic. She lifted her head to stare at the sinister heat haze that had been threatening to hide the sun since noon. The sun still burned brassily through its numerous veils, invincible, all-possessing, stifling the landscape. It could mean a dry electrical storm, with the shock of thunder and little promise of moisture, but somehow she didn't think so. The atmosphere was heavy with a nameless blend of awe and "rain talk."

No whisper of breeze moved the great shade trees of the garden. They stood engraved, breathless, waiting for the signal. The air was uncannily still, fiery against her cheek, like a blast furnace, causing her eyes to smart and her hair to cling damply in bronze tendrils to her temples and nape. She was almost sick with the heat and mounting anxieties, the core of them Paul's continuing absence. It was nerve-racking to wait; the minutes crawled past at a snail's pace, allowing her mind to range freely over all potential disasters. She was creamy pale, her forehead beaded with perspiration, her dark eyes shadowed in a delicately determined face.

It was well before eleven when Paul had gone out with a few of the stock men to settle the cattle and turn the restless, sweating beasts to the nearest lagoons and billa-bongs. Trouble was brewing, he had pointed out laconic-ally, and all forms of life seemed to know it. She remembered his short laugh, the flash of his smile as he rode out to keep at least one step ahead of it. Paul could look after himself, none better, but the knowledge did little to comfort her.

She sighed, almost beaten by the enervating heat, filled with the curious, useless sensation of marking time. Screwing up her eyes didn't make her brother's form materialize. No lanky lean figure swung into sight, slouched and relaxed in the saddle, blue eyes crinkling in the shade of his hat; the lean boyish face and a bright bronze head tilted at a characteristic angle, absorbed and confident.

Paul was no ordinary young man and he didn't propose to lead an uneventful life. He had certain set targets: *Mandargi*, the 400-square-mile property he managed for Damon Nyland, a man of immense property interests and the owner of the big experimental station Savannah Downs on their northeastern border.

Toni had never met the great man, as she very quickly dubbed him. The master of Mandargi had never set foot on his property in the whole six months since she had left her job and a dwindling romance to come north and join her brother. Her job was to run the domestic affairs of the station for him. But at the few hectically gay social gatherings, in the township, she heard Nyland's praises sung *ad nauseam* from buyers and agents, cattlemen and their womenfolk. No one loomed larger upon the horizon, or cast a longer shadow, than the exclusive, elusive Damon Nyland, with a name guaranteed to keep one listening.

Toni, ever the individualist, often felt inclined to tip her forehead in a simple, respectful form of homage every time she heard his name. Instead, in order to make a contribution, she listened with an air of pleasant interest, trying to look appreciative as though Nyland's exploits made her think very deeply. Even in the seclusion of the wilds, man must have his idols.

Once or twice it crossed her mind to question the illogical antagonism she seemed to have settled into without a qualm, but lacking the interest, she was forced back on the old standby: the man's telltale activities, the tangible and tantalizing aura of dynamism that clung to a name. Damon Nyland was quite simply a big wheel, a man of prestige and power, the kind of man "the State could well do with" as she'd read somewhere in the newspaper and put it down very smartly. One could hardly expect such a man to dance attendance on his run-of-the-mill employees. He had a reason for everything he did. There was no harm at all in being prepared: she wasn't going to fall on the great man's neck. All this reverence and mutterings of approval touched some perverse nerve in her.

Paul, on the other hand, wouldn't hear a word against his employer, bristling unaccountably at Toni's mocking jibes so that after a while, she learned to hold her tongue, feeling herself as wise as an ancient spirit grandmother. Her twenty-two years seemed double her brother's twenty-seven. Her tender mouth was compressed, giving an indication of what lay behind her thoughts. Even Damon Nyland would be awed by the primeval quality of this vast, empty land, the weird quicksilver effects of the great haze.

She nibbled on her underlip with growing disquiet, her eyes on the frowning, ragged line of the ranges, purple and blue ramparts rising against the sky. The peculiar

subtlety of the silence was penetrating her bones, making
her turn away with a forlorn little gesture hoping that
Paul would beat the storm in. It would be a long, hot ride.

At three o'clock, great curling cumulus cloud came up
from nowhere, its purple black form crossing the horizon
with great speed like an angry tide in reverse. Toni
gauged the ceiling height at about six thousand feet and
speculated that if its depth was comparable it indicated
heavy turbulence and electrical surcharge. She watched
the swift, oncoming masses from inside the battened-
down house, her blood stirred to fever heat. Behind her on
the wicker sofa sat Tikka and Leila, their slight arms
entwined, speechless with anticipation. Soon the wind
would blow up with great force and Paul wasn't in. Toni
felt her own stomach muscles knotting with her sheer
inability to do anything. Everything seemed to be waiting
for the storm to take over.

Within minutes the sun went out, obliterated by the
fantastic cloud barriers. Lightning forked through the
pearly black mounds, brilliant, and quite terrifying,
sizzling with livid fury into the huge coolibah that stood
at the end of the pebbled drive. It split asunder like so
much matchwood, falling in the darkened, windswept
landscape, endlessly resounding, rocking the bungalow to
its foundations and sending birds screeching; shadows of
kites and eagles and falcons, the shrieking sulphur-
crested cockatoos and the rose-pink galahs almost helpless against the force of the wind.

Toni shook her head dazedly, not even aware of her
movement. The spell of unearthly quiet was broken. All
hell broke loose with amazing rapidity. The first giant
spatters of rain came down on the corrugated iron roof

like a fusillade of artillery; then a driving deluge mixed with the lethal hail. Massive chunks of ice as large as emu's eggs bounced and struck. Small forms of bush life, half blinded by the rain and flying gravel, streaked erratically across the garden only to be killed or maimed by the icy grenades that ricocheted off a bigger animal to strike yet another in its frantic flight. Toni shut her eyes, her face pale, her ears assaulted by the deafening racket on the roof; yet her fears were not for herself nor the homestead, but her brother. Hail like that was dangerous to man and beast. The cattle so carefully mustered would be petrified by the storm, moaning horribly, stampeding to the densest scrub, dangerous in their panic.

She couldn't bear to look out at that beautiful barbaric scene or listen to the savage throbbing of the wind and rain. Strange that so much beauty could come out of so much terror. The two housegirls were moaning now with a paralyzing sense of calamity, their curly heads bowed. All about them, along the exposed side of the bungalow, came the splintering break of glass as windows shattered and blew in, drenching large areas in minutes.

Toni had endured enough of this. Something had to be done: she was tired of coping with such enforced inertia. She tilted her head, the muscles under the young curve of her chin tightening in a quick acceptance of possible disaster. Would the roof hold under the ramming force of the hail or give way before the storm had spent itself? Resolution seized her. She ran on through the house to the study with its massive buffalo horns mounted over the door, but her attention was riveted on the radio transceiver. It stood on the desk between two shovel-nosed spears fixed to the window wall. She almost flung herself into the swivel chair, threw the switch, pushed the send button on the mike, gave the station's call-sign. "This is MTW . . . Mandargi. . . ."

Then as she drew her breath sharply, the whole window frame seemed to plunge at her. There was a harsh splitting sound, then the world went black.

Something's happened, she told herself, something's happened to me. She lay there, a warm and sticky sensation crawling over her skin. A long way off, a dog barked. It was Rebel, she was almost sure of it. Rebel! Then Paul was back! The sound seemed to hang in the air. She opened her eyes suddenly, with a small, bewildered exclamation. It was so very still she could hear the thud of her heart. She turned her head, her dark eyes flickering, and it all came back to her. She was lucky. All about her was chaos. Scattered, drenched books and papers; an upturned chair and a fan ripped out of the wall. Splintered glass lay like a giant diadem around her head and the shattered window-frame lay half across her body. She could remember the moment of impact like a pistol shot in her head.

Blood covered the side of her shirt and the sight made her sick and nauseated beyond belief. It was only then that she became conscious of a violent headache and a searing pain in her arm. She looked down dazedly, unsurprised by the bad gash on the inside of her right arm. It must have happened as she flung it up instinctively to protect herself.

She lay still for a few more moments, then made a supreme effort to raise herself, only to fall back as black waves of sickness threatened to ride her down.

Ridiculous! She was almost too weak to move. She ran a tentative hand down her arm and felt the stickiness of blood. She swallowed, her eyes widening.

Where were Tikka and Leila? They would assume she was dead for sure! That would be their unanimous verdict. Their fear of her certain death would be sufficient to keep them well clear of the study until Paul came home. Even in the midst of the critical circumstances she found herself in, Toni had a moment of wry humor. Well, she was far from dead. No bones broken either Just a rather deep wound and a bad crack on the head.

The storm was over with the abruptness of all tropical storms, the rain turned off as suddenly and completely as a tap. A steady flow of washed-clean air was coming in through the great, open gap where the window had been. Perhaps it would serve to sober her up. She bit her lip and turned an ivory pale face toward the cool after-rush of the storm, almost in the same moment passing out,

When she opened her eyes, she felt better, almost comfortable, lying on the old black leather sofa in the lounge room, staring into a face. Dark, disturbing, different. She knew that face.

"Welcome back!" he said sardonically, and the voice matched the face.

Toni didn't say anything; her eyes roamed over his face as though condemned to look at it for the rest of her life. Various expressions—irony, ease, authority. Ice-green eyes that seemed to mesmerize her so that she blinked a little, irritated by the discovery. Then faint spirit returned to her.

"Well put!" she murmured with a ghost of her usual delicate mockery. "How long have I been out?"

"You were unconscious when I arrived about half past five. And," he glanced at his watch, "it's now seven o'clock!"

"Good grief!" she said soberly, her face tautening. "Where's Paul? Where's my brother?"

"Paul's all right!" he underlined crisply with an air of finality, watching the agitation mount in her face. "He's looked in several times, now he's gone out again. You're the patient! Apart from the concussion, that was a bad gash in your arm. I've put in a few stitches. Don't talk, if you please!" he added tersely, his mouth hardening, evidently unused to the faint mutiny he saw in her face.

"And if I don't please?" She eased out her breath rather painfully, wincing at the first incautious movement of her arm.

"I can't say I wasn't expecting it!" he said, studying her, his eyes gleaming with a kind of, I know you, but you don't know me, superiority. "Even out cold, you betray a certain nervous intensity. One way and the other, it's been a devil of a day. I suppose it's too late to tell you, you should never have come up here. The wrong temperament—too volatile for the tropics. You'll wear yourself out!"

"Not quite!" she replied, with self-mockery, not bothering to hide her thoughts from him. She returned his gaze, her dark eyes critical and appraising but scarcely hostile. A man like that would always take one's breath away. One had to be braced for almost anything, and her recuperative powers had always been good. "Perhaps it was worth it, just to meet you . . . Mr. Nyland, isn't it." It was hardly a question and he responded briefly to the point of curtness.

"Yes!"

"Strange, to remain unimpressed!" It was out in one awful minute before her head cleared, triggered by that taut monosyllable. But what did he expect? A song of joy and welcome! He seemed to, for his green eyes glittered like a flame sprung to life and she knew a stab of pure panic. She had gone too far, and what did she really know of him? However, his voice, when it came, was a smooth drawl, brushing aside her negligible opinions.

"You'll get over it! In fact, once you accept your change of environment, you may even learn a healthy respect!"

She turned her head from the brilliance of his strange eyes and his dark controlled face. "Are you warning me?"

"Of course!"

"Then I suppose I deserve it!" A smile touched her mouth and she fingered the bandage around her arm, realizing for the first time that she owed him a good deal, this local autocrat by his own admission. "For what it's worth, I apologize. It's a failing of mine, charging in where angels fear to tread!"

"The hit on the head, or perhaps you're nervous?" His gaze was cool and faintly amused.

"Nervous?" She shrugged that off delicately, but she was still wary of him. It would be impossible for him to forgive her impertinence however well he concealed it. Reprisals at some stage would be second nature to him.

He was looking at her directly, his eyes playing lightly over her face, and she felt oddly shaken. "As well as talking too much!" he said smoothly. "A charming weakness in a woman. It's a good thing I can see beyond all the bravado and you have had a time of it. One must make allowances!"

Her voice was low and faintly husky in the quiet emptiness of the room. Ridiculous to think of him as an adversary; yet the sensation persisted. "You have a very direct way with you, Mr. Nyland!"

"So have you! It must be catching!"

"I don't imagine I'm quite so . . . disconcerting, but thank you for this," she gestured to her bandaged arm "and for coming. It must have been quite a risk!"

"You're welcome!"

"But the storm . . .?"

"As you can see, I'm here!" he said crisply, chopping her off. "The details aren't important."

"No, of course not. Why should I trouble my sweet little head?" She was rambling a little, her voice faintly slurred. Her dark eyes, shadowed in the pallor of her face, struggled to hold his, but those strongly defined features were blurring. It worried her. The room swung in her view and a sickening wave of giddiness passed over her. "I think I'm going to faint!" she murmured with something like horror.

He gave a faint sigh more sardonic than sympathetic. "Suits me, you'll be easier to handle!" His mouth twisted in a smile. She felt his hands touch her—sure, very certain. "A beautiful piece of timing. A true feminine gift! Relax, child, there's nothing whatever to worry about!" Then he was lifting her, cradling her with no effort at all, protective of her arm, flicking down at her a mocking smile that still held a degree of indulgence.

Lights seemed to be bursting under her eyelids. There were so many questions she wanted to ask. Why wasn't Paul there? She didn't want to go with this stranger at all, for all she accepted his presence as an entirely natural thing. But all she could manage was a soft, plaintive cry, the tears of weakness beading her lashes. Clouds of cottonwool were suffocating her. She tried to slant a glance at that lean, hard jaw, the infernal tilt to a night-dark head; then she slid into darkness again.

CHAPTER TWO

She awoke very early from a deep sleep. Turning her face toward the mother-of-pearl light, she had no more than a faint headache and a heavy sensation in her right arm. On the dawn wind, soft singing came from the direction of the willow-hung billabong, wafting in through the bungalow windows. A song of an old, old race, a women's chant to attract the goodwill of the spirit folk. Toni listened, moved and enchanted, still so new to all that was alien and exotic about the far north.

Her wandering eyes moved drowsily about the room. There wasn't much she had been able to do about her bedroom except re-paint the old tongue-and-groove walls in a pale blue color with a glossy white trim, and add some odd bits of old-fashioned furniture in an effort to match them. The curtains, the cushions and the bedspread she made herself, in a vibrant contemporary print, an attractive enough contribution, as were the few favorite ornaments she had brought with her. But it was essentially an unpretentious room, of modest proportions, clinically cool and fresh, and no amount of know-how and imagination could make it brilliant. With the view of feathery, magnificent poincianas and the distant grape-blue of the ranges she needed beautiful, airy windows, but the single multi-paned window blocked almost everything. At least the glass in it wasn't shattered. Still under the effects of the sedative, she closed her eyes and drifted off again.

The first rays of sunlight slanted dusky-gold, through

the venetian blinds, falling across the bed. Their warmth stirred her. She looked up at the pale canopy of tropical netting that enveloped her and kicked the light sheet from her legs, looking down the length of her elegant young body. Her right arm was bandaged in a very professional fashion, an incongruous note, for she was wearing an exquisite froth of nylon and lace in a muted coffee shade; a birthday present from their unfailingly romantic maiden aunt and a garment she had no recollection of ever taking out of its box, scorning its obvious lack of practicality. Clearly some hours of her life were missing. She would never have chosen it herself.

She remembered the storm, the series of incidents that led to the one wholly unexpected development—the appearance of Damon Nyland. One more shock in a series of shocks. She knew with some certainty he was a man she would clash with. Her awakening mind raced ahead, foreseeing the difficulties, almost ticking off points on her fingers. Much better to do the fashionable thing and fall down adoring, but she couldn't see herself doing it. The man already had more followers than a tribal chief.

Uncompromising masculinity had always set her teeth on edge, a physical aversion that made her feel vaguely uncomfortable. It was unsettling, that peculiar blend of charm and hard arrogance.

Her mouth tilted in faint self-mockery. Lying so quietly, it was not necessary to suppress her thoughts, so she let them run on. Seen in the light of cold reason, the answer was simple enough—avoid the man. It shouldn't prove difficult, if only a crisis merited a visit. Hard as she tried to disavow the idea, she had to admit he played his part with enormous conviction—a strong suggestion of the *grand seigneur* with perhaps a streak of cruelty thrown in. Extraordinarily impressive and profoundly attractive. Men out of the ordinary mould were dangerous. Damon Nyland, as such, was a natural suspect, but such knowledge was better kept in reserve.

Surely she wasn't becoming cynical?

She'd never really been hurt by a man. A few rapid charades with little time for understanding on either side. No stars that fell from the skies. No love lost at all. In fact, she knew very little about love.

Strange how a dark face lodged in her mind. Skin a deep copper, the shock of light eyes, cool as mint, glints in a thick twist of black hair. Her mouth curved with irony and sweetness, visualizing the odd six-monthly encounter when he invariably came off second-best. Some men wore an air of bright challenge impossible to ignore. At least she was lucky in having an inbuilt warning system, one that could sum up dark, impatient men at a glance.

Morning sounds broke through her imaginings; the beautiful, carolling bird song, lilting voices, the sound of someone sweeping up the pebbles in the drive. Quite near the house Rebel barked and was immediately shushed by a very loud voice with the crazy notion it couldn't be heard. Toni smiled with deep amusement, feeling a wave of love for her brother. Even his voice had an eagerness and glow in it that promised well for his future. She didn't appreciate fully that she and her brother were identical in many ways; ways that were apparent to even the most casual observer. The bright bronze heads, the clean bone structure, shapely, sensitive mouths with the half-smile each wore. The inner excitement was there and the lively intelligence, only Paul's eyes blue and Toni's darkly brilliant, but the light challenge shone from both, reflected in the rather audacious tilt to their heads.

In another minute, Paul tapped on her door, scarcely waiting for her bright, answering: "Come in!"

He walked into the room with swinging grace, smiling at her. "Rebel woke you, I suppose. I looked in on you earlier and your color was good. How do you feel now?"

"Not too bad. Bit of a head and this feels heavy, but I suppose it's the bandage." She fingered it tentatively.

He nodded and came to sit on the end of the bed, anxiously scanning her face. "Honestly, if anything else had happened to you, I'd have to crawl away and die of grief!"

"How fantastic!" she smiled.

"No one could help liking you. Anyway, you gave me an awful fright. Savannah picked up your call sign and the boss flew in. Damned good of him! He's a big man and they don't usually do that kind of thing!"

"Oh, I don't know!" she pointed out brightly, "business men have been known to protect their property interests. Still, it must be marvellous to be admired!"

Paul raised his eyebrows and kicked at the rug. "You'll never do. Too much spunk. Here's my story . . . Mack's horse came down in a melon hole and rolled on him. He's broken his leg, I'm afraid—Mack, not the horse. The horse I can spare. But Mack's a careless ass; it's the only word I can find for him. By the way, the flying doctor is due in this morning. He'll take a look at you too. I tell you, girl, some days it just doesn't pay to fall out of bed. My best man out of action, and the cattle spread to the four winds!"

"Not to speak of your sister! I've been wondering why you called in. At any rate, I intend to stay in bed all day; I'm not moving an inch!"

Paul made a snorting sound and ran a hand over his head. "I should say so! The boss would have my hide if you tried to get up today. But what's a few teeth more or less? He's fairly certain you won't have a scar. The prettiest, neatest job I've ever seen."

"Don't tell me the great man's still here?" she asked in amazement.

"Of course. He's going to take a good look over the place—a report on my stewardship, no less. Now that you're awake, I'll get a few of the men to clean up the debris about the place. We've a few too many windows to replace and little time to spend on them."

"Well, now that we do have to replace them, let's make them bigger!"

He gave her a look that could have been approval. "Anything you say, you're the Missus."

"Until you marry!" she answered him carelessly, unprepared for his swift double take.

"Who, me?" He stood up, squaring his straight shoulders. "Not of my own free will, anyway. No woman is going to get me in her clutches until I'm good and ready!"

"That's what they all say!" she murmured dryly. "I'll remind you of it when the time comes. By the way, how did I get into this fabulous gear?"

He smiled in amusement, enjoying the moment, proud of his sister's good looks. "Tikka, who else? Now why don't you give it to her? That would be a nice gesture. Think of the repercussions. Poor little beggar thought you were dead, you know. She nearly passed out when I asked her to help you out of your clothes. More like a mortuary rite. But there's no doubt about it, she has a great sense of what's suitable. That's some nightie. Trust poor old Rose—four times round the world and not one proposal!

"Now, if you're sure you're all right, I'll get going. You never catch up with the work on a station and I've the feeling Nyland's not the man to keep waiting." He walked to the door, pulling a wry face over his shoulder. "He certainly took charge last night!"

"Who got here first?" she called after him, trying to sound detached and disinterested. "I remember precious little, flaking out all the time."

"The boss beat me in by about forty minutes. Hauled me over the coals a bit, but what the devil! Superman wouldn't have risked that hail!"

"Nyland did!" she pointed out, her affectionate smile contradicting the tart note in her voice.

"He flew over it, dear. The bright spirit. Do try to be fair. Besides, the storm was over almost as soon as it'd begun. Just as well! The roof took a battering. I'll have some work to do there. Poor old Mack bit the dust long before the storm broke. He's so damned mad at himself none of the men will go near him. It was you or him and I thought you would be safe enough. I just hauled him to shelter and sat it out. Jimmy D. left the jeep out, and it's pitted with holes. I'll skin him alive if he's ever game to come back again. It was his job to bring it in, but. . . . Well, make the most of it, girl," he flashed his white smile, already preoccupied, "I need your assistance around here. Those two little twits in the kitchen won't organize anything without direction. It's not the work that appeals to them. Lord only knows what we had for breakfast. Even the boss didn't ask. Didn't eat it either!"

"Dear me!" she said, the tart note back in her voice again. "I guess he'll survive!"

"So will you," he reminded her. "You were losing a fair amount of blood."

"I'm ashamed of myself!"

"That'll be the day! So long, kiddo!" He moved swiftly away. "Back before lunch."

"I only hope Mr. Nyland will like it!" her voice floated after him, almost triumphant.

For a little while after he left, Toni savored the comfort of the soft, old-fashioned bed, conscious of a dull ache in her head. She threw up a hand to shield her eyes from the bright sunlight. A slanting shaft fell across her thick, silky hair, lighting it to a radiance, flashing out all the bright reds and the ambers. She would give herself a little while longer; then she would get up. Extraordinarily privileged as they were with Damon Nyland on the premises, it wouldn't do to be laid low at the first impact. Less than one hundred per cent.

Tikka, moving along the hallway, tray in hand, let out a soft cry as a teaspoon clattered to the polished floor. Toni sat up, giving all thoughts of relaxation away, watching the young woman in her best blue housedress move slowly into sight. She took one look at Toni and gave a short gasp.

"You're awake, Miss Toni?" For some reason she spoke in a near whisper and Toni smiled.

"Happily, yes!" she said positively. "Hours ago. Is that breakfast? It's a cup of tea I want more than anything else!"

"Tea it is!" Tikka was thinking hard. She came into the room and placed the tray on the bedside table, fussing a little over the important business of pouring the tea. "Lucky you're still here, Miss Toni. I thought you were dead!"

Toni shook her bright head. "You were about half way right! Dead? What next?"

Tikka suddenly chuckled, pointing at the coffee lace nightgown. "I could work all my life for something like that!"

Toni glanced down wryly, moving her long, slender legs, tanned to a deep gold, beautifully conspicuous beneath the short, foaming hemline. "It's yours if you want it that badly. It makes me feel like a cross between a Botticelli lady and a racehorse!"

Tikka drew in her breath hoarsely as if she needed air. "Mine? That's rockin' the boat a bit. I don't know what Albert would say, but I'd feel like Sheba!"

Toni laughed aloud. A persuasive look came over her face. "Surely Albert wouldn't see it. Not yet, anyway. It might pay to keep that in mind!"

Tikka looked back at her rather helplessly, caught between being fickle and devout. "When Mr. Paul promotes Albert, we're going to be married!" It came out with great deliberation to hide the wobble of emotion.

"So the rewards will be great! If I were you, Tikka, I'd have no compunction. A wedding present, if you like. Think it over."

Tikka plucked a flower from the vase on the table and

waved it in some agitation under her face. "I'll talk myself out of it for sure. I'd be too scared to wear it."

"Because of Albert?" Toni reached for her tea and a finger of toast.

"Sort of!" Tikka explained haltingly. She took a jerky step backwards, not without a quaint grace. "More ...." Something in her face looked utterly defenceless, a denial of some basic fulfilment. She left it up in the air, without an explanation.

Toni smiled at her lightly, with affection. "I think I know what you mean. One way or the other we're all captives of what life hands us out!"

"And it's not fair!" Tikka shifted her weight to the other foot, standing like a stork at a waterhole. She looked to Toni for confirmation, but Toni only smiled.

"In any case, it is rather grand—the nightgown, I mean. One needs the right setting and certainly to be happily married. The chances are you'll make it with Albert. I hope so."

"He's crazy about me!" Tikka said and paused. Toni finished her cup of tea, then turned and sat up.

"Officially, I'm supposed to spend the day in bed, but unofficially I'm getting up shortly. See what's left of the vegetable garden, would you? The talent I threw into it—and for what? One good hailstorm and annihilation! I daren't ask if either of you two brought the tomatoes in, not to speak of all those beautiful lettuce!"

"I surely did!" Tikka clenched her hands in her lap, her face self-righteous.

"Splendid! I'm spellbound," Toni said in her normal voice. "The best thing you've ever done, and to think I questioned your efficiency!"

Tikka looked up quickly, very earnest, her curly head cocked to one side. "Yesterday was bad. Bad of me, I mean. I'm sorry, Miss Toni. I've never felt so scared!" Remembrance made her expression crumble and Toni, under the burden of that glance, answered swiftly before the apology misfired.

"Forget it, Tikka. We're all frightened of something or other. Often things we can't explain. I, for instance, would hesitate to make a pet of a snake."

"Catch 'em by the tail. Simple!" Tikka explained.

Toni shuddered, considering the consequences, then she gestured to the tray. "Take this back to the kitchen, like a good girl. Mr. Nyland is here for a while, so there's work to be done!"

"Yes, ma'am!" Tikka smiled, displaying her beautiful teeth. "That sounds just fine! He's a big man!"

"He's certainly tall!" Toni conceded and wisely changed the subject. "Now, about the vegetable garden, we'll rebuild in stages. I'm not sure if we won't even hire a few men—Albert, for instance. He might welcome the opportunity to work nearer the house for a day or two."

"As long as Albert's about, everything will go all right!" Tikka promised, pure unalloyed pride and delight in her face.

"Good, then it's all planned. Fixed in my mind." Toni relaxed her back, enjoying the lassitude of the moment.

"Shall I get that lazy Leila moving? Don't know what's eating her. She took two hours to get breakfast and then no one ate it!" Tikka looked across at the small Missus with an obvious desire to please.

"Yes, you do that," Toni nodded, fighting the impulse to laugh.

"Right, miss!" Tikka looked hard at the tray, rehearsing her lines; then she looked up and smiled. "I'm sure glad you're all right! Never did tell you the Big Boss breathed hell-fire all over us, Leila and me. But we were so scared. I thought you were dead and Leila never thought at all!" The black eyes glinted with merry humor. "I'll go and chat up that girl! See you, miss!"

Toni watched the slight figure disappearing, then she began to laugh softly. She would have given a pretty penny to hear what Tikka had to say. Out in the kitchen, anything could happen and often did, but Tikka was, unquestionably, the dominant personality. Breakfast didn't bear thinking about, but she would have to supervise the lunch. If Tikka was to be believed, at least there was enough for a salad.

Thoughts of a menu began to claim her attention. What could she give the man, accustomed as he was to perfection? Grilled chops and spicy grilled pineapple rings with a tossed salad? There was plenty of cold beer. Freshly caught barramundi barbecued on the spot might do. She could stuff it with breadcrumbs and a mixture of seasoned chopped boiled eggs and anchovies. It seemed only fair to make up for lost ground. Even Tikka had admitted that breakfast was a disaster.

There was still a residue of pain and discomfort in her body and brain, but on this day of grace she was determined not to remain in bed. The master of Mandargi was in residence, for however short a duration. Toni kicked the sheet aside and her long legs flashed enticingly, neat and quick as a cat. She turned to grope for her cotton robe and the sunlight fell in a silky gold stream over her young face and bare shoulders, gilding the bright, matchless bronze of her hair. She looked at that moment a fragile, rather exotic beauty with the piquant touch of a bandaged arm.

A man halted in the open doorway, studying her with relaxed interest, the cadence of his voice betraying amused appreciation.

"Good morning, Miss Stewart. About to disobey orders!"

As usual was implied, but not said. Toni swung her head, looking confused and briefly shocked, and he knew it. The fluid grace of her body seemed to vanish as she stiffened, her back as taut as a bow string, clutching the printed robe defensively. He swung the door wider, the swift brilliance of his eyes moving over her, experienced and detached as if she were a fine piece of glass—a unique piece, from the quality of that light, probing glance.

Color stirred in her cheeks, a sensuous curve to her mouth. If he continued to look at her in that precise fashion she would surely fall in fragments at his feet.

"Mr. Nyland!" she returned with equal smoothness. "This is a privilege! I'm bound to say I wasn't expecting you."

"Nor I you!" he countered, closing the distance between them, giving her a minute to slip her arms into the robe and gather it about her. "Why don't you hop back into bed?" he suggested. "You're rather precariously balanced at the moment!"

She made no attempt to rise to that jibe, but watched him lower his long length into a chair with an air of possession and utter familiarity, a rather stunning nonchalance. "May I sit down?" he asked with mild sarcasm. "Now I'm here, I'm looking forward to a little chat. How do you feel this morning?"

"Fine. Just fine!" she said warily, reacting to an odd note in his voice. "Ordinarily I'd curtsy!"

He seemed amused, the cool green glints in his eyes again. "I'm trying to decide whether to believe you or not. That nightgown is pure fairytale, Rose-Red."

"You can't condemn me for that!" Color swept into her face and she tilted her chin trying to ignore it. "It was a present."

He received that in silence, then laughed. "Really? Then that explains it. It's not the sort of thing one expects to see in the wilds. Neither are you, for that matter. Good-looking women don't usually bury themselves."

"If you could call it that!" Her dark eyes sparkled a challenge. "But tell me, Mr. Nyland, what really brings you away from your office? Did it catch fire?"

"I didn't expect such charm, either!" He laughed in his throat. "Apologize!"

"I can't. My head aches," she said shortly.

"Plus your arm," he said sympathetically. "That bandage gives an engaging but entirely misleading impression of . . . helplessness!"

She flushed a little under that quick lick of green fire. Above the masculine severity of his bush shirt, his darkly tanned face appeared very handsome and vital. Classic really, she thought, determined to be fair. High cheekbones, interesting hollows. Straight nose. Good mouth and a decisive chin. It was the kind of face you want to keep looking at, exciting yet inexplicably familiar. She knew with a great certainty that something was starting for her, but she scarcely knew what to call it.

"Let's change the subject," she said pleasantly, "if only to avert a scene!"

"Why not? You won't admit it, but you're the type to

hit out at the first one to come along. I got it with both barrels as soon as I came through the door. Why do you dislike me so much? May I ask?" The tiny smile that touched the corners of his mouth both mocked and pitied her.

"Dislike you?" She uttered the words with such cool surprise that her self-esteem came back. "But I don't dislike you at all, Mr. Nyland. In fact I'm covered in admiration!"

"Now why should I have imagined it?" He tipped back precariously in the chair, very self-assured, his lean body faultlessly arranged. "Perhaps it was the effect of the shot I gave you. You had quite a bit to say last night!"

She drew a deep breath, startled, a topaz sheen caught in her eyes.

"Careful! It's coming pretty close to the surface again!" he warned her. "You were quite funny really, rambling most of the time, but I got the general drift. One piece of news, good or bad I can't say. The strip won't take a plane for the next forty-eight hours or so, so you're stuck with me. It shouldn't bother you unduly; you won't be allowed up in any case. I've been on to the flying doctor base for instructions. You're not the only casualty, but you're the one under observation for a while!"

"Do you mean to tell me I'm not allowed up?"

"That's right!" he said repressively.

"Well, who would have thought it?" she said in a low, mocking voice. "Twenty-two and I'm still a baby, but if you want it that way, Mr. Nyland, there's no more to be said."

"I want it that way." It was a plain statement of fact that she could accept and obey. She lifted her eyes and encountered his very direct gaze and a strange perverse excitement moved in her. How idiotic to ride the see-saw of attraction and antagonism. It would be folly to allow herself to like him. It simply wasn't safe. But what exciting man was ever safe?

"I feel perfectly all right, you know," she said swiftly, to cover her confusion.

Her tensions must have communicated themselves to him, for he smiled, poised yet wary. "I'm sure you do!" he nodded, his eyes narrowing, "but you mightn't feel quite so well if you started racing about again. I know how anxious you are to impress me. And I am impressed!

"You've worked wonders on the house since I last saw it; curtains and cushions, rugs and whatnots, floral arrangements and bookcases. You're by no means the usual showpiece." The glance that slid over her was keen and amused.

Something about him, the set of his head and shoulders, the ironic amusement that deepened the curve to his mouth, awoke a faint apprehension in her. But for what? It was difficult to achieve any degree of normality.

"I can see it's going to be horribly difficult!" she said passionately.

"So stop fighting me!" he laughed in genuine amusement. "You can't expect me to encourage this schoolgirl animosity. What was it you said? King of the castle. Master of Mandargi. The great man and the rest." His voice was dangerously soft and Toni had an intimation of what to expect should she ever really cross him. She drew an audible breath, wondering what else she had said, and just as suddenly he was the Big Boss again, very crisp and to the point. "Now, let's have a look at that arm. Not a bad job, if I say so myself! I certainly haven't heard anything from you. The unkindest cut of all, if you'll forgive the pun!" Professionally he bent over her arm and she felt herself draw away a little, a new tension bearing down on her. His glance raked over her and his bearing altered just enough for her to resurrect a surviving sense of caution. She fixed her attention on a small pearly button near his lean brown throat.

"A pity to leave a scar on this silky skin," he said lightly, "but it shouldn't be much. Marvelous to be young and healthy. Healing begins almost immediately. We won't disturb anything for the moment. I'll change the dressing this afternoon." He was looking down at her in his own arrogant fashion, head up, eyes narrowing.

"You're a man of many accomplishments, Mr. Nyland!"

"Don't I have to be?" he retorted, hard and direct.

"And a millionaire to boot, if the papers are to be believed!"

"You might remember, in the process, a few people get rich along with me, and quite a lot of *other* people depend on me for their livelihood."

"Oh, I'll remember!" She reached up a hand and thrust it through her hair. "Message received and understood, never fear."

His mouth suddenly relaxed its tension, his teeth very white against his deeply tanned skin. "You were never smacked enough as a child. Too pretty for your own good, I suppose. Never mind, the day of retribution is at hand!"

"I'm sure of it!" she said without hesitation. "I can't help thinking I don't deserve it, but this is your country, not mine, Mr. Nyland."

"Terrifying, isn't it?" he countered, standing up and whisking the chair back a few feet. "At least, it's a great help to get acquainted. Now suppose you atone for your past misdemeanors and lie back. I'll organize the staff for the rest of the day. I'm an old hand at it."

"I'm grateful!" Carefully she made her voice blank, fighting her resentments.

"Now that, I find incredible. Right at this moment I'd say you're seething, you ungrateful brat!"

"My attempt to curry favor didn't quite come off!" Despite herself she smiled, and his eyes dwelt on her mouth.

"It would seem not, but keep trying. By the way, was that your first storm yesterday?"

"In the tropics, yes."

"You'll get over them," he promised with complete unconcern. "Everything up here is so much more unpredictable. Savage in every way!"

"I'm not frightened!" she said, controlling the few nervous tremors.

"No, you're not, are you, and you should be," he murmured with dry mockery. "That's the red hair. A mixed blessing!" His eyes slipped away from her lustrous head. "Well, I'll push on. There are a few other things that can wait. If I were you, I'd try taking it easy. An indispensable attribute in this climate!"

She watched him move to the door with his lithe, effortless paces. "Meeting you has been an unforgettable experience, Mr. Nyland," she said, yielding to a fatal impulse for mischief.

"For which you'll get no more than a simple thank-you. For the present!" He paused, one hand on the door knob, something indefinable glinting in his eyes, "There's plenty of time for drama, if that's what you want!"

She gave an involuntary gasp, tingles of warmth running down her arms. He left her feeling young and uncomfortable and badly outmaneuvered. At best, it would be an unequal struggle, but she was determined to hold out as long as she could. With practice she might be able to achieve a degree of immunity. She felt like throwing up a wall between them; yet she was haunted by the thought that he was about to wreck everything. Perhaps she should never have miscast herself to the extent of imagining there was a place for her up here. There was no place for her in the city either, not in the seven long years since their father had remarried. Mandargi was a hundred times better than sharing a flat with two other girls; a monthly duty visit home, the line of least resistance that placated her father and exhausted Myra's limited supply of feigned good fellowship. More frequent trips would only have proved troublesome all around.

In the early days of the marriage when things were pretty desperate with Myra's jealous possessiveness, Paul had very smartly left home, leaving Toni to go quietly mad with the loneliness of it all. As soon as she was able, she too had fled the nest, as Myra put it, "with largely herself to blame." A survivor of many lone battles, where words hit like blows, Toni kept her stock of grim stories to herself. Her father would scarcely have credited them in any case. A young girl, however high-spirited, was no match for a mature woman who knew when to pick her times.

It had been difficult, but she made it through, possibly

in the process strengthening her character. When Paul had written, so many months ago: "Come up and really see the sun set!" it came at a time when the circumstances of her life demanded a change. She had gone ahead making arrangements, swiftly withdrawing from the old life, the social round. Martin promised her a fixed way of life and a certain success. But she had never looked back, or regretted the break which was one of her typical characteristics, shared by her brother. Mandargi was a hundred times better than all that!

Bright indolent sunshine streamed through the venetian blinds, leaving gold bars to balance the shadows. Great lazy butterflies drifted by the open window with sweet languor, velvety black against the blazing blue sky, and the air was heavy with the scent of unseen flowers crushed and bowed by the hail. The brilliance and exotica were compensations for life in the wilds; the wild gorges, the jungle, the lily-strewn lagoons, the jade-green blady grass that rose man-high; the remote river crossings where the crocodile basked in the sun, the shadowy thickets of tea-tree and bush wattle, the giant banyan trees. Gardens were filled with crimson poincianas, the yellow cascara trees, the heliotrope orchids, the brilliant parasite, the bougainvillea that climbed in such profusion everywhere. Even a tulip tree broke out its orange blossom outside the kitchen window. The wet was a time of revival that set new life seething in the warm soil. And always the birds around them, the prolific wild life.

No wonder at all that men who lived so richly and urgently with elemental forces assumed a far different character from their city counterparts. They were tough, self-sufficient and superbly resourceful, at home in the

440

remote, least visited places. Though no woman was expected to match them, for Paul's sake, Toni could put up a moderately capable performance.

A vision of Damon Nyland filled her mind. She couldn't have ejected it, if a fortune depended upon it—the price of always thinking in pictures. Indeed it was difficult not to think of him without highly colored pictures and phrases. Perhaps the hit on the head had undermined her resistance, inducing an "acute anxiety state" in up-to-date jargon. It was a not infrequent case, and here she was falling an easy victim to cool, calculating charm, the concrete advantage that the man enjoyed over everyone.

She closed her dark eyes, heaving an exaggerated sigh of protest. Having him in the house was like waiting for another storm to burst. It took heart and imagination to combat that. A growing lassitude closed around her like a mist, leaving her temporarily without strength or resource. Oddly enough, she slept.

CHAPTER THREE

By the late afternoon she was aching with boredom, nearly mothered out of her skin by Tikka, bent on making amends for the previous day's shortcomings. From the end of the hallway came the wheezy chimes of the old grandfather clock. Somehow it brought everything to a head. Since she couldn't lie around any longer, the only way to resolve her dilemma was to get up. She moved slowly, a little stiffly, but fortunately seemed unaware of it. It took her a little longer than usual to get dressed, but the short buttercup yellow with its brief halter top was easy to get into and left her arms bare.

She paused for a moment before the sparkling mirror. She was pale, all eyes and obvious cheekbones and glowing hair. Always slender, it didn't seem possible she had lost weight overnight, but she was fairly certain she had. Perhaps a touch of lipstick would brighten up her appearance? She searched out a tube from the drawer and touched her mouth a glossy sand-rose, but it only drew attention to her pallor. With only half her mind given to the operation she blotted it nearly all off, leaving only a satiny suggestion of color.

Outside in the hallway, the house was so utterly still that her own quickened breath seemed an intrusion. She moved along the passageway as silently as any shadow with the oddest notion that she was involved in some dangerous game. The very listening quality of the silence added to the delusion. A drift of rich scent wafted in from the garden: frangipanni, a cloud of honeysuckle and oleander. She lifted her head and her delicate nostrils flared. Something else—cigarette smoke, an expensive brand. A hot quick tingle ran down her spine. She wheeled about and looked into the study, her voice a little shaken.

"Who's there?"

"So the game's up!" A deep, mocking voice reached her and she was looking at the back of a well-shaped head, the intense blackness of thick hair. He swung around in the swivel chair and stood up in one lithe movement, an object lesson in tigerish grace, she thought, trying to project antagonism into what was, undeniably, a cetain wry admiration. Across the space of the room the faint mockery dissolved into a swift look of intent. His face at that moment was a curious paradox, a mixture of cool arrogance and an overlay of a disarming gentleness.

"You're still pale!" he said, and smiled at her.

"Perhaps, but not, I think, in a state of collapse!"

"How's the head?" He reached back to the desk and slammed a report shut.

"Variable. Like a weather bulletin. It comes and goes. I'm not going back to bed, at any rate!"

He shrugged with that hard, baffling charm. "Do as you please! You're going to anyway. Is it really so necessary to set an example?"

"It's necessary not to go mad," she said feelingly, leaning against the door jamb, very young and slender. "About four o'clock I gave up. Nothing odd in that, really. I detest waiting around!"

"All life is waiting!" he said calmly with superficial tolerance. "You should know that. Waiting for this, waiting for that. Waiting for something, someone, to happen." His mouth twisted sardonically and he began to walk towards her. "In any case, I can't say it limps along here!"

Illogically Toni's eyes widened and her bones seemed to melt, realizing his personal magnetism was strengthening by the minute. She'd better stop caring what he looked like or how he behaved or learn what compromise was. Her eyes searched beyond his wide shoulders to the windowless study, restored to some semblance of order.

"I'm lucky it wasn't worse!" she said with a throb of emotion.

"You are," he agreed dryly. "but let's not dwell on it! Now, if you're going to do the thing at all, you might as well do it properly. Come along like a good child, and I'll take you for a run around the property, get a breath of fresh air!"

"But this morning you said. . . ."

He shifted his glance, studying her with maddening detachment. "Never mind what I said. That was this morning. In any case, you must make these charitable little gestures. I am the boss, after all."

"*Droit du seigneur?* Or you call the tune and we'll all dance!" She was leaning back, looking directly into his face, her body curving sideways on its narrow waist. His low spurt of laughter filled her with confusion, his glance so level and intent she couldn't break away from it.

"What a wicked, wild way of talking! I never implied that—you did!"

A glow brightened her dark eyes, contradicted by the assumed expression of sweet innocence that had worked very well in the past. "You're very tough, aren't you, Mr. Nyland?"

There was a gleam of pure malice in his green eyes and behind the malice unswerving attention. "*Firm,*" he corrected. "I don't often deign to discuss it, but I am. Especially with women."

"And all I can do is stand around and agree!"

His glance glittered over her face, startlingly candid. He looked a little hard, arrogant eyes and mouth, master of limitless horizons. "I think you ask questions for the perverse pleasure of being able to contradict!"

"It's possible." She bent her head and locked her hands together, surprised to find they were trembling slightly. "I'm sorry. I'm a nuisance, I know. Don't let me interfere with your plans." She turned and walked away from him, her slender back straight. He caught her up easily, his smile faintly cynical.

"Are you suggesting some way you can? Unexplored possibilities are always fascinating!"

Something odd and compelling stretched between them so that she had the terribly strong premonition that she must not touch him. Just talking to him was a kind of unabated excitement. He was a past master at this game. In fact, she was coming to realize he had a practised way, a sure knowledge of women. Her brain was telling her now what her senses had done. Her hand fell away abruptly from her temples with their sensitive modeling.

They walked from the deep cool haven of the porch into the golden shower of late afternoon sunlight, an excess of illumination. Yellow gold trumpets of allamanda, droves of birds fluttering everywhere. The air was warm and sweet with the overpowering scent of tropical plants, the tangle of shrubbery starred with tiny white blossoms. He glanced down at her bright head, the heavy sweep of dark lashes that swept her cheek.

"What really brought you up here?" he asked crisply, straight to the point. "A thwarted love affair?"

There was an ironic slant to her feathery dark brows. "To my endless chagrin, I can't actually lay claim to a real love affair!"

His downbent glance was spiked with amusement.

"You ask me to believe that? Women, the attractive ones, are always in love, or not in love. Not a one of them's able to resist the compulsive urge to complicate their private lives!" His hand descended lightly on her shoulder as he steered her towards the parked station wagon. She felt the shock of it right through to her bones, but she wouldn't give in to the weakness of the sensation.

"As for me," she said hardily with a great deal more conviction than she was feeling, "I don't exactly know when that will be!"

"Then you can't see very far at all!"

"That's what's bothering me." She averted her face in a rather childlike gesture, moving ahead. Flowers were everywhere, strewn all about by the storm, bird song warm and full, and above all the sun, the tropic sun. Quickly she went to open the car door, but his hand beat hers to the gleaming chrome. "It's all right, I can manage," she said a little tersely, perturbed by his near-ness—humiliating, but there it was and no way to deny it.

His voice was faintly bantering. "Of course, you're all grown up, beset by the problems of equality. Why don't you stop resisting and see what it's like?"

She didn't answer him but slid across the seat as

fastidious as a cat. His cool glance moved lightly over her long legs, then he shut the door after her and came around to the driver's side of the vehicle. A man like that could play hell with a woman, she thought, every intuition grasping at the fact, but not this one. She had too much common sense for that!

In another second he was beside her, making a jumble of all her resolute notions. His glance slid over her, light and knowing; then he reached across the glove box to extract the keys and fitted them into the ignition.

"I don't know what sort of job you did," he said sardonically, "but there you have one good reason why women are no good at the big jobs. Routine suits them better. They like plenty of scope for mooning about their love lives!"

She regarded him solemnly, all eyes, her mouth faintly parted with an unspoken protest that died on her lips. Swinging dark vitality. Rock-hard masculinity. Why wouldn't he talk like that? What else could she expect. Yet perversely these were the kind of men women were drawn to. It just didn't add up, like most things in life. The only weapon she had at her disposal was a slow, subtle smile that had worked very well in the past.

"Very cordially put, Mr. Nyland. I quite see that I for one lack the serious, responsible, objective approach of the male!"

"No doubt about it! And don't look at me like that, little one. I'm impervious to black eyes and long lashes, though I have to admit they're a nice combination!"

The amused patronage in his tone made her eyes sparkle, brought color to her cheeks. "Well, that's cleared up a few things very neatly, if they even needed clarification. You're a woman-hater!"

He gave a low laugh and slid his arm along the seat, turning his dark head to reverse out of the shaded area. "Which just goes to prove my point," he stopped and changed gear, "you're showing a fine instinctive contempt for pure logic!"

Toni turned her head swiftly so that her hair fell forward in a rose-amber sweep. "The feminine instinct, Mr. Nyland," she said sweetly, "is at least twice as good as a man's training. If women were no good at all the human race would have scrapped them and started again!"

"Good God!" his smile was very white, quietly amused. "Who said they were no good? Why, in lots of ways, Miss Stewart, I think they're incomparable."

She made a decision in a split second, knowing she would never win with him. "Oh!" she said softly, disarmingly, her creamy face still. "I thought you were all set to criticize and criticize!"

"Why should I? You look as if you've had enough!" Something flickered in the clear depths of his eyes and he gave that white, very devastating grin.

"I know the older I get, the less I know about men!" she said with some melodrama.

"There's always a sure cure, sunflower."

"Which is? I must know the truth."

"Give yourself a little time," he said lazily, "and you'll come to it all by yourself. Who knows, every last hope may be realized." His glance flickered over her and she shook her head as if warding him off, fairly caught by the devilry that flared in his eyes, that mysterious force that seemed to leap out at her.

"You're a strange man!" she said slowly, driven by some compulsion, her dark eyes touching each separate feature of his face.

"More complicated than you think!"

"Is that a warning?"

His voice was idly amused, his eyes mocking her. "My dear child, I never meant to imply any such thing." Sunlight struck obliquely across his dark copper skin, his eyes in the shadow jade green. They were moving in a swirl of dust down the bush track and she touched a hand to her throat, some weakness, part physical, moving over her, but she refused to give in to it.

"It doesn't mean anything to you, does it, scoring over women?"

"So now you know my secret! I wish I knew yours."

"I haven't got one!" she protested, over-quick.

"Oh yes, you have! We all have one, and I have inexhaustible patience. Now, enough of this nonsense. There's something I want you to do for me."

"I might have known!"

He turned his head swiftly, catching her unguarded glance. "That's how it is, little one. I'm not the big wheeler-dealer for nothing!"

"With terrible implications for myself, I feel sure."

His narrowing eyes lightly mocked her. "Such clear-sightedness! With luck, Miss Stewart, you'll go far!"

The gentle raillery piqued her, for it seemed it had a slight edge, an unnerving perceptiveness that saw inside her heart and head.

"The storm didn't do as much damage as I thought!" she said, not quite accurately, striving for a safe, fruitful topic.

He smiled, amused by the turn in the conversation, and she noticed again how the smile lit the somber, rather imperious cast of his face. The miles of Mandargi flew by, fence and grassland, the grazing cattle, pure-bred Herefords for the most part. The frost-cool green eyes seemed focused on nothing in particular; yet he saw everything to right and left, strong hands on the wheel, relaxed yet alert like a steel spring.

"The property looks good," he said almost off-handedly. "When I first bought it, it had been allowed to run down. The former owner had lost all interest in it, wouldn't spend any money on improvements or even its upkeep."

"Perhaps he didn't have any! It does make a difference."

"He had it all right," he pointed out with the cool emphasis of a man who knows his ground. "But he had some private problems he found hard to live with. His wife ran off with the first footloose adventurer to offer her a good time. At least she made it back to the city, and she was lucky to have made it at all. He was a very poor type and extracted a 'loan' from just about everyone for miles around."

"Not you?"

"A rhetorical question, I take it! No, not me, marigold. I don't listen to hard luck stories."

"I'll remember!"

"Courtesy will get you nowhere," he said dryly, "but to

return to my story . . . apparently the wife found the loneliness intolerable. No company, no taste at all for the wild
and melancholy times."

"Yet it's so beautiful! A compensation, surely?"

He turned on her swiftly, in his eyes a mixture of irony
and a deep cynicism. "You surprise me. I've collected a
lot of significant data, and in the main, I've found women
to be extraordinarily gregarious—community-minded.
They want noise and chatter and lots of friends in, a life
of cushioned ease. The better looking they are, the bigger
the ideas. Gracious living at the very least. Who cares
about the necessities, it's the luxuries that count! But for
contentment, they all need a husband with a safe job,
never mind if he likes it or not, a comfortable house and
healthy kids. A woman's values!"

"Not bad ones, surely?"

"As far as they go. They won't admit it, but women set
their own limits on their achievements. In a way they
condemn themselves to a life of mediocrity, then they
have the gall to blame men for it. They live for the here
and now, not tomorrow. Even when they are trained to
something big, they pull out at the last ditch and get
married. Race off and have six kids!"

"Not six!" she said faintly. "Not these days!"

"No, they even set a limit on that particular accom-
plishment!" he exclaimed illogically. "We've lost all our
pioneers."

For a moment her dark eyes, large and liquid, seemed
to absorb her face. "How infamous and unchival-
rous—and you needn't smile! It absolutely proves you
have an ingrained prejudice against women. Like most
men!" she finished off roundly.

"Dear me, dear me," he said, gravely mocking, insufferably high-handed and domineering. "A very shrewd hit, Miss Stewart. Twenty-two and a spinster! But I'm far too wise a fox to be baited, so don't use those velvety eyes to outwit me. I'm merely trying to point out that a man still builds for the future, and he doesn't mind roughing it, going without, for just as long as it takes."

"Have you roughed it, Mr. Nyland?" she asked sweetly, her eyes on his lean clever hands.

"I didn't always have what I've got now, honey tongue, and precious little help and encouragement." His green glance slipped over her with the degree of arrogance of a man who always got his way. "A word of advice, little one. Watch the tongue! It could scare the wits out of the local lads — something of a handicap in the matrimonial stakes. Still, they might be prepared to overlook it for the more exhilarating qualities. You're absurdly chic for the Outback. Your hair, what color is it? A rose bronze? Very unusual with dark eyes and a camellia skin. I quite expected your brother's brilliant blue eyes duplicated. You must have enjoyed considerable success in the city. Swarming all over the place, like bees with wild honey!" He didn't think it necessary to add that his ear was caught by her voice, which was lovely, warm and vital. It came to him now, for a hundred reasons, trying to jar his composure.

"I thought you implied that they'd all run the other way! In fact, you sound as if all one could reasonably ask of a woman is that she be good-looking!"

He looked at her directly and she had a moment of devastating uncertainty. "I've known quite a few," he said dryly, "yet I'm always surprised when they say the right thing, always supposing they manage anything very much at all."

"When they endorse a few of your golden words, you mean!"

"Brat!" he said gently, and laughed in his throat. "Opinionated women are never popular. Remember it, my impudent young friend!"

"So now you're disenchanted?" Her brilliant, youthful face confronted his dark, controlled one.

"Stone cold!" he said lightly. "In fact, if I didn't want a son to carry on all I've built up, I'd never marry at all. Failures are so damned expensive."

"You're rather a case, aren't you?"

"Hard as nails!" His eyes met hers and her heart gave a great lurch. The eyes were completely baffling, as was everything about that contradictory man. The visionary: benevolent dictator, shrewd and calculating, the shattering, unsettling glimpses of near-tenderness.

"But very attractive!" she managed at last. Complete detachment of the impartial observer.

His smile fetched a white line in that darkly tanned skin. "So I've been told! But not nearly so attractive without my more concrete lasting assets. Savannah, for one. A man doesn't reach my age with many illusions intact about your sweetly unscrupulous sex. Avid little fingers, cased in velvet!"

Toni started to quote lightly, lowering her lashes over a malicious sparkle. "Give crowns and pounds and guineas, but not your heart away! And you won't give either!"

"Do you blame me? You know, little one, I like you. You even appear to be honest, but I've been tricked before—by brown eyes, as it happened!"

She drew a hand over her face as if she were brushing away cobwebs. "I don't relish my position then. Trying to prove myself at every turn just as though you'd washed your hands of all of us!"

"I certainly don't bear you a grudge," he remarked blandly, his eyes on her face. "In fact, I never rush into judgments. It's a dangerous habit!"

A pity about his smile, she thought, feeling hopelessly at a disadvantage. It hovered somewhere between mockery and a sensual element as strong as an electric current. She obeyed an irresistible impulse and smiled at him, using every bit of her not inconsiderable charm. But his firm mouth only relaxed into a grin. Top marks for effort. The glittery gaze slid over her half disparagingly.

"You must have been a ravishingly pretty child, but you've got too much to say for yourself!"

"You can't have it both ways!" She looked back at him, flippantly, unwilling to concede him a victory.

"Who says I can't!" he drawled with exquisite distinctness. "At this juncture, I've got it made!"

She was on the defensive now, excited, a little moody, perplexed by some odd shift in his manner. "This is an insane conversation!"

"Isn't it, and I've the feeling we're going to continue it every time we meet. You may be wild in your ways, but your face is beautiful. A very exotic butterfly!"

The sun struck across her eyes and she turned her head away. "I'd love to see Savannah," she announced in a politely enthusiastic voice.

"Now there's a cunning, opening wedge and no mistake! All right, then, you will, and sooner than you think, which is what I wanted to talk to you about. Let's get out." He ran the car into the shade of a grove of low, shrubby trees, with light leaves and coarse bark, the aromatic sandalwoods. In another minute he had her out of the car, powerful, quiet and purposeful, with that disconcerting dash of diablerie, a light steely grip on her wrist.

"It has a sort of listening quietness, hasn't it?" she asked, over the swift, fiery beat of her heart.

He looked at her thoughtfully, seeing the pull of the place in her fine, dark eyes. "That's it, exactly. The particular spell of the tropics!" His gaze shifted to the distant line of the ranges, stretching for untold distances like a sea of blue green; the rain forest, honeycombed with cliffs and ravines, wild creeks and gorges where waterfalls rushed and tumbled into rock pools. Vibrant, flutelike calls punctuated the stillness and a flock of corellas fluttered like flags overhead. Long massed grasses lay tossed by the storm, still glistening with moisture in the places not penetrated by the bush sunlight. The smell of the earth was good, with the elusive tang of airborne flowers, and an underlying exquisite scent, almost like freesias, white-petalled and very sweet.

"Not so very long ago," he said quietly, "in my father's day, this was the wild north—still is, in lots of respects. I grew up on tales of pearls and gold and tinfields; of clashes between white and black, bloody and to the death; land grabs and cattle duffing and herds of magnificent wild horses that made their kingdom in the grasslands; tribal murders and black magic and crocodile shooters who went mad with the loneliness and isolation, the near-inaccessibility in the wet. Plenty to keep a small boy going. No wonder at all I had to come back!" His gaze descended on her, delicately practised; yet she saw clearly that a woman was no more than a piece in a pattern to him. The land was his real life. "If it's freedom you want, pretty bird," he said lightly, "then you've got it. I know I feel hemmed in almost any place else!"

She was looking back at him with an unconscious air of expectancy. The breeze skeined her hair across her face, silky and lucent, pointing up the flawless perfection of young, healthy skin. The sheen and the shimmer, the one against the other. Dark ardent eyes. The silence seemed infinite. It was impossible to break that ice-green gaze. So much for her good intentions!

He was only trying to subjugate her with the force of his personality—an easy task. The mighty male, and she the second-class citizen. Power and arrogance, she thought wryly. A great big do-as-I-please, that was Damon Nyland with his lean, hard body and stark, exciting face. His eyes were brilliant with life, clear and glittery, mistakenly placed in a face far too dark for them, an extraordinary contrast, startling to the beholder. They narrowed suddenly, and the corners of his firm mouth dented with amusement.

"What's on your mind?"

"Rebellion," she said.

His dark head came up like a thoroughbred and his aspect changed as if he had accepted the challenge. "For a moment there, I thought I'd committed every crime in the calendar. For some unknown, undeserved reason, you appear to have taken a firm dislike to me. A crushing blow!"

"Indeed I haven't!" she said with some irony.

"Women invariably betray themselves in a thousand

small, eloquent ways! Yet your brother praises you to the skies—your beauty, your accomplishments, the sweetness of your disposition, charming and docile. I can only assume he's prejudiced. So far as I can judge, you've been pampered and spoiled out of all reason. The red hair makes it worse, of course."

A new wisdom told her to say nothing. She moved away from him quickly, with a unique elegance and no clear idea of where she was heading.

"You're full of a demon energy all of a sudden!" He was beside her, studying her with great interest like a museum piece under glass.

"I didn't want to be provoked into any unwonted admissions!" she said with some truth.

Instantly he dropped a restraining hand on her shoulder, laughing in his throat. "You won't beat me, little one, but if it seems any recompense, you stand a better chance than most of getting the odd hit home!" He glanced down at her bright head and his voice sharpened. "You're trembling—what the devil!"

He gave the impression of great force and vigor and she had to smile. "You've an unusually vivid personality, Mr. Nyland. Perhaps you were getting to me!"

"My *darling* child! Forgive me." He said it with the easy, careless charm of long practice. "Now how can I make amends? I know, we'll walk on a little way ahead. We Christians must share our treasures!"

Then they were walking across the untracked, mildly sloping part of the run, treading a thick, cushiony sea of bracken. The storm had brought up from the earth a sweet freshness that was extraordinarily restful. Ferns rose tall as a man with strong brown stems and bright green fronds outstretched like arms. He went on ahead, holding them before her face, the two of them united by the cool spell of the pre-sunset hour.

They were ringed with ironwoods, bush mahogany, chalky-barked poplar gums, the graceful tea-tree and acacia. Trees, so benign and beautiful, showing a new lushness with the approach of the wet. Once a long, somnolent snake, curiously marked, slithered away from the man's foot, but he said nothing. His companion had missed it, as indeed, most would have, and besides, it was harmless. Bee-eaters swooped in low formation, the sun glancing off their blue green body feathers, the coppery sheen of their heads.

They had gone about a quarter of a mile before they commenced the ascent of the sloping butt of the cliff face. The country was rougher, but they took it in easy stages. Stones dislodged by their shoes bounced away into the thick vegetation, but there were numerous anchors of saplings and ferns to cling to. Nearing the top, a spring spouted out, a silver fountain, marvellously picturesque, making a cool splashing sound.

"Storm water!" he said briefly, and turned to take her hand, drawing her up the rest of the slope. At the top, she stood beside him, bright head on a level with his shoulder, an apricot flush in her cheeks, panting slightly, pleasurably, from her exertions.

"Worth it?" He looked into her upflung face, then pointed to a strikingly semicircular entrance, framed by cool saplings in the freshest, palest shade of almond. It was a cave, and over the rock face drooped a long, lovely

cascade of bush orchids: waxy cream into gold, speckled
at the heart with magenta. A tumbling mass of blossom, a
florist's dream, almost faultlessly arranged.

He reached up a long arm and plucked a flower,
pushing it into her thick, silky hair with unerring fingers,
surveying his handiwork with faintly sardonic eyes.

"Woman magic! It sizzles and burns! You're a pretty
thing, young Toni, but let's go inside. Duck your head,
like a good girl."

She bent almost double to enter the cave, but once inside she found there was plenty of room to stand upright.
For a few moments it was almost impossible to
distinguish anything after the brilliant sunshine. There
was only a cool gloom, tinged with the lingering scent of
herb smoke. The gloom merged into a soft, glimmering
light.

"Why, it's marvellous!" she said in a young, entranced
voice. "The perfect hidey-hole. Children would just love
it!"

His brief laugh was indulgent and impatient at once.
"Hidey-hole? God, you're closer to the schoolroom than I
thought!"

She scarcely heard him, her eyes widening in awed
amazement. "But this is a sacred place! On Mandargi."

"It is," he said rather dryly. "You're in the presence of
the gift-bearers of the Dreamtime." He tilted her chin
with one finger and she looked about her, her eyes circling
the dim interior.

Around the walls and roof of the rock shelter glowed
the good spirits of the Dreaming, mythical beings, some
wearing ceremonial headdress, others with concentric
circles for heads, surrounded by easily recognizable

animals and trees, some abstract symbols, few, if any, understood. There was no sound, yet she heard spirit drums and tap-sticks and chanted prayers. A closed world of live magic, its psychic effect remarkable.

"Why, how perfect!" she said, her voice scarcely above a whisper as if she were in church. "And I never knew it was here!" She turned up her face to him, and her skin in the gloom had a visible, opalescent shimmer, her dark eyes wide.

"No one does, brown eyes," he said rather brusquely. "Only you and I know the secret, and the aborigines, of course. I only came on it by sheer chance and I'm insatiably curious. So here's your reward for being a good, uncomplaining child. Many a lesser woman would have taken to her bed for a week after your experience."

There was a smile in the depths of her eyes and she turned to him with slim, curving grace. "Why, thank you, Mr. Nyland. Sometimes you can be so unexpectedly nice!"

"Then's the time not to trust me!" he said abruptly and began to laugh. "Well, have you seen enough? You've had enough adventure for one day. See you don't try to come here by yourself. It's way off the beaten track and you might get lost. Is that clear?"

Toni lifted her head, still caught in the magic net, anxious to please him, when from the deep, shallow recesses of the cave flapped a great, ugly bat, hardly moved from its pristine state, its inky black, membranous wings spread.

"Oh no!" She flung up her hands in an agony of fright and revulsion, not conscious of having walked or run or made any movement at all, but somehow she was locked within a hard protective circle of linked arms, her fore-head pressed against the crisp, clean fragrance of his shirt. She hid her pale, incensed face with a little muffled exclamation.

"Don't panic!" he said above her head, his deep voice faintly mocking her. "Our friend just guards the place."

"Ugh!" Her slim shoulders shuddered involuntarily. "Hideous!"

"That's taken the shine out of things!"

"No, of course it hasn't! Really. . . ." She lifted her head framed in the bright disarray of her hair, anxious to proclaim her true feelings and as suddenly fell silent. Feathery waves of excitement mounted in her, beating about her like hidden wings. The whole of her melted into a look of complete femininity, willow-slender, and infinitely desirable.

"Don't do it!" he said, and the old mocking light was back in his eyes again with a new wariness.

"I don't understand!" She drew back from him, his dark face blurring under her eyes.

"You see how it could be, don't you?" His voice was hard, a shade reckless.

Her eyes sparkled like jet against the creamy pallor of her skin. It was impossible to mistake his meaning, excitement flaring like sheet lightning between them. "I feel shut in. Claustrophobic!" she said, speaking very rapidly.

"You can say that again!" There was a decided edge to his voice now and he seemed very tall and menacing, a complete stranger. Then his tone lightened. "Come along, flower face; you're obviously too young for it!" His fingers closed about her wrist, pulling her closer, holding her still. "You're perfectly safe with me!"

Why, he lived for domination. For mastery, she thought wildly. She was trembling slightly under the terrible toll of sexual attraction, fearing it a weakness.

"You'd like to see me grovel, wouldn't you?" she burst out, the soft, furious color flooding her skin, adding to her look of abandonment.

"Why, you perverse little witch!" His eyes were no more than glittery slits, slashing at her. "You almost convince me!"

Then he was swinging her into his arms, kissing her, like no civilized man but a sorcerer. She was defenceless, without the power to resist, her mouth clinging, her body fluid and yielding, no thinking creature, but feeling . . . sheets of it, a burning, never-to-be-borne enchantment . . . a magic circle of fire.

When his mouth left hers, she could have cried out. It was like being bereft, cut off from the life force. Electrifying pulses throbbed through her. Toni turned away blindly, so filled with new bewildering emotions that they overflowed in her. She had nothing to say.

His lean frame barred the entrance. He bent his dark head to her. "Why so frantic? I'd have thought you were kissed every other day!"

"Not like that!"

Now why had she admitted that, unless her self-control had gone racing over the moon?

"Then it's my turn to apologize, though you asked for it!" His manner was so sardonic, so assured, so wildly at variance with the preceding shattering minutes, she found it hard to believe that she had experienced them at all.

His green eyes mocked her, like some jungle cat's. Perhaps it was a form of magic. Love potions. Anything. He was marvellously gifted to be able to turn it on and off like that. She was rather frightened of him. Perhaps he knew it and found it necessary, for his attitude relented, a resigned indifference to her emotional lack of growth. He turned and led the way out of the cave into the voluptuous beauty of a tropical sunset.

She sighed deeply, her eyes enormous, purplish black.

"Give everything its exact value," he said crisply. "That way you won't complicate life for yourself. It's all a question of psychology."

She stared at him, still trembling, and rubbed the false, sweet kiss from her mouth. "I've no head at all for serious things."

"Quite right! I knew we could follow this to a logical conclusion. Forgive me, Toni." He seemed to be amused, and it depressed her all the more.

"I don't know why you should find that important," she said a shade bitterly.

"I thought I told you. I want you to do something for me, but that can wait."

She stared back at him, hopelessly; then she started to laugh, the little break in her voice less than controlled. He reacted at once.

"We'll go back—you're tired. That's a sign of fatigue if ever I've heard one!"

There was no way around it but to go back with him, suffer his strong arm for ever by her side. They covered the distance in silence, the very silence unnatural, accentuating her feeling of utter unreality. He was oddly untamable, this cruel cat-man with his almost mesmeric attraction, his slanting dark brows and saturnine expression, the strange leaping lights in his eyes.

On the western horizon all the magic in the world was

harnessed. Great billowing clouds of crimson and rose and gold, shot with an unearthly radiance. The Great Earth Mother was all about them, joyous and vivid, surging with new life on the edge of the wet. Cassias and acacias and bauhinias, heavy with blossom spilled color all over the bushland. The song of the wind. The calls of homing birds as they flew into the lovely chain of waterholes.

With not a word, her young face slightly averted, Toni glanced everywhere but at the man beside her. A silent, insistent rhythm throbbed through her veins, but she couldn't put a name to it. It clamored within her like an urgent ecstasy, faithfully reproduced by the flowering wilderness that was Mandargi.

CHAPTER FOUR

After dinner they sat out in the cool of the porch, the night wind filtering through the verdant screen of vines. The vast and velvet sky was spangled with diamonds, flung almost haphazardly across the heavens, and over the banyan tree hung the Southern Cross.

Toni, sunk in the shadowy depths of a bamboo chair, seemed alien to the men's conversation. It revolved leisurely but purposefully about the affairs of Mandargi and on to the last word in advanced techniques —Savannah; experimentation, breeding, feeding, crops. Cattle-mad! Toni thought wryly. All their thoughts and energies were devoted to quadrupeds. Ice tinkled in squat tumblers, soothing to the touch and the senses.

She studied them thoughtfully; one with love and affection, a considerable degree of sisterly pride. The other with a frustrating jumble of emotions. Certainly not love, but perilously close to an obsession. Both men were handsome, intelligent, vital. One, super-assured, worldly, successful. Despot. The other, up-and-coming, ambitious but basically not all that tough. No Nyland. Both of them were dedicated men. They would never change. Indeed, they thought themselves perfect, or near enough to matter. It was their womenfolk who had to change. They were the ones who would like it or lump it, make the sacrifices.

Occasionally she leaned forward over the low table to pick up her own tall, frosty glass, and the light fell in a pool over her burnished head, her simple sea-colored dress, her face and throat rising above it almost translucent. She was pale, worn out by unaccustomed emotions. Dinner had been a success, though it had cost her an effort. One look at the vast, hot boiled mess of chicken Tikka had thoughtfully prepared in advance had been enough to make Toni give up all ideas of mere supervision. She had picked up the cooling saucepan there and then and thrust it at the astonished Tikka, who was struggling to interpret her young employer's seeming extravagance.

"Take it! Go on, take it! Take it away!" Toni still heard her own voice sailing around the kitchen. Tikka had smiled and nodded, bewildered but pleased, bearing her steaming burden to the uncomplaining Albert, who eventually tucked it away. In spite of these handicaps, the urge to present a decent meal was strong in Toni. She cared about good food, from its preparation to its presentation, and she knew quite a bit about it, or liked to think she did. At any rate no one complained. The compliments flowed from the men over dinner, free and unfeigned, and she brushed them aside with a small smile. All in a day's work.

In the end they had rather an interesting appetizer in the form of Gulf prawns with a tangy sauce and garnished with lemon. Steak, because time was short, but good Mandargi beef, crisp on the outside, faintly pink on the inside, juicy and tender and thick, served with a tossed salad. Afterwards, she brought out strawberry crêpes with ice cream, for no other reason than she was a rare hand with crêpes and the big turquoise strawberry pot had been brought into the shelter of the porch while the fruit was ripening, thus saving it from the birds and, better still, the storm. Coffee, black and strong. Cheese if the men wanted it—they did. The two girls, very quick and neat in freshly laundered uniforms, waited at table, their merry black eyes bright with a delicate delight. It was a great treat to serve the Big Boss, who responded admirably, white teeth flashing in his dark, handsome face.

It was an effort, Toni reasoned, but well worth it. Mandargi's reputation had been sustained. It was a fantastic luxury to sit in the cool of the porch, the familiar night sounds around them; laughter and shouts, the odd restrained swear word, a card game in progress over at the stockmen's quarters. The persistent warbling of a nightbird. Soft crooning voices not altogether in tune with a current pop record on the old gramophone. They had to speak to her twice before she heard them; then she turned to her brother with a faint start.

"I'm sorry, darling, I was listening to the recording. Tom Jones, isn't it?"

"Hardly. He'd get over that din. I'm sorry I ever gave them that old piece of junk. They never let up. I'd like to know where they get all the new records."

"Buy them, of course. With their wages. Mack used to order them in. *Chacun à son gout*, you know!"

"Yes, indeed!" Nyland supplied suavely, as though asked his opinion. "I like women with a touch of vinegar. Lends a flavor!"

Paul looked at him with mild surprise, then laughed. He had been aware of the cross-currents during dinner. "Mr. Nyland . . ." he began.

"Damon!" Nyland corrected with some charm and right at the precise, psychological moment.

"*Damon*," Paul saluted the older man with his glass and a lazy smile . . . "wants to ask a favor."

"I've been trying to get around to it all day." Nyland picked up the cue neatly. "Toni, there is a way you can help me if you would." His green eyes watched her with a challenging stare. An "I-know-you-damn-well-dislike-me, but say-it-if-you-dare" look.

She met his gaze readily enough, her face slightly frozen, and he smiled.

"Encouragement is what I want! I do wish you'd try to hear me out, little one!"

"Of course!" she said, as outspoken as ever.

"Thanks." He tipped back in his chair and the light fell across his face and she wished it hadn't. "I'll try to be brief. A woman relative of mine is coming to stay with me. In the nature of a rest cure. Peace and quiet, that sort of thing. She's had rather a bad time of it, but she's been very brave with that screwed-up kind of courage some women have. Her husband, my cousin, was killed in a car crash about eighteen months ago. It was all very tragic. He was only thirty-one, leaving Elissa and one child—a small girl, Anne or Annette, I'm not sure. I gather she's something of a handful and Lissa's not strong. Fragile, I suppose you'd say."

"And where do I come in?" Toni asked faintly, but straight from the heart. A fragile, introverted mother? A difficult child?

"I think your company," he said with careless grandeur, "would do Elissa the world of good. She's become very withdrawn. Bad at her age, and whatever else you are, Toni, you're bright company. It would only be for a week or so. My solicitors are handling the hiring of a governess for the child, but it will be some time before she arrives. In the meantime I don't want Elissa to be on her own. I know she'd be glad of another woman's company and the child is too much for her. Missing the man's hand, I suppose."

We all are! Toni thought wryly, at once and forever on Annette's side. The initial shock had worn off. He might crack the whip for miles around, but she had other ideas. "Please, Mr. Nyland," she said lightly, her dark eyes sparkling, "you're asking for the moon! Mandargi needs me. Paul needs me. Paul?" She turned her high-spirited face to her brother for confirmation, but he was studying the level of the whisky bottle with the complete absorption of an alcoholic. Diplomacy was one of his great assets.

Nyland, in turn, looked back at her with the cool self-containment of a statue cast in bronze. "Paul," he said suavely, "has been good enough to suggest that he can struggle along for a fortnight, but rather than let him do that, I'll send over one of my own staff to handle the cooking arrangements. He won't starve, never fear. Neither will the men. Mrs. Carroll mightn't approach your excellence, but she's what is known as a good, plain cook and she's very strong. She'll cope, not to speak of managing the staff. I think you'll find she'll perform some small miracles there!"

She stared back at him as if they had just exchanged insults. Nothing in her life had ever prepared her for such cool insolence. The trouble was, she dreaded domination, and he had a remarkable talent for riding roughshod over all opposition.

"Bullied and beaten!" she said frankly. "I wonder you

think of me, Mr. Nyland. Surely there's someone else you'd much rather ask?"

"Absolutely not! The truth is, I knew it the moment I laid eyes on you." His eyes touched her face, effortlessly able to fascinate. "You will do it, Toni? Help me out. It's all in a good cause, and you're such a good-hearted little thing. Paul's been telling me!" There was a hard, mocking glint in his eyes that suggested that he really thought her an unruly brat with reckless impulses but was too polite, or too cunning, or both, to mention it.

She was very still, her slender body tilted, looking out over the star-spangled night. "In that case, Mr. Nyland," she said with a touch of his own superb irony, "I'd be pleased to. Shall we drink to it?"

"You're very kind!" His dark-timbered voice dropped to an intimate undertone. "You've no idea what it means to me!"

"None whatsoever!" she said with a swift return to her old pugnacious self, thinking it rather mean of Paul to desert her like that. Her idea of Mandargi as a refuge was no more than a fantasy. This invitation, this *summons*, to Savannah, was symbolic, a demonstration of authority.

"I'll pay you, of course, so you won't think it's charity!" he said, gleaming eyes shadowed with some knowledge she found unbearably exciting. And she was being sent into enforced daily encounter with him! He continued to study her, very experienced, very cynical, very sure of what he wanted in a woman, a twist to his mobile, provocative mouth.

"You beast!" She withdrew to the safety of the shell-backed chair, her dark eyes melancholy, admitting her vulnerability and not caring.

"Always when I discuss money." He reached over

lazily and tipped a little ginger ale into her glass. "Here, let me top up your drink." His eyes flicked her face briefly, daring her to speak again. Toni had this wild, irrational impulse to flail her fists at him, hammer him with puny blows.

Acting in her interests? However could she believe in such a myth? She fell silent. Out-witted, manipulated, probably to play gooseberry on Savannah. Ashamed of herself, she cancelled out that last idea. What had come over her? Some weird personality change? The woman was a widow, only recently bereaved. A small child missing her father, needing an emotional outlet. She was ashamed of herself. She would go to Savannah and give her very best and she wouldn't accept a penny for it. She would make sure of that. Damon Nyland had a woman of consequence and character to reckon with.

Apparently it didn't bother him unduly, for he was already fathoms deep in conversation with Paul again. In another minute she would excuse herself for the night. They would never miss her, in any case. Probably they wouldn't even hear her say goodnight! Words impinged on her ear, making her change her mind. A dawn mustering! To ride out in the cool, mother-of-pearl light. Coffee round the camp fire, a circle of tanned faces. The flame of dawn in the sky. Very early sunlight, pale as honey. Tree shadows. Hooves stamping, impatient to be off.

"Can I come?" The words flew out, in brilliant animation, heightened by a rare susceptibility.

"No!" Nyland said very calmly. "You'll only get into trouble. Women and cattle don't mix. Besides, you have to watch your arm."

"My arm doesn't bother me in the least!" she said rather emotionally.

"You'd be the last to admit it if it did!"

"It's pretty rough work, honey," Paul broke into the conversation, his eyes on his sister's vivid young face, the lustrous sheen in her eyes. "You haven't seen too much at all as far as that goes. We'll be mustering, separating, branding, that sort of thing. A welter of noise and confusion. You've heard the calves bellow, and there's danger too. It gets terribly hot as the day wears on, and the dust and everything. . . ."

He knew, from experience, he was fighting a losing battle. Toni had a trick of getting her own way, especially with him. Many was the guilty moment he had endured on her behalf, leaving her to Myra's tender mercies when she was little more than a child with thick, glossy pigtails and never a sign of reproach in those great dark eyes.

Nyland, looking at his face, knew the younger man was weakening. A mistake with young things that needed kindness but plenty of control. It was easy to recognize his opposition, for he had dropped all pretense, his autocratic dark face set, suggesting argument would be useless, much less a private feud.

"I know I'm going to love it!" Toni found herself saying. "Ordinary riding clothes be all right?"

"Drop it, little one, while you're ahead," Nyland said easily, with only a token attempt at placation.

"Another time, perhaps, when you're more used to our way of life and you haven't had a hit on the head. It's hard riding and you're unaccustomed to it. You wouldn't stay the distance and you'd have to ride back in the heat." He paused for a moment and his eyes seemed to change subtly. They were cooler, clearer, very frank. A half smile hovered near his mouth. "You go right ahead and go to bed. You look tired and tense. We'll just take our time." He said it as if he had spent a lifetime considering her wellbeing.

Oh, he was clever! A clever, dangerous, urbanely affable antagonist. She had known it all the time. "Do you know it's the oddest thing!" she said almost incredulously, then broke off, conscious she was talking like a woman in a melodrama. She wanted to be alone, more than anything in the world. "Really, I intend to go," she said quietly, firmly, no silly girl-child. "That's my final word!"

"Why, that sounds fascinating!" Nyland gave a low laugh. "Mutiny?"

"Oh no! Give up, kiddo. Looks like you're defeated on this one!" Paul said in his charming drawl, thinking it not all that important.

"How very friendly of you!" Toni said sweetly. *Give up?* She'd show them! They had no right to discriminate against her. With a jolt she realized she was on the verge of losing her temper. That would never do. She had to save her energies. In any case, she simply didn't care enough to feel insulted. She surveyed them bright-eyed, spreading her hands in an appealing little gesture. "Forgive me, I am a little tired. I'll say good night."
am a little tired. I'll say good night."

Their faces relaxed, softened. They came to their feet, smiling, as though they found her enormously engaging. In the half-light, half-shadow, they looked exaggeratedly tall, powerful, graceful too. Wide in the shoulders, lean in the hips. Cattle men, to be treated with caution. Good friends and neighbors. Nyland sketched an elegant little salute and she felt a surge of murderous rage that carried her in a fine blaze to her room. With any luck at all she would beat them out onto the track!

The moon was still in the sky when she rose, a silver sickle. She was happy, exhilarated, keyed up like a child about to start out on an unauthorized adventure. The pre-dawn wind was cool and moist, stroking her skin and making her hair curl. It fanned out the curtains and made her whisper to herself: This is the best time of all!

She dressed swiftly, her movements keeping pace with her quickening pulse. Presently she was ready—riding pants, glistening riding boots, pale cotton shirt, spotted silk scarf to protect her nape and later on, her face, against the dust, a rakish gaucho hat, wide-brimmed and silver-strapped. She felt wide awake, diamond-bright, able to beat the opposition. It was an extra luxury to be able to sip at a cup of still-scalding black coffee poured from the stainless steel thermos she had smuggled into her room the night before. Such foresight! She finished it up, then put the cup down, turning to smile at herself in the mirror with great affection. Everything was going according to plan. She had even beaten the birds up!

It was impossibly risky to go back through the house. The window was the answer. It was only a short drop to the ground. In a flash she was through, landing lightly on the thick, springy grass. It was a magical morning, pearl gray, mystical, like being reborn. No shafts of opal light yet invaded the sky, no hordes of birds. Only the sweet, penetrating scent of some tiny white flowers she had crushed underfoot.

Her first thought was to reach her horse—no quiet little working horse, but a sweet-tempered mare descended from the Arab. Toni rode well, correctly, taught as a child. Not as the hands on the station, born in the saddle, centaurs, part-man, part-horse, or they certainly gave that impression. Experts indeed, but she had nothing to be ashamed of.

She moved warily, always looking behind her, with any number of dodges, her heart hammering, as if she was on some guilty mission. She cut through the screen of trees, head down, until she came out on the pebbled track that led to the stables. Suddenly, like some mysterious sun-signal, a great frieze of birds came flying up through the first flush of light, rising from the lagoon, straightening out their V formation, gliding in line. Shell parrots, hundreds of tiny green birds, the orange and crimson chats, unwound like some multi-colored bolt of silk across the sky.

Toni lifted her face, vivid with pleasure, her melting dark eyes filled with an intense love for this wild, fresh land, this paradise of tiny, chattering birds that seemed to ring her round, a shining massed escort. Up, up, up! A soft, swishing sound of wings, like the dawn breeze. She held up a hand, very young, very slender, with a dangerous vulnerability, an acute sensitivity that deepened her capacity for pleasure and pain.

Intent as she was on the birds' antics, it was doubly shocking to be caught up in one smooth, unhurried lunge, held in a sprung-steel trap. Off guard: she thought, her heart flipping in fright. Off guard. *As always*. Struck into an awed silence.

"You've heard about bushcraft, I take it," he said with

great distinctness, his eyes on her defenceless face. "Invaluable, I've found. Some sixth sense that always leads the hunter to the quarry. He knows exactly which path to take, which track to follow. He almost sees into the mind!"

"How clever!" she said dismally, wise enough not to struggle, feeling the first fright of reaction.

"You've changed your mind, I gather."

"Yes, but surely I have a good reason?" She ignored the sarcasm, her dark eyes searching his face, wide and alarmed. How could she ever have imagined he would never guess her secret? Alertly on guard, his supreme self-assurance was never to be shaken.

He pulled at a short bright curl and wound it around his finger. "You're practically begging for it, aren't you? You don't think you fooled me with that little girl act last night? I saw the fine blaze in your eyes. A terrible weapon!"

Some deep running physical attraction was threatening to engulf her. She leaned back against his arm, her heart knocking against her ribs, seeing the gleam in his eyes and disliking their expression.

"I'm going! Yes, I am," she said intensely. "If you don't let me, I won't help you with your cousin, and you can't make me, so there!"

"Blackmail?" He seemed poised like a hawk, a sensual twist to his mouth.

"Something like that!" she said in a terse undertone. "If you can't lick 'em, join 'em!"

"Nothing doing!" He dropped his hands pointedly, never more heartless.

"Damon!" It was almost a cry from the heart,

completely unpremeditated, and she could have bitten her tongue out.

"Mr. Nyland to you, brat!" He turned, his green eyes sweeping over her sensually alive.

"Mr. Nyland!" she corrected herself, and drew a deep, shuddering breath.

Inexplicably amusement leaped in his eyes. "Don't look so desperate!" He moved slowly back to her. "I was only fooling. Damon will do. It sounds altogether different the way you say it!"

Her hat hung down her back and her bare head glinted like the rise and fall of fire. Deliberately she pitched her voice to a bell tone, her feelings showing very plainly in her face. "Please let me come. I won't be in the way. You can trust me not to panic or lose my head. I have the right hat on and I'll come back as soon as I've had enough. I'll even . . ."

". . . if you'll allow me to get a word in edgeways," he said quite pleasantly, for him, so that she stood rapt and still staring into his dark face, her soft mouth faintly parted. "You're very polite, very persuasive all of a sudden. I shouldn't be so surprised!" His lids came down, masking the brilliance of his eyes. "You agree to come to Savannah?"

"I do. One good deed deserves another!"

He gave a short laugh, not without humor. "Yes, and I can see the effort it's taking! All right, then, come. Probably we'll both live to regret it, but I can't help myself. I'd have to be a wooden image to ignore your assets, and that's the proof!"

"Sarcasm before the sun's up, Mr. Nyland?" she asked him and smiled, holding out her hand with a sudden impulsive motion.

"The simple truth, ma'am." He took her hand briefly, sounding brisk and factual, the hard arrogance back on him, then he spun on his heel. "Well, are you coming? Or determined to waste time? I can't pretend I'm doing the right thing!"

How like a man never to give in gracefully. "Oh, don't turn your back," she burst out impulsively. "Please look at me!"

"I know better!" he said briefly, charging ahead. "Excessive bravery is beyond me!" He was burning up the ground, moving lithely, with long, lengthy paces, aloof, self-contained, so that she had to run to keep up with him. Nearing the stables, he stopped so abruptly that she almost slammed into him. He caught her by the shoulders, lowering his dark head. "Now listen to me, flower face. I don't care how seductive you are. Behave. Do exactly what you're told today. Got it? Exactly, or there'll be hell to pay!"

Color flooded her face, adding luster to her eyes. The urge to defy his authority was moving inexorably in her. "Yes, of course, Mr. Nyland. I do beg your pardon. Is there anything more you care to say?"

"That's it. That's the end!"

"That's enough!" Toni said with a helpless little cry. "You're hurting me!"

He drew back from her instantly, a disturbing element in his soft drawl. "I'm sorry, but you will stand so close to danger!" His eyes in the green gloom mocked her, his mouth twisted sardonically.

"I suppose you know you're going to get directly in the line of fire?" he added.

"Am I?" she asked rashly.

He took a quick step toward her and her eyes went

enormous. Whatever course of action he had in mind he obviously thought better of it. "Never mind!" he said with a hard, mocking grin. "We can always pick up the pieces later. Come along, velvet eyes, so sweet and simple and demure, I *don't* think!"

She thrust her hat on her soft fall of hair, tilting it to a dashing angle as a matter of course. Now perversely she wanted to please him. How could she be so changeable? "Please don't let's quarrel and spoil things," she said, twisting to look into his dark face. "I'm a pacifist by nature!"

He laughed outright. "You're extremely clever and very disrespectful, but I suppose a woman can't have everything! Now, come quietly and don't dance around me like a five-year-old or I might change my mind."

She slanted a glance at his straight profile—a good profile. His expression as usual, baffling, a faint curve of self-mockery to his shapely mouth. All at once she wanted to touch him, so badly she dared not think about it. What a fool, ruled by her emotions! She didn't even know him, so why this sense of affinity as if she'd known him in some other lifetime? A shower of excitement was tightening inside her like a closed fist. Damon spun his head as if she had thrown something at him, pinning her gaze. For a stricken minute she felt herself transparent. Every thought, every desire, everything she had ever felt, there for him to register.

"Well, well, well!" he said softly, in such a way that she turned and ran as if he were the devil himself.

CHAPTER FIVE

Cattle—rivers of them, great thundering torrents of cattle ran from everywhere. Joining up, they became jam-packed; you could have walked across their backs to almost anywhere. A big muster, thousands of head, a surging, living sea of liver and white hides, white faces, pink-rimmed eyes. Close-packed, churning hooves sent dense cloud castles spiralling to the skies. The bellowing was frightful, bouncing off the eardrums, to live on for hours after all noise had ceased.

Every hand on the station had been called into action, black and white. Scarves, folded triangular fashion, covered their faces to provide some protection from the all-pervading dust. They swung in the saddle with an easy slouch, appearing to hardly touch the reins, the work horses trained to the point where they needed little direction to flank and press back the surging, solid walls of flesh.

The sun was up, full up, burning with great brilliance and power through the successive layers of red dust that fell back from the skies. Toni, in a near-frenzy of heat and strange sights, sat on the white fence at the cattle-yards, her boots hooked through one of the lower rungs. Perched up beside her was Albert, the aboriginal stockman—commentator, bodyguard. Both of them, like the men, wore their scarves tied under their eyes, but the dust was everywhere like an insidious fog.

Dust, daring, danger, Toni thought, soaking it in. Men moved with seeming indifference and expert precision through all three. Calves separated from their mothers were frantic with fear. Anti-human. Womanlike, their agonized bellowing upset her. Roped, tied, branded. The sudden stench of singed hair and burnt flesh. The branding was not cruelly excessive but hard enough to leave a clear imprint of the stylized M. Ear-clipping, dehorning, castrating—but Toni didn't watch that. Not in any circumstances. Enough was enough, she thought, her small nose wrinkling. She swallowed constantly, convulsively, determined to learn something and not fall off the fence in sheer horrified revolt. At the very least, she learned she was no cattle woman. Perhaps she never would be, though the whole spectacle had a savage, barbaric splendor; the aboriginal stockmen performed some weird ballet as they danced before hostile horns.

In the center of the arena of noise and heat and confusion stood Paul with the Big Boss by his side. Their deeply tanned faces were almost obscured by their scarves and wide-brimmed Stetsons, their eyes narrowed against the glare and the grime. They were locked in an all-male world of decision and danger; on all sides protesting beasts flexed their great muscle power.

It was strange, utterly strange, quite unreal. The sun was slamming right into the small of her back.

"All right, Miss Toni?" Albert's voice came at a soft muffle through his bandana. "You're not asking questions any more!"

Under her scarf she gave a fixed little smile that tautened the silk across the bridge of her nose. She'd had enough, definitely enough. The question was, how could she admit it and not lose face? As it happened, help came from an unexpected quarter. One of the hands in charge of the barbecue suddenly took hold of the old dinner gong and hit it with such force that it nearly stopped the charging cattle in their tracks, reverberating above the general yelling and bawling and pounding hooves.

To Toni, it was the ultimate act of aggression. It was her savior too, for almost immediately Paul came over to her, pulling off his scarf from his dust-grimed face and wiping it carelessly.

"All right, kiddo? You look a bit green around the gills!"

A bit green? She eased off her own scarf, trying to appear jaunty and confident and never for one moment succeeding. "Perfect!" she said lightly, lying for all she was worth.

"You will be when you've had your lunch," Paul said comfortingly, assessing her with a doubtful eye. As it was, she had stuck it out far longer than he thought she would. He was proud of her. He turned to wink at Albert who had jumped off the fence, dead keen to obey the gong. "Did she ask many questions?"

"Sure did, Boss!" Albert's face split into a grin. "At the jump, at any rate. Don't think she made much of the answers, eh, miss?"

"You were a great help to me, Albert," Toni said carefully, spacing her words carefully. "I think you could safely call it a profound experience!"

Albert let that one sail over his head. He made off with a grin and a backward wave of his hand. Now for the worst! In a half-fearful agony, Toni watched Nyland's approach, bracing herself like some sapling to resist the storm. Even at a distance he had tremendous natural authority—alert, hard, all flowing muscle, he possessed a dark frightening energy that made her feel positively lifeless.

Within a few seconds those strange light eyes were turned on her full battery, studying each separate feature of her face, her undeniable sick tinge for all the apricot sunspots.

"That spirited little air of yours is sadly out of evidence," he said crisply. "How do you feel?"

She gave a funny little quirk of her mouth, not daring to open it, lest the ground come up and hit her in the face. She had wished it all on herself. She had no one else to blame for her present dilemma, though she might wish she had. How he would *crow*!

Watching the expressions chase across her face, he suddenly reached up with barely controlled impatience lifted her clear of the fence, holding her lightly until she had regained her balance. "Perhaps you're looking in the wrong direction for a bit of excitement," he said, his voice terse, overlaid with a degree of . . . anxiety? It couldn't be. He kept his hand on her shoulder, pacing her gently toward the shade. "Are you hungry?"

"No!"

"Stay cool, sweetie, and you'll emerge triumphant!" Paul promised her, loping along easily beside them, his eyes very bright and observant, going from one to the other. "Never let it be said Toni Stewart sets her sights too high! It *is* a damned cruel, messy business to a woman, I suppose," he conceded with utter fairness.

"Please!" she held up a restraining hand, then pushed off her hat. Her hair slid forward in a gleaming arc, drawing the sun, flashing out highlights.

They walked into the broad pocket of green under the

coolibahs. A wide, deep cavern, an oasis of peace and calm. Toni's mouth felt dry, the muscles of her throat almost locked rigid. She lifted a pale hand to her cheek. It was burning hot. The heat, that was it! She had been a long time in the saddle before that little lot. She needn't think too badly of herself.

The men smiled and tipped their hats respectfully. Some of them had already taken up positions on the ground, not even bothering to seek the shelter of the shade, gazing with great gusto at their heaped-up plates. Others were milling about wordlessly around the long trestle that had been set up a little distance from the barbecue, pouring various condiments over their charcoaled steaks, picking up great hunks of crusty newly baked bread; they would wash the lot down with lashings of billy tea before they were back on the job again until it was finished, and never mind the time!

Left alone for a few moments, Toni leaned against the trunk of a tree. She tipped her head back, feeling strangely lightheaded. She was enormously grateful for the faintest zephyr of breeze that stirred the fine hair at her temples, for a cold dew seemed to be gathering across her forehead.

"Here, lovie, try this. It'll make a new woman of you!" Paul came back to her, appallingly fit and healthy, hungry as a hunter, but women and children first. He thrust a great steak at her. liberally doused in the tomato sauce she loathed. Toni opened her eyes to thank him, the smell of the food overpowering and extraordinarily distasteful, desperate to prove herself equal to it all, when the trees seemed to tilt then make a great leafy swoop for her.

She gave a small, frightened moan and found the only way possible out of her contretemps short of being violently ill. She fainted.

When she opened her eyes she was lying on the grass, some sort of blanket under her head.

"God, love!" Paul was staring into her face in the most peculiar fashion as if he had just been presented with a living truth: Women really were the weaker sex! Above him, dark and inexpressibly forbidding, stood Nyland, a quick lick of flame from his eyes: I-told-you-so!

Toni touched the tip of her tongue to her mouth, her eyes huge and distressed. Without a word Nyland dropped to his knees beside her, his face a teak mask. "Get some water from one of the canteens, Paul!" he said in a taut, clipped voice.

"I'm all right," she said huskily, into the shocked silence, as if they none of them had seen such a thing.

"Like sweet hell you are!" he said vibrantly. "Someone will have to restrain your adventurous urges!"

"It was the steak. The food, the tomato sauce or something," she said fretfully, trying to absolve herself. "The unseen factor. It gets you every time. I'd have been all right if it hadn't been for that."

Paul came back at a run with a tin mug full of cold water. Nyland took it from him, put a hand behind the back of her head and held the mug up to her mouth.

It had the funniest taste!

"Was that water?" she croaked.

Paul made an about-face, thunderstruck. "God knows! You've even got me befuddled. Yes, of course it was water. Wasn't it, Ed?"

Ed, the leading hand, took a quick swig of his water canteen, just to make sure. "Sure isn't brandy, Boss!"

Nyland's downbent gaze was comprehensive, frankly accusing. To bring a woman along on such a session was to invite a farce. He needed his head read!

"Well, I tried," she said with a faint return of spirit. "And I think I learned a lot. We can't all belong to the master race!"

"No, indeed!" Nyland retorted very smartly. "But never mind, your motives are excellent, Toni. It's your judgment that's bad! I had the certain feeling all morning that something unusual was going to happen."

"Her color is coming back, at any rate," Paul murmured, sounding faintly unnerved. He looked over his shoulder to where his leading hand was hovering. "Ed, run Miss Toni back to the house like a good chap. Take the jeep."

"I'll take her back," Nyland said in a voice that settled all opposition. "I was fool enough to say she could come in the first place."

"As you like! It's very good of you, Damon." Paul straightened, tucking his shirt into his lithe waistline. "Well, what a funny old time you've had, kiddo. I always said your impulsiveness would get you into trouble!"

So they were closing their ranks on her! A fascinating insight into the male mind. "I'll go back by myself," she said hardily. "Believe me, I'm able to do just that!"

"Lady, we'll never believe you again!" His hands hard and steely, Nyland helped her to her feet, a wholly masculine look of superiority on his dark face. "Learn to give in gracefully, if nothing else. You're coming with me!"

"Yes, Mr. Nyland," she said respectfully, conscious all at once of the sea of interested faces.

"Right-oh, boys, back to work!" Paul spun on his heel, a suggestion of roughness in his voice.

Rather sheepishly the men choked down what was left on their plates and took themselves off, no doubt to discuss the whole thing at a later date. Toni had long discovered, contrary to the popular myth, that men did have their own private gossip sessions. A multitude of expressions played across her small face. Nyland looked across at her silently, some dark emotion too violent to be analyzed in his own face. One thing was certain, he was fed up. Her eyes met his for a split second. His were frosty, faintly hostile, bright with this emotion that could have been anything. Most certainly indignation was thrown in.

She took a few compulsive steps forward, moving into a segment of light, her hair a glowing dark flame.

"Are you coming?" she asked over her shoulder, an imperious lilt to her voice.

His mouth thinned and his eyes glittered. He caught up with her, taking her elbow in a light, inflexible grip, dropping his voice to a mere thread of sound. "Whoever said mastery was primarily a masculine trait? It isn't, you know. Ever heard of a henpecked husband? God, you should have! There are enough of them. Peace at any price, but not me. No one, and I mean *no one*, speaks to me like that!"

"I'm sorry. I'm sorry!" she said over and over again, undergoing a curious transformation. "We'll never get on, will we?" she said mournfully. "Truth *is* stranger than fiction. We're two of a kind—pig-headed. Shared identities are always electrifying, but I couldn't bear to struggle to maintain my independence!"

They were almost at the utility and he stopped dead, listening to her half-incoherent muttering. As on a previous occasion when she had least expected it, he burst out laughing with the true ring of amusement—a lightning change.

"Look, little one," he said, sobering abruptly, "any relationship between a man and a woman is pretty fragile at the best of times. The thing is, do you want to get along with me? If you do, you have to work at it. I can't, or won't, I'm not sure which. For some unknown and quite unexpected reason, I happen to care what happens to you. You've slipped under my guard with all that nonsense you talk. Stirred up some sort of protective instinct I didn't know I had!"

For a moment she stared up at him, a gauzy moth infatuated with a flame. "Is that why you resent me, because you don't want to like me? Tell me!"

"I'm sorry. I simply can't. I suppose I do resent you in a way. We'll have to see a psychiatrist about it some time, but for the here and now, let's leave it. I came to Mandargi on a purely neighborly action, not because I happen to own it. Now look what I've found. It almost persuades me never to lift a finger to help anyone again!"

It was his way to be flippant, to taunt her. She knew this, because it was her own way; yet she felt crushed, her breath uneven as if she were in dreadful pain. A queer little sob tore at her throat.

"Why, you little ass!" Damon's fingers dug into her curls, tightening over the nape of her neck. "Don't be so damned ridiculous. Don't you dare cry. I'd hate that!"

488

"How worrying for you! Don't be alarmed. I won't cry.
I'm beyond tears!"

"Good!" He put her into the jeep, flicking her one
piercing glance before losing interest in her.

Her look of helpless femininity, had she known it, was
ravishing, the glitter of tears in her wide-spaced dark
eyes, the faint tremor in her curvy young mouth. In many
ways he was a damnable man, she thought, relaxing her
back against the seat and feeling a kind of exquisite,
exhausted sweetness steal over her.

He kept the vehicle moving very fast, bent on not
wasting too much of his precious time. His profile was
without expression, remote even, for all its splendid dark
arrogance. Toni drew in a long breath and released it
shakily. His hard, masculine mouth curled slightly at the
corners in a faint expression of amusement. His brief,
sideways glance was brilliantly alive, shocking really
against the dark copper mask of his face.

"That's the whole trouble, isn't it, Toni? Nothing is
easy. Everything has to be paid for, some time or other.
What happened this morning wasn't really your fault, so I
don't blame you entirely. I should have sent you back a
good hour ago. That's the whole, plain truth of it!" His
tone was a hard mixture of exasperation and self-
contempt.

She clenched her small fist in her lap, wishing she had a
quarter of her old vitality. "You know, Mr. Nyland, I
really believe you should have been a preacher with a
great message for the world. Women are a plain blasted
nuisance—all the Lord intended them for. Waste no
further time!"

He gave his white, devastating grin, doubly effective

after so much arrogance. "Not again! What does all this go back to, flower face? When you were a little girl? Who was the tyrant then? It's fairly obvious someone or something has left an indelible mark on your mind. You're incredibly mulish and you can't bear even the lightest hand on the reins. In short, you're wild!"

"Even a mule has a soul, Mr. Nyland!" she observed with brittle scorn.

"After which observation I hardly know which way to proceed!"

"Neither do I." A sudden smile played across her face like a patina of light. "You'll always put me in the wrong in any case. A trying position, you must admit, but it's in the nature of things."

"Yes! Too bad, isn't it, and we still haven't seen the end." His glance whipped at her face with amused malice. "Never mind, this kind of experience won't hurt you. It may even be the making of you; otherwise you'll grow into one of those women who like to rule the roost!"

"I'll be glad to accept that any day!" she said recklessly, her creamy skin glowing with color.

"My notion is, little one, you don't even know what it means! That kind of arrangement wouldn't suit you at all, but I'll let you come to it all by yourself. By the way, we leave in the morning!"

"In the morning? I can't be ready by then."

"There you go again!" he said with soft mockery. "The girls will pack a few things for you. I want to be back on Savannah!"

"You drive a hard bargain, Mr. Nyland."

"I do that!" He looked very sure of himself, darkly relentless. "Now we're a little older, a little wiser, a little further along in our acquaintanceship, we'll have to be on the lookout for disturbances. The promise of proximity is enough!"

"Yes, indeed!" she said tightly, a pulse beating in her throat, her lashes motionless against her flushed cheeks. "We can't alarm Elissa or the little girl."

"That's the deal!" he stressed briefly. "So try to inject a little civility into the set-up!"

Her eyes sparkled like jets. "I'd be glad to. In fact I want to make a real contribution. I'll put you right at the center of things, though you might find it hard to believe, and I promise to behave beautifully. If you will!"

He bit off a laugh. "Perhaps I will! After today, There's no doubt about it, you push me right off the deep end!" Without any further warning, he turned the utility off the track, running it into the tall columns of paperbarks, shutting off the ignition, a hard recklessness in his face.

"I can see that!" she said, greatly daring, excitement and tension feeding on itself.

"Shut up, you graceless, bad-tempered brat!"

"Oh, how you love to cut me down!" She was hurt, and she had borne so much valiantly. She hit out then, a token blow, like a small suffragette, but he caught her wrists, his fingers biting into her flesh.

"I'm losing my mind. I know I am!" There was an element of wry amusement in his tone. "Get a hold of yourself. Haven't you ever been told it's unseemly for little girls to hit back? Besides, it never comes off. Too unequal a contest!" He looked down at her flushed face. "Well, what are we going to do now? There's no profit in your idea!"

He was looking at her with such cool sensuality that she burst out in passionate refusal, "Don't you dare!"

"All these great big threats!" There was a reflection of her own mood in his face, the underlying antagonism. Damon pulled her into his arms, his hand threading through her hair. "I'm glad you don't have to put up with them. You'd never have the patience. Women! What hopeless propositions! You expect them to jump one way and they jump the other!"

Toni's heart was racing so that she could scarcely recover her breath. The spark between them was so strong it was almost crackling. Her stretched nerves could stretch no further. Everything inside her was mounting to a crescendo. It was useless to deny it. Her eyes, huge and velvety as a faun's, filled with tears and her lower lip trembled. Damon muffled some exclamation and bent his head, fully aroused, parting her mouth, twisting her head, kissing her with such calculating artistry that her capacity to respond was brilliantly, effortlessly exploited. She was mindless, weightless, spinning in a void without end. Every sensation, every longing, everything she was. Wave upon wave of brilliance broke over her so that she shifted in his hard grasp, an instinctive, half blind, yielding movement that brought her closer against him, seared by a surge of wildest delight.

It didn't seem possible, but she yearned for him. A frightening, impermanent elation. Yet she responded as if hypnotized, her mouth under his irresistibly sweet, very young and ardent, with no taste for freedom at all. All barriers were gone, all conflicts, all differences; yet it was slavery of a sort, for her own personality was subjugated.

When he lifted his head, his voice was pitched low enough to deceive her.

"What's it all about, Toni?"

She didn't try to answer him. She couldn't. Unquestionably he had the advantage, her hair fanned out over his wrist. He gave a mocking smile. "You don't dissemble very well, do you? I would say that was the only area you haven't found a complaint for."

Her mouth was still sensitized, pulsing with color, a physical mark he had left upon her. She answered finally, pushed to the limit to match his sophistication.

"Does that apply to you as well, Mr. Nyland?"

He hesitated in brief indecision, unusual for him. "Sex attraction, Toni," he said in his beautiful voice. "A signal beacon, and you have it stronger than most!"

She stared at him fascinated. "Don't think for one moment I'm offering myself as the next victim!"

"Really, you could do worse!"

She wanted to hit him, so badly—turn primitive, retaliate against that cool, mocking drawl, but his hands were ready, waiting, in case she had the same urge to repeat past mistakes.

His eyes were full of a brilliant irony, seeing her abandon her tormenting desire. "All right!" He straightened abruptly and shrugged his wide shoulders. "A lesson for both of us. We all do mad things. That settled, we can proceed with my plan. And don't you dare doublecross me!"

There was a shivery, destructive quality in his voice. Toni had to defend herself. Pointedly she withdrew to the furthest edge of the seat, but he only smiled.

"Needless to say you can trust me from now on, if that's what's worrying you."

"I trust no one. Not even myself," she said very quickly, trying to smooth her tangled hair. "Certainly not myself. You know so well how to exploit a weakness!"

"Weakness?" He injected a terrific amount of mockery into the one word. "Why, my sweet little innocent, what you've got is a great strength! You're winning all the time!"

His face was vivid with satire, his eyes on her mouth a caress by remote control. Her skin tightened electrically and she looked away from him with extreme temperament, her small face intense. *A piece in a pattern!* She was no more than that. All the hard, disturbing charm in the world couldn't dissuade her of that. From now on, every minute, every hour, she would be alert to the danger of his appeal. To her mind. To her senses, more persuasive than reason ever could be.

What she hid from herself was it was already too late. Much, much too late. To face it would have been to look into some magical, terrifying mirror that revealed events before their time. Day-to-day living was a series of little concealments behind which most men and women chose to hide.

CHAPTER SIX

The Savannah cattle kingdom lay basking in the sun, casting its giant arms to left and to right; verdant from the onset of the rains, dotted with lagoons and lakes and a long silver chain of billabongs. In the months to come these would link up, each floating its lively waxy burden of lotus blooms; ivory and hyacinth and palest pink, ecstatic with the sounds of the wild waterfowl. The whole landscape was not so very different from Mandargi, Toni argued, if one left aside the obvious superiority of the all-weather airstrip.

Five minutes later they reached the massive wrought iron gates that led to Savannah's big house and its satellite buildings, and she was jolted into an immediate revaluation. A curly black head loomed up behind the lacy grill, there was a quick responsive smile, an alert half friendly, half formal salute, then the gates opened like magic without human aid and they were through.

Up the long drive they went, like the wind, past sentinel rows of coconut palms that waved their long fronds to a blazing blue sky. Flashes of the outbuildings came through the screen of trees, a longer glimpse of a bungalow about the size of Mandargi's homestead, surrounded by its own gardens in full, flaunting color. Toni missed nothing, as she looked through the windshield and side window, trying to keep pleasant interest and not just plain envy firmly implanted on her face.

"Satisfied?" Damon asked, the first words he had spoken in the five-mile trip from the airstrip.

"Your fame went before you!" she said lightly. "I hardly expected modest surroundings."

"You haven't seen the house yet," he pointed out rather dryly. "It was only completed about two years ago, on the site of the original old homestead. Not unlike Mandargi's, but bigger. That had to go. Look now, that's the best angle of all."

They made a broad sweep in the drive and Toni did as she was told, the breeze coming in warmly against her face.

"Oh!" she murmured, totally inadequately, but it was the best she could manage for a while.

He slanted a glance at her profile and she turned to meet his gaze. "It's never a good idea to fall in love with someone else's property. I was trying to remind myself of it."

"Chancy, indeed!" he agreed. "But realization usually comes slowly if it's allowed to come at all!"

"Well, I'm lost, and I might as well admit it. Right from the beginning. This could be Mandargi with a spare fortune poured into it!

"This, my girl, is Savannah, and don't you forget it!"

"How could I?" she asked, surprised by the crispness of his tone. "Savannah is beautiful." Or more accurately, beautifully dramatic, she thought. A big house in the Spanish idiom, well suited to the rugged terrain, the climate, and a particular way of life.

Damon Nyland, the cattle baron, she thought with wry admiration. The do-it-yourself king of the castle. *Savannah! My more concrete assets,* as he'd put it. Well, he had a pretty good life going for him. Handsome, wealthy, ultra-sophisticated, a benevolent big landowner, a type all but extinct in modern times.

They were within a few hundred yards of the house, sweeping past the great spherical clumps of pampas grass with its shining silver gray spears held meticulously to attention. Toni looked her fill. The house was big, very big, covering a considerable area, built on the highest point of the land, almost a hill, a curious mixture of stark and ornate. High white walls, arched windows, cool quarry-tiled colonnades, the decorative black ironwork repeated everywhere. It was a fascinating blend of the old world with all the vigor and know-how of the new.

They pulled into the inner court and he helped her out of the vehicle in silence, letting her absorb her surroundings. The "outer" entrance, or garden court, was paved with patterned ceramic tiles in a rich amber and brown. One ornamental wall of black wrought iron contrasted with the stark white façade; an open timber pergola, stained black, competed with white wrought iron furniture and huge brass pots full of the lush tropical plants of the north, some of them flowering profusely. Trellised vines, giant ferns, beautiful hanging baskets, massed succulents.

"Well?" he asked.

"Fabulous!" Toni swung her bright head to smile at him, a smile with its own subtle excitement. "Nothing to be gained by adding to that!"

"Slow coming," he drawled, his eyes on her mouth, "but a very gratifying response, Miss Stewart. I've been holding my breath, up until now. Come in by all means. I'll have someone take your luggage through in a moment."

She took a little anticipatory breath and walked into the formal entrance. It was coolly beautiful and she could have clapped her hands like a child at a wholly pleasing spectacle. A superbly hand-carved mirror, a matching table beneath, a flanking armchair in the same style—all antiques. A brilliantly colored ceramic plate about eighteen inches in diameter stood on a stand; and a Malayan weeping banyan was lodged in a dully gleaming brass pot, an integral part of the decoration.

The quarry tiles extended right through to the living area with exotic scatter rugs that she took to be in the Moorish style but were, in fact, as she later found out, aboriginal, specially commissioned. Paintings galore, a lot of modern abstracts, glowing like jewels, wonderfully illuminated, against the stark white walls. Above her head were light fittings, in brass and bronze glass, works of art in themselves. There wasn't a square inch that didn't excite the attention. Pieces of sculpture placed strategically here and there.

"Someone has an unerring eye!" she said with unfeigned fervor. "A very special way of doing things!"

"Me!"

She smiled at that, thinking it typical, and touched a reverent finger to a beautiful chest decorated with inlaid ivory. "I'm not in the least surprised. Oriental?"

"Chinese."

"If you've got it, you've got it, and if you haven't, I suppose you can always pay a decorator."

"Not me, flower face. I choose what I have to live with. No one else has unloaded their ideas on me. So far!"

"With stunning results, Mr. Nyland!"

"Damon, from now on, if you don't mind. You give

that 'Mr. Nyland' double value as if you didn't know. No, spare me the wide-eyed look. I find independence in a woman intolerable!"

"Faint wonder you're a bachelor! Which is a pity. A certain amount of training is necessary for all of us!"

"Oh, I agree," he said suavely, "but some men are just too plain dodgy to ever get caught. Anyone who lives with a woman will tell you the whole situation is fraught with difficulties, like walking through a minefield! As for myself, I've always found women either regard me as a wonderful meal ticket or . . ."

". . . please don't undersell yourself!" Toni burst out tartly, and with considerable candor.

"Either way you can't win." His eyes were brilliant with amused mockery roving over her face, sparking an immediate response.

"Perhaps you're right at that! Trying to domesticate you would never prove entirely satisfactory. It almost calls for a silent tribute to a lot of brave women, and I'm sure there have been a lot of them!"

"The usual kind of thing," he agreed suavely. "That's the really great thing about women, their endless tenacity. That appears to be an undisputed fact. Anything else is in the region of folklore, I'm afraid."

"Then you'd better watch out for yourself, hadn't you?" she said pleasantly. "You will marry?"

"I said so, didn't I? I would dearly love a son to inherit all this, without causing the most impossible scandal!"

She moved away from him in a series of graceful little swirls, coming to rest beside a brass inlaid cabinet. "You may not even have to pick out a wife," she suggested blithely. "She might pick you out. Wouldn't that be a surprise?"

"The inevitable must come, by any one of the various methods. Who knows, you may be trying out one yourself!" He had come up behind her and she felt the strength draining out of her limbs, her heart hammering against her ribs. She swung to face him, tilting her chin.

"Oh, that's brilliant! A charmingly sentimental theory. There's not a man from nine to ninety who doesn't think somebody's after him!"

"You have a lot of disastrous ideas yourself," he said in a voice that panicked her for all its light mockery. "Now why the long, desolate look? You've got beautiful eyes, Toni, large, lustrous, long-lashed. A pity you're so difficult and quarrelsome. You'll be all the better for being surpervised and directed on Savannah."

The faint indulgence melted all her resentments away. She laughed, a pretty three-noted sound. "Don't expect me to flinch away, though I can see you're going to be pretty much in control of things. Around here, at any rate!"

"So act accordingly," he warned, "even if we can expect a certain amount of trouble during the adjustment period. You'll have to admit we haven't hit it off all that well, up to now. Come now, Toni, tell me, what do you think of the furniture? You can't ignore it any more with our usual chit-chat."

She slithered away from him smoothly, away from those baffling light eyes. "Custom-designed?" she asked lightly.

"Yes, it had to be. Scaled to the volume of space, if you know what I mean!" He made no attempt to follow her up, leaning an elbow on top of the cabinet, only his eyes tracking her.

She replied in mocking imitation. "I do, indeed! In

fact, I don't think I'd move anything six inches either way."

"A fantastic admission for a woman!"

"Maybe." She let her eyes run over the grouped sofas, the deep armchairs, the fabrics, linen and silk and wool.

"I hate clutter," he announced almost to himself. "Being hemmed in."

She turned to regard him in some astonishment. "Well, you've plenty of space here. I'd be more likely to clatter in a place this size!"

His clear green eyes lit with amused malice. "My darling girl, perhaps we move in different social circles. On Savannah we have twenty guests at a time, every other weekend. Spare a moment to take that in. I don't usually accommodate them one on top of the other; not unless they specifically ask for it!"

"The more the merrier!" she said, effortlessly sweet. "I've always taken that with a grain of salt myself. I stand chastised!"

"For how long?"

"That's up to you, in my opinion!" she said, refusing to look at him.

Damon always did what she least expected. He laughed. Evidently she amused him. He uncoiled his elegant length and came toward her. "I'll take you down to the wine cellar when I know you better, but for now, we'll content ourselves with the pool area."

Like an exasperated but intensely preoccupied child she followed him through the curving archways of tinted glass backed by black wrought iron, the glass reducing the glare from the aquamarine pool. They were out on a roofed terrace, an idyllic and secluded outdoor living area. A dazzling and fascinating array of the lovely

Donna Aurora, a tropical flowering shrub, creamy and more compact than the ever-present bougainvillea rose behind them. They were arranged in green glazed Chinese pots beside the smooth white steps that led to the pool.

"It's a nice old place, isn't it?" Toni asked with some humor, looking into his dark, sardonic face, lit by the same brand of taste. "I'll never be able to settle down again. Savannah will be too difficult to forget!"

"Maybe I won't let you forget me either," he said, low and mocking.

"As long as we can still be friends afterward!" She avoided his eyes, feeling softly shaken, her own eyes brilliantly dark, fully conscious of the terrible burden of attraction.

He smiled unexpectedly and ran a finger down her small, straight nose. "I ought to be ashamed of myself. I'm forgetting how old you are. Still, Elissa and young Annette will be here by this afternoon. They tell me children make the best chaperones!"

His voice was so very attractive, with that hint of a laugh in it, that Toni smiled, her mouth curving rather dreamily, had she known it.

"Damon, you're back!"

A woman was behind them, standing at the top of the stairs, one hand shading her eyes. She was tall, rather angular, very plainly but neatly dressed. A competent, no-nonsense type with intelligent, understanding eyes, anywhere between fifty and sixty, exceedingly plain until she smiled; then her face lit up in a quite remarkable fashion.

"Clarrie!" Damon turned to her with ease and considerable affection.

"I did so want to make a good impression standing by

the door and all that, but a few other things claimed my attention!" She smiled directly into Toni's face and Toni felt her own face softening. There was a genuineness about that smile and it impressed itself on her mind.

Damon introduced them serenely, watching his housekeeper come down the steps, her hand outstretched.

"Mrs. Chase—Clarrie, when she comes to accept you—Toni Stewart, our young neighbor from Mandargi and house guest for a week or so."

"How are you, my girl?" Clarissa Chase took Toni's hand in a terrible grip and looked intently into her face. "None the worse for your adventures? We all listen to the galah sessions, you know."

"I'm fine, thank you, Mrs. Chase," Toni said, unobtrusively flexing her numbed fingers. "Mr. Nyland put a few stitches in a gash in my arm and it's almost right again."

"You look simply beautiful," Clarissa Chase said firmly. "I'd have given my eye teeth to have looked like you as a girl. That brother of yours wasn't behind the door either. Good-lookers, the pair of you. Good bones. Good blood. We'll marry you off in no time!"

"Clarrie always speaks her mind!" Damon said in a calm drawl.

"Don't worry, I'm going!" Clarrie turned on him. "I just came to say welcome and hello."

"Thank you, Mrs. Chase," Toni said quickly. "That was very kind of you."

Clarissa Chase didn't hesitate for a moment. "We can't go on like this. Clarrie it is. We must think of the future! Now, if there's anything you want, any time, call me. I'm never out of the kitchen, though some days I'm sure

Damon here is only waiting for me to turn in my notice so
he can get a more suitable replacement."

"No, now, Clarrie, after ten eventful years, even I can't
turn you out!"

That proved more effective than the most flowery
metaphors. Mrs. Chase went off beaming and was
presently out of sight.

"Clarrie's just that little bit outspoken," Damon said,
his attention returning to Toni. "In fact, some of my
guests have found her downright odd!"

"That's all right, I like her," Toni said simply. "I was
brought up to speak my mind!"

"You can say that again!" he said in full, round tones,
turning to smile at her. "You're a determined little cuss,
but don't let's wrangle about it. I'll show you your room.
A girl like you would be quite particular where she
sleeps."

"For the most part, I can take good care of myself,"
she said quite without thinking, a challenging set to her
glittery head.

"We all make mistakes from time to time," he supplied
smoothly, a flash of sarcasm in his vibrant voice, "but
come along and tell me what you think. I like to gather as
much information as I can about my house guests."

He turned and led the way across the central court, tall
and lean, with his powerful shoulders, his dark masculinity. She followed more slowly, watching him open the
sliding glass doors of a room that opened out onto the
pool area.

"All the guest rooms are essentially the same," he said,
looking down at her, one arm on the side of the door, a
taunting kind of courtesy in his cool eyes. "Color

variations, that sort of thing. You can take your pick. I thought you might be happy here, but I suppose you'll settle for something else purely as a gesture of defiance!"

He had his back to the light, his height exaggerated, almost hypnotic in his stillness.

"Now that would be a dead giveaway, wouldn't it?" she said, edging to get past him, to no avail. "I thought it took years and years to know a person as well as that."

He relented his position, shifting his arm, pushing the door to its farthest limits. "I don't think so, Toni. You're relatively simple, to follow, that is. I don't mean for a moment you're dim-witted. Never that!"

"May I see, please, Mr. Nyland, you dreadful man?" Her dark eyes sparkled up at him.

"Why not?"

She brushed past him, on line with his shoulder. A rare coordination of movement, as slender as a tulip. "I'll be well and truly incommunicado out here!" she said, coming to rest in the center of the room.

"The point is, you won't bother me any," he supplied sardonically.

"Point taken! If it's of any consequence, I'll be more than happy here. In fact, I'm greatly indebted to you."

"I'm so pleased!" He glanced at her tilted young profile, his green eyes shimmering with amusement. "Elissa and the little girl will stay in the main wing. I thought you'd appreciate your own private world. As you can see, it's entirely self-contained. If you scream at night, just make sure it's loud enough!"

Toni shook her bright head and her hair made magical moves against her cheeks. "That's very unlikely!" she said loftily. His eyes had the power to transfix her, so she avoided them carefully. "Tell me, why did you think this was me?" She gestured around the beautifully appointed room with its teak, inbuilt furniture, a deep armchair, a small bookcase, a writing desk and a chair.

"Autumn leaf colors!" he supplied in a silky drawl.

She smiled and her eyes moved to the thick, luxurious bedspread, deeply fringed and patterned in rust and gold, a rich brown and a bright orange. "Woodsy, in fact!"

"Anything but! I think you're very bold and adventurous, for a woman, not to speak of eye-catching—but for now I must leave you. It's high time. There'll be plenty to catch up on even after a few days' absence." He threw up his head, preparing to leave, and Toni surprised in herself an odd kind of reaction. She pressed an instinctive hand to the base of her throat. He was still talking, his dark head in silhouette against the brilliant light.

"Don't be afraid to wander around at will. There are quite a few things to interest you, I feel sure. The pool—always supposing you can swim!"

She smiled, a little ironically. "Float, at any rate! Which is what I'm doing right now. I daren't go with the tide!"

He turned to flicker her a look of urbane charm. "You're quite a girl, Toni. I only hope Elissa likes you."

"So do I," she confided. "I couldn't bear to offend your family."

"I honestly think you'll make out, if you try hard enough," he said soothingly. "Well, so long, little one. Clarrie likes you, at any rate. No small thing. I can't speak for myself, as yet!"

A full thirty seconds elapsed before Toni felt able to

move again. If the worst really came to the worst and
Elissa found her less than compatible, she could always
make a bolt for home. One thing stood her in good stead:
she had come to Savannah with the best possible intentions!

Elissa was pure Meissen, a petite aristocrat, a delicate
piece of porcelain to round off a collection. Annette, her
little girl, was pure Nyland, a holy terror of six going on
seven, completely inexplicable to her mother, but very
pretty with glossy dark curls, a peachy skin and the now
predictable light eyes. They flew in toward late afternoon
on a charter flight in the company of Keith Hammond, of
Hammond, Hampshire Sinclair, the Nyland family
solicitors. It was unthinkable that Elissa Nyland would
have travelled alone.

From the very first instant Toni met Elissa's Siamese
stare, she knew it was an error to have been invited, for
Elissa had no need of female companionship, never had,
never would. Elissa Nyland was a very calculating feline,
and one of her quirks was never sharing with anyone. She
had a whole bag of tricks that further enhanced her
fragile, boneless elegance, one of them being to let her
hand hover tentatively in the air for a moment before
coming to rest in the crook of a man's arm—Damon's,
Keith Hammond's, a pleasant, well-spoken man in his
early forties, who met this little endearing gesture with an
expectant look. It was immediately apparent to everyone
that Keith Hammond was smitten, enslaved.

Toni stood well back admiring while Elissa trod
delicately through the house in a pretty, mysterious

manner, pale silver head bobbing, surveying her new home, all the while purring how "extravagantly tired" she was, the upshot of which was that Toni was left with the child, who had slept on the plane and as a result was now as tranquil as a firecracker.

An hour later in the kitchen, Toni's spirits had reached a rock-bottom low as the child gave a consistent "Yuck!" to everything that was offered to her in the way of light nourishment. Clarrie, busy with her own preparations for what promised to be a banquet, watched the small circus in a telling silence, until finally, well ahead with her own duties, she trained on Annette a look of extreme practicality.

"You're a little miracle and no mistake. A mix and match angel!" She shifted her gray gaze to Toni's flushed young face. "You go and have a swim. Cool off before dinner. It's hot enough. I'll deal with young madam here!"

Whether the old terminology was entirely new to Annette or because she could detect a certain look in Clarrie's unswerving gaze, she fell to drinking her milk with saucer-eyed attention, intensely curious but not unfriendly after the initial moment of sceptical surprise. Unconcernedly Clarrie broke eggs into a bowl and frothed them up with a dash of milk and a sprinkle of salt.

"Scrambled eggs on fingers of toast be all right?"

"Yes, thank you, Mrs. Chase," said Annette, in every way a most amenable child.

Toni reached the kitchen door and saluted Clarrie over the glossy dark head. "You have a very useful personality, Clarrie. No wonder Damon won't part with you!"

The glance she had returned to her was amused and disarming. "Didn't you know I had four of my own?"

"No, really?"

"Three boys and a girl. All married, all on the land. Eight or nine grandchildren. Even I've lost count of them. After a while you get to know every trick of the trade. All this child needs is a little home psychology!"

"Don't we all!" Toni was looking at Annette's bent head, startled by the radical change in the child's manner. It was complete surrender, for she had calmed down and was ready and actually willing to dive into the fluffy yellow pile.

"There's always a way round a tricky situation," Clarrie said complacently, placing the plate before the child.

"Well, you certainly solved my problem. Thank you!" Toni said with a spontaneous smile.

Clarrie looked for a moment at the gay, laughing face. "Don't thank me. You'll do. Now go off and enjoy yourself. I'll look after Annette. Not that I know it's either of our jobs!"

The light fell across the curve of Toni's cheek so that her skin seemed dazzling. Both women exchanged a look that said plainly Elissa couldn't have cared less. There was a silence; then Toni cast a sidelong look at the little girl's tranquil profile.

"I haven't had much to do with children, but they certainly appeal to me. My first attempt at managing was pretty hopeless, though!"

"You'll come to it. We all do," Clarrie promised strongly.

With an odd half defensive, half excited look, Annette

opened her beautiful, rosebud mouth. "May I come for a swim with you, please, Toni?"

Clarrie laughed and suddenly pressed the curly dark head against her breast. "There, what did I tell you? Not tonight, my lamb, tomorrow perhaps. Now I have some nice vanilla ice cream. Sauce on top, do you think?"

"Chocolate, thank you," Annette said in a dainty voice, shoving her plate away. "Goodbye, Toni."

Toni smiled at both of them and walked out of the room in a much more mellow frame of mind. The rest of the house was quite silent, like a household in thrall. As she walked slowly and lingeringly through the beautiful rooms, a vision floated out into the hallway. A fairy child. No, too much sex appeal for that, Toni reasoned with reluctant admiration, gritting her teeth for the moment of encounter. A wonderful omen for the next few weeks.

"Don't rush away!" the vision said, swaying toward her.

Pretending a warmth and friendliness she did not feel and vaguely ashamed of herself, Toni gave her lovely, natural smile.

"How are you feeling now, Mrs. Nyland?"

Elissa tinkled into a little laugh of admission. "Quite bleak, actually, but you could make life just a teeny bit easier for me, if you would."

"I'd consider it a privilege," Toni said pleasantly, steeling herself to avoid her own ironic reflection in a gilt-scrolled mirror.

"That's nice!" Elissa responded in her silver-clear, well-bred voice. She eyed Toni speculatively, as though trying to penetrate her façade. A queen, who had acquired a new and unlikely lady-in-waiting.

She was very petite, a porcelain figurine, an inch or so over five feet, so that she was obliged to lift her violet blue eyes to Toni's. "I've tried to be tolerant, but really; the house girls! I know they're well trained, but . . . would you be a darling and unpack my things? I honestly can't face it, and I don't care to see. . . ." She snapped off right there with an air of extreme fastidiousness, which was, nevertheless, entirely natural, generous in her adversity, leaving it to Toni to decipher her meaning.

Toni saw only too well. No slim brown hands among the silks and the chiffons and the laces. The shining ash-blonde head was still tilted, the arching throat white as a swan's, the narrow tilted eyes steady and unswerving, one hand gently stroking the pale, soft hair at the nape of her neck. Her peignoir was exquisite, an indescribable mixture of blue and hyacinth, enfolding and caressing the slight figure in the subtlest revealing fashion. It was hard to say exactly how old she was, for a whole world of sophistication gleamed out of the narrow eyes, upsetting Toni's first verdict of about twenty-seven. Elissa, was, in fact, thirty-two, and even she had forgotten it.

"You haven't said, how is Annette?" Her smile was bright, her voice sweetly amiable, so that Toni wondered why she doubted its genuineness.

"Mrs. Chase is looking after her," she explained. "She's settled down quite well and she's having her tea. I've just come from the kitchen now."

"I'm very, very grateful. I did wonder, Miss Stewart, if you'd come now!"

"Yes, of course." For the first time, her true role on Savannah hit Toni starkly in the eye. There was more than a touch of regal arrogance in the request. Well, she had agreed to come!

Elissa turned away, her negligée swirling in a mist about her feet. "I do hope you won't be bored to tears in the next week or so. There's so very little I shall require of you. Rest is all I need, peace of mind—precious, up until now unattainable commodities. But you could be of great help with Annette, if you'd take her off my hands. I did want to ask you if you would mind having her beside you at night until the governess arrives. She's been very restless at night. I have such indifferent health—hard to accept sometimes!" She gave a little expressive movement of her hands, obviously waiting for Toni's assent.

"I wouldn't mind in the least," Toni found herself saying, mildly enough, "but I'm sure, Mrs. Nyland, she'd much rather be beside you."

"Of course, but it's not possible at the moment. You do see that? I must get a full night's sleep or I'm good for nothing. Honestly!" Elissa paused for a moment, her mouth smiling softly. "Damon is so good to me—too good, really. I'll never, never be able to repay him, but of course he won't hear a word of thanks. I think he loves doing it anyway, and he's so terribly taken with Annette!"

For the life of her, Toni couldn't come up with an answer to that, since it was complete news to her. Elissa, however, was indifferent to her reaction. She reached the door of her room, smiling across at Toni, her Siamese blue eyes conveying some wonderful secret she was not as yet at liberty to tell. But once inside the room, she drooped with childlike weariness into an armchair, a dispossessed princess, tapping a very white hand to her lips.

"I do so envy you your robust health. You're quite a good-looking girl!"

Toni, her dark eyes amused and just a little bit cynical, looked about her, hardly hearing Elissa's barbed compliment. The room was a tribute to Elissa's beauty and graciousness, fitting for "family." One of the two master suites, it comprised a bedroom and bath-dressing area beyond, the height of luxury in terms of space and furnishings, glowing in its white and gold shell. In a house of collections, here and there, reposed some exquisite "object" such as would never have found its way into a guest room, elegant as they might be. And looking, Toni knew beyond all doubt that Damon Nyland had gauged correctly the guest of honor. Elissa fitted all this as though it had been planned for her. Shocking to think it had! But of course it couldn't. Time was against her. Suddenly, passionately, Toni wished it might have been hers; then cold reason came to her rescue and she resolved never to have that particular thought again.

Elissa lifted her slim brows and gave her shoulders the tiniest shrug. "Perhaps you could run my bath, dear, before you start on my clothes. I know you'll be careful. I do have such lovely things!"

You beaut! Toni thought to herself dismally. *Run my bath*? Almost for a moment she nearly told Elissa what she could do, then in her apathy decided she didn't care. She disappeared into the room beyond in her dual role of nanny and unpaid lady's help.

It was a sacrilege to walk on the pale, lovely rugs, so she didn't, keeping to the tiled part of the floor. While she ran water into the oval tub set with pale opaline tiles, she heard Elissa's silvery voice, raised in summons, just loud enough to be heard above the rushing water. Toni walked back into the bedroom just in time to see Elissa point out a largish vanity case that contained her lotions and perfumes and creams. In another minute an elusive expensive fragrance wafted through the two rooms as Toni emptied bath salts into the running water.

On the tiled counter that ran the length of one wall she set out jar after jar, each promising eternal beauty, not one of them able to bestow the vaguest illusion where there was none. At last it was all over and done with and abundantly clear that Elissa disregarded not one inch of herself in the relentless war against time. Back in the bedroom, Toni walked briskly back and forth, from the bed to the wardrobes, and bureaux, taking the greatest care of Elissa's "lovely things," her luminous eyes wide and pensive.

Elissa, in a brocade armchair, sat, a creature apart, and indeed it was impossible to believe she could be anything else. Her taste and her clothes were perfect, Toni learned. She must have also a great deal of money, which meant that one inevitably escaped the more menial tasks like unpacking for oneself. As well, she made no attempt to spin a web of small talk or enliven the proceedings with a small smile of thanks, but sat thinking her own thoughts, or perhaps a plan of campaign, like a woman at the hair-dressers, her beautiful robe pulled about her excessive fragility.

"There, that should do it." Toni pushed the bureau drawer shut and turned to the silent Elissa. "Perhaps since Annette is to come with me I should shift her things now; or would you rather keep her this one night so she can settle in?"

"No, no!" Elissa came right out of her brooding trance, her words so nearly shrill that Toni was momentarily startled. "That will be quite all right," she smiled in the sweetest possible fashion, putting the brakes on. "For all my vigilance, Annette has become very naughty lately, and on top of all my own problems, I've found it rather a strain. It's not as though I'm strong, and we won't be isolated. I shall be seeing as much of her as I can."

She spoke as if her child was a natural hazard, not without love, but more as if her own offspring acted at times as a parasitic vine to pull Elissa down.

"Well, in that case," Toni said dryly, "I'll take her things now. Where are they, by the way?"

Elissa lifted her left arm in a purely balletic gesture. "The two blue cases over there. One is full of her toys. She won't go anywhere without them, and of course I have to give in to her on every point. It's not as if they were her best either. She has magnificent things!"

Lovely things! Magnificent things! Toni returned to the chatter . . . "the *Gregory* Nylands, that is, my late people. They spoil her dreadfully. She's such a beautiful child. I think somehow Damon imagined she would be beside me, but of course he's not familiar with our pattern. It's very good of you, Miss Stewart, to do all this for me, though Damon explained that he's paying you for your services, so I don't feel so badly."

With an effort Toni controlled her runaway tongue. "Actually, Mrs. Nyland, you've been misinformed, but don't let it bother you in any way. I'm here in a purely friendly capacity."

"You are?"

From the height of Elissa's silken brows and with a rising heart Toni grasped intuitively that Damon had mentioned nothing whatever about payment. That was Elissa' own little testing thrust.

"Neighborly, that's all," she continued, in a light, even voice. "My brother Paul leases Mandargi from Mr. Nyland. It's on Savannah's boundary."

"Yes, I know. Quite a jump up for a young man."

"Paul is extremely capable, a very go-ahead young man. I'm sure Damon told you that!"

"Actually, no," Elissa pointed out, regarding her shell pink nails. "He said very little beyond the few necessary facts. There were so many important things to catch up on. My husband was Damon's first cousin, did you know? I only met Damon at my own wedding. He'd been in the States before that. I believe he was always the bright boy of the family. Naturally I inherit my husband's shares in Nyland Holdings. Who knows, in a sense, I might be your employer as well?" She looked up at Toni with a bright smile.

"I think you'll find Mandargi is listed among Damon Nyland's private assets," Toni said quite matter-of-factly. "I imagine that would apply to Savannah as well, although I wouldn't really know."

"Yes, Savannah's Damon's. I checked," Elissa admitted artlessly.

"How interesting! Did you ever see the old homestead, Mrs. Nyland?"

"My dear!" Elissa used her hands again in genuine horrified remembrance. "It was frightful. Primitive by my standards. I couldn't have borne to have stayed here then. Believe it or not, Damon did, on and off for years while he developed all his projects. It was one of those old, old, shambling buildings, a Colonial-type bungalow. I can't imagine, knowing what kind of man Damon is, how he tolerated it!"

"First things first, I suppose," Toni said, seeing the funny side of it. "I rather like the old bungalows myself. We have one on Mandargi. I hope I've made it attractive and comfortable, though it would probably fit into Savannah's swimming pool. Speaking of swimming pools, do you mind if Annette takes a dip with me? Can she swim?"

"No, she can't!" Elissa lightly pointed out. "I can't either, for that matter. I'd detest all those chemicals on my skin. But teach Annette by all means, if you can!"

"There shouldn't be any problem about that. I had a whole sideboard of silver cups in my schooldays."

"How nice!" Elissa smiled up at her doubtfully. "Then I feel quite happy about leaving her with you. I'm anxious to learn as much as I can about Savannah. It's Damon's life, you see."

"A very isolated life in many ways," Toni said rather flatly, trying not to see.

"But my dear!" Elissa gave her high, sweet laugh. "Damon is here, there and everywhere. You simply don't know where he'll turn up. No one could ever say Damon Nyland stays in one place. He just uses Savannah as a jumping-off point. It's a very profitable enterprise, I understand. I know nothing, but nothing, about livestock. Breeding, that kind of thing." Some new sensuous intonation crept into her voice. "Not that Damon would care. He only likes very feminine women. He has superb taste in everything. He had a marvelous education and he's travelled so widely. It does make a difference!"

"Yes, he certainly has more than his fair share of everything!"

It was Elissa's turn for a setback. Her eyes narrowed and she glanced up in surprise. "But, my dear, you sound as if you don't like him?"

"I admire him tremendously, Mrs. Nyland," Toni said portentously. "It doesn't really matter whether I like him or not. Now if you'll excuse me, I'll take Annette's things and unpack them before dinner."

"Good idea!" Elissa's gleaming eyes were abstracted, falling on Toni vaguely as though she hardly saw her. After a moment she stood up, her slight body arching, her silvery head lifted, smiling patiently at Toni, obviously waiting for her to go. The small, boneless hand was deftly touching the soft hair at the nape of her neck again.

"If I have to," she promised sweetly, "I can testify that you're an excellent lady's maid! Thank you again."

Toni was less than amused, but it would be impossible to defeat a woman like Elissa. Somewhere along the line Elissa had lost the capacity or the interest to talk to her own sex, or perhaps she truly thought Toni was of no consequence, just another person on the Nyland payroll. It was rather terrible to be judged by the criterion of money and success.

Gently she said with impeccable courtesy, "I'll see you at dinner, then, Mrs. Nyland."

For the first time Elissa allowed herself to survey the younger woman thoroughly. Her tilted eyes traveled all over Toni from her feet to her face, her small mouth quirked. Finally her face assumed an expression of wanting to help.

"You know, dear, you'd be much more of a success

with a little more dress sense, though I don't suppose it matters up here!"

For some reason Toni was seized by the wild impulse to laugh. The calculation behind the apparent artlessness! The beginnings of a smile touched her mouth. "I can't take all the blame, Mrs. Nyland," she said lightly. "Damon picked this. We were in an awful rush to leave Mandargi."

Elissa's face was a study, a series of expressions rippling over her face, but Toni had missed them. She picked up the cases, one in each hand, and walked unhurriedly out of the room.

CHAPTER SEVEN

It was a beautiful day, golden and friendly, just a few curls of cirrus cloud marred the perfect peacock blue of the sky. The water of the Blue Lady billabong was made warm and lazy, idling along, a life-giving stream, secretively beautiful, very deep in spots with a pandanus palm that grew crookedly over the bank to make a splendid diving board. Toni had already made use of it, enjoying every moment of her swim, but now she sat with Annette, further upstream where the water shallowed, for here there were lots of polished stones for Annette to play with.

She sat beside Toni, childishly absorbed, dabbling her toes, her pink dress crumpled and damp around the hem, stained with the bright green moss that grew all over the big boulders. She was happy and content, one of her good days, may-it-last, endlessly rearranging her pile of stones with a few wild flowers thrown in and some bright, shiny leaves. The bank under the trees was cool and fragrant with the scent of the acacias, the bush boronia and a narrow-leafed shrub that was heavy with pale lavender flowers.

High above them, a herd of cattle were making the journey along an established cattle pad, the young bulls thudding, a rhythmic drumming, thrusting boughs aside with their wide horn-span. A flock of rosellas that lay along the branches of the paperbarks, sunning themselves and chatting gaily, took to the skies in a clean, shining sweep, a bright, alarmed cloud that swirled upwards effortlessly. Toni looked from the lovely flash of colors to the child, surveying her tender nape with a kind of wry affection. Funny little scrap she was, all but impossible most of the time. Elissa would be horrified by the state of her pink dress.

In fact, Elissa's views on child raising differed widely from the norm. On the odd day she showed an obsessive interest in the child: her looks, her clothes, her health, her intelligence. Then for the rest of the week she appeared to give up the whole business for a bad job. Small wonder Annette knew no stability at all, and Toni used up every bit of her ingenuity in keeping the child harmlessly amused.

In many respects, Annette had been spoiled rotten, in others, starved of the tried and true old-fashioned methods of child management. In the fortnight or so since she had been on Savannah, the household had been treated to a dozen temper tantrums and frequent impudent, equal-to-equal exchanges with a mother who offered no form of parental opposition. Only the droop of Elissa's slight shoulders indicated the true state of her physical and mental health.

Toni, involved, but not deeply, felt reluctant to interfere. Incredibly, so did Damon, now without a doubt the intended stepfather, although Toni had seen him eyeing the child thoughtfully, while her own hand itched to administer a few telling slaps. More often than not Elissa appeared locked in her ivory tower, powerless, under the spell of her own child, though it was obvious to all that Elissa would benefit from a spot of physical activity even if it were only to catch up a slipper.

But at night, with Annette a sleeping cherub, Elissa came into her own, making Toni a daily witness to a masterly display of technique in how to fascinate a man with the object of winning him, a purpose for which she was admirably equipped. By day she slumbered, attended to her beauty program, chatted on and off to a rapt Keith Hammond, drove around the property with Damon, went on one trip to the coast with him, though they were back well before nightfall. She didn't ride and she wouldn't be caught dead within 300 yards of a steer or a cow. But at night, with the men free to enjoy her company, she performed certain feats of magic in suggesting a warm friendliness between herself and Toni, relying heavily on the natural gullibility of the male. They were charmed and impressed and thought it no small thing that two such good-looking woman should share a bond of camaraderie. If they found Toni's rapid-fire deliveries and volleys a trifle too brisk they wisely said nothing. Undoubtedly she had style. Elissa had the grace.

Elissa's attitude, however, was promptly sacrificed, dropped like a stone, on the isolated occasions when the two women stumbled on one another unawares, for they had established an unspoken agreement of scrupulous avoidance.

Every day Toni regretted her position, but regrets offered no solution. Her release would come. The governess had been hired—an English girl, doing a two-year stint of Australia and New Zealand. Her qualifications were excellent. She would arrive at the end of the month, and privately Toni mourned for her. On one infrequent occasion when she saw him alone, Damon had said he would force her into accepting a token payment, but she was not engaged in any employment and told him so. Let the Nylands look to themselves. All she wanted to do was get out, away from Savannah with no harm done,

It was unbearable to watch him being so attentive, so darkly, charmingly, suavely urbane with his exquisite cream-fed relative, for far from being introspective and withdrawn as Toni had been led to believe, Elissa had come out of her shell with unprecedented abandon, witty and so slightly malicious, night-blooming, every evening in a different hostess gown, specially designed for her tiny form. Wonder of wonders! as Clarrie put it, her eyes raised to the ceiling, for Elissa had a very healthy appetite. "Glory knows where she puts it!"

In short, Elissa was almost exclusively self-orientated, with a faithfulness that transcended the necessary expediencies of bringing up a small child. It would be a bitter, empty battle to goad Damon into seeing her as she really was, and in fact, Toni lacked the heart and mind for it. It would be an impossible contest in any case, for Elissa had great natural cunning and contrary to her appearance she was very strong and single-minded when it came to getting what she wanted.

Toni, motionless, sat beside Annette staring into space, her body slightly bent, like a flower on a stalk. Now and again, with a barely perceptible motion, she passed Annette another stone to add to her collection and Annette lifted a flushed, smiling face to say "Thank you!" Poor little Annette! Nothing on Savannah was as it appeared to be. Behind Elissa's small enigmatic smile lay a scheming mind. Behind the sweet graciousness, no living warmth.

Why don't you admit it? Toni thought painfully. You're licked. Admit it and take the easy way out. There was nothing drastic about announcing that she had to be back on Mandargi. Paul had relayed a message which, decoded, said plainly that he was missing her badly. Probably Tikka and Leila didn't take kindly to being "straightened out" by a well-meaning Mrs. Carroll.

She thought too of Damon. Suddenly she was sickened, as much by her own endless mulling over the problem as anything else. It was none of her business in any case. She smiled to herself with some derision. She just didn't care. Now, too late, she discovered she just didn't care. Elissa's sweetness carried a wasp's sting. Damon's practised charm, which he used with such devastating success, meant nothing, absolutely nothing and she would do best to forget it. She would have to struggle alone with her own private devils of disillusionment.

Toni ran her hand over Annette's glossy curls and the child looked up inquiringly. For a moment Toni was lost in the clear, limpid green of the Nyland eyes, feeling submerged by a quick wave of self-pity. She would have to get over it. She rose with decision.

"Come along, darling," she said lightly. "We'd better make it back to the house. It's almost four o'clock."

Annette gave an enchanting little smile and rose to her feet. "We had a good time, didn't we? May I take the stones back, please, Toni? I *adore* them. Mummy won't look at them, of course. She's like that."

"Mummy's a wonderful person when she feels well," Toni said, trying to be gallant.

Annette stretched luxuriously as she watched Toni collect the pile of stones. "Mummy hates people. That includes me. She told me!"

Unable to believe it, Toni protested, "Oh, Annette darling, she doesn't. She loves you. All mothers love their children."

Annette's clear eyes were shadowed by her lashes. "You love children," she pointed out. "And dogs and horses and cows and everything. I'm going to stay with you, always. You're my best friend. You make up such lovely stories I want to go to bed."

Toni smiled back at her, irresistibly trapped by the Nyland charm. "When you're good, you're very, very good," she said lightly, and caught Annette's hand, holding it close and warm. "Now, *en avant!*"

Annette threw back her head. "What does that mean?"

"Get going, my pet!"

At the top of the ridge poincianas broke out like a sweep of fire, flaming everywhere one looked. The land fell into quiet—yet not quiet. The silence was enhanced by a symphony of little sounds, the rustle of the soft cane grass, the multi-throated insects, the slow slither of a lizard, wild geese that honked overhead. A breeze came and set the millions and millions of leaves sighing.

Ever afterwards, Toni never knew what focused her attention on a gaunt dead gum, bleached to the color of bone, stripped of life, of leaf, of everything. It was picturesque in a way, surrounded by pale green saplings.

It moved! Unable to believe her eyes, Toni blinked. It did move, coming down slowly like a stage prop on wires, directly in their path. Blood and brightness beat in her head. She could see it all happening with dreadful clarity. She jerked up a hand to fling away the stones, made a grab for the little girl.

"The tree!" she gasped and started to run, her heart in

her mouth lest they be running in the track of the falling giant, nearly lifting Annette off the ground. She tripped and fell and Annette came down heavily on top of her. They rolled together, as with a great rending roar the great bleached column crashed to the ground, smashing saplings and anything that lay in its path.

Twigs and leaves and bits of dead timber rayed through the golden spray of dust. It clogged the atmosphere, making them both cough. Toni sat up, dazed, gathering Annette onto her lap. Shaking, the child looked back at her silently, round-eyed.

"That was a close go!" Toni breathed, and gave a funny little choked laugh. "Those trees stand for years and years and suddenly they come down. I suppose it was the rain loosening the roots. Either that, or I'm accident-prone!"

"It's a fearful thing to happen!" Annette suddenly announced, her sense of hospitality outraged. "I shall tell Uncle Damon!" And up she got and made off at a spanking rate that Toni in her jittery state couldn't hope to match.

She felt her heart hammering against her ribs as she visualized Elissa's tilted eyes appraising her in open hostility. Even an act of God would take some explaining. "Look here!" she gasped, running after Annette and gripping the child's shoulder. "We won't alarm anyone. I'll tell the story myself, simply. It could have happened to any one of us."

"But it didn't!" Annette insisted doggedly. "It happened to us. I shall tell Mummy and Uncle Damon. I hurt myself when I toppled down."

The Land Rover was parked on a patch of grassy turf.

Annette clambered in and Toni surveyed her ruined cotton slacks, pulled on over her brief swimsuit. Pieces of twig still reposed in her hair. Annette looked a sorry sight. Elissa was legally entitled to an explanation. Toni said as casually as she could, starting up the engine:

"Don't worry about it, darling. It's past history already. We were lucky! I do have a good after-dinner story!"

The tires hummed and the wind cooled their cheeks. In ten minutes they were back at the house with Toni for the first time in her life as nervous as if she had conceived some monstrous plot to do away with a Nyland heiress. Annette jumped out of the Land Rover and galloped off as fast as her legs would carry her, evidently not as hurt as she thought. Still brushing her hair, Toni followed with the uneasy suspicion Annette was about to make great capital out of the incident, in the process, making a lot of questionable statements, for she had abruptly reverted to her *enfant terrible* mood.

A chain of physical reactions was taking Toni over. It had been close, too close. No passing fear. Her nerves simply weren't up to it, not after her own accident, and they said things come in threes! The idea of a scene with Elissa made her feel weak in the knees, distasteful in the extreme. Very likely only Keith Hammond would be there. A typical bachelor, he was comfortable in male company but serious and shy with the opposite sex. Whatever virtues he possessed as the Nyland family solicitor, on the home front he was no match for Elissa, or indeed any woman.

In silence she entered the house, in striking contrast to Annette's cavalry charge. She caught sight of herself. She looked a mess—dust and heat and beads of perspiration that spiralled down her back. Her bright tousled hair was blown all about her face. Her blue cotton slacks had a great tear in one knee. Perhaps if she looked hard enough she would vanish miraculously like the mirage. A golden beam of sunlight fell through the door and she thought fright had blown the whole situation up into ridiculous proportions. Sunshine was beautiful, cheering. Nothing sinister could happen in sunlight. Toni tossed up her head, like a thoroughbred filly, a bold, proud gesture.

From the living room came a high shrill squeal—anguish, Elissa's. From her manner and the set of her glistening, disarrayed head, Toni advanced toward the sound as if she were dressed by Givenchy. All four faces turned directly toward her, impressing themselves on her mind. Damon, in the act of standing up—instant authority, a stunning physical elegance even in narrow jeans and a faded cotton shirt. Elissa, shrunken into the armchair, peering round the side, lavender blue eyes staring in unwinking hostility, a spitting cat. Keith Hammond leaning protectively toward her setting up some sort of sympathetic vibration, a muted there, there! Annette, a head full of dusty curls and a shocking pink dress, in her bright green eyes a look of unholy bliss, the center of the stage, by *any* means. Her audience of adults clustered about her.

Serenely, like a mannequin, Toni walked to them. "It's not as bad as it looks," she said lightly. "I hope Annette hasn't alarmed you. We had a near accident."

Elissa's voice shattered like glass and as dangerous. "You look dreadful. Simply dreadful!"

"Yes, and you look so fresh and nice!"

"What happened?" Damon cut across this exchange, his voice unexpectedly hard. "You're as white as a sheet. If Annette's to be believed at all, you threw a tree at her. Here, sit down!"

It was useless to argue with Damon, useless to stand on her dignity, for he crossed the space between them in two long strides, giving her a little push into a chair. "Any time you care to start. We're all friends here."

"Yes, I know," she said, upset but as outspoken as ever. "It's wonderful to be home. Actually, if you really want to know, we were coming up from the Blue Lady lagoon when one of those old dead gums decided to bite the dust. I can't think now how I came to be alerted to it. There was no warning. It seems like a miracle. I suppose next time I go out, you'd better notify my next of kin."

"There's an idea!"

"You joke about it?" Elissa's voice sailed over the top of Damon's dark drawl. In one concerted movement she swept aside Keith Hammond's restraining hand and lunged at her avidly-interested-in-the-proceedings child, gathering her into a close, maternal embrace. "My little girl could have been killed, and you joke about it!"

"It's dear of you to leave me out. I was there too, Mrs. Nyland," Toni protested.

Almost on cue, overcome by the tortured, touching look in her mother's eyes, Annette burst into hysterical tears, engulfed in the near-atrocity as suggested to her by her mother, screeching until the room was deafened and even Elissa had let go of her.

"Now, now, what's all this to-do?" Clarrie Chase demanded from somewhere close at hand. She walked into the room, wiping her hands on her apron, her fore-head knobbling at the decibels of sound. "The way that child carries on is nothing short of disaster!"

"Who wants your opinion?" Elissa shrilled, rigid with indignation, her narrow eyes misty with tears of frustration.

"You'd better take it, Mrs. Nyland, while there's still time!" Clarrie retorted, much irritated by all the fuss.

"Clarrie, would you be good enough to take Annette to her room?" Damon requested in a superpolite voice, very much the male and bored to tears with such stuff. "Give her a bath and settle her down. Especially settle her down!"

"Good as done!" Clarrie said, glancing down at the child.

But Annette was not Annette for nothing. She couldn't do anything halfway. Always extremes: one minute angelic, the next in a rage.

"You beast!" she shouted as Clarrie reached out for her. "You beastly, wicked old woman!"

Without breaking her stride, Clarrie, a strong woman, tucked the child under her arm and administered a thumping whack on the frantically wriggling bottom. "Don't worry, I won't hurt her," she said calmly. "That was just in the nature of a well-deserved slap—the old boarding school variety from my matron days. It was the 'old' that did it. We all have our vanities!"

"You beast!" Annette continued to shout, scarlet in the face from mingled rage and her head-down position.

"That's enough of that!" Clarrie tucked her still more firmly under her arm, preparing to walk with her.

Elissa was frantic, hitting away Keith Hammond's hand with a vicious side-swipe. "Who is *she* to dictate to my child?"

"Come now, Elissa," Keith Hammond said in a surprisingly firm voice, "you can't condone the child's naughtiness. She had a shock, I know, but there are times when children need punishment, and that was one of them."

Transferring her attention to Toni, Elissa was a figurine no longer, but a lady panther measuring her cage. "How dare you precipitate this crisis? You've never liked me. I can't think why! I trusted you to look after Annette, now I'll never have a moment's peace again!" She broke off in her pacing and drew a ragged breath. "If anything had happened to Annette, because of you. . . !"

Toni spoke before she could help herself. "You must be out of your mind, Mrs. Nyland. I wouldn't hurt a hair of your silly child's head!"

"How dare you!"

Damon turned on his relative with a look of extreme boredom. "You appear to be stuck in a groove, Elissa. Calm down!"

Whatever else he said Toni didn't wait to listen. She spun on her heel in silent rebellion, unable to bear it a moment longer. You might as well tell a startled horse not to bolt, her inner voice cried. Halfway across the terrace she was caught up, hard, pushed back against the trellised vines.

"Isn't this wildly unorthodox?" she said, wildly struggling. "All this physical violence?"

"Not with someone like you," he said harshly, reducing her struggles to impotence. "Some women never create a ripple, but you!"

"Oh, damn you!" she stormed at him, seared by conviction. "You don't have to tell me what side you're on. You'd throw me to the lions for that precious lot. Playing gooseberry to a triangle," she said rapidly. "What a fool I was! What a job! What a dreadful mistake!"

"Face up to it, sweetheart!" he said grimly, pinning her chin and holding her face to him. "If that's the only mistake you've made, you're a very lucky girl!"

She struggled, as stubborn as a dozen contrary donkeys. "No wonder that child is hysterical. Have you seen her mother when she gets into her stride?"

"Be reasonable, Toni," he said, shaking her, losing his own temper. "Whatever Elissa is, I'll take full responsibility. You don't have to worry about it."

"You're damned right I don't!" she said swiftly, her eyes brilliantly dark. "I'm going to seize on any old excuse at all. I'm going home!"

His eyes remained inscrutable, but his touch changed in some subtle, mystifying fashion, melting her bones. "Jealous?" he asked.

The sudden shift in his manner, that spark of devilry, blurred her vision. She couldn't think clearly. She couldn't think at all and he knew it. A kind of helpless anger rose up in her like a huge silent tide.

"You hit me, my girl," he said tautly, anticipating her, "and I'll turn you over my knee here and now!"

"You're definitely mad!"

"Quite! I cheerfully admit it. Just mad enough to call your bluff!"

She was breathing quickly, staring up at him, locked in some savage battle for survival. His hands tightened and her nerves stretched a fraction tighter. "You witch!" he said in an odd undertone. "Even my mind has begun to accept the disaster!"

She was swaying toward him, her fingers winding themselves tightly around his, interlocking, a crackle of electricity, a fork of lightning in a summer sky.

"I say, Damon!" Keith Hammond broke out on to the terrace, his pleasant face agitated. "Would you come? Elissa's had a nasty turn."

"The devil she has!" Lines of irritation were etched about Damon's mouth.

"That's not very loverlike!" Toni taunted him.

"I'll catch up with you," he gritted out, twisting his dark head back to the anxious Hammond. "Go back to her, Keith. I'll get Clarrie. She's a trained nurse as well as everything else. I tell you, the saltmines beat Savannah hands down these days with hysterical females!"

"You wanted us here!" Toni said recklessly, discretion never a virtue.

He surveyed her for a second in silence, one hand tightly clenched on the side of the trellis, the flash in his eyes as cold as winter steel. Her mouth trembled and her teeth went unpleasantly on edge.

"Oh, Damon!" she said half fearfully, ashamed of her own retreat.

"Don't 'oh, Damon' me," he said in a merciless voice, swinging her high into his arms to hold her against his lean, hard body, leaving her too dumbfounded to speak. Master of the situation. He could do as he pleased. Across the inner court he walked, thrust open her door and threw her on the bed, his green eyes startlingly brilliant.

"The onset of the rains is the target I set myself!" he

announced casually with his customary arrogance. "Then look out!"

Her eyes were enormous, highly antagonistic in her warmly tinted face. "Look out yourself!" she said childishly, then flung herself back on the bed.

He glanced down at her in a relaxed, idle way. "It's times like these I realize I'm dealing with an adolescent."

"In a way, yes," she said in a soft shaky voice. "Go along and chat Elissa up. She'll soon put you wise. After today she doesn't strike me as all that much of a paragon!"

"Maybe Elissa hasn't got what you've got!" he said in a light, amused voice and left her while the wild apricot color mounted to her cheeks. What a fiery, shattering finish to a terrible day! The only sound was his receding footsteps across the paved court. At the very least, she'd expected fire engines after Elissa's display. One thing was certain, in no circumstances would she be persuaded to stay another day. She blew a wisp of hair away from her mouth, wilful and ardent. In the meantime she would sublimate her feelings. It was her only salvation. Away from Savannah she would be free of these troubled longings, the memory of the shape of a mouth on her own, the imprint of lean, strong hands. Damon Nyland was a forbidden commodity. She would, in time, find someone jolly if dull, but someone who would never expect her to forfeit her privacy and freedom. Savannah's sphere was a jealous and demanding one; she craved to be her own woman. It was monstrous to have Damon Nyland take control of her life.

Almost for a minute Toni gloated on what his future

534

with Elissa would be. For all her shortcomings, she was a
rare creature, a narcissist, in psychiatric terms. Then her
eyes flashed in sudden disgust. Urge and rhythm in her
slender body, she jumped off the bed and ran the shower
hard. She would wash her hair. It was always strangely
soothing. She'd had all the stimulation she needed.
Mandargi was home, a haven, a snug harbor. Who
needed the Promised Land?

CHAPTER EIGHT

In the end, Toni agreed to stay until the governess arrived, for Elissa really did suffer a minor brainstorm or the like that held her captive in her beautiful bedroom for three days; tempted by light delicious meals, a number of cool drinks, a pile of glossies, nothing heavier, until the strength flowed back into her tender limbs. Toni, quick-tempered but warm-hearted, was betrayed into a kind of irritated sympathy. Elissa couldn't help what she was. Freed of all financial worry, the necessity of earning her own living and supporting her child, she was forced back on all manner of imaginary illnesses and anxieties to fill in her time. The smallest, transient blemish on her lovely skin was enough to drive her nearly demented, let alone the high winds that sometimes visited Savannah, blowing, blowing, putting her in her own words "around the bend." With the monsoon expected, Toni wondered how on earth she would fare.

The great thing was, Elissa was too fine, too fragile, too delicate to wrestle with the ordinary commonplace things, the right schools, the right clothes, the right friends, the right marriage. False ideals were fed to her since childhood so that she had come to believe in them herself, working tirelessly toward a shallow perfection, not realizing that such things in themselves were not reason enough for living.

Her husband's tragic death came as a crippling blow; not in the accepted sense of a deep personal loss, a limbo of loneliness and grief; more, the unfairness of it all, for now Elissa would have to stir herself all over again. Her second marriage must eclipse her first. She must find a man who was in every way acceptable. A success by her own, and perhaps more important, by her friends' standards. Anything else was untenable. That he would have to be a man who would fondly deprecate her extravagant follies was understood. Whether he would find it in his heart to lavish loving kindness on little Annette was immaterial. Annette's father had left her well provided for and she would be going to boarding school in any case.

In those few days of Elissa's nervous crisis, Toni came to know Keith Hammond a lot better. Always calm, good-natured, relaxed, he was in every way a solid citizen, at peace with himself and his world, standing four-square on the sanctity of marriage and the legal profession. As he confided to Toni in his pleasant, uneffusive way, his early goals and ambitions had prevented his forming a permanent alliance beyond a spot of calf love at university when he was desperately smitten and equally desperately disillusioned. But now, in his early forties, a nice age for a man, on a decently elevated plateau of material success, he wanted marriage. He wanted Elissa. No names were used, but he wanted Elissa. In fact it was abundantly clear to his audience of one that he wanted nothing more out of life than to dedicate himself to Elissa's happiness.

If Toni thought him wanting in taste and good judgment, she gave not the slightest sign of it to plague him. He was, in any event, a kindly man, ready to shed his bounty on young Annette, who surprisingly smiled whenever they met. But day by day on Savannah he fretted. It was a gruelling business to have to watch his friend and treasured client effortlessly fascinate the woman he loved. For without Elissa he had come to believe life would be as arid as the Simpson desert. It was common knowledge anyway that he had as good as chased her all over three States and on to Savannah, on what appeared to many to be a senseless mission. But of course Toni, who agreed, never so much as hinted any such thing. In fact, she subtly encouraged him in his fantasies, if only from a mistaken idea of good-heartedness.

If anyone was to blame, it was Damon. Damon was Damon: always there, always his own dynamic self, lounging in doorways, hands thrust casually into his pockets, green eyes able, in one second, to pick up the threads of any situation. Never anything else but at ease everywhere, his old mocking self. Toni wished over and over that she could tell him to go to the devil. He was maddening. She could explode like a firecracker just thinking about him. His insolence, his arrogance—he was so smug! So certain he could manipulate her like he did so many others. He really had a remarkable talent for mesmerizing people who could be of use to him.

For Damon used people, constantly, selfishly, shamelessly. Never mind if they loved it, hanging on his every word as if it were of paramount importance. But a friend? Who could ever make a friend of a tiger? Worst of all, he had the power to hurt her. She couldn't think of him without melodrama and histrionics. It was only natural, she supposed. She was a woman. She loved him and she was jealous, her heart stormy, filled with self-contempt for her fury of hurt pride.

So he preferred Elissa? What of it? In his company Elissa came to sparkling life, her silvery laugh echoing around and around the walls of Savannah. Toni couldn't bolster herself with the thought that Damon also found her attractive. She certainly hadn't flung herself at his head. The attraction was very real and it was a tiny stir of life that moved her despite herself. He hadn't deceived her in any way. She had only herself to blame if she attached more importance than it deserved to a few kisses. If she loved him, as was her way, wholeheartedly, it was her own fault again. She didn't regret it, for if she had it would have been a denial of herself.

She could even forgive him for loving Elissa. She was, after all, an assured beauty, sophisticated and knowledgeable. Love was not logical or even reasonable and definitely not fair. No justice anywhere. The most unlikely people found a smooth path to it. Love, the elixir of life; yet it took precious little to make it evaporate. Love was a cage, for she had the unhappy notion that for her, from now on, all men would wear the same face—Damon's. She knew she was hurt and the hurt would go on for a long time, but somehow she would make out. Back on Mandargi she might be free of his bright tyranny, splendid and arrogant, the devastating flashes of humor that made him so very attractive. She was young. She would try to be happy. But she would never forget Damon whatever her destiny.

Another week went by, very fast, so that Toni later thought of it as a raving nightmare. Her controls were beginning to slip and she knew it. It was sheer torture to see Elissa's hand hovering, then lingering on Damon's arm, her shining small head thrown back to meet the sardonic indulgence, never devilry, she seemed to call forth from him. No one could ever deny they made a handsome couple, an almost perfect physical foil, as arresting in its fashion as a white camellia on a black jacket. All this Toni took in at her own risk; her better judgment seemed to have no power at all, for it was a breathtaking, piercing, bittersweet delight to be near him, at any cost.

Even on Savannah with its limitless horizons, Damon Nyland was a man separate from his background. He never merged, never lost impact, but stood out clearly, very vital, very much the individual, a man with an exciting image and straightforwardly masculine. So each day Toni determined on a course of self-razzle-dazzle. She rose early, swam a few lengths in the pool, then planned a jaunt for herself and Annette. This was a maneuver designed to keep them out of the house for long hours and from under Elissa's narrow feet. But they did see a lot of the property and once they hid in a feathery grove of acacias along one of the tree-lined gullies watching the rufous-topped brolgas dance their quadrille on the reed flats. It was a beautiful visual impression that left its mark on both of their memories.

But each night in her room, long after she had settled Annette for the night, Toni reverted to some mysterious underworld of secret and impossible dreams. It was foolish, but she couldn't help it, her feeling was so complete and profound. She brushed her hair facing the mirror, her eyes half closed and dreamy, the light sheening the silken lids. From her long hours in the sun, her skin had turned from cream to a warm peach. She used little makeup and rarely wore anything but shirts

540

and flared slacks except for dinner at night when she changed into a simple dress, one that offered no competition for Elissa's meticulously worked-on perfection. What she didn't realize was that her unadorned face had distinction and character.

Her mirror image never revealed the fresh, living face, the gleaming highlights in hair that so emphatically framed her modern, contemporary young beauty. She never really saw herself as others saw her: the fine dark eyebrows, silky black lashes, thick and spiky, the fronded brilliance of dark irises with their gleams of shifting light. If there was knowledge and experience in Elissa's jacaranda gaze, there was a delicate innocence in Toni's eyes for all their touch of temperament.

The same weekend Cathy Tennant, the new governess, was due in, the whole Nyland clan arrived for a general meeting and celebration combined, for one of their senior members had been elected to the Senate. They flew in, en masse, and almost immediately started into a series of business discussions for the men, gossip sessions for the women, who were rigidly excluded with no more expected of them than to be pretty and pleasant. But a lot of fun was had in between times. There were jaunts round the property, picnics and swimming and riding; the pool was very popular, and the men played polo-crosse. There were displays of camp drafting, cutting out cattle, breaking in the best of the brumbies, wheeling, galloping, biting and lashing, snorting and pawing the ground and the inevitable rough riding from every hand on the station. In buck-jumping, the horse, Salvation Jane, emerged the exclusive reigning champion, ready and willing to throw the gamest challenger, to the sun and the wind, then the ground.

The Saturday evening the whole of Savannah would come to life with a gala party, semi-formal for the family, gaily informal for the station employees and their families and anyone who cared to come for hundreds of miles around. A great many cared, and they all came, pitching tents under the massed shade of the eucalyptus ready for a night under the blossoming stars.

So far as the Nylands were concerned, they were pretty much as Toni expected: sleek and gregarious, very "family," the young ones trendy in all kinds of fabulous gear; moving, talking, swimming, riding with practised skill and grace, the perfect assurance a great deal of money seemed to bring. The men were very friendly, very appreciative of a woman's good looks, the women a mixture of curious-wary-friendly with the occasional downright patronizing, independent of family status. The Senator's lady was far and away the most charming.

It was Cathy Tennant, the governess, who was the real surprise. A small girl, neat and fine-boned, she had fiercely red hair, deep slate-colored eyes, a pixie, not pretty face, that was still very pleasing, if not endearing, a fair share of freckles, and a smile like a sunburst, a sudden radiance that people found themselves waiting for like some heart-warming revelation. It revealed the one true Cathy, a bright self-reliant girl, but soft too and very funny.

Toni took to her at once. A natural empathy was established at once with a little humorous aside on the degree of redness to which hair could attain, from Toni's rose bronze to Cathy's almost burnt orange. When she heard there was to be a party that night, her smile broke out afresh, her gaiety and youthful high spirits ready to embrace the world. If she emerged from her interview with Elissa a bit subdued, she soon picked up again to fire a volley of questions at Toni, who sat on the end of her bed watching Cathy shake out her clothes and hang them away in the long built-in wardrobe. She was thrilled with her surroundings and didn't fail to say so in her bubbling, beguiling fashion.

"Any words of advice on how to handle Mrs. *Elissa* Nyland?" she inquired, gyrating with a party frock.

"God, no!" Toni said so emphatically. The other girl looked startled, then broke into peals of laughter. "Then we'll just have to have a little 'think' session, won't we? Now, Mr. Nyland, Mr. *Damon* Nyland, that is, there's such a lot of them, he's a super man, isn't he? A great chunk of purest gold. Gorgeous! I thought they were only like that in films. All that tall, dark, handsome bit really grabs you, doesn't it? Makes you go weak at the knees. He swung me down from the plane, you know. A delicate adagio, wafting through space. All the good times come at once!"

"Elissa saw him first!" Toni contributed soberly.

This brought Cathy to a rapid halt. "A point that had not previously occurred to me." She pursed her bottom lip. "So that's the way of it! Just as well you told me, or I'd have set out like Columbus on uncharted seas!"

"Well, it was short notice, I admit!" Toni smiled, "but do decide on my advice. I'm not saying it won't be hard, a fight all the way. But look at the broad pattern. I'll introduce you to my brother. He's a bright bachelor, but very well trained!"

"Your brother, you say? That's very generous of you!" Cathy twirled lightly, all attention. "Tell me, does he look just a little like you? If he does, my stay is complete!"

"He does!" Toni smiled, "but aside from that aspect of the matter, he's very nice. Very nice indeed! Flower-blue eyes, utterly wasted on a man!"

"How could you mean that?" Cathy cornered her with her eyes. "That statement won't bear closer examination. Know what I mean?"

"*Yes,*" Toni said, suddenly assailed by a vision. Her heart leaped, but she tried to appear calm, keeping her head down until the moment of danger passed.

"Your brother, you say," Cathy was bubbling on happily. "When do I meet him?"

"On your first weekend off, if you like. We'd love to have you. We lease Mandargi, another cattle property to the southwest, from Mr. Nyland. It's no Savannah, but we don't endure any economic hardships."

"Is such a thing possible in this country?" Cathy whirled to face her, speaking with unabashed sincerity. "Thank you so much, Toni, I'd love to come. I'm really getting my money's worth here. New Zealand was very kind to me, so friendly and such glorious scenery, but Australia! Why, you can throw in an extra dimension. It's so big! You can go on forever and still not get anyplace. That's the first thing that strikes you. Why, Queensland alone would swallow up the whole of Western Europe and still leave the Pacific coastline and all the off-shore islands. I'd say the Great Barrier Reef was my favorite beauty spot in the whole world, and I've been through all the glamorous places. Working, of course. Money is always gratifying!" She folded a silk scarf and put it away in a drawer, then broke into an improvised song:

Australia, I love you, I do, I do,
I love the blue sky above you
and your sea of sapphire blue!

"Cripes, mate, I love your enthusiasm!" Toni smiled and affected a laconic drawl. "In fact, I think you're absolutely splendid!"

"You're more splendid than I," Cathy protested, judging the completely satisfactory inner springs of the bed.

"Not at all! I will willingly concede we're equally splendid!" Toni bounced up and down, becoming involved despite herself.

"All right. Just whatever you say, dear." Cathy collapsed back into an armchair, flushed with her exertions. "This is a super house, isn't it?" she said with great conviction. "Naturally I took the trouble to inquire into the more significant facts of the Nyland biography. It must be really something to have so much of everything you never have to question yourself or your way of life. You just *are*. It's so unexpected, too, to find a place like this in the middle of nowhere. The house and the furnishings and the paintings and all those gorgeous bits and pieces I can't wait to feast my eyes on. In fact, if I didn't know I was in the middle of the Australian bush, I'd think I was back home on one of the big estates. The landed gentry and all that. I mean, he's like a bloomin' feudal lord or something, a slice of the past. It's not fair. I tell you, it's not fair."

"I believe he worked very hard for what he has!" Toni said magnanimously, striving to be fair. "It wasn't until a great many of his ideas were proven that the rest of the family came in with the backing for the big ventures."

"Money makyth money!" Cathy intoned. "It's sort of inevitable, isn't it? Half their luck! The Lady Elissa is very grand. Pure and fine and a great frontal attack. A thousand questions crowd to my tongue, but I know I shouldn't ask them. Strike that one off the record. I don't want to cause any resentment this first day off, but I feel I've known you a hundred years, and so forth. Interesting, is it not? Your people didn't pass through the British Isles, by any chance?"

"Both my grandmothers came from Ireland, if that's any good to you."

"Yes, I've heard of Ireland," Cathy said, her dark gray eyes dancing. "And they tore up their roots to come here?"

"They felt they owed it to their husbands, I imagine. They were resident in Australia at the time." Toni screwed up her eyes surveying the quaint, pixie face in front of her. "You don't look unlike the 'little people' yourself! Tell me, what are you wearing this evening? That taffeta tartan has great potential."

"This one?" Cathy went to the wardrobe and twitched out the long skirt of a halter-necked number in different shades of violet and lilac. "I thought it was a bit violent myself, for a first evening. One mustn't overdo it."

"No, I like it," Toni repeated. "And I'm hyper-sensitive!"

"Well, it has had a lot of mileage," Cathy said

thoughtfully, smoothing her flaming aura. "Which just goes to prove I like it myself. Important for a woman. Never mind what the men think. Now, what about you? What are you wearing? Not that it matters when you look like a cross between Audrey Hepburn and Ali MacGraw."

"Come and see what you think. I hate everything!" Toni got up off the bed and led the way along the terrace to her own room, where the girls fell into a discussion on the possibilities among Toni's very limited wardrobe. They both agreed she could look very much better than she probably would with what was on hand, but there was little they could do. They were not the same size. Cathy was a "twiggy" girl and Toni was three inches taller and a different shape. But what did it matter? Elissa, undoubtedly, would steal the show, with the rest of the Nyland women offering some pretty heavy challenge. They were the lilies of the field, and both girls were sensible of the distinction.

As a general maxim, Toni had long since accepted, things do not always work out as planned. Life was full of surprises, whether desirable or not, and when they were pleasant, it helped a lot. In this way she dressed for the party that evening with a feeling inside her approaching elation. A kind of triple glow, for now she had a new friend and a true friend in Cathy, one who was destined to become her lifelong confidante: Damon had withheld until the last minute the much appreciated gesture of flying Paul in, and as a consequence of having a thoughtful and far-seeing brother she now wore her one and only dazzle dress, a Jean Patou copy and an extravagance from the old days.

It became her like no other—a slither of amber paillettes on a bronze silk ground, twinkling, glittering, throwing off the most beautiful bloom on her face and her bare shoulders and throat. It was very simple in cut, being little more than a slip, but it was very sophisticated and she applied herself with great diligence to making the most of her hair and her makeup, till she blossomed into something very special indeed. She stared into the mirror with a gathering excitement and what she saw there gave her confidence.

"My, you've changed!" she said to herself. "Why, I scarcely know you. It's been a long, long time since you've looked like that!"

Almost eight months, she deducted, falling into a reverie. Ever since then she had dressed for comfort, not fashion. A little embarrassed, she tried to resurrect that evening with Martin. Good-hearted Martin! Suffering fools gladly, always turning the other cheek, nursing the one drink all evening, the possessor of many sterling qualities, yet he had gone into oblivion. A pity, because he was a nice person, but like many a thoroughly nice person he was just a bit uninspired. Perhaps he thought of her in the same way. She laughed softly, a quiet, pretty sound, and switched off the main light in the room, leaving only the warm golden glow of the bedside lamp.

Recrossing the room, she caught sight of the glamorous stranger again, and for a moment something like triumph gleamed in her eyes. "Amazing, really amazing!" She shook back her thick, shining hair and felt the heat of pleasure and excitement in her cheeks, delicately shaded and tinted. She would go down and see how Cathy was faring. There was some special magic about a party. Even the word had a little inbuilt stir to it.

Cathy, when she came to the door, did a double take, sincere and very heartwarming. "Wow!" she said softly, falling back the better to focus. "You look sensational. That's what I call a drop dead dress. Terribly sexy. Now where, oh, where did that come from, or mayn't I ask?"

Toni took a few gliding steps into the room. "Paul brought it with him, marvel that he is! Some leftover glitter from my city days. You look incredibly marvellous yourself!"

"Yes, I'm always at my most remarkable at nights!" Cathy smoothed the violet and lilac taffeta over her trim hips, very young and glowing, big-eyed and eager. "It's times like these a girl must extend herself, meet the competition. A well-groomed girl is a happy girl, I always say!" She picked up an atomizer and sprayed herself with a fresh tang of Vent Vert, emerging from the sea of fragrance to smile into Toni's brilliant dark eyes. "If it's all the same with you, old girl, I intend to do a little fascinating myself. Your brother, to be exact. I think I'll like him. Very much!"

"You go right ahead," Toni said, nodding her head in an encouraging fashion. "It's good to see young people enjoying themselves. It's no use his struggling, I suppose?"

"None at all!" Cathy preened for a minute longer before the mirror, then turned to Toni. "Come along, girl, let us go out. Shall we? The visiting team, with the play on the home ground!"

"You're a looney, aren't you?" Toni said with a soft little laugh.

Cathy patted down a fiery curl and stared across the court at the blossoming, beautiful house. "Don't worry, there's intelligence behind the looniness. Actually I'm a lot smarter than most people think. Ye gods!" she broke off to speak in a much different voice, "that's the lovely Lady Elissa, is it not?"

Toni followed the direction of her gaze in time to see Elissa, small shining head upflung, silver gray chiffon foaming about her feet, adding to her fey attractions, pale slender arms extended, as if her heart went with them, to . . . yes . . . they waited for a tall figure to come into sight. Damon. Tall, dark, devastating. Heady stuff and the main attraction. Toni frowned and made off, fast.

"Someone clamoring to talk to you?" Cathy enquired, her shorter legs striving to keep up.

"I'm sorry!" Toni slowed the pace, but only fractionally so that Cathy stared at her, narrowing her slate-colored eyes. She was not only smart, but extremely acute. Poor Toni! But who could blame her? The man was fantastic—anyone could see that—but these society types stuck to their own. Money makyth money! She'd said it herself. Still, Toni, vivid and slender, looked remarkably chic and elegant. She could hold her own anywhere and Cathy was absurdly pleased for her, having cast her staunch vote very early in the game.

"Cheer up, chum!" she said with a happy, irrepressible little laugh. "You're a success. In fact, I'd venture to take a bet no one will approach your magnificence tonight!"

"Well enough!" Toni flashed an involuntary smile, her eyes on Cathy's fiery curls, like vivid flowers around her head.

Elissa, when she first caught sight of the girls, witnessed their transformation with a certain amaze-

ment, her piercing, imperial regard moving from Toni to
Cathy and fixedly back to Toni again, in such a way as to
infuriate Cathy, who normally loved humanity. Even so,
she held on to her bright smile. Grin and bear it, if only
for politeness' sake, and the fact that she wanted to see a
great deal more of Savannah and the Outback. The
woman was her employer, but it was abundantly clear to
Cathy that Toni had an enemy, a formidable one in the
egocentric Mrs. Nyland, for all her kittenish ways. It was
a first impression, Cathy thought, screwing up her eyes,
as though it helped, and first impressions are notoriously
misleading, but her observations, in the main, were
threaded with a certain, illuminating, perception. Her
grandmother had been the same.

She cleared her throat. Her voice felt a little tight,
because she had been holding her breath, but now it
loosened. "Here's Paul!" she said brightly. "As handsome as you promised!"

He came on toward them, lean and stylish, as cleanly
cut as any young girl's dream, quizzing them with such
infectious charm the icy little splinters of Elissa's
displeasure were drowned out of consciousness—for
Cathy, at least. Her laugh gurgling, Elissa forgotten, she
turned her piquant face up to Toni's extremely attractive
brother, covering a lot of ground with breathtaking
suddenness. But for Toni, tempted to stay with them, the
swirling kaleidoscope of color, the women's dresses, the
beautiful furnishings, the lights and the flowers, everything, was a void in which Damon's dark head and face
stood out starkly. A stranger. The center of a little
universe of laughing, warmly admiring friends and
relations. For a split second she felt desperately unhappy

and lost and illogically she deeply resented him, as though he had deliberately shut her out. He was sitting talking, gleaming, amusement-filled eyes, one hand gesturing, the other holding a glass. Elissa, significantly, was now beside him, her foaming dress a transparent sea lapping the edges of his beautiful evening jacket.

Oh, why, oh, why did she hope for such impossible things! He looked up abruptly in mid-sentence, and trapped Toni's gaze. His expression changed subtly and he saluted her with his glass, his black brows lifting. She threw him the stock party response, a sparkling, quite meaningless smile, which he accepted for what it was worth, one brow tilting, his eyes slipping over her with some irony. If she didn't move, she would give the show away, but deliverance was at hand. The Senator's lady, her golden-brown eyes short-sighted, but warm and friendly, smiled across a lovely arrangement of russet and gold chrysanthemums and said to Toni, "Why, hello there!"

Simple and effective, an escape. Like a brave little soldier Toni made her way with gratitude and deliberate grace to the luxurious curving sofa, watching Grace Nyland pat the cushioned seat beside her.

"I knew you were beautiful, but not that beautiful!" she said dryly. "Come and tell me all about yourself. Precious little information Damon volunteers, though I'm grieved to admit I pumped him. He's my godson, you know. There, my dear, sit down!" The inquisitive golden eyes were pleasantly indomitable, and Toni found herself responding, yielding to a little friendly persuasion.

They continued to talk for some time with periodic drifts across the room of a distinctive, tinkling laugh;

provocative and conquering. Toni's heart quivered, but she kept a tight rein on her sensibilities. The realization that nothing had changed, had hit her forcibly. Nothing was different from yesterday and tomorrow. No bright party face and a dazzle dress could alter anything. Love for her wasn't going to be happy. She could believe it now. It was an unbearable, oppressive sensation, like going on and on through a dark tunnel. Nothing happening. Nothing resolved. Light somewhere, but how far on?

Her brilliant, wide gaze clung to the Senator's lady, seeing yet not seeing, so that Grace Nyland, nobody's fool, for all her shortsightedness, was sufficiently aware something was going on. She scrupulously examined the delicately determined young face before her and saw nothing to criticize. Over-sensitive perhaps. Rather heartbreaking, really. She continued to look and listen with infinite tolerance and understanding. In some ways it was a blessed relief to be past it all, safe in the serenity of the sixties.

She thought of Damon, her godson. Handsome, splendid really. Clever, immensely successful. Enormous sex appeal; even she could see that. Why couldn't Damon be the answer? But even as her mind framed the question, Toni's dark gaze shifted, wistfully, almost compulsively, and Grace Nyland had her answer. Her own heart moved in quick, instinctive sympathy. These young things, tearing themselves to pieces. The dramatization of the normal emotions, the normal course of events.

"Child," she said, peering at Toni through her elegant slightly ineffective evening glasses, "why don't you join the young people, though you've given me a great deal to go on with!" She swiveled her head. "Damon!" her voice had lifted to platform level, so that her godson broke off his conversation to smile at her and, extracting himself from the smart young Nylands, came toward them.

Color flooded Toni's face. She looked blazingly alive. Lit up inside, yet she could have sunk through the floor with mortification. Let the earth open up and swallow her and she wouldn't give a purple damn. Grace Nyland's bejewelled hand rested lightly on her arm, the embodiment of kindness. She looked up at her godson. "Damon, why don't you take this child off and give her a good time? See the others meet her. I like her immensely!"

"I haven't told you my secret yet, have I?" he drawled in his dark, mocking voice.

She tilted her beautifully dressed gray head. "Tell me now, not that you need to!" she said in her turn.

Precipitately Toni shot to her feet, desperate to escape both of them and their infallible pronouncements, but warm, strong fingers closed about her wrist, seeking the pulse beat.

"Come dance with me, Toni!" he said, knowing full well how she felt. "You look a dream. In fact, you swamp me. I was almost afraid to approach you, let alone speak."

"Off you go, you devil!" Grace Nyland admonished him. "I won't tell a soul!"

Damon's hand tightened over Toni's protesting fingers. Some warm, stabbing emotion took charge of her. She couldn't bear to look at him. Who was worthy of him? Handsome and arrogant. A devil, for sure, Lucifer proud and sure of himself with laughter glinting from under his half-closed lids.

"Wine to a heavy heart!" he taunted her softly, a curve

to his mouth. "Let's forget our private feud. You're not going to quarrel with me, I hope! Not with Grace's attentive eye trained on us."

Toni moved her head in denial, but didn't speak. She felt like laughing and crying at once. He steered her through the room and out on to the terrace, twisting her expertly into his arms, joining about ten other couples, who between the lot of them were demonstrating the different dance styles from a pre-World War Two frolic to the latest do-your-own thing and be damned to the rest of you.

They danced, conventionally, but his arms seemed to hold her closer than necessary, and his midnight-dark head bent over her own. She didn't speak. She didn't dare, lest the words shatter the perfect physical empathy that asserted itself between them, subduing all differences that verbal fences could devise. It was like driving on the highway in a high-powered car. The furious, reckless thrill of it. The limitless, irresistible path to destruction? It was useless to pretend to herself. He moved her like no other man and she didn't trust him for one single second.

The music stopped and someone laughingly moved off to stack new records on the hi-fi equipment. Damon slid his hand down her back, closing on her narrow waist, turning her into the curving shadow of the vine-wreathed wall.

"We're home, baby!"

She lifted her face to him, her femininity heightened, exploited by his nearness, the fascination of the unattainable. He was pulling her gently, inexorably toward him in exquisite slow motion, and she trembled.

"It's so easy! Sometimes. Simplicity itself," he said, his voice deep and lulling, narcotic even.

An iridescent insect fluttered past them. The amber and gold lights from the living room shed a magic light over her hair and her dress, her flawless, tinted skin, the small white teeth that showed between the clear crimson of her parted mouth. He heard the soft, sensuous little intake of her breath and his own expression tautened. The melancholy in her eyes deepened.

She thought of dozens of absurd and useless little tricks to hold him, keep him beside her, aching with longing, but there was nothing she could do, she thought in a burst of self-defeat. Damon would go his own way in everything. He was far too seasoned to fall for a few Circe-like tricks. She was only inflicting punishment on herself. A whole wasteland of frustrated emotions, with no outlet. Only at that moment it didn't matter. All that mattered was they were together. He was holding her, looking at her, speaking her name in his beautiful voice that turned her heart over. Her uplifted face reflected more clearly than she knew, the completeness of her surrender to the here and now. To love and not be loved. It happened, but he wasn't indifferent to her. She was certain of that. Wherever she looked tonight he would be there, even in dreams.

An imperious, silver-toned voice broke up their little idyll, making itself heard above the mingled party sounds.

"Oh, Damon! Darling!" A light and resolute step moved swiftly along the terrace, a floating smoke screen. Elissa, a jealous queen, her feline gaze all violet blue flames upon them. "Darling!" she said again, possessive and imperative, smiling a brittle smile, frozen-eyed, regally outraged, increasingly dangerous. "I need you for a moment. Do back me up on this. . . . Vivian is saying . . . and you have such influence with him. . . ." She broke off, her eyes shifting to Toni, viewing her steadily as an object, flashing dismissal, her voice dripping sweetness. "Please excuse us, Toni, but this can't wait. Family business!"

Toni's eyes didn't waver and she murmured with charming indifference, "But of course, Mrs. Nyland."

Why fight it? she thought dismally. Elissa was invincible, a cut above the ordinary decencies and in that way beyond retaliation, protected by her own curiously unyielding nature, the hard core of self-interest. Pretending a casualness she did not feel, she turned away and gave a little wave to Paul and Cathy who were circling the far end of the terrace.

Almost immediately she was snapped up herself by a pair of eager arms and a voice that inquired: "May I?" without waiting for the answer, evidently not expecting one. As a family, the Nylands didn't contemplate refusals from anyone. Quaint, really, she thought as she rejoined the crowd, listening to some very high-flying compliments which she accepted with an enigmatic smile that did wonders for her false guise of exotic mystery.

Extraordinary how immune one could be to broad flattery attacks. With nine out of ten men it was different altogether. Toni had absolutely no need to marshall any resistance, because she loved Damon—a dangerous total commitment with disastrous side-effects for herself. With mingled scorn and self-pity, she fell to giving a reasonable performance of a girl enjoying herself and her successive partners laughed appreciatively, doing their level best to stay with her until wives and girlfriends galloped in to break up such trivial matters. By suppertime she found herself the toast of the evening, a confusing and ironic turn of events when she would probably cry in her sleep; yet she took every hurdle like a thoroughbred, accepted and applauded in varying degrees.

Shortly after midnight she suddenly felt she had reached the limits of her acting abilities, the gurgly social talk, the gay repartee explicit with false delight. It was heaven and hell to see Damon at every turn verifying Elissa's every statement, his suavity and charm blatant enough to cut up with a knife and distribute around. Fatal and self-destructive to feel bitter, and she wouldn't be that, but her heart was breaking up like ice floes.

It was a release and a benediction to be out under the stars inhaling the heady perfume of the broom flowers. Lights were threaded through the trees and she could see far across the starlit grounds to the barbecue areas. The crowd had long since thinned, but there were still quite a few people about indulging the urge and the instinct to enjoy themselves.

Beyond the perimeter of the formal gardens and the house proper, small camp fires were glimmering. Down by the lagoon and all around small voices gave tongue: the possum-skin drums and the tap-sticks, the muffled drone pipe. The breeze stirred with the rhythm of their beat. Toni listened intently. Long-long-short, then stepped-up variations until her heart was throbbing in a kind of harmony. It was almost impossible to listen and not be affected. Subconsciously her body was responding to the insistent vibration, swaying slightly with rhythmic grace. It was soothing, yet stimulating, quickening the pulse.

The moon threw shadows through the leaf patterns and a night hawk whistled. She lifted her face to the sky. A limpid well of light, an avenue of blossoming stars, the deities of the Dreamtime moved in procession across the Timeless Land. The sand drums began to beat in earnest and she walked towards their hypnotic sound. She heard no footfall, yet she was conscious of a presence behind her with every nerve in her body. She swung about. Nothing in his face quietened the tumult of her mind. Even in the curve of her body there was excitement.

"Where the devil are you going?" he asked without any polite preliminaries.

"Following the drums!" she said, equally short.

"Well, it's pretty damned late and I'd like you to go carefully if you would. Don't just wander off at will. We might be looking for you for days afterwards."

"Oh, please!" she said in a pathetic little voice. "I'm a big girl now. Besides, I thought it was an old tribal custom, heading off to greet the One of the Secret Tongue!"

"All right, all right!" he said evenly. "Shall we step out into the clearing? You've said your few pertinent words. Coming?"

"No, not particularly!"

He swung on her, as alert as a hunter. "Have done, Toni. We both know this has nothing to do with anything, don't we?"

"What?" she asked huskily. Anything at all to irritate him, and she knew that she was. There was some sort of tension in every taut line of him. She tilted her bright head, thinking it ridiculous the way she let him unnerve her. A light flickered in his eyes and he shrugged his powerful shoulders.

"There's got to be a key to you!"

"There's a key to everything, they tell me, even when you can't find it."

Cynicism touched his mouth. "Well, I never claimed it as an easy existence. In fact, I've been under more pressure since you arrived on Savannah than at any time in my entire history. I sometimes think I could crack up!"

"Don't we all!" she said, shockingly flippant, "You're constantly reminding me of my inadequacies!"

"Toni, Toni!" he said under his breath. "What's up with you now? You've lost all ability to relax. Be normal."

"Why not?" she challenged him. "If you think I'm neurotic you're the underlying cause. You! What you are. Who you are, but you'll never make me feel inferior!"

Damon hit a hand to his head, looking so immensely strong and vital she almost gave in. "God give me patience!" he said quietly. "Does this mean you're stupid or is it some kind of communications barrier? I just don't understand you."

"Is it so vital to try?" she asked with asperity. "Why don't you use your authority? You've got plenty of it."

"You don't want to learn, do you?" he asked, dangerously soft. "You oppose the principle of the whole idea."

"Kindness goes a long way, haven't you heard?" Her eyes flashed and the blood rushed to her head. "I just don't like being pushed around. If you'd only relent a little...."

He made one slick movement towards her, his grip
bringing her to a shaking stop. "Let's see if we can
improve the situation, shall we? Maybe a practical
demonstration might have some value. Don't keep your
feelings bottled up. It's bad for you!" He shook her a
little and her hair moved in a thick swirling mane about
her face. "Don't struggle, Toni, I want to make friends. It
was your own idea, kindness and all the rest of it. I'll be in
it, no matter how futile the experiment."

She wasn't going to retreat, refuse the conflict. She
shut her teeth, condemning herself to a breathless,
wordless little struggle, until flushed and angry, she
slowed up, reduced to complete impotence, quick tears
starting to her eyes.

"Better to cry now than later," he said heartlessly.
"It's later than you think, anyway. You'll get over it. The
truth is, you want this. You know why, but you won't
admit it, you unremitting little mule!"

His hand closed hard under her chin, but she was
moving in a dream. Not away from him, but close up
against him, in a kind of drugged acceptance of the
strange magnetism working between them. The moon
shone briefly on his tautened face and gleaming eyes. He
gave a bitter little laugh and lowered his head. Her heart
leaped like a bird in a great agitation, but the first touch
of his mouth was the charm. Her body responded
immediately, interpreting what she really felt, a perfect
instrument, gifted with a language they could both
understand, translating the myriad expressions of love. A
matchless sensation. A remembered devouring
conflagration, fiery sparks shooting like arrowheads
through her bloodstream. Emotions too deeply felt to be

ever forgotten burned into the memory, an indestructible thing. It didn't seem possible he didn't love her, with his hands locking her to him as if he would keep her with him for the rest of his life. She responded more passionately than she knew, moving her mouth along his cheek in a slow, drowsy hunger. . . .

Damon checked abruptly, lifting his head. "Say it!" he said in a perfectly hard, steady voice.

She shook her own head as if to clear it. "Say what?" she asked him, more than a little dazed, conscious only of her burning flesh. Her voice would never obey her.

In the moonlight his face had a moody, glittery look, infinitely disturbing. For once, she sensed, he didn't have complete control of himself. If that were so, she was safe no longer. She looked up at him pleadingly, her eyes wide and dark. "Please, Damon, I swear I don't know what you mean."

He grasped her shoulders right through to the bone. "Is that the truth of it? Is it? Because I'm going to say one thing. I want you!"

There was so much fire and passion in his voice, a certain calculating ruthlessness, that she let out her breath in a long gasp of pain and protest.

"Sex isn't love!" she said fiercely, her heart sinking, utterly devastated now she knew what he meant.

He actually groaned, flinging at her a sharply sarcastic: "Doubtless! But it would be pretty damn dull without it. Anyway, I'm not interested in a debate, Toni. In fact, I don't want any conversation at all. This seems to be the only way we can communicate!"

Deftly, with fresh urgency, he reached for her, but she made a furious little movement to shake him off, spinning on her heel and fleeing as if she had no confidence at all in her ability to hold him off. He was a sorcerer offering her the cup of forgetfulness. But she wasn't going to take it. Oh no! She had too much pride for that. She had to make her escape.

She went like the wind, her hair whipping in the breeze. A tear slid down her cheek, then another. She ceased to care, driven by an elemental anger. Life was terrible, eternally lonely, one prison to another. Every last emotion was a fake, yet she loved him, and the hell of it was, she could love him forever. If so, she was beaten, sunk into chaos. Better to be a primitive woman and run at him with a carving knife, but there would be so much explaining.

The trees thinned. She was nearing the house, looking into a face so set in its strain it was almost unrecognizable, stripped of its beauty.

For a moment both women were too tense to speak, then Elissa spat out her fury:

"How dare you! How dare you move in on my territory? You jumped-up opportunist! I knew what you were the first day I saw you!"

"Oh, go jump off the roof!" Toni said clearly, the lines of her nostrils more clearly defined.

Elissa froze, her narrow-eyed stare done to a turn, depths upon depths of virulent spite. "*I beg your pardon!*"

"Oh, let it pass!" Toni said wearily. "It was only a suggestion."

Elissa moved swiftly, blocking her path, her pearly gown blossoming, driven by some deep compulsion, a curious kind of imbalance prowling in her smoky eyes.

"Oh yes, I know what you are," she hissed softly. "Out for all you can get. And that's all you will get, the intoxication of a few furtive kisses, a tumble in the dark. Men pick an easy mark. But Damon knows you—he told me. The lowest card in the pack, and that's what he said. I've never done such a thing in my life. I've too much respect for myself."

"Really! What a pity. You must find it very dampening," Toni said in an utterly dead voice, her stomach lurching. "But don't say another word, Mrs. Nyland, or I might push you in the fishpond. I'd do it for two pins, only I have too much respect for the fish!"

Elissa went paper-white, her hands shaking. "You insufferable little bitch! Some upstart from no place—no money, no background. You in your borrowed finery! Don't tell me you paid for it, but you'll pay for what you just said—you and your brother. You have everything to lose, all your bright ideas. Just tell your brother he can forget his dreams. I'll see he doesn't get another property anywhere!"

Toni could feel her revulsion show in her face. "If you do nothing else, Mrs. Nyland," she said carefully, "don't inflict your own personality on your little daughter. Give her a fighting chance. Personally I find you and your attitudes unwholesome but remarkable nevertheless. Mean as all hell!"

"Little do you know *how* mean!" Elissa said somberly, with underlying viciousness. "I've had something like this happen to me before, and I took care of it. I'll win. I always win."

"Careful your methods don't boomerang on you. Life has a way of paying us out in our own coin. Now, if you don't mind, I'll cut short this charming conversation. There's always something ludicrous about women fighting—to me, anyway. Your fears are unfounded, in any case. I hound no man. I'll leave you to do that!"

"Excellent! The very thing!" Elissa said in the most peculiar fashion, no less a merciless machine bent on revenge. "As to that, you came here trying to move in, carry on your guilty little masquerade. You didn't know how nice it was here on Savannah, did you? But what did you gain? Ask yourself. You think Damon cares for you? I don't think so. Trust in the kind of thing you've had from him and you'll go flat on your face. He's mine, part of my world, and don't you forget it, for if you do, I'll demonstrate how very unpleasant I can be."

Toni started moving then, speaking quite pleasantly, holding the shock back until later. "At the risk of repeating myself, Mrs. Nyland, go jump in the fish-pond!"

All might have finished there, had she not walked into a segment of light that flashed off her dress in a million prisms. It had a catastrophic effect on Elissa, bringing her to crisis point. The look of the girl! Her beauty, her élan, the audacious tilt to her head, the enormous advantage she possessed of ten never-to-be-recaptured years. It was all too much for Elissa. A wild resentment filled her, a burning desire to wound, to "get even."

She made a frantic little darting movement toward the girl, like a hysterical cat, hand upraised, her delicate face frighteningly colorless. Toni's eyes came wide and alert, too late. She wrenched herself aside, caught up in a monumental aversion to the situation, her loathing of scenes. She couldn't bear to come into physical contact with Elissa. Her hand went backward, clutching at air. She shut her eyes in sheer self-defence. There was no time to brace herself. She had little warning. Elissa came on with a rush of movement, exquisitely fragile no longer, but strong and thrusting, her eyes two pinpoints of violet blue flame. She looked quite mad.

Toni didn't know what to do, so she threw herself backwards away from the shallow marble steps in terrible slow motion that lasted seconds and tumbled into the empty dark. Black bat wings swooped to embrace her as they did in the cave on Mandargi. She fell heavily, but even then allowed no scream to tear up from her throat. It all had to be done in silence. Her head cracked into something agonizingly solid, sending waves of brilliance shooting through her brain, then a rush of crimson. On the edge of consciousness she heard Elissa's voice, shocked, frightened, out of control.

"It was an accident, Damon, I tell you. She fell . . . she fell. . . !"

The words struck like blows and Toni surrendered to the abysmal black void, an anodyne to all pain, when in that moment she would have cheerfully died.

CHAPTER NINE

There were lights and voices spilling down the stairs.
Toni opened her eyes and looked into Damon's face. She
floundered for a moment at the expression in his eyes,
shimmering like jewels in the grim mask of his face. She
knew that love had many other guises. He might be cruel
and careless, but it was still love she felt for him. Damon
was love. It didn't seem to matter how much he hurt her.
The thought lasted only a moment. Clarrie Chase, in a
robe, with tousled hair, joined him, kneeling beside her on
the grass.

"Saints alive! Is there some conspiracy on? What
happened, dear child?"

Past her shoulder Elissa hovered, ghastly pale, tiny and
frail, supported by Keith Hammond's broad shoulder,
embraced by his encircling arm. She turned her head a
little, wincing, trying to smile into Cathy's shocked and
anxious face, her expression mirrored by Paul. "Sweetheart, are you all right?"

Toni gasped a little and her breath failed her. There
was a brief silence.

"Toni missed the step!" Damon retorted, his imperious
dark face shadow-marked, his words evenly spaced, yet
underscored by some kind of menace. "She fell in the
dark and she's cracked her head. Again. I just don't like
to think about it. I'll get her to her room if you'll all stand
back. No, it's all right, Paul," he said briefly as the young
man closed in, brushing back his sister's tumbled hair,
"I'll take her. Clarrie, you can come along."

Cathy's hand swung forward and pressed into Paul's shoulder. He looked backwards, wondering whether he could believe the message he read in her slate-colored eyes. Damon lifted Toni into his arms, glancing briefly into her pale face as if he had himself on a tight leash. "All right?"

She didn't answer; she closed her eyes, turned her head into his shoulder, giving herself up to the sweet protection of his touch.

She awakened suddenly. There had been a sound, but now listening, drowsily, she heard nothing. She turned her head along the pillow, her eyes piercing the long shadows. She hadn't known he was there. He came toward her, lithe, as graceful as a tiger, his green eyes a startling shock of color in the polished bronze of his face. His ruffled shirt was carelessly unbuttoned, the cuffs turned back.

"Toni," he said in a mock despairing voice, "what is it? Are you trying to drive me insane? All these accidents!"

Oddly, even then, she was drowning in sweetness. The sight and the sound of him, the thrilling shock of his compelling gaze. She lay very still, lest he vanish. Such things have been known to happen after a knock on the head.

"What time is it?" she whispered to the vision.

He threw up his arm and glanced at his expensive wrist watch. "Almost three in the morning! I expected you to sleep through the night, but you always do the different thing."

"What are you doing here?" She was still whispering as if they were enveloped in a golden cocoon.

"Drinking myself to death!" he replied, as mocking as

ever, but there was a bottle of Scotch on the dressing table and an empty glass. "I prefer to keep an eye on you," he said dryly. "I don't like all these cracks on the head, though I suppose it could have been worse, knowing you and your liking for high drama." He came to her side, adjusting the lamp so that it fell in a lustrous pool over her face and shoulders. She stared back into his eyes the lamplight had called into sharp brilliance.

"What really happened?" he asked softly, persuasively, touching the gentlest of fingers to the tiny pleat between her brows. "Did you fall or were you pushed? Elissa was giving a Jekyll and Hyde performance when I arrived. It was all I could do not to shove her head first into the fishpond on the offchance!"

A flicker of astonishment staggered her eyes. She was completely confused, clutching at a remembrance. Shove Elissa into the fishpond? That didn't add up in sentiment or gallantry. There was something sadly amiss here.

"I fell," she said at last, slowly, distinctly. "I lost my balance. No question about it, I must be bumble-footed!"

"Bravo!" he said in terse sarcasm. "You're a brave one. I'd like to know what she'd been saying to you, all the same."

She didn't answer, though he paused, waiting for her to go on. "Toni?"

They weighed each other carefully, utterly intent, the one on the other. Her eyes were black and velvet through the thick density of her lashes, and evasive. "I didn't like it then and I like it less now," she volunteered, "but I'm not saying! It was just a bad dream. It might be a good idea if you go away, though!" she added unsteadily, avoiding his expressive gaze.

"Why?" His gaze pinned her down.

"Well, heavens, you shouldn't be here!" she pointed out, her heart thumping sadly.

"I'll be where I damned well please!" he said with complete arrogance, on course again as the master of limitless horizons. "Besides, you'd better get used to it—seeing me here whenever you wake up!" He looked into her enormous eyes, startled and unbelieving. "I hope you don't mind, not that it makes a great deal of difference."

The cadences of his familiar voice fell on her stunned ears. "You are real?" she said faintly. "You're not a wish fantasy? I'm not still dreaming?"

"No!" he said lightly, and his lean brown fingers twined through her own. "Here we are, together again. Real people. Hearts and minds. These odd things happen in life, but if you're none too sure. . . ." He bent his dark head and dropped a hard kiss on her mouth that was a mixture of desire, reassurance and utter possession.

Life surged through her veins and color swept into her face, lending her a breathtaking beauty. "I love you!" she said aloud, when she thought she had cried it out silently.

"That's what worries me!" he murmured, and ran a tantalizing hand down her cheek. "It's a big responsibility!"

"I mean it!"

"I know you do."

She turned her face into his hand and kissed the palm. "I love you, Damon. When did you find out?"

"Oh . . ." he narrowed his eyes thoughtfully. "The first time I kissed you, perhaps. On Mandargi, certainly. You were just what I expected—a fireball, but very sweet nevertheless. I knew it was all over for me, though I struggled a bit as a matter of form. I don't like to make it too easy for any woman!" He was looking down at her, his face spiked with humor. He stirred slightly, a sensual twist to his mouth. "Don't keep nuzzling my hand, child. All this calm indifference is only a front, a very thin piece of camouflage." He shifted his hand and slid it under her creamy chin, kissing her once more, as light an enchantment as a windbell.

"I love you too, baby! Didn't you know?"

"No!"

"So much for a woman's intuition! I thought it was pretty glaring myself."

"And Elissa?" she asked, longing to hurdle that obstacle and be done with it.

"You have a lovely mouth!" he was saying rather vaguely, then, apparently just hearing, he lifted his head in mild irritation and surprise. "How the devil did Elissa get into this bedroom? Bring Elissa into it and it will prove you're quite mental. To the best of my knowledge and with my fervent blessings, Elissa intends to put poor old Keith out of his misery, God help him. I've even gone so far in a rash moment as to suggest to him that Annette can stay here on Savannah in the event of a honeymoon. Apollonian benevolence, wouldn't you say? Cathy can look after her; I've got other plans."

He was in deadly earnest, Toni could see that, and any lingering seed of doubt vanished. The insistence of his gaze, the quality and depth to it, told her all she ever needed to know; the tenderness he no longer bothered to hide, the endearing light touch of his hand as it threaded through the thick silk of her hair. Sudden tears sprang to her eyes.

"Don't cry, darling!" he warned her abruptly, his

tolerance deserting him. "I can take anything but that. You're a sick child and I'm the loving uncle. I've got to remember that!"

He studied her face in detail as though he sought to impress it indelibly on his brain. His green eyes narrowed and he got to his feet, his voice low but quite audible. "I'm not saying how long that could last, so I'll go!"

Handsome and mocking, collecting the whisky bottle, he prepared to depart, his green eyes gleaming into hers, his voice shaded with a slow excitement, a promise for the future. "Sleep tight, my lamb."

She smiled and blew a very real kiss along her hand, feeling a great warming tide of peace and elation. Savannah seemed to settle and sigh happily around her. Her eyelids began to droop and she turned her face into the soft hollow of the pillow. She had found her true haven.